FERAL

AN ANTHOLOGY OF FERAL CHILDREN STORIES

EDITED BY

ROBERT ALLEN LUPTON

WEST MESA PRESS
2020

The First Book of Feral is dedicated to the contributors who wrote the stories that appear in this volume.

Special thanks and acknowledgement to three of the writers who inspired this volume, Edgar Rice Burroughs, Rudyard Kipling, and Plutarch, one of the earliest, if not the earliest writer to tell the tale of Romulus and Remus. No matter whether Momma walks on two legs or four legs, swims in the ocean, flies through the air, lives in the swamps, slithers through the jungles, or tunnels underground, no matter how she looks, Momma would be proud.

FERAL

AN ANTHOLOGY OF FERAL CHILDREN STORIES

Edited By

Robert Allen Lupton

WEST MESA PRESS

Table of Contents

INTRODUCTION

This stories in this anthology were solicited from a select group of writers around the world. This is a 'By Invitation Only' collection of short stories and I think that the writers did a fabulous job.

The contributors are from Canada, Great Britain, Australia, and the United States. Folks in those countries don't always spell things the same way. A person in Great Britain uses 'labour,' while in the USA, we spell it 'labor.'

Words don't always mean the same things. In some places a truck is a lorry, a caravan is a recreational vehicle, and an elevator is an escalator. I'm not even going to get into the whole "first floor' thing.

When a writer from Australia spelled a word the way it's spelled in Australia, I let it stand. I made no effort to change word usages that reflect the dialect and meanings from the writer's home county to those in use in one designated location.

I think various word meanings and spellings from the writers' homelands are part of the charm of the world.

I did try to ensure there were no misspellings in this book and that 'their,' 'there,' and 'they're' were used correctly. Any mistakes are my fault. Apologies to the authors and readers.

Enjoy.

MOULTING

BY STEPHANIE ELLIS

"Mia, what on earth are you doing on the floor? Get up, girl. How many times have I told you? I really thought you'd grown out of that habit."

Her mother's eyes bore into her. Mia wished her mum would understand how she felt much more comfortable, much safer, when lying down. Usually she remembered to have a magazine in front of her or headphones on, then she was just being a typical teenager and her mother would tut, but leave her alone. Today, she'd forgotten her disguise.

"Sorry, Mum." She didn't mean it. Her words came out as a hiss, another trait they'd tried to beat out of her. To be fair, that had been Dad and he wasn't around anymore.

Mia pulled herself up and onto the sofa, a slithering movement which caused the frown on her mother's face to deepen.

"Mia, love," she said. "You're seventeen, you'll be an adult soon. I know life's been tough on you but it'll get even worse if you don't put this behind you once and for all. I mean it's not as if you lived your whole life down there."

Down there. Down in the basement. Not this mother's basement, but another. One in a farmhouse miles from anywhere. One she'd found and hidden in when her grandparents had vanished and no one had come looking for her. In the dark, she'd found another mother, her First Mother, as she thought of her. First Mother had loved her, raised her, and taught her how to fend for herself.

"Two years, love," said her mum. "And you were so little. You should've forgotten by now."

She had been one. They had found her when she was three. An impossibility, they had said. They had assumed someone had abandoned her down there, her behaviour simply mimicking the snakes as a way to cope with the trauma.

"At that age, children copy what they see, it's as simple and straightforward as that," had said the paediatrician and the health visitor. "She'll grow out of it. Don't try and force it."

Her parents hadn't listened, her behaviour unnerved them and they would swing between rewards and ever more extreme punishments. None of this stopped it completely but she learned to hide her habits from them sufficiently so they thought she was 'cured'. Any resurfacing of old tics and habits was easily ascribed to episodes of stress and anxiety.

They had killed First Mother. It was a scene she'd never been able to forget. Soft sunlight had sent its beam down into the farmhouse cellar and illuminated the two of them. She remembered the glitter of dust motes, the beauty of First Mother's skin. The serpent had wrapped itself around her in a protective coil. She had not been in any danger. The new arrivals thought otherwise and after those few seconds of shock, when they'd stood stunned at the basement's threshold, they had rushed down. The man who became her father had grabbed an axe and decapitated the python in one fell swoop. The woman who became her mother had swept her up in her arms and tried to soothe her. She had been terrified they said, when they recounted the tale. Yes, she had been terrified, but not of First Mother.

Her new father had dried First Mother's skin, turned her into boots, and wore her cloth jewelled in brown and bronze and black. Beautiful patterns of life turned into death. She hated him for that, had finally made her feelings clear the last time she saw him, the last time she embraced him.

Mia wrapped herself around her mother, coiling her arms and legs around her body, only for the woman to shrink away from her. Another misstep. She rearranged herself to offer a more acceptable hug.

"Perhaps we should think about counselling again?"

"No, Mum," said Mia. "I'm ok, promise. Just stress probably, you know. What with Dad and all."

Her mother sighed. "Yeah, sorry, love. I went to the police again but they've heard nothing. They think he's just another man having a mid-life crisis and gone AWOL. You sure he gave you no clue he was thinking of leaving?"

Mia shook her head. The last time she had seen him, she had hugged him. The years had shrunk the man, his drinking had weakened him. She recalled his surprised look at this apparently affectionate action. He had even started to smile.

"Seems we're finally alright, love," he'd said. "After all this time …"

She had coiled herself tightly around his body at that point, hadn't wanted to listen to him anymore, didn't want him thinking he'd won her over. She had squeezed and squeezed and he'd said nothing, was unable to say anything. She had taken his boots, rescued the remains of First Mother, and tucked them away in her wardrobe. The only person who would be wearing them was her.

Did this 'mother' think they were finally 'alright'? Age hadn't been kind to her either. She should be a more considerate daughter. Play the role at least.

"You need to rest, Mum. Go and have a lie down and stop worrying. Wherever Dad is, I'm sure he's fine. Now leave me to start the dinner."

Her mother's hand felt soft against her cheek as it stroked away a loose hair, held her gently for a second. Mia loved those moments, they were rare, but enough to remind her, her mother did indeed love her, despite everything. Grey eyes studied her anxiously.

"It's only because I worry about you," she said. "You know that, don't you? I know we're not your 'real' parents, but we've loved you like our own. You *do* know that, don't you?"

Loved her like their own. Except they had none of their own and she had been their only one. A surprise discovery they had claimed for themselves and no one had ever challenged it. Newspaper clippings from the time had lauded her parents for giving the 'Snake Child' a loving home rather than putting her at the mercy of the state system. To take on a young girl who could not speak and would only hiss, who did not walk but would slither across the floor was regarded as nothing short of saintly. Nor did her parents object to follow-up stories over the years, her adoptive father in particular taking advantage of any freebies or interview payments coming their way. That some monies were intended for Mia was glossed over or ignored. She never saw any of it.

"Sure, Mum. Go on, go and rest."

Mia watched her mother trudge out of the sitting room before she headed into the kitchen to start chopping the vegetables for dinner. The repetitive action was soothing and soon her mind had drifted back to those early days, to the memory of being held so closely, so tightly by First Mother. So cocooned was she in that long-ago darkness, it took a while for her to register the sound of screaming from above. Mum! Mia ran up the stairs, unaware she was still clutching the knife.

Her mother's room was empty. With thudding heart, she turned to her own room and found her stood in front of the wardrobe, its door open. She was holding a pile of clothes in her arms and staring into its depths.

"Mia, I ... what ...?"

Slowly the woman turned her horrified gaze on her daughter.

"What are you doing in here, Mum?" How could she explain what her mother had discovered? She kept her tone level, calm, a struggle as she felt the serpent rise up inside her.

"I thought I'd hang up those clothes of yours from the airing cupboard before I lay down. You hadn't got round to doing it, so I …"

Mia moved to her mum's side. They both looked at the boots.

"Your dad's boots. What are they doing in here? He never goes anywhere without them. He certainly wouldn't have left without them. Mia …"

Mia watched her mother's gaze turn from the boots to the knife in her hand, watched her face pale.

"Mia, you … what did you do?"

Despite the truth of her assumption, it stung she had immediately presumed Mia guilty of some horrific action.

"What are you assuming I've done, Mum?" asked Mia. "Leave them alone!"

She grabbed her mother as the woman reached in to pick up the boots, but wasn't quick enough to stop her seeing the dried blood inside. The snake inside her was coiling itself around her heart and her memory, reminding her of who, and what, she truly was. It was getting harder and harder to keep the two sides of her separate.

"Mia, love. Tell me what you did. I'm sure it was an accident. We can get you help."

Mia felt herself sway slightly, a weaving motion she used to use as a child to comfort herself. It took her back to that basement. The dark. It was safe down there. Where First Mother looked after her, taught her how to survive.

"Don't, Mia …"

Something inside her snapped and she was no longer two, had become one. The serpent inside had reclaimed her totally. It was with relief she gave herself up to it.

"Don't, Mia. Stop, Mia. Shut up, Mia. Don't hiss, Mia. Don't, don't, don't. That's all you ever say to me. You never wanted to talk to me about that time. Left it to the counsellors, the therapists. You never tried to understand." Her words were coming out in an unending flood, a continuous hissing, vowels and consonants merging into a stream of sibilance.

She tried again but normal speech proved elusive. Her mother was backing away, making for the door.

"Mum!" She tried again, but it came out as another hiss. Her tongue flicked the air, tasted fear.

"I'll get help, Mia," said her mother, from the doorway. "I'll tell them you had some sort of breakdown, that you, that you …"

Mia stepped forward as her mum turned and ran for the stairs. Mia shot after her, reached out, but mistimed the action, and instead the contact sent her mother tumbling down the stairs. She watched in horror as the woman fell, finishing with a sickening thud at the bottom.

She rushed down to her mother's twisted body. Her eyes were closed and blood was trickling from her ear, the rise and fall of her chest indicating she was still breathing. Mia needed to get help, an ambulance, but if she did that, they would start asking questions, start digging.

Her mind went back to the basement. It was safe down there. That was where she would go. Mia took hold of her mother's shoulders and dragged her to the door, opening it to reveal the stairs leading down. The air smelt cold and clammy, spiced with an underlying scent of decay. She hauled her mother down the steps, choosing to ignore the knocks and bumps to the woman's head, the floppiness of her body. She could think of nothing beyond getting her down into the dark. When she finally reached the bottom, she left her mother and returned upstairs. Any signs of the fall were quickly cleaned up, the vegetables she'd prepared for tea were swept into the bin and soon it was if nobody had been around, as if the occupants had gone out.

Satisfied with her efforts, Mia returned to her mother's side and stretched herself out alongside the woman's body. First Mother! With a jolt, Mia started up. She had to bring her down here. Back up the stairs, peering around the basement door to make sure all was clear. Nosy neighbours had a tendency to pop in. The doors! Mia locked both front and back, then made her way to her bedroom and collected the boots, held them in a reverent embrace.

Once more in the basement, she took off her trainers and slipped on the boots. When First Mother had looked after her, she had shed her skin many times and given them to Mia so she could wrap herself in them and keep warm. Curled up within that discarded cloak, decorated with its beautiful patterns, she too had become a serpent.

Mia stared at the woman she'd dragged down to the cellar. This woman was supposed to be her mother and so she too should clothe her, like First Mother had done. Her skin however, was pale and old but it would do until she could claim those of others, those dripping with ink and swirls of rainbow colours on their flesh.

"Mia."

The sound of her name startled her. She slid over to the mother's side, felt the rub of dirt and dust against her arms and face, the occasional chill of metal. It felt good to be herself, to be as First Mother had raised her.

"Mia." Her mother's voice was fainter.

She was beside her now, coiling herself around the prone body, wrapping her up with her arms and legs. She could feel the desperate fight for breath beneath her, the weakening pulse. She couldn't wait anymore. It was the duty of the mother to shed her skin for her young, clothe her. First Mother had taught her that.

She could taste the woman's age on her tongue, her sweat, her pain, her fear—her death. Her mother was scared of her.

"I'm here, Mother," she said, but her voice continued to hiss her words. It was as if all the intervening years hadn't happened and she was that child once more.

Mia curled herself even tighter around her body, squeezed hard, a final embrace between mother and daughter. Except the woman was not her mother and she was not her daughter, she never had been, although everyone said she was. The woman was silent now. She would never speak Mia's name again.

This mother was old and her skin was tight. It would need loosening before the moulting. Reluctantly, Mia rose to her feet and made her way to the small bathroom in the corner of the basement. Before her father had gone, he had been in the process of converting the basement to a living space, had got as far as an ensuite bathroom. Mia turned on the hot tap and soon felt steam on her face. The water needed to be boiling for her purposes.

When full, she dragged her mother's body over to the tub and undressed her before hauling her up and dropping her into the water. It would take a while to work on the skin, loosen it up for what she had to do. She didn't mind though. She peered over the edge of the bath and saw her mother's eyes wide open, gazing blindly at her.

Mia yawned. The warmth from the steam was making her feel drowsy. It was time to rest and so she curled up against the side of the bath, allowing its heat to seep into her body. An hour had passed before she woke again. She stretched herself and yawned. She felt good, truly herself for the first time in a long time. And her mother was waiting to clothe her.

She pulled the body from the bath and dragged it over to the old tarpaulin she'd thrown on the floor to cover her father's bloodstains. Then she picked up the kitchen knife from before and made the deep cuts needed at wrists and ankles, and around the neck. These incisions would allow her easier access to peel away the skin from muscle. She would leave the face however. For now, she still preferred to wear her own.

Picking up the freed edge of skin, Mia started to pull it down and away. It took some effort, although she found this body easier to work with than her father's, his skin had been much tougher. Occasionally, it tore as blood loosened her grip, but she kept at it until eventually, she had two sheets of skin which she hung up to allow any blood to drip away. The body itself, she rolled up in the tarpaulin.

Then she set to and cleaned the basement and herself as best she could, until her stomach's protesting growl reminded her she needed to eat. With no one to forbid her, she crawled up the stairs and wriggled across the carpet, feeling small burns caused by the friction between her skin and the carpet. It was easier for her on the kitchen laminate which she slithered across easily, finding herself suddenly eye-to-eye with their cat. Her stomach growled louder. She loosened her jaws as First Mother had taught her.

Silence reigned.

Back in the basement, her mother's skin had dried sufficiently for Mia to strip and wrap herself in it. The skin was not enough but it would do for now. She had been reborn as First Mother had made her.

Her father's skin hung from a nail on the far side of the cellar. She would not wear him.

Mia crawled slowly back up the stairs to find the day still warm even though dusk was not far off. She reached up and unlocked the back door, peering out into the garden to see if anyone was watching. Satisfied no one was around, she continued to slither her way down the garden path, ignoring the sting of grit. She kept her new cloak wrapped tightly around her, moved slowly so it would not be torn or damaged. The grass however, was kinder and she enjoyed its soft, cool feel. It soothed her small cuts and burns.

As she basked in the late afternoon's heat, the strains of a familiar song drifted through the air. Mia wriggled carefully over to the hedge and peered through its gaps. She could see Terri, their neighbour's daughter. Mia couldn't stand her but she coveted the girl's colours. Terri was sprawled out on a blanket, her skin exposed to catch the sun. She was an iridescent butterfly, tattooed in gorgeous tones of turquoise and crimson, pink and yellow. Mia clutched the knife to her chest, watched as Terri's eyes drooped and closed in sleep. Then she slithered through the gap in the hedge. She wanted to wear those colours too.

***

Stephanie Ellis writes dark speculative prose and poetry and has been published in a variety of magazines and anthologies. Her latest work includes the novella, *Bottled,* published by Silver Shamrock, who will also be publishing her novel, *The Five Turns of the Wheel* in October. She has recently been published in Flame Tree Press' *A Dying Planet* anthology with "Milking Time" and is included in Silver Shamrock's upcoming *Midnight in the Pentagram* anthology with "Family Reunion." Her poetry can be sampled in the Horror Writer Association's *Poetry Showcase Volume 6*. She has collected a number of her published, and some unpublished, short stories in *The Reckoning*, her dark verse in *Dark is my Playground*, and flash in *The Dark Bites*, all available on amazon. She is co-editor of *Trembling With Fear*, HorrorTree.com's online magazine. She is an affiliate member of the HWA and can be found at https://stephanieellis.org and on twitter at @el_stevie.

THE CURSE OF MIDDLETON BISHOP

BY RJ MELDRUM

I have waited so many years to tell this tale. The circumstances of what occurred are so bizarre and so tragic that it bears telling, but I wanted to wait in order to spare my dear friend Percy the heartache of reliving the trauma and tragedy, even though it is now three decades since it occurred. I have been informed that Percy passed away last month and the sawbones tells me my own time is limited, so I must tell the tale of the Curse of Middleton Bishop before it is too late. I suspect you will have never heard such a story before.

It was 1789. I had returned from the colonies in 1782, having been part of Cornwallis's defeated, but not subjugated, army at Yorktown. A year later I read the news of the signing of the Treaty of Paris with disgust. Those of us who had fought and surrendered our arms at Yorktown were adamant that we could have forced those damn colonials with their ungentlemanly tactics to eventually yield to the King's army. If it weren't for the damned French we would have succeeded, may that race be cursed for eternity. But, I digress.

I returned to these blessed shores without a clear purpose. I was signed off on half pay, a situation that many brother officers found themselves in. I was lucky, my family wealth allowed me to continue my life as I always had, and my record of fighting in the colonies provided me with a veneer of bravery and adventure, not shared by the officers who never left these shores. I settled back into my old routine quickly, but became bored with mundane family affairs after a time. I resolved to take a trip to clear my head. I was at a crossroads, I could continue my military career, hoping for a posting that would allow me once more to assume the role of command, or I could resign my commission and focus on the family business. The choice was not clear to me, so I decided to take some time to consider my future.

By pure luck, I happened upon the village of Middleton Bishop in the county of Wiltshire after a dreary and uneventful tour of the southern counties of England. I lodged at the inn, as was my custom on this trip. My horse was taken by one of the lads to the outbuildings at the back of the inn, while my bags were taken to my room. In the main room, I noticed a family crest above the fireplace, one I half-recognized. I asked the landlord of the inn which family it belonged to.

"The Lord of the Manor, sir, Lord Somersby."

"Somersby? I know a Somersby; Percy is his name."

"Yes sir, that's the young Lord."

"Why, I served with Percy in the regiment back in '79. I wasn't aware he resided in this area. Can I get your man to pass a message to him?"

"Of course, sir."

I quickly penned a short note and it was sent on its way. I was delighted, young Percy had been a subaltern in the regiment, when I was a young Captain. We had served together for a year in Boston before he had been forced to sell his commission and return to England after the death of his father. It would be delightful to renew our acquaintance.

It didn't take long to get a response. Percy's note suggested I pack up and come to the manor house to spend a week or so as his guest. It was an easy decision.

I asked for directions from the landlord and rode over to Somersby Manor the next morning. After a ride of perhaps half-an-hour I found myself at the manor house. I rode through the open gates into magnificently manicured gardens, with a stunning Baroque mansion as the centrepiece. It was quite delightful.

I was met at the door by a footman and a stable hand. My horse was led away and the footman picked up my modest baggage. I was met on the threshold by Percy, my old friend. He had hardly changed in appearance, except for some wrinkles round his eyes and some grey hairs.

"It is wonderful to see you George," he said as we shook hands.

"And you too, Percy."

"Come in, let me show you around my modest home. I have some guests you'll want to meet."

I was led into the library and introduced to a number of people, most of whom I recognized from various society balls and hunts. They were all members of the gentrified class, as one would expect. Time has faded some of the names and faces from my memory, but I remember there was the Lady Hamilton, beautiful and elegant, Baronet Bowater, recently returned from Italy, and the young Lord Vansittart.

After introductions and lunch, Percy escorted me to the drawing room and invited me to sit by the blazing fire. As this was October and the air was chilly, the warmth was most welcome. He pulled a cord to summon the butler, then sat opposite me.

"You have come at a most opportune time, George."

"I have?"

"Yes, by Jove! I was saying this morning over breakfast that we could do with some military men to help solve this problem and behold you appear, unbidden and unsought, but very welcome."

"Well, I was planning the pursuit of leisure, but now I am under your roof and accepting of your hospitality, I am obliged to offer whatever help I can. I cannot help but wonder why you need a military presence, are the peasants revolting?"

"I see time has not diminished your sense of humour," laughed Percy.

"So, in all seriousness, what can I do to help?"

His face grew sombre.

"It is a hard thing to relate George. It is my responsibility to the tenants and the others of the manor to provide protection to them."

"Indeed, it is the duty of any Lord of the Manor, even though we no longer live in feudal times."

"Well, there seems to be a curse on this particular manor my friend."

"A curse?"

"Just in the last year, fourteen villagers have disappeared without trace. Men, women, and children. Livestock too, seemingly snatched away in the middle of the night. There is also talk of merchants and other folk who travelled through the area and who never reached their destination. The villagers speak of a curse from God."

"Poppycock!"

"Of course, but you know how these country folk are, uneducated and superstitious. Even the Reverend Thomas cannot change the villagers' minds. As Lord of the Manor, I am charged with investigating and solving these disappearances. Hence my unbridled joy when I saw your note."

"You've searched?"

"Of course, I arranged for my men to search the area, especially the forest that bounds the eastern portion of the manor. It is wild and largely unexplored, but we did our best. Nothing was found, at least nothing was found in the places they looked."

"So why the need for military men?"

"My men are all locals. They won't go into the deepest part of the forest, no matter how much I press them. It has an evil reputation, there is an ancient legend of a supernatural creature that lives there. The villagers naturally have made the link between the disappearances and the legend. I need brave souls to venture there, to see if we can seek the truth. Men of stout heart and no imagination."

"An apt description of a military man."

"Who else could stand fifty yards from the enemy and withstand a cannonade without blinking an eye?"

"Well Percy, I have accepted your hospitality and now I offer my stoutness and courage. I will aid you in your quest, although it does seem unpleasant and possibly dangerous."

"Excellent, my friend. Now, where's Peabody with that port?"

The next morning, Percy assembled a party of twelve stout, dependable men, all persuaded to enter the darkest part of the forest by the reassurance that I, an English officer, would accompany them and provide military advice. The men were lined up and Percy addressed them, as if he was back on parade.

"Men, I know we have a grim task ahead of us, but we have been charged by the good people of this manor to find the source of the curse and destroy it, if we can. We have searched the majority of this manor, except for the deepest part of the forest. Today, we will search there."

He gestured to me.

"I know you men fear that part of the forest and have so far refused to enter. One of you requested I form a militia or even request the garrison at Bristol to provide men. I refused since both suggestions were impractical, if not frankly impossible. Well, the matter is now settled. We have been joined by Captain George Manning, a veteran officer who served in the Revolutionary War. He is highly experienced and has seen combat. You can rely on him to see you through this quest and bring you all safely back home. He is the man we have been looking for to ensure a successful search."

I felt inadequate in the face of such praise, but if my presence gave steel to these men's backbones, then so be it.

Percy and I mounted our horses, the others would follow behind on foot. I held a Brown Bess, the beloved, trusted weapon of the army that I had borrowed from Percy. My pistols, the ones gifted to me by my father, sat snugly against my waist and a sword, loaned from Percy's collection, bumped against the saddle. Lorimar, the Master of Hounds for Percy, brought up the rear with two of his best sight hounds.

We headed out along dusty roads, bordered by fields tended by the villagers. It was a bright, beautiful autumn morning. Mist lay between the trees as we followed the trail that would take us into the forest. As we entered, the sun was cut off and I shivered at the sudden change in temperature. I looked to Percy, beside me.

"How long until we get to this forbidden part of the forest?"

"Perhaps three or four hours."

We spent the entire morning travelling through pleasant woods. I managed to enjoy the experience, even though the thought of what we might find weighed heavily on my mind. Images of monsters and supernatural creatures occupied me. I was called back to reality when Percy halted his horse.

"George, we've arrived."

I glanced at the route we had to take. Previously, I had silently mocked the villagers for refusing to enter this part of the forest, but now that I saw it, I understood. The landscape changed quickly from pleasant English woodland to the type of untended, rough forest I had seen in Massachusetts. I don't know what freak of geography or nature caused this change, but this part of the forest had an evil atmosphere. It was dank and dark, no sunlight could penetrate the canopy above us. Moss grew thick on the forest floor, making the going slippery and treacherous. The horses were uneasy, their eyes flicking back and forth; the hounds whimpered, cowed. The men were silent, no-one wanted to wake the evil that dwelt in this place, for surely, evil must be present.

We travelled in silence for perhaps an hour, the tension building with every step we took. The going was so hard Percy and I had to dismount and lead our horses. I sent a man out in front of us to scout the trail.

One of the men behind me screamed. I turned, raising my musket. He pointed.

"I saw a creature in the trees!"

"What did you see, man? Tell us!"

"It was small, stunted like a dwarf."

"A human?"

"No, its face was contorted, evil. I'll swear it was holding a lump of flesh."

"You managed to get a good long look then?" asked Percy. "But no time to fire?"

"I was frozen with terror, my Lord."

"Did anyone else see this creature?" I asked.

The men shook their heads.

"It must have been a deer or something similar. Your imagination turned it into a creature," said Percy.

The man shook his head.

"I know what I saw, my Lord, as God is my witness."

The man was clearly terrified.

"Well Percy, we are looking for creatures, so it is possible he might have seen one. Men, keep your muskets primed and look to the tree line."

We moved more slowly from then on, each man carefully watching the trees. It reminded me of the war, constantly checking for snipers and bushmen. I must be honest, I was now terrified, but the cause of my fear I could not say.

We moved through the forest for another hour or so until the man at the front of our tiny column halted and beckoned me forward.

"Sir, rocks."

He was correct, there were a number of huge boulders sitting in a clearing just ahead of us. They towered above us, perhaps some twenty feet high. It was a perfect position for an ambush, whether the foe be human or devil. I turned to the men behind me.

"I will go alone. Be prepared to support me if I'm attacked."

I crept forward, my sweaty hands clutching my musket. It was primed to fire and my finger gently pressed the trigger. The boulders were shrouded in darkness; it was still only the early afternoon but the position of the sun meant they were in shadow. There were plenty of places I couldn't see. I was well used to fighting men, but I was used to open battlefields or well-armed columns. I was leading a dozen men, poorly armed and poorly trained, against an unknown enemy, one rumoured to be supernatural. Would a musket ball kill or even stop a supernatural creature? I asked myself, what creature did Percy's man see? I was scared for my life and began to regret writing the note to Percy.

I crept closer. Two of the boulders leant against each other, forming a natural cave. It was a perfect refuge. I motioned to Percy and he was soon by my side. I pointed out the cave and he nodded. I took the left flank and he took the right. We arrived at the entrance at the same time and entered.

The inside of the cave was thankfully empty, but within was a scene of utter carnage and horror. I felt the bile rise in my throat as I surveyed the devastation. I had seen men's limbs being blown off, musket balls rip through flesh, and comrades dying slowly of disease and infection, but this was far worse.

The cave was full of bones, some were animal, but others were clearly human. Some of the bones were picked clean of any flesh or sinew, but some still had meat attached. In one corner of the cave, furthest away from the entrance, lay a fresh corpse. I could see the flesh was torn and bitten, parts of the face and hands already eaten. The remaining part of the face was a mask of agony and I could see the throat had been torn open.

Percy called his man over to examine the bones.

"What caused this?"

The man spent some time examining the bones and the corpse.

"I can't work it out, my Lord. Some teeth marks are clearly a large animal, but others are smaller and I ain't never seen such a thing before."

He paused, absentmindedly stroking a human skull that had a large hole in the top of the cranium.

"But I tell you, my Lord, this wound wasn't done by no animal. Something sharp made this hole. I swear, this ain't no work of an animal, my Lord, nor is it a devil. This was the work of a man."

Percy looked up at me.

"So, the tales told by the villagers are wrong, this is no devil. There is a human element to this curse."

"It would seem so."

"The creature in the woods that your man swears he saw? He said it had human form."

"I was thinking about that. It might have been the perpetrator of these crimes."

Percy looked to his man.

"Call Lorimar to fetch the hounds. They have tracking to do."

"Yes, my Lord."

The hounds were brought into the cave. They sniffed around, finding a scent. They pulled on their leads, dragging their handler out into the daylight.

"What time is it?" asked Percy.

"Half past the hour of two," I answered, checking my pocket watch.

"We still have a few hours before dark, but we will need to watch our time. I don't want to camp out here tonight."

"Agreed."

We followed as the hounds tracked the scent they had found in the cave. We walked deeper into the forest, the men behind us grumbling over every stumble or every shin grazed on a fallen log.

We walked through this unholy place for about an hour. The trees pressed close to us and there was no clear trail, but the hounds clearly knew where they were going. We just had to hope they had the right scent and we would soon track down our quarry. I was more reassured about what we were likely to find. The contents of the cave, however horrific they were, dispensed with the supernatural theory. We were dealing with an entirely human foe.

The dogs were panting, straining at their leashes. Percy glanced over to me.

"We must be getting close."

He looked back at the men following.

"Men, prime your muskets!"

We emerged from the dense forest into a clearing, perhaps five-hundred yards wide. We stopped at the edge, despite the hounds pulling to continue.

"By God, look at that!"

A bear was loping across the clearing, with what were clearly human children running alongside. One or two of the youngsters clung to its fur to keep up. Percy gasped in shock.

"Egad George, do you see what I see?"

"By God, I can't believe my own eyes."

"How many children?"

"I count eight or nine."

I could hear the men behind us cursing and praying. I turned to them.

"These are your devils, gentlemen. This is your curse."

I looked to Percy. His face was as pale as death.

"Your orders, my Lord?"

"I...I..."

"As the Lord of this Manor, you are duty bound to rid the place of this curse."

I raised my musket.

"Shall I fire, my Lord."

He nodded.

The bear was now two hundred yards away, so I knew I had no chance of hitting it, but I couldn't let it leave the clearing and be lost in the forest. I fired.

The noise was enough to stop the bear, it turned and snarled at the threat it now perceived. The children stood close by, some still holding onto its fur. I had a premonition.

"Men, it's going to charge. Wait until it's fifty yards from us, then bring it down."

I was right, the bear started lumbering towards us. What shook me to the core was that the children did the same. I heard gasps of shock and horror from the men around me. I quickly reloaded my weapon.

"Hold your nerve!" I called to the men.

"But the children, sir."

"Shoot or be damned, man!"

"You must shoot. I command it," gasped Percy.

The bear and its terrible offspring were a hundred yards away now. I could see the enraged visage of the bear, huge teeth and a blood-red tongue. The children ran beside it in a rough line, some ahead and some behind. Their faces were blank and their eyes glassy.

I waited until I guessed our foe was fifty yards away. I waited a few more seconds.

"Fire!"

I heard the discharge of a dozen guns. I pulled my own trigger and watched with no satisfaction as the musket ball hit the bear. The bear continued to run towards us, then faltered. The children started to slow their run, as some of their number fell. They looked confused, scared.

I knew I wasn't commanding soldiers, but I yelled for the men to reload. I could see some were already getting ready to fire again, as my own fingers fumbled with ball and powder. I fired once more, as did some of the other fellows. Percy was frozen.

The bear stopped and reared up on its hind legs, a full ten feet high. It gasped then slumped forward, crushing one of the children standing in front of it.

The smell of powder was acrid and smoke drifted across the clearing. I knew it was over. The bear was dead. There were three children still standing, one clutched his arm. There were five crumpled figures lying on the ground, including one partially hidden beneath the bear.

Percy shook his head, as if waking from a nightmare.

"Men, capture those children."

Two of his men ventured forward, their muskets raised. The children did not resist and were soon bound with rope. Percy and I examined the bear.

"The children, the bear…I don't understand," said Percy.

"It was looking after them."

"I saw, but why?"

"It's a female. Perhaps that explains why. They say the maternal instinct is strong in all creatures."

I glanced over at the captives, being watched carefully by the two men.

"These children, look at their clothes, what's left of them. They're gypsies. "

"That would make sense. The bear must have come from a travelling fair; we have a number of them during the summer months. The gypsies follow the fairs, palm reading and fortune-telling, and the like."

"Did the children run away, I wonder? Did they take the bear with them for protection?"

"The gypsies have a fierce regard for their children, and while we will never know for sure, I suspect it's more likely the bear escaped and the children followed it, perhaps thinking they could claim a reward for recovering her. They likely got lost in the woods."

"I'm sure their parents would have searched for them, but why didn't they contact you, as Lord of the Manor?"

"You know the Romany people; they don't go outside their own communities."

"Tis true, they keep themselves to themselves. But, those poor children, lost in this forest, all alone."

"Aye, no doubt their kind searched long and hard for them, but eventually gave up, thinking the children dead. The children found the bear at some point. She adopted them, cared for them. They followed her, learning from her how to hunt, how to survive."

"And eventually, they forgot they were human, and started to kill and consume their own species."

"A terrible fate."

I walked over to the scene of devastation. The bear lay in the mud, bloodstained and battered, her life extinguished by a dozen musket balls. Her face was still and dignified. The studded collar, used to confine her before she escaped, was still round her neck. The peace that had been denied her in life had come to her in death. The child she had fallen on lay crushed under her, his/her face contorted in agony. There was no humanity in that face, only feral hatred. Even in death, the child had no peace.

I stared at the three remaining children; filthy, partially naked, and covered in sores. They ignored the armed men watching them; they were little more than animals.

"What will happen to them?"

Percy grimaced.

"Executed I dare say, or confined to an asylum."

"A fate as bad as death."

"Yes, I fear so. They won't survive for long, whatever happens."

I glanced around the muddy clearing.

"So this was your curse Percy. Just children."

"So much destruction, so much tragedy."

"It reminds me of war. They are destroyed and we are cursed with the knowledge of what we have done. There will be no happy ending for anyone."

***

R. J. Meldrum specializes in fiction that explores the world through a dark lens. His subject matter ranges from ghosts to serial killers and everything in-between. He has had over one hundred short stories and drabbles published in a variety of anthologies, e-zines and websites. He has had his work published by *Midnight Street Press, Culture Cult Press, Horrified Press, Infernal Clock, Trembling with Fear, Black Hare Press, Smoking Pen Press, Darkhouse Books, Breaking Rules Publishing, Tell Tale Press, Kevin J Kennedy and James Ward Kirk Fiction*. His short stories have also been published in *The Sirens Call* e-zine, the *Horror Zine* and *Drabblez* magazine. His novella "*The Plague*" was recently published by *Demain Press*. He is a contributor to the Pen of the Damned and an Affiliate Member of the Horror Writers Association.

Facebook: richard.meldrum.79
Twitter: RichardJMeldru1

THE FOUNDLING

BY ALYSON FAYE

The figure crept on all fours to the boundary of the woods. This was his evening ritual, as dusk settled on the lawn of the big house, kissing the grass and giving the figure shelter in the shadows. He was enticed thus, to stare at the glittering glass windows and the stick figures who passed behind them. He didn't know their names, instead he recognised them by their gait and their build. There was one, who fascinated him the most because, like him, he was small, quick moving, with a mop of long dark hair. This mirror boy often appeared on the stone steps, and the smooth lawn, throwing sticks for a yappy dog, or running around, yelling, making dens in the bushes and, most excitingly, coming right to the edge of the woods although never crossing over into them.

He'd whispered to the mirror boy on several occasions and once, greatly daring, had thrown a rock at him. It had missed and had landed at his feet. The boy had picked it up, looked around him in surprise, before rubbing the rock's surface and pocketing it.

He thought the boy from the big house knew he was there, but no one else did. The taller figures from the house never walked down to the woods. They stayed on the stone terrace drinking, eating, talking, or puffing smoke from their mouths.

This particular evening the lights in every room in the house were blazing, and it was buzzing with laughter and activity. He could smell horses arriving and departing, and hear the carriage wheels rolling over the gravel on the drive.

He drew back deeper into the trees, stealthy, sliding from trunk to trunk, seeing clearly in the dusk, chewing on a piece of bark and finally heading back to his den, where he knew he'd be safe.

***

Bertram was bored. Deadly bored. The party was the total utter end. He was all gussied up in a starched linen collar, velvet pantaloons, and a crisp white shirt. He looked, he thought, just like, his sister Gwendolyn's favourite doll. Having long curly hair at eleven years old was a real disadvantage as his Mama loved to have him wear it loose to his shoulders and worse still, parade him in front of her friends. He'd already met more adults in the last hour than he ever desired to for his entire life.

Stuffy stuffed shirts. Boring old bores. Inside he sniggered at his own wit.

Mama's parties lasted for hours and he knew soon the guests would start gathering around the pianoforte with Gwendolyn being encouraged to warble a version of *"Everybody's Darling"* in her high screechy voice. The sound of which he personally detested, as it had pursued him in condemnation for most of his young life.

Time to escape.

He edged towards the open terrace doors, breathing in the cloying mix of the ladies' scents and the gentlemen's cigars one last time before sidling outside, where the night smells of jasmine and mint assailed his nostrils. He plucked a sprig of mint from a nearby clay planter, and chewing it enjoyed the fresh minty taste burst on his tongue. Bertram yanked up his lacy shirt cuffs, hearing one of them tear and tucked them under to secure the fabric, before heading off across the moonlit lawns.

He had a plan.

For a few weeks now he'd had suspicions there was someone living in the woods – his Papa's woods. Therefore this person was trespassing and probably illegally poaching. Bertram didn't care about any of that, what he wanted was the glory of the capture and the proving that his suspicion was correct.

He'd heard sounds, human-type whispers and observed bare footprints in the dirt. Then there had been the rock which had come at him from the tree line one evening, followed by a flurry of giggles. He'd caught the odd flash of movement, but whomever it was, was swift, climbing like a monkey and stayed in the shadows.

Tonight he'd decided was the night. The party was the perfect opportunity to bring back his prisoner and, another bonus, cause a scene. He'd brought bait with him, stowed in his pockets. Sweet treats: Cook's marzipan cake and chocolate truffles. His mouth watered.

At the tree line Bertram hovered, jiggling from foot to foot. He smelled something feral on the breeze and heard a rustling. Carefully he placed the marzipan cake two steps inside the tree line and then he backed away.

"It's safe. You can come out. They are otherwise occupied at the house."

The brambles nearby moved, a skinny dirty arm shot out and snatched at the cake. It vanished, before Bertram could move. He smiled to himself. Success. Next he laid out a chocolate truffle, but this time placed it nearer to himself.

'"Did you enjoy that? I have more. But you have to come out and let me see you."

The bush rustled, he could hear snuffling. It didn't sound human more like a wild pig. For a moment Bertram was worried he'd misjudged the situation. He edged backwards. Then to his astonishment a pair of bare filthy legs appeared, followed by the torso then the head of a boy topped off by a thick mass of long, tangled dark hair.

The boy was naked, scratched, and dirt encrusted but his eyes were bright and sharp with intelligence.

Bertram gulped, and watched what he had lured out grab at the truffle and chew it. The boy never took his eyes away from Bertram. He wiped his mouth, then stuck out a scrawny hand.

'"Do you want more?"

No reply.

"Do you even understand me?"

No reply. Just the dark brown eyes watching him, never looking away.

Bertram pulled out a shortbread biscuit and offered it to the boy. He grabbed it from his hand, crouching on his haunches, he ate it in one gobble. Then he reached out and stroked Bertram's velvet pantaloons, sniffing his fingers afterwards, before continuing to touch his shirt, his skin, and his hair. Bertram stood frozen, not daring to move. The stink coming off the boy was powerful; a mix of urine, mushrooms and something else he couldn't name – was it blood? God knows what this creature ate. He was skinny but wiry, however Bertram knew he had the extra height, weight, and muscle strength to win in a tussle.

'"Sorry, old chap. I have to do this. You'll see, it's for the best."

The boy cocked his head to one side, listening, but not moving away. Seizing his moment Bertram grabbed the boy's skinny right arm and shoulder and began pulling his trophy towards the lawn and the lighted windows. The boy fought back, twisting, wailing like an animal, and trying to bite, but Bertram held on, fierce and determined. He endured the kicks and using his superior strength and weight slowly manoeuvred his prize towards the house. The ruckus brought Papa's guests onto the terrace, his Papa at the forefront, closely followed by his wife.

"Bertram! What the devil are you doing out there, boy?"

Bertram had no breath spare to reply, his muscles ached with the struggle, but foot by foot he was winning ground. Two of the menservants rushed out to help him and soon the forest boy was being held firmly between them, head forced down, arms stretched out in their tight grip. Subdued. Overwhelmed. He was a pitiful sight.

"'Oh my goodness, is he naked?" Bertram heard one the ladies ask, before his Papa ordered one of the servants to fetch a blanket. He noticed the ladies huddling in a corner well away from the boy, as though he would contaminate them.

The boy was hauled onto the terrace, where he gazed around himself in panic, wriggling like an eel between the two servants, screaming and wailing. Bertram walked up to him, thrust his own face into the boy's who immediately went still. The two boys stared at each other, several tense moments passed. Bertram reached out his hand to touch the boy's hair, just to give him reassurance. The forest boy spat fully in his face, the gobs of spittle ran down Bertram's chin. Without a second thought, Bertram lashed out, slapping his prize hard on his right cheek. The sound cracked around the terrace and several of the female guests squealed in fright including his mama.

The boy cocked his head like a sparrow, his eyes burning with what Bertram recognised to be hatred.

***

Eight months later . . .

Bertram sat facing his tutor in the chilly schoolroom in the East Wing of Heraldine Hall. He watched Thaddeus copy his letters in chalk on to a hand-held blackboard and repeat them.

"'A for Apple . . . B for Box . . . C for Cat . . .''

He could hardly recognise the boy from the forest in this clean, sweet-smelling, besmocked lad who sat by his side every day, for schooling, at meal times, playtime, and bedtime. The doctors, the vicar, and Papa's money had wrought a miraculous transformation. The boy had put on weight, learned and also remembered from "before" a smattering of words, spoke instead of cried, had been baptised as Thaddeus, regularly attended church, and was learning to read and write. He had a new wardrobe, a new home, a new brother and sister, though Gwendolyn spent very little time with "that filthy creature Bertie dragged into our home", and new parents all wrapped up with the promise of a bright shiny future.

The Reverend Charles Leland never ceased to lavish praise upon Bertram's parents for taking in the "poor abandoned waif" and he regularly visited, armed with his Bible, and lessons in Christianity. Bertie heard the low drone of the vicar's voice leaking through the nursery door and the long silences from his brother, who said very little in response. He sympathised with Thaddeus on that count.

Bertram also worked hard to forget those nightmarish first few weeks when "the forest boy" had howled for hours, torn at his own flesh, and pulled out his hair in clumps, so eventually "for his own good, sir" the doctor had intoned, he'd had to be restrained in a straitjacket, from where he still spat out his food and milk at everyone and urinated wherever he stood or sat.

Yet, it became obvious, he did understand a modicum of words and eventually he did speak – his first words were "ball" and "dog." Clearly he had lived with humans at some point but despite extensive newspaper advertising and an expensive private enquiry service – no leads were forthcoming as to the boy's identity. He remained a blank.

Doctor Gregson, Papa's personal physician, estimated Thaddeus to be seven or eight-years-old and said he had probably been living "as one with nature" for a significant period of time, maybe two or three years. Enough time to forget language skills and, thought Bertram bitterly, toilet skills.

He overheard his parents and their friends discussing the boy's origins for hours. It was the new parlour game for the local gentry.

"'Probably some tart's offspring, who grew too big to feed and clothe, and was tossed out. You know what women like that are like."

"'Perhaps his family all died of the cholera and he ran away."

"Or he was sold into service and ran away."

"Perhaps a foreign girl brought him here on a ship and then she died. He has very dark hair and eyes. He doesn't look English."

The theories kept coming but not the answers.

Bertram also remembered the day when Thaddeus had seemingly capitulated to the new regime and his new life. The miraculous day when he'd eaten his breakfast oats, drunk his milk, used the latrine, and held Nanny's hand in his own small fist. He'd learned quickly after that, soon joining Bertram in the school house, and then the nursery, full-time.

His speech grew more fluent and he enjoyed simple card games such as *Old Maid* and *Happy Families*. He became attached to Bertram's cocker spaniel, Layla, and followed them both around, copying every mannerism and gesture of the older boy.

"'It's adorable how he apes you, darling," Mama pronounced to everyone. She would parade the boys at her afternoon tea parties, before the twittering ladies of her social circle, pointing out how alike they were.

"'Every outfit I buy for Bertie, I now buy in a smaller size for Thaddy, don't I, darlings?'"

Thaddeus would beam and bow, which the ladies loved, while Bertram stared into the middle distance wishing he was somewhere else. It should have been flattering and for a while it was, but Bertram soon felt smothered and also began to suspect there was an insincerity to his newly acquired younger brother's act. He glimpsed a curl of the lip, a glint in the eye, a smirk which quickly disappeared in front of the adults.

Boys know all the tricks of other boys and Bertram was getting to know Thaddeus very well. Better than their ageing, easy-going Nanny who just wanted a quiet life and her bottle of gin, which she kept in her underwear drawer, as Bertram knew all too well. Better than Papa who paid the bills but was rarely at home, except for dinner, where as long as the boys did as they were bade, he was satisfied. Better than Gwendolyn who was busy receiving, at sweet sixteen, her first beaus and attending her first parties and who was interested only in her frocks and her hair.

Their tutor, Master Henry Hocking, whacked his cane (more for show than use for he was a kind-hearted young man) on the desk. "Right lads, time for lunch and a brisk promenade around the grounds. This afternoon we will be studying mathematics." He beamed at his charges.

Bertram and Thaddeus stood up in unison and headed to the nursery where they ate their light lunch of boiled eggs and soldiers in silence whilst Nanny scurried around them.

"Lovely sunny day today, boys. Off you go." Nanny gazed longingly at her underwear drawer and the hidden bottle of gin.

In silence the boys trooped out. Thaddeus made straight for the woods, as he always did and today Bertram let him go. He was supposed to restrain him but he couldn't be bothered. He was sick of being his brother's keeper. The June sunshine was making him sleepy and he wanted to dip his bare feet in the pool and watch the tadpoles cluster around his toes. At the trees' edge his brother turned to stare at him and then he dived into the viscous greenery. Bertram glimpsed splashes of his white shirt before he was swallowed up. Removing his black button boots, he dipped his toes in the blissful chilly water, wiggled them, and felt his eyelids close.

Just a little nap.

He awoke with a start. A shadow stood over him and his skin felt chilly.

"Thaddy is that you?" he asked, rubbing his eyes.

His brother stood, beaming at him, holding something in his hand. Something liquid dripped between his fingers onto Bertram's discarded boots. Bertram staring up, blinked and realised at that moment it was blood smeared over Thaddy's mouth and hands.

"What the Hell have you been doing?" He was so shocked he used the forbidden "H" word which he'd heard Papa shout in the study late at night when he'd been at the whiskey decanter.

Thaddy stood unmoving, his smile faltering. Bertram could hear the soft plop, plop of the blood.

"'Look at you! Oh Mama will be so angry."

There were blood spatters all over the expensive French white linen shirt, so carefully laundered by the servants. "For you, brother." Thaddy held out his hand.

In it Bertram espied a broken corpse, a squirrel, he guessed. It had been ripped apart. He turned and vomited into the frogspawn lying across the pond. His mind raced, calculating the effects of this version of "show and tell" upon the household, against hiding the evidence. He knew how much his parents had invested, both emotionally and financially, in their new adopted son. He knew how their status had risen in county social circles and how a knighthood was being proposed for his father. He knew, in his heart, how it would destroy his Mama if she ever found out about this aberration. She had lost two babies after him, both had been agonising stillbirths, and he'd never forgotten her grief.

"Why did you do this?" He stood up, grabbed Thaddy's hand and tossed the gutted squirrel into the shrubbery. He plunged his brother's arm into the pond to wash it. Thaddy stood, saying nothing, a dazed but content expression on his face.

"Here, wash your face too and let's hide that shirt. Quick, take it off."

He helped his brother undress, then balled up the linen and buried it beneath the rhododendron bush.

"We'll sneak you in through the back entrance and fetch you a clean shirt. Tell no one about this. Do you understand?"

Thaddy stood, nodding, then smiled showing blood-smeared teeth. Bertram shuddered. "For God's sake, brush your teeth before the lesson. You must never ever do this again, do you hear me? We don't eat raw meat or rodents."

The boys bypassed Nanny who was lying snoozing, gin-sozzled, in her usual chair in the nursery. Ten minutes later Thaddeus appeared, as before lunch, smartly attired, in front of Henry Hocking in the schoolroom.

"Boys, ah there you are. Excellent. You're a tad tardy today. Let's not make a habit of that sort of lax behaviour. I do hope you both enjoyed your repast and exercise. It is so good for the mind and body. Now let us turn to the tricky business of division . . ."

He handed out the chalkboards and turned away. Bertram's now empty stomach roiled. He glanced at his brother, who was focussing on the numbers drawn on the tutor's blackboard, with a frown, with nary a drop of blood upon him. Indeed he appeared the model student.

Over dinner that evening Papa folded his London newspaper, sucked in his gut, and drew a breath. This meant an official announcement was coming. "Ladies, you may leave us. I have a matter of some importance to raise with the boys."

Gwendolyn and their mother vacated the dining room in silence, pulling in their wide skirts, edging sideways through the door whilst both radiating disapproval. His sister was smirking as she retired. Bertram sighed and his guts clenched in fear.

"Certain items have been vanishing from the er – er ladies' rooms lately. Do you know anything about this matter, boys?"

Bertram was puzzled. His father appeared mildly embarrassed, which was a new development. Thaddeus' face remained a blank. Silence followed.

"'Can you tell us what these items are, sir?" asked Bertram.

His father shuffled in his seat. "Ladies er – er undergarments. Corsets. The like."

Bertram was astonished. The look on Thaddeus' face was identical.

"The ladies are becoming rather concerned about this, as you can imagine. I suspect it's just a jolly jape, but it must stop now, boys." Their father stood up. "You are dismissed and may go to the nursery."

They marched upstairs in silence. Inside the privacy of the nursery walls Bertram turned on his sibling. "What the Hell have you been doing?" He rather liked the sound of the "H" word. It made him feel big and strong.

Thaddeus shrugged, smirked, and turned away. Bertram grabbed him by the shoulder and like a snake, the younger boy turned, swift, agile and bit Bertram on the right hand in the fleshy part between his thumb and first finger. Letting go, he licked his lips. Bertram yelled in pain. There on the back of his hand was an exact indentation of Thaddy's teeth decorated with droplets of blood.

"You little animal!"

He threw himself at his brother, pounding him with his fists, banging his head on the floorboards until Thaddeus cried out, "Help! Nanny! Help me."

The door opened, heavy slow feet pounded across the bare boards and Bertram was yanked backwards off his brother's skinny frame. Thaddy promptly curled up into a ball, in the foetal position.

"Stop this now, Bertie! You boys mustn't scrap."

"He started it, Nanny." Thaddeus looked up, pointing a finger, as a timely bruise flowered over his right eye, which was also beginning to swell. "He called me an animal." Thaddeus got up and rushed over to Nanny, grabbing her skirts and sobbing. "I'm trying so hard to be a proper little gentleman."

Bertram rolled his eyes and gave up the fight. He knew he was going to get the caning of his life off his father.

Hours later as the boys lay in bed, Bertie hissed, "What are you doing with the ladies' undergarments, you little freak? I know you have them."

Thaddeus giggled in the darkness. "I smell them. I like the smell of ladies."

Unpleasant pictures arose in Bertram's head, evoked by the giggle and the words. He balled his fists.

"I like Miss Gwen's scent the best. She is my favourite." His brother chuckled and turned over to face the wall.

Bertram heard him scratching his fingernails along the wallpaper, a nightly ritual, as though he was trying to claw his way out. It calmed him and he usually fell asleep mid-scratching. Nanny said nothing of this habit to her employers, not wanting to risk her comfortable position nor did Bertram, but for different reasons. He knew his mother would worry herself sick over it.

Under the covers Bertram lay awake, shivery and anxious. Once, years ago, he had longed for another brother, and had prayed, each time his mother fell pregnant, for a baby to join him in the nursery. Now he dreaded what each day would bring and resented how much time he had to spend with Thaddy.

You'll never be my brother. Never. Not as long as I live. You are nothing but a foundling.

***

The weeks passed in the usual rhythms and routines of the household, above and below stairs. Bertram kept a close eye on his brother, but apart from him slipping away into the woods as usual, nothing else untoward happened. The ladies' undergarments reappeared in the laundry room and the matter was closed. His father spent increasing amounts of time away in The Capital on business matters and Bertram understood from the whispers of the staff and his mother's interminable social gatherings that his father's star was on the rise and a knighthood would be forthcoming in the new year.

His mother began a new habit of taking her sons out with her on visits, in their carriage to their neighbours' homes for tea with their offspring. It was part of Thaddy's "social grooming," Bertram had overheard her saying. It was during one such visit the next incident occurred, a more public one than before and one which couldn't be hidden away.

Bertram was sitting with Miss Jemina Roding taking tea in the family's nursery, when he realised he hadn't seen his brother or the younger Roding's girl for half an hour or more. He felt a fluttering in his heart and stomach.

"I will go and see where Thaddy is," he murmured to his miniature hostess and trotted off around the upper floors' rooms.

He heard a whispering coming from one of the bedrooms, a small one tucked away near the end of a corridor. On pushing open the door, he stood frozen in horror at the scene before him. His brother and the youngest Roding girl were both semi-dressed, sitting with playing cards lying around them, but worst of all was the sight of numerous locks of the girl's blonde hair also strewn on the red carpet. She sat, six-years-old, cross-legged in her chemise, beaming, whilst Thaddy kept hacking at her hair with a pair of silver scissors. A pair, which Bertie guessed, he'd brought hidden in a pocket, from home.

In silence, he shut the door behind him and wedged a chair beneath the handle. They must not be discovered like this. It would cause a scandal beyond anything they had previously known and it would ruin his parents.

"What have you done, Thaddy?" his voice quiet and furious.

He'd forgotten the younger Roding girl's name, but walking forward he grabbed the silver scissors off Thaddy who pouted and spat at him. He missed and the spittle hit the carpet. The girl giggled, ignorant of the rights and wrongs of this behaviour but enjoying the drama of which she was, not her sister this time, the centre of.

Thaddy picked up one of the blonde locks and sniffed it, his eyes closing as if in ecstasy, then he carefully tucked it into a pocket of his waistcoat.

"'I want to look like a boy and Thaddy- said he'd help me," the nameless girl lisped, still grinning. "Boys have more fun."

Bertram gazed appalled at the wreckage of her scalp, where some of the hair had been cut away at its roots but in other sections sprouted longer. Mama Roding would have a heart attack. His family would be banned from every household socially in the county. He wielded the scissors and trimmed as much hair away as he possibly could to even it out. Then he turned to Thaddy, "Your turn," he hissed. If you have yours shorn off too, we can say it was a game, not an – assault. Do you understand?"

His brother shrugged, but kept still, while Bertram cropped his long dark hair down to the scalp. The effect was to bring out Thaddy's dark eyes and sharp cheekbones, causing him to appear more waif-like and far less genteel.

"You can say you wanted to be like twins," he told the Roding girl, who looked thrilled at this idea.

She laughed and rubbed her hand over her scalp then did the same with Thaddy, who to Bertram's surprise, allowed her to do so, before he pulled her hand to his lips to kiss and ended by bowing to her.

In the ensuing ruckus of the revelations of the new hairstyles to the respective Mamas, Bertram forgot about what his brother had pocketed, until he brought it out that night in the nursery, after Nanny had departed. He held it to his nose, sniffing and licking the blonde strand of hair, before sighing, he stowed it in a metal box, which he kept under his bed.

"You are such a freak," Bertram hissed at him. "You're no brother of mine. Is that clear?"

Thaddy shrugged. He turned over and began his nightly scratchings at the red flock wallpaper. Bertram pulled the pillow over his head, his anger turning to sobs of rage, before he fell asleep.

The social visits to the neighbours slowed somewhat after the hair cutting incident but overall it was regarded as an amusing jape and the Roding girl remained unconcerned and cheerful, so no real blame or retribution was brought to bear upon Thaddeus.

"Boys will be boys," his mother had trilled to everyone, her shrill laugh several notes higher than usual.

Thaddy turned eight or maybe nine-years-old, Bertram turned twelve and both of the boys' birthday parties went off without mishap. Their father received his knighthood and spent even more time away in London leaving the household run by the women. Bertram noticed how sad and tired his mother appeared, rising later and later each day and venturing out less. The Vicar visited her often, but his Bible readings did not seem to raise her spirits. Nanny drank more, slept heavily and kept a looser grip on the boys' activities, so Thaddy was able to give her the slip.

At night Bertram watched his brother stare out of the window at the woods, his lips moving with no words coming out, just tears falling. He followed him at night when he slipped out and plunged into the guts of the forest, returning hours later at dawn to his bed, smeared in earth and blood, beaming happily, snot dribbling from his nose, his clothes torn, and his grown-out hair speckled with leaves. Bertie would hustle him into the copper bath and make him bathe. In silence. Thaddy refused to talk about these night-time adventures. But on the nights when he didn't venture out he was more agitated, picking at his own skin and hair, speaking less, and miming more. The woods calmed him, it seemed, and gave him peace.

After a half dozen of these episodes Bertram decided to follow Thaddeus into the woods. He lay awake listening to Nanny snoring, whilst giving his brother a decent head start. Then stalking through the shrubberies bordering the lawn, he pursued Thaddeus into the woods and into unknown territory for him.

He knew the woods stretched for miles, were as wide as they were broad and they bordered onto the moors which the servants said were "blighted and full of wild creatures." Beyond that he was ignorant. Clearly though his brother knew his way intimately through the forest landscape, skipping ahead, jumping from one fallen log to another, and swinging over other obstacles, nimble and confident.

It was tough for Bertram to keep up and keep his distance but he was thankful there was a sliver of moon that night to guide him. Unlike Thaddeus, he needed it. His brother's night vision was remarkably acute still.

He sensed forest life around him, twitching, rustling, and breathing, but he saw nothing. The air was chilly and he wondered at how Thaddeus, wearing just his pants and nightshirt, could be warm enough? He didn't seem to feel the cold whereas Bertram loved to snuggle by the fire with a book and a drink of cocoa.

Badgers, squirrels, that's all. Nothing bigger. Maybe a deer or two. Bertram tried to comfort himself.

The walk through the woods lasted longer than Bertram had expected or wanted - he soon regretted his decision to follow Thaddeus and wished he'd stayed in his warm bed.

Who really cares what the little freak is doing out here at night? Probably eating bugs and chewing grass.

The trees began to thin out ahead and Bertram glimpsed flatter land beyond, dotted with giant rocks and boulders and acres of heather and gorse.

The moor. The blighted moor.

He watched his brother's skinny figure shadow-walk over the rocks and climb up onto one, shaped like an elephant, there he threw back his head and howled.

Bertram froze, because, to his gut-churning horror, the howl was answered by another. This one definitely from an animal. He crouched in the low-growing shrubs fringing the moor, and shivered. His brother was calling to something or someone of that he was certain. He watched as Thaddy stood rigid, on top of the rock, staring into the darkness and waiting. He seemed calm, and unafraid. At ease even.

Bertram smelt it before he glimpsed it. The feral stink of a large animal approaching. The rustling of the heather as the sprigs bent before it, the whisper of paws on rocks, the glint of the moon off its black eyes, and white teeth before a cloud took away the light. It was climbing up towards Thaddy.

Bertram hunched down into a ball and tried to be soundless. He prayed the wind was blowing the wrong way. The moon rolled out again, and there on the rock was his brother, kneeling, his arms hugging the thick fur ruff of a grey wolf. Boy and animal were as one, still, silent, intent on the other. The wolf lowered its massive head to Thaddy's face and licked him. He laughed. He stroked the beast and tickled it behind the ears. He behaved as if this massive wild animal was their pet dog, Layla. He sat down beside it, and the wolf sat on its haunches. Together they stared out at the night moor. Thaddy kept one skinny arm thrown around the wolf's back. They sat for several minutes, until Bertram, stiff and clumsy, moved and a stone rolled beneath his foot down the slope. Boy and wolf turned as one, the wolf ready to leap and attack, Thaddy more cautious.

"Hello there, brother," he seemed unperturbed, but he kept a hold of the wolf's neck ruff.

Bertram stood up. He was more terrified than he'd been in his life and he sensed warm urine trickle down his leg.

"Come closer," Thaddy invited him and slowly Bertram stepped forward into the brushy masses of the heather, smelling the wolf and knowing the wolf smelt him.

"'This is my mother," Thaddy said. "She found me, fed me, and kept me warm and dry. Many seasons passed. I lost count."

The wolf's dark eyes watched Bertram. Its tongue lolled, long and mobile, wet, from its jaws.

"You know that cannot be so, Thaddy, You are . . ."

"'. . . human? Like you and your parents? I have tried to fit into your world, brother." He sighed and his face fell, so he looked much older. "It is a sad, silly world you live in. Here - there is -" he threw out his arms, "there is this. The wind, the rain, meat, shelter. I can be myself. No teachers, no God, no rules."

The wolf growled as though in agreement.

I am going mad, thought Bertram. *I must be, because I understand what Thaddy means. Mama's silly friends and empty parties. Papa always away making money. Me being raised to be a gentleman with the right education. What is it for?*

"Look up, brother. See the stars. Taste the wind. Feel the earth." Thaddy bent down and smeared his face with dirt. "This is living."

The wolf turned away, as though bored by Bertram and trotted off, waiting at the next cluster of rocks. Thaddy jumped down and jogged over to Bertram. He took his hand, sniffed it, and licked the palm.

"I will be well here, brother. Do not fear for me."

Bertram watched the boy and the wolf lope away, the wolf pausing to wait for Thaddy to catch up, until the night took them from his sight. Bertram wiped his face, surprised to find tears there. He didn't know he felt so much affection for Thaddy. He thought he hated him.

***

Bertram endured the ensuing weeks of the police investigations, Papa's questioning, Mama's hysterics, and the newspapers' hyperbole with great maturity and fortitude. He said very little. Thaddeus had slipped away in the night and he knew nothing more. Nanny had to be forcibly retired of course and Gwendolyn's proposed nuptials postponed until the scandal died down. But die down it did, as there was no fuel to fan the flames. Bertram felt most sorry for his mother who relapsed into morbid melancholia at losing another child, albeit an adopted one, and never recovered her former "joie de vivre."

Bertram suspected his father found comfort in the ladies of London's night-life and there he died, in the arms of one such, a few years later, just after Bertram had come of age. So the timing was fortuitous. Bertram inherited the estate, the title, the money, the house, and the woods verging on to the "blighted moors" at the age of twenty-one.

He split his life between London and Yorkshire, but made sure he was more often in the country than his late father had been. He rather enjoyed long walks alone, taking hours to explore his land. He was a solitary man, not given to attending or hosting parties, but much prone to charitable acts towards his employees and he always kept pet dogs, often several in his household, upon whom he lavished much affection.

Stories did percolate, through word of mouth from the inhabitants of the outlying villages, of sightings of the Master, out late at night hiking, a pet dog at his side, oft times accompanied by another male figure, lithe and agile, running with a larger beast. The word "wolf" was whispered after a few pints of ale in the inns, but no one seriously believed that.

In time the stories passed into local lore and legend and became after Bertram's demise, his legacy.

Alyson lives in West Yorkshire, UK with her husband, teen son and four rescue animals. Her fiction has been published widely in print anthologies - *DeadCades, Women in Horror Annual 2, Trembling with Fear 1 &2, Coffin Bell Journal 1, Stories from Stone, Ellipsis, Rejected* ed. Erin Crocker) and in many ezines, but most often on the Horror Tree site, in *Siren's Call* and *The Casket of Fictional Delights*.

In May 2019 *Night of the Rider*, was published by Demain in their *Short Sharp Shocks!* E book series and later that year Demain published her 1940's crime novella - *Maggie Of My Heart*.

Currently she has stories appearing in the *Strange Girls* anthology (ed. Azzurra Nox), *Colp: Black and Grey*, and a selection of charity anthologies, *Burning Love* from *Things in the Well, Amongst Friends (Gypsum Sound Tales)* and most recently in the amazon e-book best seller *Diabolica Britannica* (raising funds for the NHS).

Her work has been read on BBC Radio, local radio, on several podcasts (e.g. *Ladies of Horror*), posted on YouTube and placed in competitions.

She performs at open mics, teaches, edits for an indie publisher and hangs out with her dog on the moors - in all weathers.

You can contact Alyson through her blog:-

https://alysonfayewordpress.wordpress.com/

A full list of her publications can be found via her author page on amazon:-

https://www.amazon.co.uk/Alyson-Faye/e/B01NBYSLRT

THE DOLPHIN GIRL:
A STORY OF THE DROWNED WORLD

BY ROSE STRICKMAN

I was ten years old when I first met the Dolphin Girl.

I'd swum out into the mangrove swamp alone. My tribe, the Reina Solis, had only recently arrived in the region, our boats sailing up from the southern continent, and there were no other people there, either Land or Sea. We had spent the dry season fishing among the islands, but, as the hurricanes approached, we headed west to among the mangrove forests that bordered the shore of the vast, unexplored northern continent.

We'd only arrived a few days earlier, setting up camp on a sandy island, anchoring our wooden ships and draping our tents with sheets of plastic, scavenged from ruined built before the Drowning of the World. It was a sunny, clear day, belying the storms to come, and the sun shone on the water channels, the mangrove leaves, and the rusted ruins, choked with vines and branches, poking from the forest. Splashing and happy, I went exploring, hunting crayfish and playing, and didn't think to be afraid until I got stuck.

I had reached an arm in among the tangle of mangrove roots, reaching for something shiny. It was a piece of Pre-Drowned metal, potentially valuable; but then I couldn't pull back my arm. I tugged, dropping the shard, but couldn't get my arm free. I was trapped underwater.

At first I was only a little afraid. We Sea People cannot drown, of course: my gills supplemented the oxygen in my lungs, and I was able to move, to pull at my arm, then, in increasing desperation, to thrash and struggle, trying to get free. But my arm was well and truly stuck.

After ten minutes, I found myself getting woozy. This was bad, I knew. We Sea People may not be able to drown, but our gills can only do so much. If we're kept underwater too long, we lose consciousness. And then it was only a matter of time before the tiger sharks that cruised these swamps found me. I wished desperately that I'd never swum off alone as I yanked at my imprisoned arm, the water turning dark around me. I was losing consciousness, I realized as the whole scene flickered before me.

There came a sudden high-pitched whistle, and something large darted past me. I bobbed from my arm, half-lying on the mud of the swamp bottom, and watched through the waving fronds of my luminescent hair as the dolphin pod swooped and squeaked around me. They poked me with their snouts, darting near and then away.

When the girl appeared, I thought I was hallucinating. A Sea girl, about my age, her entire body rippling as she swam through the jade-green mangrove-water. Her silver hair flashed with rainbow colors, venom pulsing along the passive tentacles threaded through the shining mass, as she inspected me, squeaking and whistling like a dolphin, face impassive, silver eyes looking at me without recognition, without any human emotion.

I'm trapped. I used my free arm to sign out my plea in the underwater gesture language. She watched the movements without recognition, and I let my arm drift, dark clouds drifting across my mind.

A pair of strong webbed hands took hold of my trapped arm. I opened my eyes to see the girl hovering before me, emotionless face only inches away. She pulled at my arm, she levered up the mangrove root. With a wrench, my arm pulled free.

I drifted underwater, too disoriented and oxygen-deprived to swim toward air. A hand on my back, and the girl pushed me to the surface, just as a dolphin will nudge an injured pod-mate up.

I took a great gulp of air, lungs hurting as they expanded, the sunlight blinding after so long below. I filled my lungs again and again, dizzy with relief. Around me, the pod surfaced, whistling, dorsal fins flashing, great black eyes gleaming at me across the waves. Then a pair of silver Sea Person eyes appeared, and the girl bobbed up beside me, seawater flowing down from her hair.

"*¡Gracias!*" I gasped when I could speak. She didn't reply, but looked at me with those strange, inhuman eyes.

I hauled myself aside, gripping a mangrove trunk, and pulled myself out of the water, shivering with exhaustion and delayed reaction as I sat, dripping, on the mangrove branch. The girl stayed in the water, swimming closer, the dolphin pod circling around us.

"Thank you for saving me," I said. "I'm Cesar, of the Reina Solis tribe. Who are you?"

She just looked at me, face blank. Then she flipped away with a high-pitched dolphin whistle, flashing among the pod.

I stared after her. She was clearly a Sea Person, from the gills on her throat to her outspread flipper-feet to her mass of silver hair, threaded through with venomous tentacles. She was one of my people. But she was utterly different from anyone I'd ever known. She was naked for a start, and I blushed to see a girl without so much as a single bracelet or necklace. But as I looked closer, I saw there was more to it than that. She was swimming among the dolphins like she knew them, nudging and sliding against them like they were her family. And she was *acting* like a dolphin, I realized, spinning around with her pod-mates, circling back to look at me with one eye and then another, just as they did. She even swam like they did, with her whole body, rather than kicking like a normal Sea Person would.

"Can you…understand me?" I asked the next time she circled back.

She just gave another squeak and dived away. She couldn't, I realized at last. She spoke no human language.

I watched her swim among the dolphins, rubbing against them, nudging them as they nudged each other. She was a dolphin, I realized at last, but also a person. She was a Dolphin Girl. And she'd saved my life.

"I'm going to swim home now," I told her the next time she flashed around. "But maybe I'll come back tomorrow, *claro*?"

She let out a laughing whistle, and I dived into the water. The dolphins, and the Dolphin Girl, swam with me awhile, flying through the water, but then peeled away, disappearing into the depths of the swamp, well before I reached the moorage where our boats were anchored.

I hesitated in the water, watching them go, the Dolphin Girl's hair shining silver in the shadows, glittering rainbow stars in the dimness, as she left without a backward glance.

***

Mind full of my adventure, I made it home without incident. Perhaps the dolphins had guided me more than I realized, as I did not become lost in the mangrove forest, but soon swam up to our boats, lolling in the crystal-clear waters. I told no one of what had happened, not even my frantic mother when she demanded to know where I'd been. I was roundly and justly scolded for wandering off alone into the mangrove swamp, and sent to bed without supper.

I barely noticed. My mind was full of the Dolphin Girl. I kept a watch over the darkening bay, but didn't see her that night, and the next day I was kept confined to the camp, helping my mother with repairs and cleaning. Around us, our tribe worked and explored, harvesting what they could from the swamp, led by grim-faced Rodrigo, our headman. I was terrified that one of the explorers would see the Dolphin Girl—I felt instinctively that she was *mine*—but no one returned with stories of a mysterious girl living with a pod of dolphins.

My own mind was awhirl with questions, though. I sidled up to my mother that night after supper. "Mama," I said, "are we the first Sea People here?"

"Yes, as far as I know," she said, barely looking up from scrubbing the cookpot. "We're the first people here in these swamps at all. Why do you ask?"

"No reason," I said airily. "I just wondered if…anyone might have been washed up here or something."

"It's possible," she shrugged. "People get separated from their tribes, washed out to sea…It happens. That's why you should be more careful, Cesar. If that happened to you, you'd die."

"*Maybe* not," I said, thinking of the Dolphin Girl. "I *might* live. A pod of dolphins might save me or something."

Sitting nearby mending a net, Rodrigo snorted. *"That's* not likely, Cesar. People can't live with beasts."

My mother bent her head and blushed, as she often did when Rodrigo spoke to her or me. Sonia, Rodrigo's wife, glared at her, face set with old resentment. I shifted a little, uncomfortably. Mama's husband, my older brother's father, had died well before my birth, and, though no one would say so, it was an open secret that Rodrigo was my father. One might have thought, in that case, that he would have taken an affectionate interest in me, or taken pains to care for me and my mother—but, though he made sure my family was always provided for, he was a cold, remote man, and we had an uneasy relationship.

"Why not?" I asked, a bit defiantly. "If a baby was swept away and a pod of dolphins found her—"

"They'd probably eat her." Rodrigo held up his net to the firelight and grunted.

"They might not," I said. "They might raise her as one of them."

He looked up with a raised silver eyebrow. "Where'd this come from?"

"Yeah, Cesar," said my half-brother Jaime. "What are you on about?"

"Nothing," I said hastily. "I was just thinking."

Mama laughed softly and kissed my cheek. "That's enough thinking for one night, Cesar. Go to bed. You've got a big day tomorrow. We've found a good ruin in the forest."

***

There were, as I have stated, ruins in these northern forests, ruins from before the Drowning of the World that had not yet been picked over. We marvelled over them: all the ruins to the south had been scoured of any useful materials long ago. Even our plastic had been in our tribe for generations. I wondered that the ancient people had placed buildings in such a swamp, but of course it hadn't been a swamp back then: the rising sea levels had drowned so much of the lost civilization.

The one Mama guided me to, along with a group of other women and children, was choked with mangrove trees, but its cement and metal walls still rose high, and even the roof was still intact in some places. We scattered, exclaiming over our finds, scavenging metal, glass and plastic, stowing away our loot in the baskets and leaf-bags we'd brought along.

I worked my way some distance from the others, careful not to cut myself on the many sharp objects, and emerged out onto a cracked concrete platform in the open, along which the water lapped and murmured. I came to a halt, taking in the view: a wide expanse of open water, bordered with mangrove forest, and overhead the dark heavy clouds of an approaching storm. The air hung heavy and intense.

There came a splash, and I looked down to see a dorsal fin cutting the water. It was the dolphin pod again, swimming toward me, their freckled bodies easily visible in the clear water, babies flying alongside their long smooth mothers. And they weren't alone.

The Dolphin Girl trilled up at me as she glided past. I laughed aloud in delight and sat at the platform's edge, legs dangling. "*¡Hola!*"

She did not smile at me—I don't think she knew how to smile—but she whistled invitingly and splashed me as she passed. I splashed her back, kicking the water, and she glided away, as smooth and swift as her fellow dolphins. A large female gave a warning whistle that I could recognize as maternal concern, and clacked her jaws angrily at me as she glided past. I held up my hands in self-defense.

"I won't harm her," I promised the Dolphin Girl's mother. The Dolphin Girl swam back, treading water near the platform, but not pulling herself out. Her hair fanned out around her, luminous venom pumping.

"This is a Pre-Drowned ruin." I patted the cement. "From before the Drowning of the World. Do you know about that? They say people changed the climate, warmed things so much that the sea levels rose…That's why the Land People created Sea People, they say. People who could live in the ocean, so humanity could survive. But Mama says we were created by Iemanjá the Queen of the Sea, and Land People were made by Mother Mary, so I don't know…What do you think?"

She let out a long, whistling squeak and dived away. I laughed again and, putting down my bag, pushed off the edge into the water.

There my hair came alive with venom, tentacles reaching out, flashing with color. My feet spread out, becoming flippers, and my transparent inner eyelids closed as my hands spread their finger-webs wide. I swam after the Dolphin Girl, among the flash-fast whales, and we played together underwater, above the undulating meadow of seagrass studded with submerged fragments of ruin, whirling around each other and around the dolphins, riding the bubbling wakes left by their tails, swimming among the ruins and through arches of mangrove roots. I gestured to her underwater, and spoke human language at the surface, and she trilled at me, and the dolphins whistled to both of us, and it did not matter at all that we couldn't understand each other.

At last, as the first hot raindrops fell hissing into the sea, each one a silver splash on the surface, I pulled myself reluctantly out onto the platform again. I could hear my mother's voice, anxiously calling my name from the other side of the ruin.

The Dolphin Girl swam to the edge, looking up at me. I stood, taking up my bag, and waved to her. "*Adios*. I've got to go. See you later."

I turned and ran back to the scavenging group, with only her loud splash and whistle to bid me farewell, through the growing storm.

***

After that, I often met with the dolphins, and with the Dolphin Girl.

Somehow, I was never discovered. Of course, it did help that I was the youngest of my family and always somewhat solitary and prone to wander. The other children might have noticed, but they were in the habit of avoiding me due to my ambiguous social position, and never tried to stop me. It was always a relief to put the tribe behind me, with the unspoken truths swirling around me and my parents. Life was simpler with the dolphins and the Dolphin Girl.

The Dolphin Girl and I played, along with the young dolphins of the pod, exploring the channels and islands of the forest, spinning around one another in underwater games, the wavering lines of light patterning our skin. We explored the great murky roots of the mangroves, hid from sharks, and whirled with the young dolphins in dizzying games. We even helped the adult dolphins hunt, the Dolphin Girl and I hovering underwater, our hair spread out in glowing nets, while the dolphins drove schools of fish to be caught in the multicolored strands and die. I took my share home to cook, and earned a growing reputation as a good fisher; but the Dolphin Girl ate her fish raw as her pod-mates did, tearing them apart with her fingers and teeth. I showed her how to hunt crustaceans too, and she ate them in the same manner, claws snapping and bits of chitin drifting slowly to the seafloor.

She never left the water. I climbed out all the time, of course, exploring sandbars and islands at low tide, and climbing into the tree branches to throw down fruit for her and the dolphins to play with. But the Dolphin Girl never once tried following me, never showed any inclination to come out on land. The one time I tried to pull her out, hauling on her arms, she resisted, screaming and breaking away, buffeting me hard with her shoulder before swimming away, the pod escorting her off. She was a truly remarkable swimmer, even for a Sea Person, as fast and graceful as the dolphins, and she easily outpaced me underwater, hair flowing behind her as her whole body kicked and undulated.

I grew to know the dolphins, over the course of the season, their personalities and distinguishing features. I had been right: the large female was the Dolphin Girl's adopted mother. They were very affectionate with each other, constantly trilling to one another, embracing in the dolphin manner by rubbing their bodies together, and swimming together in tandem. The Dolphin Girl's mother was gentle and accepting of me, which was fortunate, for I don't think the Dolphin Girl would have gone against her if she'd tried to drive me off. On the whole, the pod was accepting toward me, welcoming me with clicks and squeaks whenever I showed up, and letting me play with the Dolphin Girl as long as I wanted.

I tried to teach her human speech, gesturing underwater and pointing things out and telling her the words at the surface, but she could not comprehend my lessons. She just stared, or flashed away, clicking, buzzing, and squeaking. Human language had no meaning for her, any more than human customs or human concepts. She truly believed herself a dolphin, I realized, and maybe she was: a dolphin in a human body, living as a dolphin should.

Perhaps that was why I felt no urge to tell my family or tribe about her. She didn't need rescue or help: she was living the life she was meant to, and it was my privilege to be her friend and share that life, just a little. Perhaps she had been born a Sea Person with a dolphin's soul, or Iemanjá had willed her into being as a wild thing, or perhaps she'd just been swept out to sea as a baby, to be rescued and raised by the dolphin pod—but in any case, she didn't belong in my world.

***

The storm season came to an end. The hurricanes grew less frequent, further spaced, and the sun came out more often. Rodrigo decided now was the time to head east, back to the islands, there to harvest what bounty we could find.

I managed to track down the Dolphin Girl one last time before we left. "I'm leaving," I told her sadly, floating in the water with her, our heads above the surface. "We're heading east tomorrow."

She looked back, face expressionless as always. But in her eyes was a sad, wordless comprehension.

"Maybe I'll be back next year," I said. "Will you be here?" Dolphins do not have set migrations, but it's no sure thing that they'll be in the same place all year, every year.

She let out a long mewling whistle in response and rubbed against me in a dolphin hug, body strong and sleek. I rubbed back, smiling.

"I'll miss you." I waved at the other dolphins, swimming around us. "You too. Take care of her."

They whistled and clicked after me as I swam away, clouds casting fleeting shadows over the water and the mangrove trees.

***

We set sail, heading east into the islands. I was quiet the first few days, missing the Dolphin Girl; but at age ten I couldn't stay sad for long, and was soon fishing and playing with the other children, swimming around the ships, and avoiding the heavy splash of the oars.

The islands were forested, with the remains of cities and farms lying wrecked in the wilderness. The sea washed in and out of broken old buildings, stained with rust, and in some sheltered places we even found skeletons of the people who had lived and died there, stained with algae and patched with sponges, sloshing back and forth in the water. But there was life too: wild pigs, fat for hunting, slipped through the bird-singing forest, and the turquoise waters lapped and surged over coral reefs rich with fish. We were the first tribe to arrive, and we reaped a good harvest, of fish, fruit, and scavenged materials. I kept an eye out for dolphins, but though I saw several pods, there was no sign of any Sea People living among them.

Midway through the season, another tribe unexpectedly appeared, the Estrellas Rojas, the red stars on their sails clearly visible for miles. Starved for company after long months in isolation, we rejoiced at their arrival. The feast went on late into the night, around the sparking fires, adults talking and exchanging news while the children ran and played. Someone struck up a flute, another a drum, and soon the young people were dancing, the girls swaying in a graceful line across from the boys.

I saw my brother, Jaime, exchanging looks with the girl across from him in the dance set, and my mother noticed too. She went over to talk to the girl's mother, both of them very friendly while their children danced and laughed in the firelight.

Within a few days, all was arranged. Jaime was wed to the girl, Rafaela, standing hands-linked in the dawn's light, up to their knees in the surf while they draped shell necklaces over each other's heads and kissed. Jaime moved into the hut our families built for him and his bride, and, when her tribe moved on a few weeks later, my brother went with them.

"Why must Jaime leave?" I asked my mother, plaintively, as the ships sailed away, Jaime on board.

Mama sobbed, and that frightened me. All Sea People constantly shed tears, to rid our bodies of salt from the seawater we drink, but to cry tears of emotion is much rarer. I took her hand, pressing close. "Don't cry, Mama."

She sniffed, wiping away her tears. "It's the way it has to be, Cesar," she said thickly. "Young men go with their wives' families. Most of the time," she amended.

"But why?" I demanded.

"Men don't raise children like women do," my mother explained, "so they don't need their mothers and aunts and sisters at their sides. Any hardworking young man can forge a place for himself among strangers; but women need their relatives' help."

"*You* don't have any relatives," I pointed out with the heartless honesty of the young.

"They're all dead." Mama glanced at Rodrigo, who had already turned away from the sea and was heading back to camp.

"Oh. Right." I shuffled uncomfortably. I knew the story. Mama had been young, only fourteen when her family, an offshoot from a larger tribe, had been shipwrecked in a terrible storm. Only she had survived, and adopted by the Reina Solis. She was married to a much older widower of the tribe, Jaime's father, only to see him die too a few years later.

And now, with Jaime gone, Mama and I were truly alone. "So…when I marry…*I'll* have to leave?"

"Yes, Cesar." Mama smiled and nudged me playfully, though her own expression was still sorrowful. "Don't look so worried! You're a good boy. You'll do well."

I said nothing, but the thought of leaving my mother all alone was a dark shadow in my heart.

***

As the storms approached, we headed west again, back to the sheltered mangrove forests. I kept a more eager watch than ever, my heart leaping at every sign of a dolphin, only to sink again as I saw only ordinary whales, bounding alongside the ships or riding in our wakes, with no Sea girls swimming among them.

We made camp on the island where we'd stayed before. I snuck away and swam off repeatedly, to places where I thought I remembered meeting the Dolphin Girl. But I did not see her, for long weeks, until after the first major storm.

She and her pod happened upon me unexpectedly. I was out fishing, my hair full of wriggling, dying fish, when there came a high-pitched, blinding whistle. I turned eagerly, hair undulating in the murky green water, and cried out, a great bubble rising from my throat, as the Dolphin Girl flashed near, squeaking, and clicking to see me. Around us, her pod swam and danced, her dolphin mother and dolphin aunts crooning, her cousins bouncing among them.

The Dolphin Girl and I hugged dolphin-style, rubbing against one another, and after that it was as though I'd never left. We played and fished together, just as we had before, exploring the forest and helping her pod with the hunting. The Dolphin Girl was just as I remembered: just as great a swimmer, still naked, face still expressionless, but her vocalizations just as varied. She'd grown, of course, just as I had, and must have had an encounter with a shark sometime during my absence: I could see the scars on her legs, still red and raw-looking. But she was in perfect health, stronger and faster than I was, and always greeted me with a splash and a whistle of delight.

All through the storm season, we played together, just as we had last year, and never were we caught. We parted only at the end of the season, when the Reina Solis migrated east once more. I spent the dry season happily anticipating the storms, and my return to the Dolphin Girl. But the next year, when my tribe returned to the mangroves, the dolphin pod wasn't there. They'd moved on.

I was miserable to miss the Dolphin Girl, and kept an eye out for her all through the season, hoping to see her or her pod. But I wasn't able to sneak off as I had before. I was twelve that year, and Rodrigo took a sudden interest in me, insisting that I start learning all I needed to know as a man. My time was thus consumed with learning to sail, to mend the boats, to craft tools, and to fish and hunt with the other men, particularly Rodrigo. I had mixed feelings about this. Part of me was proud and happy to be learning how to be a man, but I still dreaded leaving home.

And any hopes I'd had that my father and I would develop a real relationship were crushed quickly. Rodrigo was a cold and impartial teacher, and that was all he was to me: my teacher. He never invited me to the fire circles, as other fathers did with boys my age and he never told me stories or joked with me or even held a real conversation. I watched the other adolescent boys with their fathers, jealousy aching my heart, and I worried more than ever for my mother once I was gone.

Time passed, and storm chased storm across the sea. The next year, I was thirteen. I was taller than I had been, though I had not yet hit my growth, and I was more awkward and clumsy by the day. I had lost my childish grace, but not yet acquired a man's strength, and I seemed to have no place in the world; a child who was no longer a child, a boy with a father who was no father, and a mother who had no family. The other boys were friendly enough, but distant, and I longed more than ever for the Dolphin Girl, the one aspect of my life that was actually *mine*.

A few days after we arrived at the mangroves that year, I managed to sneak off. It was a hot, still, overcast day. The mangroves hung limp and the water seemed uneasy, lapping ominously at their trunks. I pressed deeper into the forest, giving the high-pitched whistle I'd learned could summon the dolphins—if they were here.

They were.

There came a flurry, a series of clicks, and the dolphin pod came flying up, the Dolphin Girl among them. She swam up to me, body longer and stronger than ever, and I saw that she had changed: tiny breasts sprouting on her chest, a dusting of hair between her legs—and still entirely naked. The sight made me feel strange, especially as she arched up against me in the dolphin-hug. I twisted away, and she looked at me with her expressionless face, her fathomless eyes.

We explored, all together, searching for fish among the mangrove roots. The Dolphin Girl bent and twisted sinuously among the roots, seeming with no fear that she would get caught. The scars on her legs were old now, and she swam with greater strength and assurance than ever, squeaking and calling to her cousins, who leaped and danced around us. Further out, the adults swam sinuously, clicking as they flashed in and out of sight.

Later, the Dolphin Girl and I hovered underwater, hair splayed out, while the dolphins dashed away to herd a school of fish into our glowing net. It was then, lurking underwater, that I heard the splash.

Twisting around, hair swirling around me, I saw the long, slim underside of a canoe. Another splash, and a paddle made lightning-bright bubbles rise as it dug forward. They were heading in our direction.

I turned to push away the Dolphin Girl, to warn her, but she was already gone, swimming in that amazingly fast way of hers, hair flashing as she fled after her pod. Within seconds she was gone.

Another, larger splash, and Rodrigo came swimming toward me, the beads of his bracelets and anklets trailing in the water, his long hair flashing bright. *Who was that?* he asked in the underwater sign language.

I don't know what you mean, I lied in the same language.

His eyes narrowed at me, and he made the *surface* gesture. We broke the surface together, lungs pulling in air as our gills sealed and our inner eyelids slid back. Our hair coiled around us, lighting the dull gray water.

"Don't *lie*, Cesar," Rodrigo snapped at me. He glared at me with far more emotion than he'd shown me in a long time. "There was somebody there. I saw their hair glowing as they swam away. Who were they?"

"The Dolphin Girl." I whispered it, soft and miserable.

"The *Dolphin* Girl?" he echoed incredulously.

"She lives with the dolphins," I muttered, shaking with shame at my betrayal and crumpling inside that my secret was out. "It's like she *is* a dolphin. She acts just like one…I think she thinks she's a dolphin."

Rodrigo stared at me. "How long have you known about this Dolphin Girl, Cesar?"

"Three years." I could barely squeeze it out.

"Three *years*?" he nearly shouted. "And you only just tell me *now*?" He cuffed me around the head. "Waves of Iemanjá, Cesar, have you no sense at all?"

"She's *happy*," I said desperately, holding my aching head. "The dolphins are her family. They take care of her."

"She's a lost child," Rodrigo said grimly. "We'll have to capture her."

Horror seized me. "No!"

"Rodrigo's right," called another man from the canoe. "We can't just leave her there." He peered keenly into the forest, after the Dolphin Girl.

"No, please—!" But Rodrigo had already caught hold of me under his arm and was hauling me back to the canoe.

Back at camp, Rodrigo made me tell the tribe everything: how I'd met the Dolphin Girl, how I'd snuck off to meet her, how she behaved and lived like a dolphin, and how she was unaware of her own humanity. The children seemed fascinated, edging close and listening with shining eyes, but the adults were all horrified at my tale, and I was in dire disgrace for not telling them years earlier.

"A lost child living with animals and you don't tell anyone?" Mama hissed after Rodrigo finally let me go. She slapped me, though not very hard. "What were you *thinking*?"

"She's happy living with them," I muttered, clutching my slapped face. "She really thinks she's a dolphin."

"Well, she's not," Mama said flatly. "And it's up to us to save her."

No one would listen to my frantic attempts to explain that the Dolphin Girl didn't need saving. Rodrigo organized a search party to patrol the mangroves, and everyone was instructed to look out for girls living with dolphins—everyone but me. I was confined to camp, under my mother's eye, and strictly forbidden from swimming off.

The other children sidled up, eyes bright, half-repelled and half-attracted by the one who was in such trouble. "What's she like?" they asked. "How'd you meet this Dolphin Girl? What's she look like? Does she have a snout? Does she have a blowhole?" I didn't have the heart to answer, and my mother eventually drove them off.

I gave offerings to Iemanjá, the ocean goddess, protector of the Sea People, setting flowers adrift on the waves. I whispered prayers, begging her to protect her dolphin-daughter, to send the Dolphin Girl and her pod far away to save her from the hunters.

Iemanjá didn't answer my prayers. On the third day, Rodrigo and the hunting party returned with the Dolphin Girl.

They approached through the channels, in one of the long canoes, the men paddling and swimming ahead as they pulled the towlines. And in the bottom of the canoe, as they hauled it ashore, was a bound figure, mewling and struggling against her fetters.

It was the Dolphin Girl. For the first time ever, out of the water, lights and venom fading from her hair as she flopped around, helpless as a caught fish.

My mother, the children, and everyone else still in camp gathered to gape as the men swung the Dolphin Girl out of the canoe onto the beach. She writhed around, sand sticking to her damp skin, trying to get back to the water, and letting out high-pitched distress squeaks. I scanned the bay, but saw no sign of her pod. Had the men driven them away?

"We caught her!" announced Rodrigo. "We caught the Dolphin Girl." He bent to untie her, careful to avoid any flailing limbs, but she didn't strike out at him. She just lay in the sand, staring at him, at us, with huge, terrified eyes.

"How?" Mama leaned forward, fascinated. "How did you capture her? Just look at her! It's like she's half beast."

"It wasn't easy," grunted Rodrigo. "But we finally cornered her among the mangroves. Come on, girl, on your feet…" He took hold of her arms, pulling her up. She shrieked, struggling against him. He was stronger, though, and set her on her feet.

She collapsed immediately, falling helplessly to the ground. Out here on land, surrounded by ordinary Sea People, I could see her differences more clearly than ever: her nakedness, her scars, her expressionless face, even in her terror. She didn't contract her flippers into land-feet—was she even able to?—and the muscles in her legs were strangely shaped, arranged in all the wrong places. She couldn't stand up at all, I realized: she had never stood up on land in her life. She really was like a caught fish.

"You have to let her go!" I surprised even myself with my loud shout, and everyone turned to stare at me. "Please," I begged. "You have to let her go. She doesn't belong with us. She can't even stand!"

"We'll have to teach her, then." Rodrigo came over to lay a hand on my shoulder, and I fell very still. This was the most affection my father had ever shown me. "And she does belong with us, Cesar. She's a Sea Person. We can't leave a child of our people lost in the mangroves." His grip tightened on my shoulder, and he smiled warmly. "You did the right thing, Cesar, telling me."

His hand was warm and callused on my bare shoulder. It felt so good. I looked up at Rodrigo, into his approving eyes. He had never touched me for so long a time before. He had never shown me such warmth. In that moment, he really seemed like my father.

So I stood back. I stood back, and I let them drag the crying Dolphin Girl away.

***

She could not walk, but she thrashed toward the sea so violently that Rodrigo finally had her tied to a pole of his tent. She might have untied the fetter—it was just rope, not tightly bound—but she didn't know how. She thrashed and struggled until she collapsed with exhaustion. Even sprawled out, sides heaving, she stared toward the water, keening, squeaking, and clicking, but her family did not appear.

My mother tried to get her to eat. She ladled hot fish soup toward her mouth, roasted clams. The Dolphin Girl turned her head away, breath sobbing in her chest. Her hair hung lank around her, wrong and ugly after I'd seen it lit up and dancing in the water.

Her cries disturbed the camp all night, and the next morning she slept like one dead. She lay in the shade of the cover Rodrigo built for her, ribs barely moving, her terror and despair evident even at rest.

Being near her hurt, but I couldn't bring myself to leave her, even though nothing I tried helped to calm her. My mother watched us both with troubled eyes as the day went on and the Dolphin Girl awoke and tried yet again to escape, only to be pulled back by the leash on her leg. She cried out, a long, keening wail.

"Rodrigo," Mama said when he returned from fishing that day, "are you sure this is a good idea? What if she ends up killing herself?"

"It will be fine, Ana," he growled, and that evening he took out his flute and played it to the Dolphin Girl, long, low, soothing notes. She actually seemed to calm down, falling still to listen. The music soothed me too, still sitting rigid nearby as night fell and the waters lapped and played around the island, invisible in the dark. But when Rodrigo's flute fell silent, the Dolphin Girl let out her cries again, straining on her bindings, yearning toward the sea.

I spoke then, for the first time all day. "Please," I said to Rodrigo. "You have to let her go."

Rodrigo's flute lowered. He looked at me, and in his eyes there was no hint of the warmth I'd seen yesterday: only chill determination. I wasn't his son in that moment, if I ever had been. I was just something in his way.

I was shaking by the time he got to his feet and strode away. I watched him go with a sense of helpless hurt, helpless despair. Beside me, the Dolphin Girl struggled and whimpered.

He's never going to love me. I'm not sure why that was the moment I realized the truth, after avoiding it for years. Rodrigo would never love me, no matter what I did, and he would never be a true father to me.

I looked up, shaking with the finality of this realization, and met my mother's eyes. She knew. She'd always known. She gazed at me sadly for a long silent moment, before getting up and leaving me alone with the Dolphin Girl.

I looked at her: sprawled on the sand, helpless and caught. I had betrayed her for nothing. I had destroyed her life for nothing.

I clicked at her: my few, clumsy dolphin sounds. But they seemed to soothe her. She fell still, eyes reflecting the dim light of the dying fires, panting with pain and exhaustion.

I looked back at her, shame and sorrow crowding my heart. I scanned the camp—perhaps I could get her away right now—but there were men on watch, sitting by the light of planted torches. I could not free her without their noticing.

So I let out a long, high-pitched whistle. Sitting on the sand beside the captive Dolphin Girl, I whistled, long and loud, over the creeping tide. The mangroves rustled in the evening breeze. The water lapped and murmured. And I could only pray that the dolphins, or Iemanjá, had heard my call.

***

They heard.

The next morning, the camp was woken by splashes out in the bay, and the Dolphin Girl's frantic whistles. We all came out of our plastic-draped tents, blinking sleepily in the dawn's light, to see what had happened.

It was the dolphin pod, swimming back and forth in the sparkling waters, calling to their daughter, who struggled to be free, to get to them. Her dolphin-mother came very close, surging almost onto the beach, and Rodrigo charged at her, shouting. She lurched off, squeaking, snout opening to reveal rows of sharp teeth, and splashed him as she swam away.

"They're not acting naturally," said Sonia, shaking her head at them uneasily.

"They want her back," I said quietly. No one heard me but Mama. She looked at me sharply, but said nothing.

The men, led by Rodrigo, tried to drive the pod off, lunging spears at them from the boats and shouting. Nothing worked. The pod shied away from the spears, but always they returned, keening and crying out to the Dolphin Girl. She keened and cried out too, in desperate response, her gaze fixed on them. Rodrigo tried playing music again, but nothing could soothe the Dolphin Girl, not when her pod was within sight. Her bound ankle was turning bloody from her struggles.

I heard my mother pleading with Rodrigo that afternoon. "Please, she has to go back," she said quietly inside his tent. "If we don't give her back, the dolphins may start attacking us."

"They will forget her, Ana," he said. "And she will forget them."

"I don't think they will. I *know* she won't. It isn't proper, but I think maybe she's lived among them for too long, Rodrigo. Cesar's right: she's more dolphin than human now. We can't change that."

Rodrigo would not yield, but I saw the troubled looks the tribe gave one another, the frightened glances toward the water, where the dolphins waited. No one dared go in the sea that day. An angry dolphin is a formidable creature; and there were other uneasy whispers spreading through the camp. Perhaps the dolphins would curse us so our nets would never fill again, the tribe murmured, or perhaps the Dolphin Girl was a daughter of Iemanjá, and we were risking the goddess's wrath by keeping her from the sea.

But Rodrigo stood like a rusted spike from a Pre-Drowned ruin, facing the dolphins and the heavy storm clouds beyond, and I knew that the struggle had seeped into his soul and he would not yield.

The Dolphin Girl curled up under her shelter as the first raindrops fell, drawing her scarred legs to her chest. I stood under the fall of warm rain, my hair half-reacting to the deluge, pulsing faint colors sluggishly as rainwater ran down its length. Around me, raindrops soaked into the sand.

Across camp, Mama stood, her hair also half-awake, glowing faintly like a beacon in the dark afternoon. She met my gaze, and I knew she knew what I planned.

I nodded to her, once. And she nodded in reply.

***

That evening, the rainclouds cleared away, and the sun set in a glory of red and gold over the mangrove forest. The Dolphin Girl had stopped struggling, worn out from exertion and despair. But she didn't sleep, merely lying on her side, staring blankly at the water, where her family paced and waited.

Darkness fell and the full moon rose over the ocean's horizon. Its light silvered the backs of the dolphins as they rose to the surface, spume puffing from the tops of their heads. The ocean surged in response to the fullness of the moon, rising over the beach in strong waves. The camp lay quiet: it had been a sorry, subdued sort of evening, riven with anxiety over the dolphins, with no stories, music, laughter, or song. Everyone had retired early, and now only the watchmen stayed awake, skin and hair glowing orange in the light of their torches.

From the darkness, I watched as Mama walked up to them, limbs loose and easy, carrying a pot of fruit wine. "*¡Hola, muchachos!*" she called cheerily. "What a day it's been, hasn't it? Why don't we have a drop to warm ourselves, after all that's happened?"

The two men looked at her silently. They glanced at the Dolphin Girl. They knew exactly what Mama was up to. But they chose to turn away, to my mother. They took the wine, and she sat down with them, laughing and drinking.

I moved then. I crept through the jagged black shadows and the moonlight until I groped my way into the Dolphin Girl's shelter. It was completely black in there, the shadows made obsidian by moonlight. But still the Dolphin Girl's eyes gleamed, her breath ragged.

"I'm sorry," I whispered then. "I'm sorry for what I did to you. I'm sorry for my selfishness, and my weakness." It occurred to me that this was a very adult sort of thing to say, and I felt a pang of utter loss: I would never be a child again. I would never be innocent again, never yearn for my father's approval, and never play with the Dolphin Girl, not ever again.

The Dolphin Girl crooned, and in that sound I heard a sort of forgiveness. Or perhaps I only wished for it.

I laid a hand on her leg, warning her to hold still. And I untied her, fumbling apart the knot in the dark.

The Dolphin Girl let out a triumphant squeak as her ankle fell free. Inside the tent, Rodrigo snorted in his sleep, and I whispered, "Shh! Shh!" as I took the fetter from her ankle, gingerly peeling the fibers from her bloody flesh.

The watchmen let out a loud laugh, covering the noise. They knew. They knew what was happening, but they looked away, focusing on the amusing story Mama was relating, as I pulled the Dolphin Girl toward the sea.

She could not walk, but neither could I carry her. We made slipping, stumbling progress down the beach, me walking backward as I hauled on her arms, her crawling awkwardly after me. After days on land, she still had not contracted her feet, so her flippers plowed clumsily through the sand, throwing stinging particles over my legs.

Behind me, the voices of the waves grew louder, and the dolphins squeaked, splashing as they came awake, sensing the approach of their daughter. The Dolphin Girl whistled, and I frantically hushed her again as I hauled her further down the beach.

The waves surged against my legs, and the Dolphin Girl broke away, flopping down onto the wet sand and writhing into the water, just like a beached dolphin. I took hold of her again, pulling her into deeper water, and her hair lit up, the venom flowing, her gills opening, as she kicked forward and dived into the sea.

My hair glowed as it floated in the water around my waist, sand shifting beneath my feet. I watched as the Dolphin Girl swam forward to meet her family, her hair gleaming with a hundred colored lights, shining like stars in the water. The dolphins whistled and sang for joy, swimming and arching around her, and she clicked and sang back, eyes shining in the dark.

At last, when the pod had greeted her, when they had all sung their joy, they began to slip away, arching below the surface, tails leaving dim white splashes. Only the Dolphin Girl and her mother remained, swimming to and fro, looking at me with their huge eyes in the moonlight. They knew what I had done. That I had led to the Dolphin Girl's capture, but that I had freed her.

I raised a dripping hand to wave goodbye. "*Adios*," I said softly.

The Dolphin Girl let out one last whistling click. Then she dived below the waves, following her mother, and the lights of her hair faded away as she swam beneath the moon's shimmering trail.

Then she was gone.

***

That was the last time I ever saw the Dolphin Girl.

The next morning, when Rodrigo awoke to find his captive gone, he was furious. He turned on me, shouting that I had let the Dolphin Girl go. The watchmen, perhaps a little bleary-eyed from a long night of wine and entertainment, blandly denied any such thing. "The rope must have frayed," said one of the watchmen mildly. "She *was* struggling quite a lot."

Rodrigo glared furiously. He knew I'd freed her, and he knew the watchmen had been in on it. But around him was a palisade of stony faces: the tribe had had enough. Sonia and my mother both glared at him, for once on the same side.

My father wisely closed his mouth. The look he gave me, though, would have frozen my soul had I still cared anything for his opinion. As it was, I looked at him steadily, face as expressionless as the Dolphin Girl's. He faltered, blinking in surprise, before he turned away.

I did not sneak off again that storm season, nor did I look for the Dolphin Girl. She and her family were far away by now, I knew, and they would never return to the mangroves. Rodrigo was finished trying to teach me anything, but I worked beside the other men, fishing, building, and hunting. And with every net I cast, every pole I pounded into the ground, every flash of my adze building a canoe, I felt my childhood, and the Dolphin Girl, fall further behind.

That dry season, when we went back out to the islands, the Estrellas Rojas were already there to greet us. Mama and I both fell on Jaime with happy cries, and were overjoyed to meet his new baby daughter. Mama and I spent every minute we could with Jaime and his new family, and the Estrellas Rojas. It was good to be back with my brother, and among a tribe that cared nothing for our family's history. And at the end of the dry season, it seemed very natural that Mama and I should accompany the Estrellas Rojas on their migration. After all, Sonia pointed out with a big grin on her face, Mama had no daughters, and no family left living. If she did not leave with her sons, she would have no support in her old age. That I could have stayed with the Reina Solis instead of Mama leaving was something no one suggested. By then, Mama and I were glad to go.

The last I ever saw of Rodrigo, the man who had been no father to me, was his thin figure standing on the island shore, watching our red-starred ship slip away. He did not wave, he did not call out farewells. But he stood and watched, still as a ruined tower, until the island finally disappeared from view.

So my mother and I lived with my brother and his family among the Estrellas Rojas, and I eventually married within this tribe. I have travelled far with my new tribe, and I am glad to be married to Blanca, my warm, lovable, and utterly human wife. I love our children, and I am glad to live with my brother and his family, and that our mother is here with us. But I will never forget the Dolphin Girl, and a part of me will never stop loving her.

I have no regrets for setting her free. She did not belong with humans, and she would have died like a beached dolphin out on land. Living with the dolphins, she leads the life she was made for, the life Iemanjá has ordained. She has a dolphin's soul in a human body, and nothing could ever change that.

I have not seen her again, and I don't look for her. But sometimes, late at night or early in the morning, I think I hear her. Perhaps it is only wishful thinking, or a fragment of dream, but I hear her click and whistle, feel the slap of waves as she sloshes water against the boat, and the cries and squeaks of her dolphin-kin. She is an aunt now, and her many nieces and nephews circle around her in the water, flukes smooth, tails strong, as she swims close, scarred and thin from a life at sea, but eyes shining still with joy and love.

It is only a dream. It is only ever a dream, and I always open my eyes to an ordinary day, without her in it. But I know in my heart that she lives still, and remembers still, and, somewhere far away, where humankind has not yet reached, she sings and laughs with the dolphins, her kin.

***

Rose Strickman is a fantasy, science fiction, and horror writer living in Seattle, Washington. Her work has appeared in anthologies such as *Sword and Sorceress 32, Earth: Giants, Golems & Gargoyles* and

Swashbuckling Cats: Nine Lives on the Seven Seas, as well as online e-zines such as *Feed Your Monster* and *Luna Station Quarterly*.

Please check out her website at https://aqua-wombat-29pf.squarespace.com/ or, for more Drowned World stories, see her Amazon page at: amazon.com/author/rosestrickman

ONCE FREE

BY DAVID MORRIS

CHAPTER ONE
The Storm

RONNIE

When the sirens first sounded, I could barely hear them. Downtown wasn't close. The siren poles were in the center of town and that was a few miles down the hill in the valley. Grandma wouldn't have heard it at all, but she was next to the window. It wasn't unusual to hear the echo of loud noises from the valley.

Grandma turned off the TV where she'd been watching the progress of the storm that was coming our way. When she heard the siren, she grabbed me in one arm, a few things from the kitchen in the other, ran into the makeshift hallway, and stood me on the floor. I'd been making a fuss trying to find out what she was doing, but instead of telling me she sent me down the stairs and into the cellar.

Pushing the button on the ancient light switch, illuminated the tiny cellar from a single bulb handing from the ceiling. The room was lined with shelves, each covered with turn of the century canning jars filled with the preserved harvest from the summer before.

At the time, I was six years old, soon to be seven. It was a clarification I was sure to add to anyone who might ask. I was here in this house because it was summer and I always stayed with Grandma while my parents worked, some fifty miles away.

She had yet to say a word to explain why we were running downstairs. In the corner of the room was a pile of blankets and old pillows, neatly stacked with an old sheet over them. "Ronnie, stay where you are. I'll be right back."

"What's going on," I yelled as Grandma disappeared into the hallway upstairs.

"Don't worry honey," she called back as she turned the corner. "We're having one of those big storms, might even be a hurricane. We'll wait it out down there in the cellar. It'll be fun," she said in an unconvincing tone. "You're about to hear the biggest storm you ever heard. They said it was moving real slow so we're going to be down here for a while. Those blankets over there will come in handy. I'll be right back and we'll set this cellar up all comfy."

I stood there looking around the tiny room. A small wooden door, a few boards really, secured the cellar from the outside world. I knew that door opened onto a concrete stairway to the yard. I'd used it dozens of times investigating the old house.

Grandma came downstairs with a flashlight, a few candles, and a box of matches. She set them down, walked across the small room, and locked the old door that opened to the outside by pushing the dangling hook into the little round screw in loop.

"You just remember," she said. "Don't you open that door until I tell you it's okay. We won't be leaving this cellar 'til it's over. Gitcher self comfy 'cause we're likely gonna be here all night."

CHAPTER TWO
Lost

HUNTER

When the Williams couple brought me home I must have been very young. I don't remember any of it. Looking back, I could remember the newspaper whacks from Allen when I'd pee in the house. Apparently, they were allowed to go in the house, but I wasn't. I remember the long hours at home while they left most days. For the most part it went on that way for a couple of years, then one day something changed.

That day they brought me a new baby boy. They called him Johnny and they'd already set up a whole room for him. The mattress of Johnny's crib was higher than I could see over and I knew Alice wasn't about to let me jump up to see him, so I did the next best thing. The hollow under his crib was just my size. It became my bed from that day forward until the crib was replaced with our new little bed, just big enough for me to curl up at the bottom.

For the next six years I watched him grow into a boy. I followed him to the door each day as he left for school and returned in the afternoon to await his return. I could feel the big difference between Johnny and the Millers. Johnny worshipped me. He was mine to protect and to love. To the Millers, I was a pet. To Johnny, and to me, we were a team.

Allen felt, he had to punish him from time to time. He was the Alpha and all I could do was growl, hoping he wouldn't hear me. I watched him like a hawk to make sure he didn't hurt him. There would be no newspaper whacks for Johnny. Luckily, he was allowed to pee in the house.

Late that spring the whole family went on a long trip. I was stuck in the back seat of the SUV with Johnny. From there I could lean my head out the window and smell the scenery as we continued down the road.

We visited Allen's sister for a few days. There was a lot of activity, with boxes and everyone yelling to everyone else. Then the house was filled with strange people hauling furniture and a house full of boxes in a giant truck. Then, Allen packed the car again as we got ready to leave the now empty house. This time there was a lot more to bring.

From what I could tell his sister was riding with us. There was a big sign out in front of her house and a giant lock on the doorknob.

This time he packed all of the luggage and a few boxes on the roof. That left plenty of room in the back seat for his sister and Johnny leaving the cargo area for me.

I waited for them to lift the back of the SUV to let me in, but instead they all climbed into the car and drove away while I just stood there.

I stayed in the driveway sure that they'd realize they'd left me behind. I was patient at first. I sat there waiting expecting them to return, but hours later when they never came I began to panic. I was afraid to move. I just sat there in her driveway whimpering from time to time, knowing it was getting late and would be getting dark soon. Besides, I was getting hungry.

Across the dirt road that ran in front of the now empty house was a jackrabbit. When it turned to face the other way, I took off like a bullet. The chances of catching him from this distance were small. As he realized I was coming he rose to run through the grasses, but his foot slipped on the dust by the road. It delayed him just long enough for me to grab him and give him a good shake. I wandered off into the grasses to find a place to experiment with it. Before long I was full and my face was a bloody mess.

I could smell the creek that ran nearby and before long I was lying next to it rubbing my wet paws across my muzzle trying to remove the blood and rabbit bits from my face.

It was getting dark, so I walked along the creek and finally found a big stone facing that blocked the wind, rolled into a circle below it, and fell asleep for the night. In the morning, I ran back to the house, but found no traces that they'd returned to get me.

I sat in the driveway and howled. No one heard, but I couldn't stop. My boy Johnny was gone. I had nobody to protect and I was alone.

CHAPTER THREE
Helen

HELEN

The day my new life started, my new owner, who I eventually discovered other people called Helen, came down the concrete hallway filled with built in cages just to see me. I'd been living in this cage for a month. Helen, who I'd eventually come to know as 'Mommy' told the lady who brought her into the hall that she was looking for a dog that was friendly, but fierce looking to scare away intruders. "A real watchdog," she said.

"This is the dog for you then," said the lady from the pound, He's right here." Pointing her finger at me while I examined the two of them, wondering where all of this was going. She opened my cage, assured Mommy that I was really sweet, and brought me out to meet her.

Mommy stepped back, balancing herself on the concrete wall behind her, "But that's a pit bull!" She cried, leaving me with little hope of getting out of this place.

"Isn't he mean?" She asked.

"Oh GOD no, he's a real sweetheart. He just looks mean, and from what you say, he's just the dog for you."

"Then he'll do just fine." She said.

She was a short woman, only about twice my height. If I stood on my legs I think I'd be just as tall. She was on the fat side, wore a baggy old dress and flat worn shoes. After disappearing with the lady, they both came back, fastened a leash to my collar, and walked me around in the yard. A few minutes later I was jumping into the back seat of an old faded SUV. A few minutes later she pulled into one of those big box pet stores. She returned about a half hour later with a bed, a bag of food, and a new personalized collar with a brass colored plate built into it with my new name.

"There, she said as she fastened the collar around my neck. I'm going to call you 'Hunter.'

***

I'd been picked up a month earlier wandering the streets in the middle of the night. I'd been on my own in the forest for a couple of years and game was getting scarce, so that night I'd sneaked into town to raid garbage cans. As I trotted down the street a man saw me and started to run. I followed him, mostly out of curiosity, which seemed to terrify him. He ran screaming into a building slamming the door behind him sending wonderful smells my way. It smelled like beef, chicken, and butter. Just about every wonderful concoction imaginable. I hadn't smelled aromas like that since I'd lost my boy and his family.

Losing interest in the frightened man, I ran around back where I found a giant dumpster near the back door of the place. The aromas from it were overpowering. I ran across what looked like a parking lot and leaped inside. It was filled with food. Trying to balance myself on the boxes and bags, I ate my fill not noticing a gate rolling shut blocking me into the parking lot of the restaurant.

I was full, but I was trapped, but in a way it made me feel good. Once again I was in a fenced yard, I was full, and frankly I'd grown tired of being alone. Now that I was here, maybe someone would help me find my boy.

The next morning a man in a truck pulled up, opened the fence just enough to enter, and tossed something on the ground not far from me. I wasn't very hungry after ransacking the dumpster all night, but I walked up to see what it was anyway. In another second he'd caught my head in a stick with a rope on it. Noticing I wasn't putting up too much of a fight, he walked me to the truck and into one of the cages built into the side. After slamming the door behind me he drove off and brought me here.

An hour or two later, I was released into a yard and after a few minutes interacting with the driver, he led me to this cage and except for a few potty breaks, I've been living in here since.

What they didn't know was that I'd been lost for well over a year, maybe two. I didn't need anyone but my boy. I wasn't looking forward to sitting in a house again eating turd sized pieces of dried mush, much like the crap they'd been feeding me here, but it would be worth it if I had Johnny back.

If I could have gotten out, I'd have looked for my Johnny, but we'd driven awhile to get here. He had to be far away. He was just a little thing and even though it'd been awhile I knew he still needed me. Truth be told, I needed him. Losing him hurt. He was on my mind all of the time.

Both of the ladies left the hallway full of dog cages and before long they returned with a leash and opened my cage. My heart beat harder. That little old lady was taking me! *They always take the dogs out when they bring the leash.* I thought.

A short walk and a nod and I was headed to my new home. She opened the back door to a beat up old SUV and I jumped in. I was anxious to see what was coming.

She drove that old SUV up a steep hill, on a winding road that eventually leveled out into a heavily treed area. It wasn't far from where they picked me up when I originally got myself captured.

My tail was slapping the window, hoping we'd be staying here. In a few minutes, she pulled off the road to a long driveway that ended in a little carport next to a tiny house. She led me inside, poured me a bowl full of the little crispy mush balls and another filled with water. I leaned down, took a few of the horrible crunch balls and ate them, just to make her happy. "Good Boy" she said. I'd hear that a lot over the next few weeks.

CHAPTER FOUR
The Dog

RONNIE

I heard the wind getting stronger and stronger. Soon, it was raining hard. Grandma and I sat in the cellar on two folding chairs with the blanket across our laps and the pillows behind us. Before long, water began to flow down the stairs that led up to the yard and it wasn't long before it was flowing toward us.

She took me to the stairway that wound up to the house where she laid the pillows down. We were wrapped in the blankets watching as the cellar floor filled with water as it ran down the concrete stairs from the yard and under the door. The noises outside got louder as we sat there and the stairs we were laying on were vibrating. The sound was deafening. "Grandma, what's happening? I'm scared!

She never answered. She just lay there on the stairs, covered in the blanket. Her eyes and mouth were open, but she didn't move. At the time I thought she was as scared as I was, but when I shook her to get her attention she rolled to the side. Her face was turning white and I sat there feeling her lifeless body next to mine sitting on those pillows and wrapped in our blankets in the cellar.

I stayed with Grandma and soon started to cry. If anyone heard me, I'm sure it sounded more like hysterical screaming.

As the storm stopped and the water stopped running under the door, I sat on the stairs with Grandma not knowing what to do. The water on the floor of the cellar was a couple inches deep. Eventually the line of light that came through the bottom of the door to the yard darkened and disappeared. The power had gone out earlier after Grandma died, so I just sat in the dark with the body of my Grandma, terrified.

***

HUNTER

"Come to Mommie," Helen called after I'd washed down the mush balls with water. I jumped up on the couch with her, resting my head on her lap as I'd done so many times with my boy. She didn't smell right thought.

She rarely called me 'Hunter.' She usually just called me 'Boy' or 'Good Boy.'

Occasionally people would come to the door and Mommie would answer it. My job was to stand right behind her. She'd hold the door like I was trying to get out and the person would leave in short order. She'd close the door and say "Good Boy." Usually I'd lay down after that, but sometimes, if she was feeling nervous about the visitor, she'd let me out into the yard surrounded by a chain link fence.

Sometimes while I was in the yard I'd see a little boy, much like my Johnny. I'd lay by the fence and watch him. He lived at the next ranch house, only a few hundred feet away. The lots were separated by a tiny stream that ran between them. Someone had built a little walking bridge over the stream connecting them. Today the wind started to blow, and then it started to sprinkle, so I ran back inside knowing he'd likely stay indoors in this weather. I liked watching him. He had the same hair as Johnny and he was about the same size, but with today's wind I wasn't likely to see him today. I climbed the stairs to the back door and gave it a gentle scratch. Mommie let me back in, and told me I was a 'good boy' again. I laid by the fire place and slept for the next few hours.

I was awakened by the thunderous rain hitting the old roof. The wind picked up again and Mommy ran around the house closing the shutters and checking all the windows. Then she came and sat with me next to the fire place. We lay there awake until the wind stopped. Mommy ran around and checked the windows again. I followed her this time as she opened the shutters and looked for leaks.

One of the big trees next to the house was down. It'd fallen on the dog house that Mommy bought the day after she brought me home. It also downed a section of the chain link fence.

The rain water had drained off the yard and into the stream between the properties. It was already roaring with whitewater, but the footbridge that curved over it was still intact.

What caught my attention was the boy on the other side. He stood next to the house just outside their cellar door and was screaming. Mommy heard his cries and opened the door to investigate. She was waving the boy over when something inside me just snapped. I ran by her, down the landing stairs to the yard, and took off running toward the boy easily jumping the remains of the downed fence.

CHAPTER FIVE
Ronnie

RONNIE

My shoes were wet from standing in the mud. I'd raced through the house, picked up the phone to call for help, but found it was dead. I thought I'd run next door to see if the old lady in the little house was home, but I remembered she had a giant mean looking dog. I thought of running to the road, then I thought about Grandma's body on the cellar stairs and I froze there in the mud. I couldn't help her; it was too late. I knew it, but hadn't put it into words yet. I stood there and started to scream. I had no place to go and there was no one who could help me.

When I looked up again, I saw the killer dog, Hunter, from next door running over the bridge with his eyes fixed on me. For a split second I just hoped that it would be quick so it wouldn't hurt.

Seconds later, he slid to a stop right before me, ran his giant nose across my shirt, reached up and tasted me. As I prepared to die, I saw his tail wagging so hard his behind was waving from side to side.

Once he calmed down he left, passing me by and running down the stairs to the cellar. In seconds he returned and standing beside me, looked me over for a few seconds. He reached forward and gently took the sleeve of my jacket between his teeth, pulling me toward the woods.

The lady next-door stood on the landing of the stairs to her house and called for him. "Hunter, you leave that boy alone." When he ignored her and continued to pull me towards the woods, she came down the stairs and cautiously stepped her way through the mud toward the old bridge that arched over the now raging stream. Before she got there the bank washed away just enough to drop one end of the bridge into the water. The sound of cracking wood filled the air as the other side was ripped away by the raging water.

While she made her way up the side of the stream to cross at the road, Hunter continued pulling me into the woods and beyond.

CHAPTER SIX
The Journey Home

HUNTER

It all made perfect sense to me. The boy's Grandma was dead. He was alone and too young to protect himself. I saw no reason why I shouldn't adopt him, much like Mommy had adopted me. I turned my head a minute to see Mommy standing in the mud where the bridge had been only moments before knowing that she'd never let me keep him. As we disappeared into the woods I turned to get one last look. She looked horrified, but no longer moved toward the road.

I knew I had to get my new boy back to my old lair before it rained again. I knew this country having hunted most of it before the men from the pound threw that rope around my neck. The lair was not close by and I hoped the boy would be able to make it under the terrible conditions.

He didn't resist me in the slightest. Before long, I was able to let go and he ran along side. Maybe he knew I was saving him.

At his limited running speed, I worried about his stamina. I slowed to a walk as the boy began to slow and breathe hard. He wasn't very fast, but Jonnie had been the same way. I knew he wouldn't last much longer, but one of my temporary shelters was around the bend.

Before we got there I walked him over a rocky area. In this mud we'd been leaving tracks and I couldn't let anyone catch my new boy. After a while we stopped at one of my temporary shelters held together by the roots of a tree at the edge of a hill, but it had been destroyed by a tree that apparently blew over in the storm.

I hated to drag him all the way to the old hunting cabin, one of my other temporary shelters, but I had no choice. Twice, that I knew of, a couple of old men came there with guns. I thought they were looking for deer, but I'd already cleared the deer out.

***

RONNIE

The monster dog took me by the sleeve and pulled me toward the trees. Grandma never allowed me to go there, but he seemed intent on the both of us going together. He hadn't hurt me and after a minute I reached out and touched his collar. A metal tag was embedded in the leather. On it was the word 'Hunter.' It had to be his name.

When he turned to see what I was doing, I could see that this huge monster dog wasn't mad at me at all. He looked happy and seemed to just want me to follow him.

After a few minutes he let go, and I walked alongside him. I didn't know where we were going, but he seemed to have a destination in mind. *Maybe*, I thought, *he was taking me somewhere we could get help.*

We walked and sometimes ran the rest of that day. It wasn't long before I began to think I might have to spend the night on the ground here in the trees, but before panic set in, I saw a little one room shack. It was a piece of junk, looking more like a chicken house, but it'd make a neat fort and proved to be a good place to spend the night. When we got there I pushed at the door, but it was locked. The wood was so dry and brittle that I broke one of the boards with a limb from the storm, reached in and opened the door from inside. A dusty old blanket sat folded on a makeshift table and two old army cots were folded and leaning in the corner.

I was wet and muddy. I needed to rest, but first I had to get out of these wet clothes. I stripped, hung my clothes over the edge of the table, unfolded the cots, and wrapped myself in a blanket to get warm. In seconds I was sharing a tiny cot with a massive dog, a very warm massive dog.

CHAPTER SEVEN
My New Diet

RONNIE

After a few days, I got used to calling him 'Hunter.' It proved to be a fitting name. That's exactly what he was. By now I realized he was not only able to kill when we needed food, but was otherwise full of love and affection.

In the morning he'd run into the woods to take care of his business. At the same time I'd head to the hole I dug with a shovel I'd found in the little cabin and do my own business, and then I'd return to the cabin and wait.

Hunter would usually be gone an hour or so. Before long he'd show up with a squirrel or a snake. The first few days I went hungry and watched him eat, but it wasn't long before I was butchering his finds to make them more appetizing. The shed came with a cabinet full of useful tools like hunting knives and matches. Unfortunately, a year of sitting in the shed in the elements made the matches useless.

At six ½ years old, deciding to eat raw snake takes a lot of internal struggle, tears, and disgusted faces, but over time I not only looked forward to raw whatever-animal-we-could catch, but became instrumental in its capture.

It wasn't long before Hunter and I started working as a team. Even though he was big, I was taller. I could see the rabbits and where they were going. With a quick point, I'd send him scrambling through the brush, soon to return with our dinner.

When the berries started to ripen, I spent time looking for them, but Hunter didn't like fruit, so most of our time was spent hunting. It wasn't long after that when the nuts started to open. I'd planned to spend the day shelling the nut's I'd collected, but Hunter was bound and determined to leave.

***

HUNTER

Game was scarce near the old cabin. The squirrels and turtles would soon be safe underground and my boy hadn't been able to collect eggs for a very long time. I knew if we didn't want to starve, we had to go where bigger game could still be found. Boy was not happy having pretty much staked the old cabin as his, but it was time to take him to the lair.

The next morning, I pushed him up the hill with my nose over and over, bit by bit, kicking my nose into his behind. He was seven now and growing out of his clothes, or what was left of them. His hair was longer, but not down to his shoulders yet. I worried about his survival over the winter. The leaves were already turning. Soon his clothes would be in shreds and his shoes already had cracks across the toe line and holes in their soles. He'd been barefoot most of the time over the last two months. The bottoms of his feet looked just like mine. He didn't really need his shoes, but when the cold weather came they'd keep his feet warm.

Finally after all that prodding, he gave up and jumped aside. Realizing we were moving on, he told me to "stay here" and ran back to the cabin. Before long he returned with a blanket filled with things he wanted to keep. As long as he understood we were moving on I was okay with it. *Besides,* I thought, *the blanket might come in handy later.*

On the way around the mountain, I heard a shuffle in the bush. It was downwind, so I hadn't sensed that anything was there. When I spun around to see what made the sound, I was looking at the biggest bobcat I'd ever seen. Usually a bobcat would run from me. I'd even had a few for dinner, but this one was very big and he looked hungry. In an instant he was running toward me, his jaws opening wide. As I jumped up to defend myself, hoping to get a good grip on his throat, he fell to the ground. His body trembled for a few seconds and it was over. Boy was standing nearby, sporting a grin from one ear to the other.

He'd thrown a rock the size of a baseball as hard as he could. It'd slammed into that cat's head so hard it was still imbedded in his skull. I jumped on the body, grabbed it by the neck and gave it a good shake. I was covered with blood by the time I was done. The rock had killed the bobcat, but I felt honor bound to do my part.

I'd seen boy bring down squirrels and birds with rocks before, but it never occurred to me that he might be able to protect us with those same rocks. All this time I'd taken responsibility for protecting my boy, now we were a team more than ever.

The bobcat was a good sign. We were getting closer to bigger game. Boy opened the blanket and pulled out the hunting knife. In minutes he'd skinned it, turned the skin inside out and stretched it over a rock in the sun. We spent the next hour feasting on cat. It was getting late so we laid under an outcropping, Boy emptied the blanket, found a roll of cord and hung the rest of the bobcat from a tree. In a few minutes we were both sound asleep. Before I knew it, the sounds of the birds made it clear that we'd slept hard through the night.

***

RONNIE

After stuffing ourselves on bobcat, I wrapped up the pelt, tied it with the same cord I'd used to tie the body from the tree, and stuck it in the blanket along with the other tools I'd brought. *After being filled with this pelt and the other tools I'd brought, this blanket'll need a good washing when we get wherever we're going,* I thought.

We continued on our way. By nightfall, following the stream, I saw a beautiful valley with a small lake at the bottom. We continued down toward the lake. Hunter was ahead by a good twenty yards, turned the bend toward an outcropping of rock and disappeared.

I ran ahead to see him standing, facing me in front of a hole at the bottom of the rocky hill. We were home.

CHAPTER EIGHT
Cooperation

RONNIE:

Over time we learned ways to help one another. I, for instance, was very good at scaling trees, where I could collect eggs during the spring and fruits during the fall. We also learned that when a herd of deer passed through the valley, Hunter would run ahead and lay in waiting while I appeared from behind, stampeding them right into Hunter's massive jaws. Then, when I'd catch up with him, I'd skin them up to the neck and down to the legs bringing back a wet and blood soaked future blanket for the winter. Once we'd eaten our fill, I'd cut away as much of a thigh and hip as I thought we could carry and we'd take it back to the lair.

After a couple days of feasting, it was not unusual to fast a day or two. At dawn we'd hunt, during the day we rested, and in the early evening we'd hunt again. We were not always successful, but sometimes when we couldn't get red meat, I could kill a duck with a rock. Hunter would jump in the lake and bring it to shore.

By that time, I could hit almost anything with a rock. During the season ducks were a prime source of food. I liked them because we could eat the whole thing. I didn't like the fact that food was all they were good for. I preferred collecting skins I could dry in the trees for the cold weather to come. Duck feathers were useless.

After all this time, my hair had grown beyond my shoulders. I kept it tied back out of my way in sort of a pony tail.

Hunter learned to answer to his name and over time we developed a sort of sign language. He learned to respond to sounds I'd make and I could usually read his body language and even some of his whines and growls.

When game was scarce, I'd throw fish from the creek to the shore, whenever I could. Hunter would quickly dispatch them. Raw fish was my least favorite food, so fishing meant there was nothing else to eat.

My clothes eventually fell apart. The holes and cracks in my shoes made them worthless to me. For some time I'd gone barefoot, long enough that I could run through the brush comfortably. I hadn't worn my shoes in a year or so.

I'd lived here with Hunter for five or maybe six seasons. Hairs sprouted where they'd never been before and I started to give off a scent that forced me into the pond, sometimes several times a day. In the winter months, Hunter would sometimes clean it off. Our lair was piled high with the skins I'd dried. Because the entry was small, and Hunter and I were so large we managed to stay fairly warm cuddled together under the furs.

While there was less game in the winter, the few kills we made lasted a long time in the cold so we were able to eat the whole thing. The flies were gone for the season. A deer would last a few weeks if I kept it packed in the snow. There were a few nuts I'd learned to save, but no fruit.

When it started to get cold at night, I knew I'd need to find some way to keep warm. I began to experiment with the pile of hides I'd collected that year. By poking holes in them and overlapping the edges I could tie the hides together with leather strips I'd cut with the knife I'd taken from the cabin. That knife had proved its worth over and over. At night I'd sharpen it on a piece of slate I kept in the lair. In a couple of weeks I'd fashioned an ugly pair of pants, a jacket of sorts, and even a dreaded pair of shoes. In the process of putting these clothes together, I found I could soften the leather by pounding it with the edge of the slate I used to sharpen my knife.

CHAPTER NINE
The Departure

RONNIE:

Year after year we lived a simple life. We hunted for our food, defended each other from predators, guarded our kills and enjoyed our company in the lair and our adventures in the warmer months. I spent a lot of time making my clothes. They seemed to shrink and at the same time I was getting bigger.

The hair on Hunter's head had turned almost completely white by that time and each day he seemed to grow tired faster than before. One day, in late spring, he couldn't bring himself to leave the lair. I brought him meat from our last kill and when it was finally gone, I brought a squirrel and a few eggs. He'd eat, and I could get him to crawl outside long enough to pee and leave his droppings, but he'd have to get back to the bed of hides right after.

One day he started to whimper. I covered him with one of the pelts I'd softened for a blanket and the old blanket we'd taken so many years ago, then crawled in next to him and held him tight against me. It tore me up to see him hurting like that. In time we both fell into a gentle sleep curled up together like always, keeping one another warm.

At dawn, I woke with the birds as usual, but Hunter didn't wake with me. It reminded me of my last day with Grandma. I held him against me knowing it would be the last time. I pulled myself together, left the lair, and dug a grave for him with one of the stick tools I'd created. I remembered that dead loved ones were supposed to be buried.

In time, I dug a hole large enough to hold him and deep enough to keep the coyotes from getting him. I placed him inside, crying, mostly screaming, as I dragged his body to the hole. I lined it with one of the deer pelts, lowered him as easily as I could, and covered his body with another deer skin. Then I filled it in. Watching the pelts disappear under the dirt was like a stab in the heart.

When I was done, I rolled a rock to mark the spot where he rested so I'd always know where he was.

I didn't know what to do with myself. After laying awake, missing the warmth of Hunter next to me, I dragged what had been our bed outside to the stone. I dropped it on the ground and wrapped myself with the old blanket and one of the pelts, but I didn't sleep. Instead I closed my eyes and tried to feel his presence. I lay there until the birds began to sing. I knew I was alone. It was the first time. I didn't think I could stand another night like this, at least not here, so I decided to climb down to the old cabin. It broke my heart to leave him here in the ground. I grabbed the old blanket and a few pelts, threw a few of my tools in the make shift bag, and started down the hill.

CHAPTER TEN
My Return

RONNIE

A day and half later, I arrived at the old building. It looked worse than I remembered. I hadn't thought to bring anything to eat and I didn't stop to hunt, so I was hungry. I threw the old worn blanket down outside the cabin, and walked into the forest to hunt. An hour later, I returned with a ground squirrel. The first thing I noticed was that the blanket was gone!

Something is very wrong, I thought as I opened the door to the old building, planning to prep the squirrel for dinner. As my eyes adjusted to the dark, I froze. Two men jumped up from a tiny table under the window. They looked more surprised to see me than I was to find them in my old cabin. I turned to run, but before I could, they tackled me. I struggled, but they wrapped me in my own blanket, pulled off their belts, and strapped them around me pinning my arms to my side. I walked to a chair as best I could wrapped in the smelly old blanket and sat. One of the men was short and fat. He was bald and wearing a flannel shirt. The other one was just a little taller than me. He was in a t-shirt and jeans and had bare feet. Two cups of steaming coffee sat on the table.

"Tom," said the bald guy. "He's naked as a jay bird,"

"Where do you think he came from?"

"Jack, did you ever smell anything like that?"

"Fraid so. He needs a bath that's for sure. What do you think…
he's… maybe sixteen? Tomorrow we'll take him back to town and see if
anyone knows who he is. You know, with his hair grown halfway down
his back, I'd guess he's been out here quite a while."

"Hey Jack! I'll bet that blanket's the one that disappeared. You
remember, it was years ago!"

The tall guy picked up the blanket, held it up and studied it.
"Well, I'll be damned if it isn't. You don't think he's been out here since
then do you? He'd never survive that. Hand me my backpack. I've got a
shirt in there he can wear and maybe I can strap that blanket around him
like a skirt. I don't want to march him into town naked."

"Do we have any shoes he can wear?"

"Hell no. They're what, maybe a seven? Besides, they're super
wide. He's been running around here without shoes a long time. Look at
the bottoms of his feet."

Stepping closer, the man named Jack grabbed my leg by the
ankle, lifted it and examined the bottom of my foot. "Yeah, he doesn't
need shoes," Al said. "He hasn't worn shoes for… maybe years."

It was late and the village was at least ten miles away through
the woods. One of the men picked up my squirrel, opened the door and
threw it into the brush. Then he left with a bucket and returned after
filling it with water from the stream. The cabin had a wood burning stove
in one corner and he sat it on top to heat. After they blocked the door,
and it became evident that I wasn't going to attack them or run, they
started to unwrap me. One of them wet a cloth and showed me that he
meant for me to use it to wash with. By that time, the water from the
stream was warm enough to keep from shocking me. I remembered that
I'd considered bringing that bucket when we first left the cabin some ten
years earlier. It would have been useful to carry some of the tools I'd
taken with us. Instead I grabbed this dirty old blanket, but it kept us
warm quite a while before I collected the pelts.

Dipping the cloth into the bucket I spent the next fifteen minutes
or so washing up, finally dipping my hair inside. One of the men ran
something over my head and foamed it all up while the other one threw a
few things into a big pan and set it on the same stove my water was
heating on.

I remembered my mom washing my hair years before, but I
hadn't soaped this hair in all this time. When my bath was over I smelled
sweet and the food was almost ready to eat.

After draping me in an extra-large flannel shirt that felt like a
robe and tying it shut with a piece of cord, the man named Jack put three
bowls on the table and ladled some kind of noodle concoction into each

one. In a few seconds, I buried my face in the bowl. I was lapping and sucking up the noodles and sauce until the bald guy pulled me up and forced a fork into my hand. It was not new to me, but I hadn't used one in years. He wiped my face, something Hunter usually did, and I spent the next fifteen minutes moving single pieces of noodle stuff into my mouth while re-learning how to hold a spoon.

A couple hours later, one of the men slid a bench in front of the door and piled their bags on it. The other moved the table, closed the shutters and set his bed up under the only window in the cabin. It was obvious that they were blocking all possible exits, but it was a waste of time. I had no intention of going anywhere. My goal was to return to the village and they could only be of help by showing me the way. I hoped they'd start back in the morning and I wasn't disappointed.

The next morning we started hiking down the hill. They still didn't trust me, making me walk between them, but it wasn't long before they seemed to realize I had no intention of running. I knew I could have taken off through the forest at any time. I'd have disappeared before they even started chasing me.

After we'd hiked for about several hours, I caught sight of the village in the distance. I wondered, with Grandma gone, what they planned to do with me. Surely someone had discovered her body. My mom and dad must have thought I was dead by now.

When we finally reached the main street, I had no further use for the two men who'd accompanied me down the hill into the forest, so I turned and ran down the street toward my grandma's old house.

The men just stood there. They'd never seen me run.

I got to the stairs in front of the old craftsman house, jumped to the porch, and grabbed at the doorknob. It wouldn't turn at all. In frustration I shook it back and forth. Seconds later, it clicked and opened. On the other side stood an old lady peering through the half open door in amazement. "Young man, why aren't you dressed? Who are your parents?"

I wasn't used to speaking much, so my explanation was cryptic. "My Grandma used to… I don't live here… My mommy…"

About that time Jack and Tom ran panting up the stairs to the landing, each grabbing an arm and pulling me back to the middle of the porch. They told her what they knew of me and excused the interruption.

"Could you call the sheriff?" Tom asked the old woman. She disappeared into the house for a few minutes while we sat on the steps. It wasn't more than a few minutes before the three of us were riding in the back seat of an old cruiser.

They spoke to the sheriff, explaining where they'd found me. Knowing the house I'd run to, it wasn't long before they put the story together.

"Naw," said the sheriff. "It couldn't be him."

"One way to find out!" Said the bald guy.

Before night fall the door to the sheriff's office swung open and I saw the face I remembered from so many years ago staring at me in disbelief. She was looking at a barefoot sixteen year old wrapped in a giant flannel shirt, with incredibly long hair. My wispy beard made the image even worse.

I knew her instantly, but I think at first I was a mystery to her. "Mommy?" I asked watching her expression morph as she bent down to get a closer look. Tears filled her eyes as she leaned forward and took me into her arms. My dad was silent, standing behind her. His eyes were wide and his hands were shaking.

Being held by my mother terrified me. I hadn't been held by anyone in ten years. After the sheriff and my parents filled out a bunch of forms, we left and climbed into a white car.

As Dad drove, Mom sat in the back with me. Ronnie, where have you been? How did you get like this?"

"She'd seen my feet, knew I was naked under the shirt, and since I had to leave the items originally stolen from the cabin, I had nothing.

Eventually we arrived at the house I recognized from my childhood. It looked different, but there was no mistaking it. A minute later we stepped inside and I walked around, undisturbed and getting used to seeing it all again. When I opened the door to my room, it was unchanged. A comic book still lay across the foot of the single bed against the wall. The closet was still full of little boy clothes.

"Come into the family room and tell us where you've been." She said. "We missed you so much." Worry covered her face. The different possible scenarios that she thought she might hear weren't even close.

Closing the door behind me, she led me into the family room.

CHAPTER ELEVEN
Adjusting

RONNIE

Over the next few days, Mom bought me a ton of clothes and had my hair cut. I was examined, and poked by doctors and tortured by nurses as they inoculated me for everything. I had the vocabulary of a six year old and everyone who saw me for more than a few minutes seemed to feel sad for me. I wasn't sad, but at the same time I didn't feel like I belonged here.

When Mom and Dad got me to reveal the whole story, finding out that I'd been taken and raised by a dog, they didn't believe me. For days they kept asking me where I'd really been. It wasn't easy to explain, partially because it was so hard for them to believe, but mainly because I had a difficult time coming up with the words I needed to explain it.

The men who found me in the cabin came to dinner one night and by the end of the day, I think they finally believed I'd been cared for by a dog this whole time.

A man from the local newspaper came to get the story and before long the whole town knew. Everyone wanted me to show them where I'd been, but for me the place was sacred, so I lied and told them I didn't know how we got there in the first place and finding my way back to the cabin again was just luck.

Everyone spoke so well. Even other boys my age. Compared to me, they were eloquent. Their words kept me guessing. Even the words I knew were a distant memory. I'd used a few with Hunter, but so many didn't apply that at this point most of them I'd either never heard or long since forgotten. I had a lot of catching up to do.

It was summer vacation. After I'd been home for a few weeks mom finally stopped watching my every move. I could even go outside. People would come by from time to time walking a dog, and I'd run to see it. The intensity of my interest sometimes frightened both the dog and their walker. One day a lady I'd seen before came by the house walking her dog. It looked just like Hunter, but her dog was a female, a very fat female.

While I was hugging her dog, telling her how beautiful she was, the lady squatted down, so we'd be face to face. Having heard my story, which I'm sure was all over town by now, she said "Honey, Roxy here is about to have her puppies and… if you like… I'd gladly give you one, if your parents say it's okay."

"Stay here," I practically ordered the woman as I ran for the front door.

"Mom, that lady has a dog like Hunter who's having pups. She said she'd give me one if you said it was okay." Mom could see the look on my face, knowing I'd never forgive her if she said no. She looked out the door, saw the fat looking Pit Bull standing next to the lady who'd promised me a puppy.

"Betty," she called, "I didn't know your dog was having puppies." Looking down at me once again and back to Betty she said, "Ronnie'd love to have one of her pups. It's fine with me."

It wasn't convincing, but it was the commitment I'd looked for. That day I was the happiest sixteen year old boy in the world.

CHAPTER TWELVE
Going Home

RONNIE

Roxy had her puppies about a week later. I visited them almost every day, and it wasn't long before I chose the one I'd one day take home. When that time finally came I picked him up into my arms, thanked the lady profusely, and ran home with him.

When we got to our house, I walked into the front room just as Mom was bringing my shoes down the hall. She was always trying to get me to wear them, claiming I'd have to when school started. She'd enrolled me in a special class where a sixteen year old could start to learn to read and absorb the other facts and figures that little children had to know in order to move on to the next level. The worst part, for me, was sitting at a desk all day with my feet covered in my new shoes. They were soft leather, but even though Mom bought the widest ones they had, my feet were bigger and the shoes pinched.

Wearing shoes seemed silly to me, I could walk anywhere in my bare feet and I was pretty sure everyone else could too if they just did it for a while.

I named the dog 'Boy.' Mom wouldn't let me call him anything like Jaws, or Hunter and so I settled on Boy. That's what I'd always be calling him anyway. "Come here, Boy." To me it just made sense. Mom said it was odd. "Why?" I asked. "If people hear me calling him Boy, it'll sound normal.

In the fall, school finally started. I had to get dressed up in all my new clothes and felt like I was tied up. Top that with a tight pair of shoes and I was seriously uncomfortable.

School was awful. I always found myself sitting in a class with a bunch of kids or adults. Nobody was my age. Then, when I finally got home the neighborhood boys would tease me for going to that school. I barely understood half of what they were yelling at me. I was tempted to look for a rock, but thought better of it. Most of the time I ignored them. They reminded me of a bunch of prairie dogs yelling at me as I walked by their mounds.

They were easy to ignore. By now they knew better than to attack me. They'd made that mistake once and were in no hurry to repeat it. It's hard to fight with a boy who fights to kill and bites. Apparently there are some kind of rules for fighting.

So after attending school for a few months, I had no friends except for Boy. It wasn't a popular thing to be seen with "that boy," and some of the parents even forbid their boys to interact with me at all, perhaps it was the teeth marks.

Fall turned to winter and winter into spring and Boy grew and matured. When it started to feel warm again, I made a decision. I was done. *Why would I want to be the bottom of the barrel when I could be King in my wilderness? I was once free.* I thought. *Now, with Boy, I can be again.*

One night, after everyone was in bed, I stayed awake until I thought everyone was asleep. Boy was curled up on the bed behind my legs fast asleep, not waking until I stirred to get out of bed. I was already completely dressed minus my shoes. I put on the heavy parka Mom bought for me before last winter set in. It was still cold at night and I knew it would come in handy in the future.

As quietly as I could, I slid my bedroom window open, set Boy on the ground, and the two of us ran down the street, through town and into the country.

Boy was fit. He had to be to keep up with me. The moon was full and soon we were passing by the highway that led to the little town where Grandma used to live.

I stuck my thumb out and before long a truck pulled over. "What are you doing out here on a night like this? Don't you know it's late?"

I gave him a story about going home. He dropped us at a truck stop and a few rides later, another trucker dropped us off a mile or so from Grandma's.

I ran to the old house, because I remembered that it was from there that Hunter had taken me into the wilderness. From there, Boy and I ran into the woods following the old stream. Eventually we arrived at the old hunter's cabin, but this time I didn't stop. This time I went through the cabin to see if there was anything I could use. The same knife I'd grown up with had been returned to the drawer I'd found it in when I was only six and a half.

We continued another mile until we finally lay down to sleep. The birds were already announcing the dawn. By noon we were up again and hiking up the hill to the lair. Once there I took Boy to the stone that marked Hunter's grave. We sat there a while, until something caught Boy's attention. He ran off into the bush. I trusted him by now. He wouldn't go far. I kissed the stone, then jumped up and ran after him only to find him coming back with a large lizard's tail hanging out from the side of his muzzle. *We're going to be fine*, I thought.

Once we were settled, I took Boy down to the lake, threw a rock and killed a duck for our supper. I jumped into the lake to retrieve the floating body only to find that Boy was swimming at my side. I held back to see what he'd do. He grabbed the body by the feet and turned toward shore. It was an odd way to retrieve a duck, but I knew he'd learn in time.

When we got back to shore, I took the duck from him to make sure he understood that the body was not a plaything. While he watched, I stripped it of feathers and sliced it into a few pieces and together we ate the first of many meals we would share. Boy wasn't as finicky about raw meet as I'd been, especially after traveling all these miles with only a lizard to eat.

It was going to take a little work to bring Boy to the deer hunting stage, but he was quick to learn, and I was confident that together we'd make a good team.

I was afraid to stay this close to the village, knowing I'd been captured the year before. We needed to go deeper into the wilderness, so for the next few days we hiked back to a mountain Hunter had shown me many years before. On the other side, was a lake and a new life for Boy and me. Together we'd build a new lair and I'd train Boy to be a first class hunter. The night we arrived, we dined on jackrabbit under a stone outcropping, curled up together, and drifted off to sleep. It was good to free again.

***

David Morris grew up in Phoenix, Arizona, from the time he was seven. In 2010, after moving a number of times he finally settled in Palm Springs, California where he finally had the time to write.

HIs first novel was his own biography. He'll never publish it, but it helped to give him the skills and the drive to continue. 'Once Free', is his first short story.

He writes Suspense/Romance and what he likes to call Science Fiction of the Possible. He has five novels available.

Spots Book One: The Youth Tablets
Spots Book Two: The People at the Pond/Second Chance
Spots Book Three: The Finale/The Lost Tablets
Jason's Virus
The Time Ship

His eBooks and paperbacks on Amazon can be purchased here:
https://www.amazon.com/s?k=David+Lawrence+Morris&i=stripbooks&ref=nb_sb_noss

His eBooks at Barnes and Noble can be purchased at:
https://www.barnesandnoble.com/s/david+lawrence+morris?_requestid=9614216

Kobo
His eBooks at Kobo can be purchased at:
https://www.kobo.com/us/en/search?query=David+Lawrence+Morris

Facebook Link:
https://m.facebook.com/david.morris.54390876?ref=bookmark

FLAMINGO DAWN: THE LEGEND OF KERI FLAMINGO

By Robert Allen Lupton and Robin Lupton

Amy woke up before her parents on Sunday morning. Her room on the second story of their home in Tupelo, Mississippi faced the east and the bright August sunrise was directly in her eyes.

She brushed her teeth and dressed. She hurried downstairs and quietly opened the front door. The Sunday paper was in the driveway. She read really well for a nine year old and the Sunday funnies were one of the high points of the week.

She took two hurried steps from the front porch, dodged the sprinkler system, and stopped dead in her tracks. She stared at the house across the street. The McIntire's front yard was filled with plastic flamingos, hundreds of plastic flamingos.

Mr. McIntire opened his front door, spotted his newspaper, and shuffled sleepily down his driveway. He picked up the paper and turned toward his home. That's when he saw the flamingos.

He threw down the paper and screamed at his wife. "Martha, get out here. Help me! We've been flocked. He jerked one flamingo after another from his lawn and flower beds. Martha stood in the doorway and put her hand to her mouth. "Oh, my sweet Lord, Mike McIntire, what have you done this time?"

Mike McIntire shouted, "Martha, this is no time to talk. Get me a box of trash bags. These flamingos have to go. Now, woman! Don't just stand there."

His screams woke the neighborhood. Amy's parents joined her on the front porch. Her dad said, "I'll put on some coffee and be right back. I'll get some lawn chairs. I want to watch Mike try to clean this up. Putting a flock of flamingos in trash bags is almost as hard as straightening a couple of hundred tangled clothes hangers."

Amy took a glass of orange juice from her mom. "Why would anyone want to untangle a bunch of clothes hangers?"

Her Dad laughed. "No one would. That's the point. In college some people would fill a dorm room with several hundred coat hangers as a prank. Takes forever to untangle them."

"I think the flamingos look fun. Why is Mr. McIntire so upset? He's using some bad words."

Her Mom snickered, 'Yes, he is. Someone thinks he's done something really bad. He's a City Councillor, you know. It could be the way he voted, or perhaps he's taken advantage of his position. When elected people don't do the right thing or when other people behave like pompous asses..."

Dad put his hand on Mom's arm. "Language warning, Vickie."

"Yes, dear. When people get too big for their britches, a flock of plastic flamingos is just the thing to cut them down to size. It's hard to look important when you have a plastic bird in each hand. Someone flocked the McIntire's last night to teach Mr. McIntire a lesson."

Across the street, Mike shoved another flamingo into a large black plastic trash bag. The big bags would only hold two or three of the plastic birds. He put the bag down and jumped on top of it, lost his balance and rolled across the yard knocking over flamingos as he went. He stopped nose to beak with a flamingo. He jerked it away from his face and screamed, "Son of a bitch!"

His wife, Martha yelled. "There are children, Mike. Watch your language. It's Sunday morning."

Mike kicked flamingos aside. He took two steps and tripped over a pink plastic neck and disappeared under the flock. He kicked for a moment and scrambled back to his feet. He took a flamingo in each hand and threw them into the street. "Piss on Sunday morning, piss on these damn birds, and piss on anyone who doesn't like my language."

Vickie stood up and folded her lawn chair. She took Amy's hand. "I think we've seen enough. Come inside, Amy. I'll make waffles for breakfast."

Mr. McIntire stood with his back to the street and ripped one flamingo after another from the ground and threw them over his shoulder. They spun several times before they hit the asphalt. Amy's Dad laughed. "Look, honey. He's flipping the bird."

"Language warning back at you. Inside, now."

After breakfast, Amy read the Sunday comics. Her mother put the dishes away and poured herself another cup of coffee. Amy refilled her milk. "Mom, I still don't understand about the flamingos. I thought they were pretty, but Mr. McIntire was so upset.

"I know, dear. It's a long story, but a good one. Would you like to hear it?"

Amy said, "Yes, please."

Vickie said, "Well, I call the story, The Legend of Keri Flamingo. It began at the Bon Aminux Zoo in Louisiana almost a hundred years ago in 1923. Once upon a time, there was a young girl named Babette.

***

It had been nine months since Mardi Gras and Babette's stomach was getting steadily bigger. She didn't have long now. She ran her free hand over her stomach. Her zoo uniform was close to bursting. She'd let out the back twice now to make it stretch over her swollen belly.

It was hot and her back hurt. Babette tossed one of the light pink baby shrimp to the waiting flamingos, then munched one down herself. Big Daddy caught the tiny prawn in his beak, then gave her an approving flamingo squawk. Sometimes she swore she could understand them. Babette loved Big Daddy. He was a good listener.

Babette and the flamingos had gotten close during these past nine months. As her stomach grew so did her affinity for the birds. She loved all the animals in the park, but the flamingos were special. She liked that they were pink. Pink was calming. Unless it was the hot pink swill at the bottom of a hurricane or a strawberry daiquiri.

Anytime Babette thought about hurricanes or daiquiris, she was reminded of that that morning in New Orleans when she woke up next to Boudreaux. The memory made her feel hungover and nauseated again.

"Big Daddy, with god as my witness, I swear I will never drink another hurricane again."

Big Daddy squawked in agreement. Babette plunged her swollen hand back into the bucket of shrimp and chomped one down and tossed another handful to the birds. The doctor said that she would get cravings when she was pregnant, but she hadn't expected it to be for raw shrimp. She threw another to Big Daddy.

"I just hope that butthole doesn't find out I'm here and come looking for me. That Boudreaux got himself quite a temper."

Babette had told the flamingos her story on several occasions in all manner of colorful iterations. Babette was a born storyteller and she told her story to the flamingos, often punctuating the tale by either munching down or throwing the riveted flamingos another fistful of shrimp. They literally gobbled it all up, story and shrimp. The result was that they were the pinkest flamingos in North America, had anyone bothered to do a colour test.

The summation of Babette's story was as old as time itself. Babette went to New Orleans for Mardi Gras. She got rip-roaring drunk and ran into her ex-boyfriend, Boudreaux, who was out on parole. They snuck off and ended up in the back of his Packard. The seats were velvet and leather. A small stature of Jesus, carved from a cypress root, watched them from his place on the dashboard and bobbed rhythmically in approval. Poor Jesus had seen this movie before.

A few weeks later Babette found out she was pregnant and made the mistake of telling Boudreaux. He didn't take it well and Babette ended up with a black eye. Immediately after that, Boudreaux decided the right thing to do was to make Babette marry him, because he'd convinced himself that would be the honorable thing. Besides, if he broke parole and went back to jail, there was that conjugal visit thing.

Babette knew he would still screw around and the beatings would get worse. She told him there was no way in hell that she was marrying him. That's when he started stalking and threatening her. He broke down the front door to her momma's house. She ran out the back door, got in her Model T, and drove away. She didn't even tell her momma where she was going.

An hour later her car broke down in the middle of a bayou bridge just outside of a town appropriately named Big Swamp. The sign said, "Bon Animiux Zoo ½ mile."

Babette walked to the zoo and asked to use the phone. She never left. The owners, who were a nice Cajun couple, gave her a job cleaning the park and feeding the animals. She slept in a room that had been used by an old security guard.

"I just pray he don't find me." Babette said to Big Daddy. Up until last week, Babette had been pretty sure Boudreaux would never find her, but last week, homesickness finally got the best of her, and along with the fear of going into labor on her own, she broke down and called her momma.

***

Vickie continued. "Now, Amy, there were articles in the local papers that prove this story is true. One of the best known ones was in the" Big Swamp Weekly Gazette" in June of 1923. It's all about the day the flamingos escaped from the zoo. The writer, Ray Ray Matiness, later wrote a book about the whole story. We've got a copy. You can read the article, honey." Vickie took a book from the bookcase, thumbed through it, and handed it to her daughter.

Amy read it out loud.

"Bon Aminux Flamingo Flock On the Loose"
Extracted from The Big Swamp weekly Gazette, August 5, 1923: By Ray Ray Matiness.
"Tragedy struck the small town of Big Swamp last Wednesday evening when a flock of flamingos absconded from the local zoo. Witnesses report that the flamingos carried off a baby in the process. Bastion Fonteneaux said, "Them birds was like a team of storks. They was a hundred of 'em flying through the air holding a pink baby blanket. I could hear a baby crying up there in the sky..."

"The "missing" infant is said to be Keri Edmee, who is five days old, and is reputed to be the daughter of Bon Aminux employee. Babette Edmee, who is nineteen years of age and unmarried.

In a bizarre interview with Babette Edmee, the distraught mother claimed that the baby's abusive father, Bubba Boudreaux, was attacked by the flock of flamingos after he threatened to kill her and attempted to steal her baby.

In her slightly rattled interview, she stated, "Big Daddy, he's the king of them Flamingos, and right before Bubba could hit me, Big Daddy, he just swooped in like a flying knight in pink armor and bashed that no good Bubba in the face. Next, Big Daddy, bit him on the nose. Bubba sat right down and howled, "Help. I've been beaked."

"Then, Mamma Queenie, who is Big Daddy's woman, she done grabbed my baby girl, Keri, right out of the buggy and wrapped her in a baby blanket and all them birds grabbed that blanket and they plumb flew off. They saved her. Big Daddy is my hero."

"Mr .Boudreaux's version of the events was quite different. He stated that he believed Miss Edmee was mentally unwell. His exact words can't be printed in this newspaper, but essentially, he said, "That girl be crazy.""

"In his version of events, there never was a baby and Babette Edmee made up the story of the baby to trap him. He believes that Edmee led him to believe that he was the father of her non-existent child and she lured him to the zoo to confront him as part of a child support scam.

He said "The buggy was empty when I got there. I don't think there ever was no baby. Babette acted like she could talk to those birds. When I tried to get her to come home to her momma, she threw a whole mess of raw shrimp at me, and the flamingos went wild and flew away."

"Edmee is emphatic that the flamingos rescued her baby and that the birds have hidden somewhere in the bayou to keep her child safe. When asked for a description of the child, Edmee stated that the baby has bright pink hair. "It's 'cause of all the shrimp I ate while I was pregnant. My baby girl is bright pink all over. I'm gonna find my little girl no matter where she is. She needs her momma."

"Whether an infant was stolen or not still remains to be seen but there can be no doubt that the flamingo flock is still at large somewhere in the swamps of Louisiana."

Amy finished reading. "So the flamingos stole the baby?"

Vicki nodded.

"Then what happened?"

"Now, well, no one heard a word about Keri for ten long years, even though Babette never gave up hope."

***

From the minute her baby was taken Babette never stopped looking for Keri. She saved every penny she earned and bought herself a pirogue and an outboard motor. She spent nearly every hour she wasn't sleeping or working at the zoo, looking for the flamingos and ten years later, she finally found them.

Can't you imagine how she felt? There she was, floating through the hazy swamp day after day until one day, she finally caught a glimpse of pink. She cut the engine and drifted toward them, hunched low in her boat. She watched them from twenty feet away. She didn't want to spook them. The birds were grouped near the shore in the standing tree pose, balanced on one leg gracefully above the water, and their pink feathers cast rosy shadows on the bayou in a bright midday sun.

Babette got out her binoculars. She was desperate to see Keri. She knew the girl was out there. She could feel it and the feeling made her spine itch. She drifted closer and closer. She was only five feet away from the flock.

A big old flamingo lifted his head and spotted her. "Big Daddy?" She whispered. Big Daddy would be pushing thirty by then. Some flamingos, ones in captivity, can make it to fifty, so seeing him still alive wasn't exactly surprising.

Babette reached into a bucket in her boat and pulled out a fistful of shrimp. "Come on Big Daddy. Show me my baby girl." She whispered. She tossed the shrimp in the water. The splash make the flamingo next to Big Daddy turn her way.

"Queenie?"

The bird held its head up and hissed at her.

"Now Queenie. You know Keri is mine. I gonna take her back. She don't belong here with you. She a person."

Queenie flapped her wings and hissed again.

"I know you done raised her up till now, but you know I been out here every day." Babette put her hand above her eyes and searched the water. In the distance she thought she saw a gangly pink preteen girl balanced on one leg in the water, but before she could be sure, the girl disappeared behind the rest of the flock. Babette called out, "Keri, is that you. Don't be afraid, girl. I'm your momma."

Queenie hissed another warning. All the birds hissed. You might think a hundred flamingos flapping in furry would be comical with their long graceful necks and whimsical legs, but you would be wrong. Flamingos are big birds with powerful legs and mighty necks and beaks shaped perfectly for stabbing and a flock of flamingos all hissing at you is like being attacked by hundred prima ballerinas with steak knives for noses. It is beautifully terrifying.

In unison every single bird in the flock took one step toward Babette, then another and another. Their heads towered above her, beaks ready to strike. This was a fight she couldn't win, but damn it, she wanted to win, she wanted her baby girl, but in her heart she knew Keri wasn't really her baby anymore. She was Queenie's. The Flamingos raised the girl for ten years. She was one of their flock. At least, Babette knew her daughter was okay.

"Alright, I'm leaving. But Keri, baby girl. You just know I'm your real momma. And know I love you. I brought you a present. I made it myself." She reached in the boat and dropped a hand knitted doll with fluffy pink hair over the edge. It floated on the surface of the water. "I'm gonna stop looking for you now, but I may come and visit. I'm still working at the zoo and if you ever want to see me. Got my own place. You could have your own bedroom."

Queenie hissed again. All the flamingos hissed again, their beautiful mouths elegant with menace.

"Not that this swamp ain't wonderful accommodations. And Queenie, Big Daddy, thank you for saving my baby." Babette dumped the rest of the shrimp into the water and motored away leaving the midday sun's reflection on the water in her wake.

After all the shrimp were eaten in a flamingo frenzy, a hot pink adolescent hand plucked the doll from the water. Keri turned to Queenie and squawked, "What am I supposed to do with this?"

The flamingos stayed busy raising Keri and Babette worked her way up at the Zoo. Bubba Boudreaux, Keri's daddy, if you remember, worked his way to the top of a crime family based in New Orleans. That family did all sorts of bad things, but one of the things that they did was to clear swampland for oil fields and houses. They didn't care about the swamp animals or the people who owned the land. The world needs oil and people need houses, but we haven't reached a point where we have to destroy nature to have those things.

Bubba took charge of swamp clearing. He liked that. He didn't care about alligators, muskrats, nutrias, or anything else that lived in the swamps. There was a flock of flamingos living south of Big Swamp, Louisiana that he particularly disliked. He touched the side of his face and traced the scar on his cheek. A vicious flamingo had bit him when they stole his baby a long time ago.

He and his crew moved their equipment into the area and began to clear the swampland. Some of the local people objected. Fred and Karen Guidry, the proprietors of the Bon Animiux Zoo, as well as Babette, led the opposition.

Bubba and his folks weren't the kind to take disagreements lightly. Bubba and his boy's visited the zoo and beat the old couple and Babette half to death. They killed several of the animals.

Well, animals have a sense for when things aren't right and Big Daddy could tell things down at the Bon Aminux zoo weren't right. Maybe he could smell the blood in the air. Maybe he could hear the crying. Who knows? Either way he got a bad feeling and he couldn't shake it, so he flew to the zoo and got the whole story about the attack and the murders from a muskrat who saw the whole thing from a cypress tree.

To say Big Daddy was angry would be an understatement, and he wasn't the only one. The flock, including Keri, was outraged and the entire state was in an uproar. The police looked everywhere for Bubba Boudreaux and his men. They found him and he was arrested, but no one could prove anything. In no time, he was out of jail and his men were back clearing the swamps.

Keri was almost eighteen years old when this happened. She was tall and thin. Her hair was bright pink and her complexion was rosy. She spoke fluent flamingo and pretty good English, with a strong Louisiana accent. She'd learned to talk like a human by listening to hunters, fishermen, and tour guides. Momma Babette brought her boat into the swamp and read out loud for hours. Keri hid close by and listened. There was a small school house on piers over the bayou near Big Swamp and some days when the water was low, she swam under the school and listened to the teacher.

The Guidry's organized another protest and the citizens of Big Swamp gathered and tied their pirogues and swamp boats together and blocked Bubba's equipment. Babette was up front in her boat. Bubba didn't care. His equipment drove right through the boats. Nine people were killed. Babette's boat sank. The police came, but they never found anyone. Bubba and his men were hiding.

Keri stood on one leg between Big Daddy and Queenie. "Looks like those men what is trying to destroy our home has flat done got clean away from the police. Somebody got to stop them and I don't see anyone to do it, except for us."

Big Daddy squawked, "We know where two of them are, child. What you got in mind?"

Keri and the flock followed Big Daddy to a ramshackle hunter's cabin. The flamingos surrounded the cabin. Keri had two shrimp buckets filled with filthy muck and mire from the swamp's bottom. She wrinkled her nose. "This smells so bad, I bet the catfish won't eat it. Let's get those boys outside."

The flamingos covered the roof and squawked and stomped. The old building shifted and creaked. The two men ran outside. They had shotguns, but before they could use them, hundreds of flamingos attacked them. The birds ripped off their clothes and held them down.

Keri splashed through the shallow water. "You boys best not fight. These birds will do whatever I say. We ain't gonna kill you, but you're gonna be our message to the rest of your kind."

She smeared the filthy muck over their bodies and the flock covered them in flamingo feathers. The men were mired and feathered. Before Keri tied them up she handed a pen and paper to one of the men. "If you want to keep your fingers you better write, 'Follow the flamingo' on this paper."

He did. Then she tied them up and put them into the little flat bottomed boat that was tied behind the shack. The flamingos pulled the boat to Big Swamp and Keri docked it at the public pier.

Keri gave the note and gave it to Big Daddy. "Go fetch the police." Big Daddy flew to the police station and threw a ring-tailed hissy fit until the police came outside. He spit Keri's note at them and backed away. The sheriff picked it up and read it.

A deputy said, "Sheriff, what we supposed to do about this?"

Sheriff Williams hitched up his belt and pointed at Big Daddy. "What we do is follow that damn bird."

Over the next two months the flock led the police to all of Bubba's men. Sometimes, the flock mired and feathered them, but sometimes they just guided the police to them. The police quickly learned to drive around town at sunrise. If a home had a live flamingo in the front yard, it was guaranteed that one of the evildoers was inside. Boudreaux's men were captured in New Iberia, Baton Rouge, and as far north as Shreveport, but Bubba Boudreaux remained at large.

Keri's flock searched the state. Flamingos staked out bars and restaurants. They hid in the bushes near night clubs and honkytonks. Flamingos perched in trees from north Mississippi to east Texas. Queenie spotted Bubba on a Saturday morning in at the Main Street Diner in Thibodaux, Louisiana.

She sent for Keri, Big Daddy, and the flock. If folks had paid attention, the Louisiana skies were dark with flamingos early that Sunday morning. Queenie had found Bubba in a shotgun style duplex on Rose Marie Lane. Queenie and over four hundred flamingos silently filled the yard and lined the street. Big Daddy flew to the sheriff's office and pecked the sheriff's window.

The sheriff and four deputies hurried outside. The sheriff looked at the row of flamingos that lined the street as far as he could see. He said, "Mount up, boys. It's a flamingo dawn. Let's go catch a bad guy."

Bubba was arrested and the sheriff handcuffed him and led him outside the duplex. The carpet of living flamingos moved aside and let them pass. A tall flamingo caught Bubba's eye. "Stop, Sheriff. That flamingo, the big one. It looks like a woman."

The sheriff spotted the thin pink-haired girl. She smiled, winked, and clapped her hands. The flock exploded into the air. It sounded like a hundred helicopters. A hard pink wind buffeted Bubba and the officers and feathers covered them like a soft rain.

The skies cleared. The birds were gone and so was Keri. Bubba said, "Sheriff, you saw that woman, right."

"Didn't see a damn thing, me. Shut up, murderer. You going to jail."

For over thirty years, police departments in Louisiana and Mississippi woke some mornings to find a flamingo waiting to lead them to a criminal. "Follow the flamingo" became a watchword for law enforcement across the nation, but Keri Flamingo and her flock, dedicated as they were, couldn't be everywhere. Santa Claus and the Easter Bunny can't be everywhere. They have helpers. Keri Flamingo needed helpers too.

People across the country wanted to help, but ordinary people can't talk to flamingos, so they buy plastic flamingos and display them in people's yards. Now, Amy, everyone with a flamingo or two, or even a dozen isn't a bad person. Most of those people are true believers. They have flamingos in their yards as a warning to evildoers.

True believers and supporters of Keri Flamingo, Big Daddy, and Queenie keep a few flamingos displayed to warn folks like Bubba. A small grouping means, "We're here and we're vigilant. You better behave. We're watching you. Misbehave and you'll wake up and find yourself flocked some bright shiny morning."

"So Amy, that's the Legend of Keri Flamingo, and that's why Mr. McIntire woke up to find a flock of plastic birds in his yard this morning."

"Mom, is that why we have six plastic flamingos in our front yard? Are you and Daddy helpers for Keri Flamingo?"

"You'll have to ask your dad about that, but sometimes plastic yard art is just plastic yard art."

"Momma, whatever happened to Babette? Did she ever get to see her daughter again?"

"As a matter a fact she did. There is another article about and a picture in the book." Vickie flipped to the article and handed it back to her daughter.

Bon Aminux Owner Gets a Birthday Surprise
By Rhonda Myers

Babette Edmee the proprietor of the Bon Aminux Zoo celebrated her 80th birthday today. Edmee started working at the zoo in 1923 as a bird keeper. She worked her way through the ranks and eventually took over ownership of the zoo in 1957. It's rumored that she's the mother of the famous Keri Flamingo.

Babette thanked everyone for the party and said, "I know ya'll think I am crazy but I tell you, my baby girl, Keri, is out there and she and Big Daddy are the ones giving all these gangsters the run around. I couldn't be prouder of her."

To celebrate her birthday Edmee gave free entrance to the park to anyone who wore the color pink and she decorated the park with pink balloons and streamers. The staff honored Edmee by baking a cake in the shape of her favorite animal, a flamingo. The cake was topped with 80 pink marshmallows.

"The best part of my birthday," said Edmee, "was that, after all these years I finally got a visit from my daughter. I woke up this morning and found this."

Outside Edmee's bedroom window, a large heart made of flamingo feathers was on the patio table. Edmee said, "I know my baby girl made that. Isn't it thoughtful? It's beautiful, only I don't know exactly what I am supposed to do with it."

***

Robert Allen Lupton's information appears after his short story, "Swim With the Beavers, included elsewhere in this anthology.

Robin Lupton is an expatriated American, currently living and writing in England.

THE SONG OF ABBY

By Shebat Legion

"If you listen, you can hear the trees sing."

A tree sings with the breath of waving branches, the sigh of wind-swept leaves, and with roots spread beneath the fabric of the one-world. They sing to spread news or as a warning of the ax or other dangers, and then it is, "We are you. We are us. It is as it must be." A tree is a gossip – they are that *most* of all. Time passes, and with it, things occur that are interesting and true, for a tree does not lie. Most importantly, trees will sing songs of each other, for a tree lives long if left unharmed, but they do not live forever.

"The song is the immortality of a tree."

Oak was old, tall, and widespread, towering over its neighbors in a small clearing deep within the forest, overlooking a deep pool of water that burbled over rocks that sang their own song. Oak, struck by an errant bolt of lightning which left behind a deep slash against its wide trunk, hollowed over time by insects and woodpeckers, it was a wound, this knoll. Oak accepted it, for trees are a pragmatic lot.

Oak's branches sheltered many creatures, and the tree watched - and felt, for trees feel deeply, the life of its inhabitants. Countless birds and their children nested. Squirrels and their cousins do as squirrels will, and they lived, loved, and died. Insects, by the score, visited, bringing news as insects do. This was the nature of things: life, followed by its sister, death, then life again - a cycle completed, only to begin again. The song is the same and yet different each time, for that too is the nature of things.

Oak watched, year after year, and if it spread its limbs to grasp daring youngsters, the failed leap of a young squirrel or the misstep of a fledgling, the tree did so with best intentions for a tree is empathy, sympathy, and *curiosity* most of all.

Oak's roots provided its anchorage, and root hairs gathered food elements for all that mother sun did not provide. This root system connected to a vast underground of information and additional communication that combined with limbs held high, its leaves as sensitive as any whisker. Oak heard and felt its brethren fall, and sent what passed as a tree's prayer, one of commiseration, and the hope that the dying behemoth's children, whether by seed or rootlet, would grow and prosper and one day sing its own song.

"Trees sing, to each other, to themselves and to those who might listen. And so you will hear them, deep within your silence, within a dream. "

One day, a human woman stumbled through the forest, holding a young child. Oak watched as she placed the child, a tiny child, against Oak's stout trunk. "Forgive me," the woman whispered. "Forgive." With a sob, the woman hurried away, never looking back.

The child stood uncertain. She held fast to Oak, balancing carefully, patting its trunk as she walked as a toddler will, in need of support and guidance. Oak watched the child fall, having held out her hands for a mother absent. She scrambled blindly, at a crawl, to grasp Oak with small, desperate hands.

"Mama," the little girl wailed.

Oak watched with interest and certain knowledge. The child's distress would surely attract the attention of predators. Perhaps the mother would return, maybe not. Many a foundling fell to the striking of teeth or talon, and this was the way of things. But a human child was a rarity, this deep into the forest, and Oak hummed as the child held, clinging fast, taking comfort where she could, climbing into Oak's hollowed-out knoll, wails quietening to exhausted sobs that stuttered into hiccups and finally, a troubled sleep. Trees do sympathize. The young of any species is the hope of its future, and while death will strike, as it always will, life must be protected. Oak rustled its leaves loudly as if hit by a sudden gust, to drown out the continued whimpers of its newest inhabitant, however temporary.

Oak began the process of hardening his aged and injured trunk, something that a tree can do to ward off blight or as a defense, and so it did with an effort to protect the little girl.

"A child shelters within me," Oak sang.

"Death,' the other trees hummed. The child, unprotected, would most certainly die. Death brought its own reward, nothing is a wasted in a forest, not hair, nor bone.

But, Oak crooned, "I do not wish for this child to pass into its final slumber, so I must do as I must do."

The child had cried herself into a deep sleep. Oak could feel her begin to dream, and it dreamed with her, for this too is the nature of a tree.

"All trees dream."

There came the scent of salt, a taste of milk, and a warm, gentle softness like the downy breast of a bird as she covers her unhatched eggs.

Then, into the dream came fear, and darkness. There was coldness too, and the little girl shivered, although, sheltered within Oak's bough, pressed against its exposed heartwood, the child was warm.

The oak tree rocked, sighing, singing gently, and the child too sighed as she heard Oak's song and shivered no more, sinking instead into the place, surface to depths where dreams do not care to venture. And Oak found her there, and her name was Abby.

Oak sang to her about things that are, and not of what could be, for a tree is courteous, and the child was young. For now, she was safe, but Oak wondered as the child slept the deepest of exhausted sleep. It touched the child's mind with the softest of tendrils, a whisper of curiosity, and so it sank into the child's mind and never did it disturb her slumber.

Oak learned many things. The child hungered, and again the trees whispered and sang. How did a tree feed a child, who, barely out of infancy, could not forage, even though a tree is generous with its fruits?

Sap was discussed. Oak could not provide the nutrients palatable to a small and hungry human girl. But Oak could receive what was needed, and it did, painfully, from other trees, from their roots, and into his sapwood. From far and wide maples of all descriptions sent deliveries to Oak, who produced a woody bump inside of his trunk where the child slumbered and gently introducing this formula to the toddler.

"Abby," the trees sang, "she is Abby."

Oak felt the child stir, her small hands grasping, gently stroking, finding the dripping of nutrients instinctively, feeding. Oak held her fast, sending her back into a deep sleep, where errant movements could not endanger her. "Sleep," Oak sang. "Child, it is enough to do this. We are with you." Abby cooed. Oak could feel who this child was, the finding joy in the touching of things, the humor found in shapes and sounds. Deep within her slumber, Oak listened and learned and wondered what a tree could do for a small being, alone in a forest, who had no fur or claws or wings.

"I wish to keep her safe, "Oak whispered, and the other trees muttered or moaned or questioned, but Oak remained steadfast for a tree is stubborn.

Oak held Abby safe and sleeping. She fed on nutritious syrup and absorbed chlorophyll, and she remained within a deep dream where Oak kept her, while it exuded pheromones that discouraged pests. To the surprise of the forest, Oak sang of the needs of a nestling. It is not often that a tree asks for anything. There came a surfeit of feathers and fur to cover the child for, as the forest reasoned, Oak had provided much, and it was old.

And into Abby's dream, Oak planted rootlings, shadows of the knowledge that only trees can hope to attain, for this knowledge is as vast as the largest ocean. Within this tide, Abby learned of the first tree and its children, then insects and birds, mammals and reptiles – all that flew, or swam, or burrowed. Abby learned about life and death and how to embrace both. Death, like life, must never be wasted, and there cannot be one without the other.

There were questions. To Oak's delight, Abby was inquisitive.

"What is a star?"

Oak described Mother Sun, and that led to questions about energy and light, which led to its twin, darkness. Abby could not see well in the dark and then came the question of why this must be so, and this Abby argued. Oak pondered, and the trees began to sing possibilities and rule out options - for all taught Abby what she needed to know, and not a few things that she didn't. But this was different; this argument, for a human child is not a tree and will wish for what cannot be true, or could it? There came ballads of discussion, for it was one thing to know how to feed oneself, to climb, to swim, to dig, but how does one teach another to see things as they are?

Finally, the only option was an invasive one.

"We can change you," the trees hummed. "Your infant skin is malleable, we can teach your skin to see, and so the darkness will be revealed all the better."

Phosphorescence, how a tree uses it to see, was explained, and so, with Abby's permission, her skin was taught, and this change, delivered through Oak's root system, did great harm to it but it was done well.

Was it magic? Was it science? Surely it was both.

Later, much later, Abby slept. Oak directed branches to shelter the entrance, allowing for necessary light and moisture. The child's skin changed gradually, into something different, and then one day, Abby began to shine.

Oak felt the toddler stretch and turn toward Mother Sun, and it that Abby would soon outgrow the knoll in which she slept. Into her dream, Oak taught Abby of the ways of the animals who burrowed, climbed or perched. He taught her the many things a child could eat, and of what she must never touch.

Abby asked question after question. "What is a badger?" And then would come the image and the scent and what a badger could do and what it could not, and Oak was ever patient.

"There is no better teacher than a tree."

But, from within Abby's dreamscape came the questions of why - why this and why that. A tree does not question the why of things. A tree is not so much a single thing as an all thing. A tree is never an only tree, just as Abby was not an only human. But here there was a difference, and as Abby was to stumble with the concept of self, so did Oak stumble, for it did not think in terms of singularities, and she did. From what Oak could understand, humans thought of themselves as separate from each other and yet a part of their genus, and so Oak's answers were halting and did little to answer Abby's questions of who she was and why.

"Abby," Oak sighed into the dream he kept her, "people are the same but different, and there is no why, there only *is*."

A season of cold passed, Abby sheltered within lifeless branches, cuddled into generous donations of fur and feathery down brought by birds. And she grew, as a child must, and when the warmth of Mother Sun awakened the forest, Abby climbed from her knoll and began to cautiously explore, seeing not with only with weak, human eyes, but with her skin, her small arms outstretched, shining.

Abby met wolves, who loved her, allowing her to drink rich milk, for wolves too, are kind. And Abby met the badger of which Oak had spoken and learned to dig deep into the crust of the world and make for herself a small cave beside Oak's roots, never straying far. She practiced climbing, and if it could be said that a tree wrung its branches, it would be then, for Abby leaped and clung and often came close to plummeting to the ground.

Raccoons and other creatures with clever paws, or beaks taught Abby the skill of weaving, as did a medley of spiders. The nearby family of beaver taught her the art of building. Abby made a small lodge within the nearby pool into which she could escape the heat that was the summer, swimming under and into and in and away. But wherever Abby climbed or burrowed, her dream was Oak's dream, which was an all-dream, and Abby was never alone.

"We are connected. "

Oak could not teach Abby all there is to know, for that would have taken lifetimes that Abby did not have, but, as the child grew, so did her mind. Many things, Abby accepted on faith, other facts, she questioned until even a tree might be less patient. The question of singularity she pondered endlessly, it seemed. Oak sought different ways of explaining the difference of us versus I and you. Abby clung stubbornly to her selfhood, and the trees sang of this, in bemusement. They accepted that this was true, but they did not understand it.

Also, although it seemed as if the child understood death and accepted its necessity, Oak noticed an odd thing. Sometimes, when Abby slept, she dreamed of things that scared her and cried out or trembled. It was as a human thing that she did this, it had to be, for the things that

Abby dreamed were not true things at all, or things that had happened or ever could. As the oak tree touched Abby's mind as she screamed in her sleep, it discovered a separate world where death held a different meaning, one of great sorrow, disturbance, of terror and grief.

"Oak," Abby wailed.

The trees moaned to each other, for there seemed no solution. Abby was a human child, with a human mind, that saw and felt things that were not, who wished for things that could not be.

"Abby," the trees sang, "Abby."

There was a loneliness that trees never feel, and here Oak sought to do as it could. "Never alone, no. Always. Forever." Oak sang, in an attempt to quiet the child's fears. Sometimes it worked, and other times it did not and when this happened, no ballad was an answer.

Finally, Oak sang to its brethren; it was perhaps better for the child to return to her kind, for Oak reminded, a child is not a tree, as much as, and Oak had to admit to it, Oak would have liked this to be the case.

"A tree can love. It can love forever."

And so came the day that Abby set out, walking through the forest, toward where people lived, her skin shining, wearing nothing but fur and feathers.

In the town that Abby visited, people stared. They made sounds and touched her with curious hands. Abby did not have words, although she knew of them. Trees do not speak with mouths, and so Abby reached out with her mind instead. A woman screamed. Then, a man shouted and pushed at Abby, who fell, confused, to the ground. Oak heard and felt this, as did all the trees, there and everywhere.

"Language, it can be a weak thing; it can be a strong thing. But it is what they know." Oak whispered. "Speak as you would do and not as we are."

So Abby began to speak, first in halting words, then in full sentences, and some listened, but others were fearful and ushered her from where she sat on the ground, into a dwelling where they closed the door. "We will bring you food and think on what you have said," Abby heard, "we do not understand how or what you are, shining and singing. We fear you, and we may harm you in our fear."

These were not the words spoken aloud, but Abby could hear what they didn't say, and she ran out of the small house when the food was brought, running as she did in her dreams, fearful but escaping.

Abby ran to Oak and wept against its trunk until the noise of the people who chased found her.

"What are you? Are you a demon child, we are afraid."

"She is a ghost child, see how she shines?"

Others sought to reason but too few and too late.

Abby reached out, her mind to their minds, and showed them who she was. Some heard and wished to understand, but there were others who chose fear before all things. And there was a man who held the one thing that *all* must fear, fire, which the frightened man carried on a stick. He threw it at Abby, whose hair ignited and she ran to the pool and slid into the water to hide, shivering within her small lodge.

The woman screamed again, "A ghost child, a demon, see how she disappears?"

Others searched for sane answers, and they muttered together, questioning.

The fire spread, and the people, at first, did nothing out of this fear and out of this hesitation.

"The fire will kill the demon."

"The fire will kill everything, and this is not as it should be."

Abby, safe in her lodge felt the forest burn. She wept her human tears while her thoughts stormed into the world, "Why have you done this? Feel my pain." And Abby screamed and screamed.

The people tore at their faces and pulled at their hair at the song of Abby, whose grief was unlike any other, this child, raised by a tree.

And she felt Oak begin to die.

"No," Abby cried. "No."

At first, she could only feel Oak's physical pain, and she felt sorrow and so much of that. But there whispered into her distress Oak's familiar lullaby. It sang of acceptance and hope. Oak, touching her gently, respectfully, as it always did, sang, "Child, my child."

"My?" Abby shrieked. "You mean our, ore, or ..." She faltered, "I have listened. Oh, I have tried. We. We are. *Us.*"

"No," Oak insisted from deep within his blaze. "*You* are *my* acorn."

Much later, Abby ventured out into a changed landscape, with fire-stricken trees burned to blackened earth, shorn to the fabric of the world.

Some had done what they could, to save what could not be saved. At first, seeing them, in her grief, Abby thought to be angry, but she remembered herself and all that she was and she sang, "I can hear you. I. We. Us. Together." Abby dropped to her knees, shining hands upon the ground as she looked at the quiet people, the ones that reached out from their fear, filled with remorse, seeking.

"Trees sing if you listen."

***

Shebat Legion is a consummate producer/storyteller who has been printed and reprinted in numerous anthologies, including her collection of short stories called "Hubris." Legion is responsible for the creation of Vampire Therapy, which includes a full-length novel, "Jackson and Eva," as well as an illustrated collection of short stories set in the Vampire Therapy universe called "The Chronicles of The Cats Ass Boutique: Seasons and Reasons." Legion's most recent production credit is the illustrated anthology of short stories, featuring over sixty authors, "Klarissa Dreams Redux," the second in the "Klarissa Dreams" series, with proceeds to breast cancer research and awareness.

https://www.facebook.com/Author.Shebat.Legion
https://www.amazon.com/author/shebatlegion

ON A BAYOU

By J.F. Capps

Perhaps, Wallace thought, perhaps that hadn't been at all what he'd seen. Perhaps he'd hallucinated. Yes, that was it. Much more likely. That hadn't been the dome of a human head skimming along the top of the water. That'd been…been… Well, what? What on Earth could that have been? A large eye? He almost laughed. If that was an eye, one that big, he'd never go back out on the water ever, *ever* again. He'd tuck his tail and run home like his butt was on fire and the water was gas.

He slicked his hand, wet with water and swamp scum, through his hair, then fanned his hand around his face to fend off the swarm of mosquitos that gathered for the feast. They were relentless. The whirring, whining buzz of one of the little marauders sounded in his ear for the ten millionth time that night and he was ready to scream. Almost did.

Water splashed somewhere nearby. A gator, he knew. He'd heard that sound before as one came up for a moment, caught air, and then submerged. He reached out, took hold of his gun.

A gator cruised by under the boat, rocking it from side to side. He clenched; if one of those scaly monsters were able to knock the boat over he'd be screwed; there'd be no getting away in these conditions. The water and the scum were at least hip deep. He'd fall in and either stick or have to swim. Regardless, he'd make too much noise and they'd be on him. No, he couldn't afford to go into the water, to go into their territory. Here though…

He hefted the rifle and stuffed it into the pocket of one shoulder. Crickets were starting to sing along the bank and frogs were hollering in a near endless roar as if they were worshipping the fecund swell of the moon overhead.

Hadn't someone disappeared on this same bayou recently?

He cursed himself for remembering that story at the most inopportune moment.

One of them brushed under the bottom again. Wallace held an oar out and probed along the side, feeling for the beast, prepared to drive it off or shoot or…

The boat rocked again, hard. He slipped from his standing position and fell to a kneel, one knee smarting from impact. The boat made a grinding sound as something hit it, followed by a thump, and

Wallace clinched with everything he had. *Thump, thump, thump* the gator hammered the bottom of the boat. He pushed the rifle over the edge and took an estimated guess of the monster's location. He fired. There was no speedy retreat. The gator was either brave or stupid or both. It kept hammering the bottom of the boat, now rocking it dangerously from side to side. Wallace's foot slipped in the slimy algal liner along the bottom of the boat and he fell hard against the little metal bench seat that bisected the center of the vessel, feeling the hard metal dig into the soft meat of one hip. Something popped. He spilled backwards into the boat and barely registered the *splash* of the gun that he'd dropped as it entered the bayou. He'd never see it again.

His hand gripped the aching hip as he tried to flatten himself against the bottom of the boat, a filth-greased strand of hair falling in his face while his reptilian assailant jarred one side of the boat hard.

Oh please, he thought. *Oh please, just let me get the hell out of this, and I swear to…I swear I'll never smoke or drink ever again. I'll go to church and I'll help the poor and…*

The boat rocked to one side, then the other, then flipped over, dumping him into the fetid water of the bayou. He sunk, his guess of the body of water being hip deep swept away when he didn't even touch the bottom before surfacing. He did touch a huge, slimy body that was complete with fins as it swam past, and though it wasn't a gator, it was still big enough to make lunch of him and he screamed while still under the water. Screamed and let all his good air out. It circled back, brushed him, and went the other way - oh God, oh Jesus, this shark sized thing…

Something bit into his neck.

Wallace's head came up above the water as he struggled with his attacker, some sort of smooth, round head that he couldn't get a grip on burying deeper into the pocket between his head and shoulder while it fought for better purchase. Then it started to roll and, oh holy shit, the pain oh God…

Something tore loose.

Wallace stopped struggling and tried to push his hands against the injury, tried to do anything to stop the bleeding while he felt hot blood pouring from his neck. The slimy thing brushed his boots but he didn't focus on it. Instead he struggled to settle his eyes on whatever the hell it was that was attacking him, tried to make sense of it all, tried to…

He screamed one last time when he saw the animal, screamed and tried to speak even though he was already so weak from blood loss.

***

"Another body." Sheila said as she shut the door behind her. "That's two in less than a month, Harv. I know that NPD didn't want anything leaked into the public through the media yet, but we're dealing with…with…with something here! There's a serial killer or a maneater or something on the loose out there in the swamp and we have an obligation to tell the public."

"We also have an obligation to support the Nujac Police Department." Harv said. He stood and walked around his desk, taking a seat on the corner and reaching up to twist the curl back into his mustache while he spoke. "We talked about this. I need you to just let this story simmer a little longer, Sheila, and maybe then we can discuss publishing."

Sheila didn't like it when he overrode her. She also didn't like it when reminded her that he'd overridden her before. She did at least understand why though. Her lips pursed while she slipped her tongue between her teeth and bit down just enough that it hurt, but didn't bring blood.

"How much longer?" She said. Harv shrugged, pulling a Werther's Original from his shirt pocket. He offered it to her and she shook a hand at her. "No thank you. That's old man candy."

"Old man candy is the best candy." He said. He unwrapped the little treat and threw it in his mouth. She heard it click on his teeth. "Maybe…two weeks? We'll have to let the cat out of the bag soon. It's going to get out regardless. Hopefully a little patience on our end…"

"…my end…" She said, correcting. He nodded and held up a finger as if "shooshing" her.

"…your end, then…hopefully it pays off."

She was skeptical. She said so. He shrugged and smiled.

"Well, in the meantime, I suppose you can dedicate some of your time to working on real stories…"

"This is a real story!" She said.

"…and, if you get time to build the case on this one then…well, all the better."

Sheila huffed, slicking her fingers back through her hair to pull the mess of curls from her face that attempted to takeover during the negotiation. She turned, leaving the office, angry, but trying not to be, trying to remind herself that it was all business and business was all it was, but dammit she was so tired, *so tired*, of finding a story, and putting it together, and doing the legwork, and then it wasn't the right story for this reason or that and it got scrapped and then there she was, back at square one, starting all over again.

She stormed past the breakroom, glanced once at the coffee pot. It was getting near lunch time. She needed to dump it before the coffee became oil, but then decided that, you know what? It could be someone else's problem today. One of the other simians she worked with could rinse the pot out today, by God. She continued down the hall, thinking about how to do the legwork, the research, who she could interview…

Who she could interview!

The realization that she had a contact struck her like a brick to the forehead, so hard that she wondered how on Earth she'd forgotten about Detective Mortimer "Mort" Kojakski! My, but he was a tall glass of water, so handsome. Sheila liked him. He was stern, but had a kind heart and she was willing to bet that if there was anyone in this little yeehaw town that had some sort of connection to this case, then it was Mort. Well, duh. He was a detective after all, but more than that Nujac PD was small and there were two, maybe three detectives tops, and with the way they were working with the state police to keep it all under wraps at the moment that meant she had little avenue of approach when it came to pre-emptive strikes on getting an interview. If she wasn't careful one of the bigger newspapers from Shreveport or Beaumont or Lake Charles would swoop in and get the first dirt on the whole thing and then there she'd be, Sheila fuckin' Walker who'd almost made it, but, once again, managed to snatch defeat from the jaws of victory. She considered her other options; the coroner, the staties, the city council, none of them were liable to work with her on this she knew. Mort, though, marched to the beat of his own drum.

She rushed down the hall, into her office. She dug through the top drawer of her desk and pulled out the card with Mort's direct line on it.

She rang him.

"Detective Kojakski." He said. She sighed in relief in the second before it all came pouring out of her mouth, flooding out, coming with such a fervor she had to stop after her first stuttering attempts and start all over. She even went as far as to reintroduce herself.

"Okay, it's Sheila Walker over at channel 4. Remember me? I interviewed you a few times a couple years back over that officer related…"

"Yes, I remember you, Ms. Walker. What can I do for you?" He said. There was a grating in his voice, a sort of air of 'I know why you're calling but I wish everyone would just leave me alone about this crap' kind of pitch in his voice.

"Well, obviously I'm calling about the reports of a mangled body pulled out of a bayou last night."

"I figured as much." He said, his voice blown with a sigh. "You and about everyone else in the parish wants to know what happened."

"I'm sure it's wearing thin." She said.

"It is." He said for confirmation.

"The people do have a right to know, though. I'm not going to publish anything on it until you guys are ready, but I'd sure like to start picking up some of the details you've got already."

The phone shuffled in his hand as he adjusted the way he held it. He was quiet for a long time.

"Ms. Walker…"

"Sheila."

"…Sheila, you need to understand that this is a very peculiar case. A very, *very* peculiar case. It's way out of my hands for the most part, you see. NPD is really just supporting a higher law enforcement echelon's investigation at this point."

She loved it when he spoke like that. All sophisticated and authoritative.

"Come on Mort, I promise I won't publish yet. Just…give me something. An interview, anything. Come down to the office…"

"I'd rather not do that." He said. He seemed short and uncomfortable with the recommendation. "I've got work to do, Ms. Walker…"

"Sheila." She said, correcting him again. He didn't pay much attention this time.

"Sheila." He said, correcting himself again. His teeth clicked together as he sucked in air, obviously thinking about what to say next. She held her breath. "Listen, Sheila, I can't discuss this case in an official capacity yet. It's that simple. The best I can do for you is offer you a ride along, if you want. You can uh…I guess you can watch me work and draw what you think you can from that for your story later or something…I dunno."

Okay, she'd take that. It was a start.

"When?"

"I uh…when are you available?"

"Asking a police detective when he's available is like asking a weatherman when it's going to rain. You're only going to get the right answer every now and then."

"Fair enough. Tonight?"

Sheila looked at the clock on the wall. She could still squeeze in a decent meal and a nap before pulling an all-nighter.

"You know I'm a detective, right?" He said. His voice was laced with sarcasm. "I don't work past four without a reason."

"Then call me if you go in." She said.

"Hold on, Ms. Walker…"

"God dammit, Sheila!"

"Sheila, sheesh. I can't just call you to go with me if I get called out on official business."

"You just asked if I wanted to do a ride along." She said, reminding him. Her voice was firm, adamant. "So if you get called in, I want to ride along."

"Fine. I'll call you." He said. The phone beeped as he ended the call. She found that she was chewing one of her nails. Heat crawled up her neck. He'd actually pissed her off a little bit, but she tried to remind herself that there were reasons for what he was doing. Protecting the public, protecting the victims, protecting the investigation. She thought about Harv for a minute, thought about how he was always so damn accommodating for the police department. She decided she was going to leave early, get a good nap, and be ready in case Mort called.

***

Mort called.

"Ms. Wa…Sheila. It's Detective Kojakski. We've received a call and I'm going in. Where should I meet you?"

She looked at the time. 2 AM. She'd laid down for her nap hours ago. The Sandman was beating a blood pressure war drum in her head because of the crappy sleep she'd caught laying on her couch. She sat bolt upright, her hair flopping down over her face in a complete mess, her clothes wrinkled from being slept in.

"What? Where are we going?"

"Duncan Bayou."

Her heart was now hammering. She was on her feet, trying to scramble and get herself together.

"Now?"

"Of course now. That's why I'm up calling you at this hour."

Couldn't argue with that.

"Pick me up in the McDonald's parking lot on the way." She said, hanging up. She wanted to at least swish some Listerine around in her mouth before she took off. And maybe get her hair under control. Had he said, 'going in?' Wasn't that a bit…dramatic?

Already she was on the move, a throw rug almost tripping her as she pulled away from the couch with it in tow before she rushed to the bedroom and grabbed the clothes she'd laid out for the morning before rushing to the bathroom. She changed and tried to put herself together into something descent. Then she hurried out of the house, forgetting her keys, turning, running back up the steps into the house to get her keys and lock the door since she'd left in such a rush that she hadn't done that, and THEN she was driving…

Sheila couldn't remember the drive to the parking lot. It was all a blur, her entire trip washed away by her fight with sleepiness, as well as being on autopilot, allowing her brain to force her through the motions of getting their while her consciousness was elsewhere, and trying to decipher what she thought she'd see, if she was ready to see, and what questions she should ask - if any. Could she take pictures? Of course not. She'd left the little bag at home that she carried her equipment in. She cursed herself. Every time she got in a hurry about anything it always backfired and she'd left half-cocked and without everything she needed.

Kojakski was already parked and waiting on her when she arrived, a little orange light flashing on top of the car. She pulled up next to him, grabbed her purse since, for whatever reason, she had the good sense to grab it, but not her keys or any other important thing earlier, and then climbed in the car with him.

"You're fast." He said, putting the vehicle in gear and getting them rolling, the roar of the engine making her squirm in the seat.

"So are you." She said, unsure of how to respond to that. She caught the side-eye as they blew through the first red light, and then the second.

"I'm still a little sketchy on the particulars of what we're about to get into." Detective Kojakski said. "I say that to indicate that I don't know what you're about to see."

"Okay."

"If you're…"

"Are you going to turn around and take me back to my car? I doubt that, so just save your chivalry and drive."

"Suit yourself." He said.

She saw the blue lights from a mile away. Smattered amongst them were various other flashing emergency responder lights from the local Rescue Squad, the Fire Department, and EMS. They must have had good radio discipline because there weren't any looky-loos yet, and since people were glued to their scanners nowadays, it seemed improbable that she was just lucky enough to get there without a huge crowd to bog things down without some sort of effort on behalf of emergency services. They stepped out, Kojakski slipping a hat onto his head while Sheila popped open an umbrella that'd been sitting in the floorboard on the car's passenger side. The rain was weak, barely coming down at all, but it was enough that it'd mess up her hair and get her soggy enough to be miserable and neither of those options were what she wanted.

"Sorry that I had to wake you up but I knew you'd want to see this." A lithe redhead said as she trotted up. "We've already identified the body as Suzan Collins, last seen by her family three days ago before heading to the bayou to take pictures of orchids in the back country. Apparently…who's this?"

She stopped short, motioning her hand toward Kojakski's new friend. The redhead, smiled, but said nothing while waiting for Kojakski to introduce her, but he waved her on and made her start talking again.

"…*Apparently*…" She resumed, a bit indignant, "Whatever happened to her was…she has been partially consumed like the other recovered bodies. The Coroner…"

"Kowalski." Kojakski said.

"…The other *Ski*…" She said. Her words were becoming venom. Sheila squirmed, getting uncomfortable with the direction this conversation was going. Was a fight brewing? Were these two about to get into a shouting match? She hated shouting. Reminded her too much of her childhood.

"I uh…excuse me." Sheila said, stepping away. She could hear them talking behind her as she went, though about what she couldn't tell. It was obviously heated and she wanted no further part of it, and while she was no stranger to having to be stern with people, a late night argument, even the prospect of one, was enough to get her heart thundering, anxiousness gripping her by the throat.

Cops were everywhere, from local yokels to staties. They were just close enough to the park that a Ranger was on scene as an advisor. There were also EMTs, Rescue Squad, Firefighters; it was a veritable who's-who of the uniform services.

She only needed to wave off one man and explain that she was with Detective Kojakski in an advisory role to be left alone for the duration of her brief solo sortie. She wormed her way through the crowd of cops who were gathered in clusters of two and three, talking about this or that, having a late dinner or early breakfast, sharing smokes and coffee, before she arrived at the short, sandy beach where Suzan's body lay. It, *she*, had come to rest after having been washed into a small stand of river oats and swamp milkweed. The first thing that hit her, well, after the visual assault, was the smell; it was rancid, like meat left in warm water, which she guessed wasn't far from what happened. Suzan's eyes were open, still staring in horror at whatever happened to her. Her hands were out, fingers clutched like she'd died grasping something, fighting. The ends of her fingers were a mangled mess with nails bent and broken away, some sporting chunks of flesh beneath them.

A fly crawled out of her open mouth.

Sheila fought back nausea.

Her throat and the soft abdominal flesh were both torn open, probably the cause of death, and Sheila guessed that this is what a gator attack would look like, if not a little less savage. With an alligator she'd expect the already extensive damage to be catastrophic, but this was torn and chewed as if by something that wasn't a living, breathing hedge trimmer. There was a mammalian quality to the bite marks, though she was no expert.

She raised her camera and snapped some pictures.

"For record retention." She said to the first officer that tried to approach her. He nodded and stepped back. They'd string her up by her toes when they found out she'd lied.

Maybe she hadn't lied. Maybe she'd just preyed upon the truth.

Cops were talking behind her, but she couldn't focus. All she could do is look at Suzan with a million different emotions taking control of her. She was sad, scared, repulsed, angry, and mesmerized, the simple parts of her primate brain conspiring against her to make her stare at the dead member of her own species and dwell upon the fact that it wasn't her, but that this area was dangerous. The skin on her neck prickled.

More cops talking. Their voices were getting animated.

"Gimme that spotlight, will ya?" One of them said. It was the first thing she understood from their conversation. She turned and looked at the cops that were gathering on a clear section of shore maybe fifty feet or so from Suzan's body. There were some hand gesticulations and broken conversations, but the part she'd always remember was when one of them raised the huge spotlight and turned it on, shining it down the bayou until it was near a cypress that had leaned over, creating a sort of natural shelter over the water.

There was a head. A human head.

At first, Sheila thought that this was another body, and her sense of dread jumped. When the eyes blinked, however, and she realized that the head was alive, and her sense of dread jumped again, this time exponentially. It came gliding slowly, gently through the water toward them, nose just above the water, and everything below that submerged. It didn't even leave a wake.

"Hey, you, come here!" One of the Officer's shouted. He was on the shore unbuttoning his sleeves.

The silent shape continued forward.

Sheila looked over her shoulder, back at Detective Kojakski, looking for some sort of guidance or reaction. Kojakski was coming down the trail to the water to get a look for himself. One of the other officers was down to his trousers and was wading out, leaving even his duty belt behind.

"There's gators!" Kojakski said, his voice booming across the surface of the bayou and reverberating back off the wall of cypress on the other side. "Get out of...what is that?"

"It's a head!" Someone said.

"That's a person!" Another Officer said. "It's alive!"

Sheila's sense of reality skewed as she wrapped her own mind around what was happening. The head was...well, weird. It was small and pale and hairless for whatever reason. The top of it seemed to be scabbed or scarred or...well, she didn't know what. It was odd and looked almost like scales, reptilian scales. She dwelt on that for a moment. Reptilian scales. As opposed to what other kind of scales?

She watched the officer wade out, watched him as he called out to the head that glided through the water, and watched the head dip under.

"Sonofa...crazy bastard, where'd you reckon it went?" The cop said, calling back over his shoulder.

"Mike, get back up here on the shore!" Detective Kojakski said. "We have no idea..."

He never got to finish the sentence.

The officer, Mike, turned to come back to the shore, but stopped after the first step. He screamed, reached down, and grasped at something in the water. Pistols were unholstered all along the shore and officers called back and forth throughout their ranks for help or to see who was going in. Kojakski was already heading down the shore while Sheila scrambled next to him, unsure if she should follow or photograph. She was at a loss, no idea what to do, the horror of the situation and her desire to help Mike clouded her judgment. She paced back and forth, one hand covering her mouth.

Mike came up, a scream singing from his lips. There was blood in the water. His body was rolling, turning.

Another human form was stuck to his.

Kojakski didn't hesitate. He went in the water after Mike, fine threads and all, making bounds in water that was up past his hips. He reached into the swirling maelstrom where Mike went under, gripped, screamed, and hauled a small human form from the water. A naked kid flailed in his arms, his body covered in sores, scrapes, and growths like scales. His teeth gnashed the air. A chunk of Mike's flesh hung from his mouth.

Kojakski's eyes darted from the kid, from the water, to Sheila's eyes. So much passed between them in that instant; her out of her comfort zone, afraid, with no idea of how to respond to what was happening, him amazed, surprised, and inadequately trained for this…whatever this mess was. He held tight to the kid and stomped back toward the shore, the boy wriggling and thrashing. She couldn't believe that Kojakski still had a hold on him. Two more cops rushed in, grabbed Mike by the arms and dragged him from the bayou

The boy's eyes met Sheila's and she could see something cold, merciless, and calculating; something devoid of human emotions and human thoughts in those cold, steel blue eyes.

She fainted.

***

Sheila woke up in a hospital room. At first she didn't understand where she was or what was happening, but then she remembered the boy, remembered his eyes, remembered Kojakski pulling that kid from the bayou like he was some sort of water monster. She pushed herself up in the bed with the notion that she'd have to make it a point to stop waking up this way soon. Twice in one day was too many times, after all.

Her gaze settled on a clock. Noon. Sitting in a wooden chair below that clock was Detective Kojakski.

"You alright?" He said. She nodded, fireworks going off in her cranium. She winced, raised a hand, and rubbed the bandages that wrapped her head. She must have hit it when she fell.

"I think so. I'm sorry. I don't know what happened back there." She said.

"Don't worry about it. That was pretty hard to swallow for a lot of people. Even our guys who work on kid crimes were pretty uh, disturbed."

"Who was that kid?"

Kojakski squirmed around, getting comfortable in his seat. Or maybe it was because he was uncomfortable that he had to fidget? Sheila couldn't tell.

"John Doe, unidentified 12 year old male, origin unknown, parents unknown, and no known missing child report. The uh…the initial word is that he may have been out there for a while."

"How long's a while?" Sheila said, eyes wide.

"Probably ten years, as best as we can tell."

"Ten years! He'd have been two!"

"There's a theory that he learned how to hunt…"

"…how to hunt…"

"…how to hunt by watching the gators, living among them. Did you see how he moved through the water?"

"Are you suggesting that this kid was raised by alligators!?" Sheila said, one hand held up and pressed into one of her eyes. "You can't possibly mean that. Think of how absurd that sounds!"

"He uh, we turned him over to CPS pretty fast. They took him in for a bunch of tests, got some samples and stuff. There was human hair in his stool sample…"

"There was what!?" Sheila said. "How long have I been in here!? You're telling me they're already getting test results back!?"

Detective Kojakski held up a hand, motioning for her to calm down.

"You've been here for two days. You hit your head pretty hard on a rock on the shoreline. Like I said, don't worry about all that. The lady over at CPS fainted too when they gave her the stool sample results."

"Oh my God!"

"They call him Gator Boy down at the station. There's some very real talk that he was probably raised by gators, all joking aside."

Sheila lay back in her bed, pressing both hands now into her eyes, trying to force this dream, this nightmare out of her psyche, trying not to think about a child, a human being, being reduced to some reptilian existence in an environment that had to be beyond miserable. How had he done it? Why hadn't the other, correction, *real* alligators eaten him?

***

In a mental health facility a hundred miles away an orderly struggled with a boy who refused to eat anything but raw meat, a boy who screamed, threw tantrums, climbed and jumped from his bed like it was a trampoline. A boy who knew no words nor made any sounds aside from the occasional grunt or growl. A boy who bit three fingers off the dermatologist who tried to examine and diagnose the strange growths on his skin from living in the stagnant water of the bayou.

***

J.F. Capps is the author of "Ophedities and the Dragon", "Eddie," and "Winter's Orphans." He spent twelve years with the U.S. Marine Corps, both active duty and reserve components, and currently works as a professional woodsman. He lives on a small farm in the hills of east Tennessee with his wife and four kids.

AMONGST THE CACKLE

Timothy Pulo

There is such a thing as having too much money and Dalton Trench was the epitome of that statement. He made his first million, well, all of his millions, rather easily – inheritance from his mother and father that sat somewhere around the 35 million mark. He was too young to touch it when they died so the fortune lay dormant over the course of the next decade, generating interest and increasing exponentially. Unfortunately, as the money sat there dormant, Dalton's mind didn't; it raced, spending the money fictitiously over and over until it quite literally drove him insane – psychosis, anxiety and personality disorders to be exact.

Through his natural charisma, a decent chunk of negligence and the fact that there wasn't really anyone left on Earth to care about poor little Dalton, the quirky boy with the lisp, he evaded being institutionalised and, at age eighteen, the year of his actual inheritance, slipped away from the life that he knew and migrated to miserable Kolomyia. Ukraine was a weird destination for a multi-millionaire but all a part of the bigger plan that Dalton was devising and far enough away from anyone that would likely stop him.

The first property he purchased, a dilapidated farmstead in the town's north, was completely transformed in the space of six months, providing needed work to the area and an unusual splash of colour in an otherwise drab, grey city. Locals wondered exactly what the foreigner was up to. "Have you seen what *netuteshniy* is doing?" "What is it meant to be?" "Mad with money!" The questions were never ending and opinion divided the congregation, as half thought Dalton was building some kind of exotic animal sanctuary and the other, some sort of accommodation that contrasted with every other building in Kolomyia. Dalton enjoyed hearing what was said about him, even though most of it he couldn't understand and truth be told, there was an element of truth in what both groups were saying.

"Okay, now go." Dalton said to the lead builder of his project.

"Don't you want walk around?" the burly builder said in a thick Ukrainian accent that he tried to minimise when he conversed with the foreigner, "make sure finish?"

"No, you've done your job admirably," Dalton replied, looking around the finished property, "and far quicker than I could have ever imagined." He retrieved a cell phone from his pocket and swiped and prodded incessantly for around fifteen seconds while the builder looked on dumbfounded. "I have transferred another 5 million hryvnia for you to leave now and not tell anyone the specifics of the place. Share it with your men or keep it for yourself. I don't care, just forget this place."

"*Dyakuyu*, ah, thank you," the builder stammered, his gratitude obvious, "but, what is for?" he concluded, struggling with English yet again.

"My dumb friend, take your money and leave. What I plan to do here has nothing to do with you."

***

The drives to and from Korosten were the worst, a fourteen hour commute, not including necessary rest periods, but Dalton was adamant it was all worth it. "Business can't occur at the same place as pleasure," he used to say, "dilutes the results," and besides, the drive gave him time to think, time to delve further into his psyche, and continue convincing himself that he was doing the right thing, doing what science couldn't.

He pulled up at In-Taym Children's Home, his bright orange Bentley Continental an eyesore amongst the continued grey of the neighbourhood of the orphanage. Employees of In-Taym were now familiar with Dalton's visits; this was his seventh, and when a well-dressed, well-spoken man in a suit, with obvious pedigree from the States came knocking, looking to adopt a child, you best believe the workers of the children's home answered.

"Ladies," Dalton exclaimed, oozing swagger as he entered the building. One of the perks of his disabilities was the knack of quite easily portraying a man free of the anxiety that rendered his brain instable. So convincing was his portrayal of normalcy that no one ever questioned it.

"Mister *гроші*," the lady at the entry way with the best understanding of English said relieved, "you are back for another?" She was hopeful and wanted nothing more than a good home for the forgotten children of the Ukraine. She had worked at the orphanage for the best part of the decade and rarely had they seen children adopted until Dalton Trench first ventured into the building a little over three years ago.

"Yulia, I am. I still have love in my heart." His words made Yulia and her offsider weak at the knees; not only was the man wealthy and good looking but he had a seemingly endless amount of love and compassion that he wanted to offer the less fortunate souls of the country. "For me," he went on, "this is about providing the best and most stable conditions possible to as many young as possible." It was the same speech he'd said the previous time and would not doubt be the same the next time and, like last time, the women of the orphanage would struggle to comprehend, but saying it aloud had a cathartic effect, it almost justified things for Dalton. "I have been blessed with money. More money than one man should be blessed with. What is money without people to share it with?" Dalton didn't expect an answer to his rhetorical question, but nodded and smiled when he received one anyway as he happily allowed Yulia to lead him further into the building.

By now, Dalton had all but memorised the layout of the place; children with a greater chance of adoption in the front, the harder sells at the back, and the disabled upstairs in individual rooms. He followed Yulia to the back of the dwelling. She was good like that, never questioned the fact that, although he stated he had love to give, it was never enough to warrant a child with a disability.

"немовля?" Yulia asked, pointing towards the room of the orphanage containing the youngest of the children without care, "Another baby?"

"Please," Dalton replied, walking into the room lined with cot after cot, many of which contained multiple children with at least one covered in bodily fluid of some description. The conditions of the place made it so much easier for Dalton to do what he did without too much, if any, lingering guilt.

The pair stopped in the centre of the room and Yulia waited for Dalton to make his decision. They had danced the same dance many times before and she knew there was a process, a method to his madness and she watched patiently. Dalton walked up and down past each cot, clearly looking for something, a quality he was after, as he hummed a tune barely audible over the cacophony of gurgles and feeding cries. After what seemed like forever, but was more accurately only forty seconds, he stopped in front of a cot; it was no different to all the others and, like many others, contained three children, two of which were red in the face from endless minutes of desperately crying for attention. The third child, slightly plumper than the others, a rarity in these conditions, lay content amongst the noise, watching the events of the room unfold.

"This," Dalton said, pointing his index finger at the quiet, plump baby. He had become something of an expert on the matter and estimated that the child, a boy (but that was irrelevant) was definitely under the age of one, most likely around the eight or nine month mark. "This one here."

Dotingly and with the care and consideration of a mother, Yulia bent down and brought the child to her bosom, squeezing it one last time before she passed it off to its new father. Dalton accepted the baby gladly, smiling ear to ear with the latest acquisition before following

Yulia out to the entry of the building where one of the other women had already expediated the necessary forms and traded them for an undisclosed amount of money from Dalton that they would share amongst themselves.

"We will see you again?"

"Yes, one more time ladies and then I am done." Dalton replied as he waltzed the baby to the impractical family car for the return trip of his commute.

***

Dalton trampled down the narrow corridor of his purpose-built complex carrying a clipboard and a blue pen. He called it his morning rounds, likening the experience to a nurse completing duties first thing of the day at a hospital. It was how he made sure everyone was okay and progressing as he had hoped. The seventh and eighth babies had now well and truly settled into their life at his complex but, unlike baby one, two, and three, it was far too early for him to see much in the way of changes, for the more recent arrivals, Dalton simply made sure the children were still alive.

The complex was divided into eight main parts, with each part containing a darkened room resembling a den that opened into a large yard more or less overran with foliage of the area. The yards were not maintained and more accurately resembled the Ukrainian wilderness, an area devoid of human contact, and that was exactly Dalton's intention. Routinely, Dalton would arrange for food to be delivered to the yards, a combination of vegetables, carrion, and livestock to satisfy the needs of his experiment, leading to residents of the local area to incorrectly assume that Dalton was tending to exotic animals in another example of a white man with too much money.

Dalton looked at the top of his list, the same list he printed out at the beginning of every morning, the same list that would ultimately be vital to his findings.

"Number one," he said to himself as he approached the door and slid back the rectangular piece of Perspex to provide him with a view of the darkened room, "wakey, wakey," he continued as he flicked a switch that illuminated a light from within the room. The globe was not bright but provided Dalton enough light for him to easily see what was happening from within the room.

The room itself was roughly eight foot wide by around ten feet; small when you considered its inhabitants, but Dalton's guilt was always lessened when he considered the size of the adjoining yard. He designed things this way so that it resembled as best as possible, real life conditions. He looked to the far side of the room, to a silhouetted grouping of black. To the uneducated, it could have easily been mistaken for nothing, but Dalton knew precisely what he was looking at. He knew so well because baby number one had been living in his facility now for a shade over five years and the changes he had witnessed were truly astounding.

"One!" he called in a booming voice that was intended to compel, "Odyn, come to Doctor Trench," Dalton continued, calling by the name he bestowed upon the child after what he gathered was the Ukrainian word for one, "it's breakfast time."

From out of the darkened pile, a figure moved and arced its back, wakening itself from what appeared to be a deep sleep. Another, bigger and broader also rose from slumber and prodded the first figure with its nose, almost in an act of communication, goading the first to move towards the door. The creature would. It always did. Baby one still refused to eat with the remainder of the cackle, it refused the scavenger lifestyle and forced further human intervention on behalf of Dalton. He didn't mind. The creature was showing progress in other ways; like its hyena brethren, it walked on all fours and had learned to communicate through a series of whoops, giggles, and groans.

The baby, now well beyond toddler age, had long, matted hair and its skin, once white and pure, was dirtied to almost entirely brown in colour, more closely resembling the other hyenas. Being the first of Dalton's experiments, he researched as best as he could how to introduce a human into a cackle of hyenas, but, of course, no such research existed and he placed all his faith, and the life of the innocent child, in the maternal qualities of the hyenas he illegally brought to the Ukraine. After some initial resistance, Dalton was surprised at how quickly the animals took to Odyn. The natural motherly instincts of the female hyenas kicked in and they soon were saving carrion and flesh for the infant to eat. Of all Dalton's children, Odyn was perhaps his favourite. Though he swore to himself not to get attached, but it was difficult when the child so quickly adapted to life amongst the cackle. Dalton covered his hand and the bulk of his arm with a black leather glove – it was important to minimise the contact he had with the creature. Odyn came to him, as she always did, and he ever so quickly muzzled with its hair, bringing it to a point and then watching it flop back over her face. Odyn purred in delight and further arced its back, looking like the cat a hyena is often mistaken for.

"That's it, my girl," he said under his breath before passing Odyn some food; berries and a squashed banana. He was beginning to ween the child completely off being hand-reared so the portions he fed had drastically diminished in the hope of the child fully taking to carrion.

Odyn quickly took the food before scurrying away and returning to the other animals basking in their peaceful pile of darkness. "See you tomorrow," he muttered and then madly scribbled on his clipboard.

The remainder of his morning was spent dotingly checking on his other creations; DVA hadn't made the progress Dalton had hoped he would. Living amongst the shoebill storks had all but turned him into a mute as the birds rarely uttered a sound. Chotyry, number four, had quickly become another of Dalton's favourites. Though he was more or less solitary now, his time attached to his adopted leopard mother as an infant, taught him a predatory instinct that would more than capably assist Dalton with his greater vision. For as great a success Chotyry proved to be, Pyat, Visim and Shist, existing alongside dingoes, saola, and elephants respectively, were yielding less than spectacular results, almost torn between their learned behaviours on all fours, and their primordial instincts on two feet, but Dalton was not yet concerned – when the time was right, the pieces of the puzzle would align. Sim, his orangutan child, once Dalton realised that an abundance of food led to greater socialisation between the creatures, had flourished and its tendons had relaxed, almost stretched, allowing it greater freedom on the limbs of trees.

Dalton walked to the end of the corridor to the room emblazoned with a bold number three. Try had been the most curious of his cases so far and, as his number suggests, one of his earliest. Though he did his research extensively, and there was a reason for each of his choices, of all the animals he hoped to implement into his grand plan, the aardvark proved to be the most elusive. The papers he had read all outlined the animal's preference to be independent and Dalton fought the urge to populate the room with multiples of the creature and instead placed a single female aardvark in the enclosure. The female, roughly two years of age, quickly made itself at home, spending the daylight hours hidden amongst its makeshift burrow, while at night time, it frolicked under artificial moonlight, decimating colonies of ants planted by Dalton. After almost six weeks, Dalton returned to the children's home and selected the third of his specimens, a brunette male, eighteen months of age. The child was older than the previous two but everything about his experiment was still trial and error and there was something about the infant, something that instinctively made him believe it was the right baby for the job. The first weeks of the baby's immersion were the worst; they always were as the child screamed until it was blue in the face and slept purely from exhaustion. Dalton fought the impulse to intervene, he always did; for the experiment to be as successful as he envisioned, human contact needed to be all but non-existent. The screams continued for the better part of the next month, contact between Dalton and the child, and the aardvark and the child completely absent as the infant relied on primal instincts alone to survive. Dalton expected to wake every morning to discover the child deceased, but day after day, the child defied all the odds, enduring almost as though it was predetermined to do so. Try's initial contact with the aardvark came almost by accident, the infant unable to sleep one night and comically bumped into the animal. Unbeknownst to Dalton, who had well and truly retired to his sleeping quarters, Try spent the remainder of the night following the Aardvark as it frequented its usual places, binging on ants and larvae, quickly mirroring its habits and behaviours. The pair's relationship continued to blossom, the aardvark relaxing when it was around the infant, at times, even sharing its food source. In the space of the next two months, Try had completely adopted a nocturnal way of life, fossicking for food in the pitch black surroundings, becoming increasingly adept at seeing in the darkness. The time passed and he continued to evolve, to adapt to its new surroundings, but the creature struggled to truly thrive. In an attempt to put on the weight needed to continue its existence, Try began eating leaves to fill the gap left by the ants; they were in abundance but it still wasn't enough for a human child, even if, at this stage, it was barely considered human.

It wasn't until Dalton watched back the footage of the night prior that he truly understood why he now had a deceased aardvark in his possession and why it had more or less been torn to shreds. Try had sidled up to his adopted mother like it had the evening prior and the one before that. It was hunting time; a time of bonding where the pair took turns decimating the soil in attempts to uncover colonies of their food source except this time things played out differently. Try kept its distance from the aardvark, not participating in their turn taking endeavours of nights passed and then without warning launched itself at the creature, unloading its bare foot deep into the animals stomach, completely knocking the wind from it and leaving it in a lump on the earth. It was the next part that Dalton found to be really curious; instead of finishing the job right then and there, Try paced on all fours, circling its mother, fighting an impossible battle – kill the aardvark and sustain its life for a while longer or nurture the injured aardvark and continue to slowly die from a lack of sustenance. After what seemed like an eternity, and a cruel routine of keeping the creature down, Try pounced, using an errant rock to brutally strike the injured creature, surprised at its ability to use its front limbs to hold and use a tool so effectively. The remainder of the footage depicted, in gruesome detail, Try poking and prodding at the aardvark, and eventually eating from its fatty underbelly.

Against his better judgement, Dalton left the aardvark inside the enclosure, allowing his creation to continue to eat the remains of the animal while he contemplated what to do next. He realised that implanting another aardvark would be counter-productive – simply sending the creature to its death, so the decision was made to leave Try by itself, routinely providing it with smaller mammals to sustain itself and refine its killing abilities.

Dalton peered inside the enclosure and temporarily killed the lights; its effect was instantaneous as the feral child leapt into life, associating the darkness with its time to hunt, to kill. Dalton eagerly watched the frenzied display of pure, reckless abandoned as his most curious creation searched for prey that had yet to be released. "That's it," Dalton mused to himself, relishing the attitude of the one he created third, "in the darkness no one will be able to stop us, not the Giants of Japan and definitely not the Purple Guardians from the States," he scribbled in his clipboard, "it's just a matter of time, Try, then the world is ours."

***

Living in the north of Sydney, Australia, Timothy Pulo is an avid writer across many different genres. He enjoys writing short stories, longer works of fiction, and experimenting with comics, finding inspiration in pp-culture and unusual encounters experienced in his daily life. In between juggling the frenetic pace of being married to his beautiful wife and have three young spirited boys, Timothy endeavours to put as many of his atypically wonderful and random ideas onto paper as he can, in the hope of entertainment for readers. Timothy can be found on Twitter at @timothypulo.

CHILDREN OF THE ELWETRITSCHEN

By Catherine Jordan

Gretel awoke in the morning, shivering. It was the third day since Stepmother and Father had abandoned them in the abysmal forest. The morning air was white with fog and mist. She hoped it would soon clear.

Gretel picked up a stick and a sharp rock from the ground, then sat down beside her brother, Hansel. He was curled up, his thumb in his mouth, and asleep at the base of a tree, using a leaf-pile for a mattress. He had been scared and talkative, wanting to hear words of consolation from her. Gretel had complied as best she could. He had fallen asleep while talking, and she had stayed up most the night keeping watch over him.

With a rock's edge, she set to carving the tip of her stick. If it were going to serve any purpose, it would be that of a knife or a skewer. Certainly not an arrow. She'd never had good aim. She'd hit her Papa several times in the shin while playing ball. One time she'd even hit Stepmother in the head. Maybe that was why she hated them so much.

After some time, when Gretel's stick was nice and pointy, she went to show it to Hansel, and realized he was still asleep. He twitched and let out a small sob. Poor baby was having a nightmare. She patted his arm and hushed him, told him everything would be okay. But would it?

Gretel was still tired from her sleepless night and began to doze off again. Something was licking Gretel's hand, its tongue rough and warm. Gretel thought for a moment that she was back at home on her hard bed, the cat beside her, eager to play. The cat smelled raw and wet.

Gretel rolled over and opened her eyes, expecting a brown fur ball at her side. Instead, she saw... "Ah!" Gretel stabbed at the huge blur of a thing, and missed. It squawked and dashed into the brush, wings flapping wildly.

Hansel sat up. "Gretel? What's the matter?"

"I must've had a bad dream," she said, looking 'round, her stick planted firmly in the ground, but seeing no sign of the mysterious creature. Gretel pulled her stick free, got to her hands and knees, and crawled toward where she thought she saw it run.

"Where you going, Gretel?"

"Stay there," she hissed, aiming her weapon straight out from her chest.

She wasn't gone long, didn't dare venture too far from her wee brother. But when she discovered evidence of the bird, she gasped. Quietly, she crawled out from under the brush, her stick by her side.

"I found a nest," Gretel said, waving for her brother to follow. "Come see."

They hadn't got far into the brush when Hansel whimpered. "My britches are stuck," he said, his puppy dog eyes already wet with shame.

"No worries, just take them off."

"My britches? Take them off? But, what'll I do for pants?"

"You don't need them, Hansel. Our clothes are mostly ripped to shreds already. They're nothin' but filthy rags. Here, I'll take off my dress. Oh, don't look at me like that, I've got on a slipdress—you won't see my bum. And I won't see yours."

Gretel pulled her no longer white dress up over her head and dropped it to the ground. Hansel swallowed hard, still uncomfortable with the thought. The little rascal had no trouble coming home with half his clothes missing after being at play, but here in the woods, he played timid. "Your clothes aren't protection, least not anymore. They're just getting in the way. If you're worried about getting cold later, don't be. We can make a blanket out of feathers. Look!"

Gretel parted the brush with her stick. A giant nest of feathers— fat, long, thick, and dark brown, sat under a downed tree trunk. Hansel's eyes widened. He smiled, and then kicked off his britches. "Should I keep my shoes?" he asked. Gretel nodded.

Hansel climbed into the nest. "The feathers are warm," he said, throwing them up into the air with glee.

Gretel rubbed her hand over the nest's silky edge. It gave under pressure. "This feels better than our thread-bare blankets at home."

The boy lay on his side and snuggled in. "Can we live here, Gretel?"

"I don't know," Gretel said, itching her head. "This probably belongs to something, and it's a big something, that's for sure. We could drag it away. It's not heavy. Get out; I'll show you."

Hansel climbed out of the nest. He grabbed the edge like his sister showed him, then they dragged the nest out of the brush and into the forest opening. They carried it all day, tossing in their castoff clothes, Gretel's stick, and interesting items found on the journey: a sharp rock, dried kindling, a piece of broken glass, berries, a hunk of bark in the form of a crude bowl.

Hansel blabbered on and on. Gretel spent half the day shushing him.

They scrounged the forest floor, eating wild berries, chewing on bark, but it was not enough to fill their distended bellies. They walked farther on, foraging deeper into the woods.

Hansel dropped to his little bottom and began to cry. "I miss my cat," he said. Hansel had spent quite a bit of time with the cat; they were almost inseparable. "And I miss Papa. But I hate Stepmother for bringing us out here. I want to go home. I'm so hungry, Gretel." He rolled onto his side, put his thumb in his mouth, and rocked back and forth. Leaves crunched underneath him, and his hair quickly became a knotted mess of twigs and debris.

Gretel missed the cat, too. Stepmother had treated the cat better than she did Gretel and Hansel. Right now, it would be nice to have their pet bring them a fat mouse or a bird. Gretel was hungry enough to bite the head off one right now. In fact, she was hungry enough to wrestle the cat to the ground and eat it!

They slept in the nest that night, sounder than they ever had in their entire young lives. They were warm and protected from the wind and had no fear of the scurrying night foragers. Or snakes. Gretel hated snakes.

Gretel and Hansel carried their nest-home day after day. Hansel whined constantly. Gretel had half a mind to stuff her knickers in his mouth. "But I can't help it, Gretel. I'm hungry, and talking keeps me from thinking about food all the time."

"Tell you what—if I were to catch us something good to eat and fill that tummy of yours, would you shut your mouth?"

"For how long?"

Gretel stopped. She dropped her end of the nest. "Long enough to patch this thing. It's starting to fall apart at the bottom from us dragging it. We should find a place to call home, at least for a while."

"Here? In the woods?"

Gretel shrugged. "Where else are we going to go? We're lost, Hansel. We'll probably be in these woods for a long time."

The boy looked around, his eyes glossy and wet. "I want to go home."

Gretel sighed heavily. "We're never going home again, Hansel. Never. I keep telling you that. But you mustn't worry or cry. We have each other. We'll find a way out, somehow. I just don't know when. And we have to prepare for the winter. It'll be especially cold, then. We'll need this nest and anything we can store inside it."

Hansel wiped his eyes with the back of his hand. "So, we have to leave the nest right here?"

"Um, no…" Gretel put her hands on her hips. "I thought I heard water flowing—that way, I think. East."

Hansel sniffed. "How do you know which way is east?"

"By the sun, stupid. Don't you ever listen when people talk? No, you spend too much time running your mouth. If you want to live long enough to get out of here, then you have to pay attention. Father taught me lots of things about hunting and surviving. He tried to teach you, too, but…"

Gretel picked up her end of the nest. "We can't drag it much farther, or we won't have a bottom. I think we should leave it under a tree by the river. We'll have water, and we can fish. We both need to eat something besides berries and bark. I've pooped and pooped and have nothing left to wipe my butt, and I'm starting to get raw. So are you. And we both need a bath. Now, for the last time, lift."

As Gretel had said, there was a river a short walk east. The nest went under a leaning tee to protect it from the elements. They stripped off what was left of their clothes and waded into the cool river, lapping up water. "Oh, this tastes so much better than rainwater from the bark," Hansel said.

They rubbed layers of dirt from their hair and face and armpits—everywhere it had crusted. "Don't wash your feet," Gretel warned.

"Why?"

Gretel was raking her fingers through her hair, trying to detangle it. "To keep them rough. Your shoes are almost as worthless as mine. I have a feeling we'll soon be walking barefoot."

"You should cut your hair," Hansel said, quite bluntly. "You keep getting it stuck in branches. And there are too many bugs in it. I hate having to pick them out."

Gretel tugged her hand free from her hair. "Yep. But I don't have scissors."

Hansel's eyes sparkled. "Oh! What about that piece of glass I found?"

She smiled. "Clever boy. I'd forgotten 'bout that."

A short while later, they were both bald but bug-free. The children then set to catching fish. Frustrated by the small success they had with one measly fish, they vowed to try harder the next day.

Their lithe bodies dried (and the fish) in the sun while they laid on a flat rock. Hansel turned and stared at Gretel's head. He giggled. "You look silly," Hansel said.

"So do you," she said.

Before dark, they had gathered enough kindling and dry wood, and used a glare off the glass-shard to spark their first fire. "Keep this fire going, Hansel." She placed the fish in the flames. "As long as we have a red ember, then we're okay. This is your job, now, to protect the fire."

Hansel nodded as if quite pleased with his responsibility. "Let's put stones around it, and keep it away from the nest so our home doesn't catch fire."

Ah, so the boy had paid attention to Father's advice at least once in his life. Gretel rubbed her hand approvingly over his rough scalp. "Right."

"Gretel," the boy said, staring thoughtfully into the woods. "You ever think about the bird that used to live in this? We stole its home, ya know."

"I'm sure it's already built another one."

Hansel's eyes went to the nest. "How come we haven't seen any birds that big? Huh?"

Gretel smiled and rubbed the boy's head again. "Be glad. I am. I wouldn't want to tussle with a wild creature big enough to carry me away. Would you?"

Hansel's face fell. "Maybe it's looking for its nest?"

"C'mon, Hansel. We've been safe for how long now?" She thought he'd answer, thought he knew. Gretel knew.

Hansel shook his head. "No idea. How long do you think it's been?"

She'd been tallying marks in her upper thigh with a splinter of wood. She'd never imagined the tally would go for as long as it had, trailing onto her hip. It'd been six months, two weeks, and three days.

"Not so long," she said with a shrug, not wanting to worry the boy.

After they'd eaten, they laid down in the nest, rubbing their satisfied stomachs. They tried sleeping, unaccustomed to the rustling in the trees, more than usual. "Birds?" Hansel asked. Gretel nodded and told Hansel it was because they were close to water. "Birds like to fish," she said.

"Big birds?" he asked.

"Oh, for pity sake. Go to sleep, Hansel."

Later that night, Gretel woke to Hansel's scream. Her eyes popped open and she caught her breath, staring into beady eyes and a long, long beak that reached her nose. The mammoth bird's head cocked this way, then that. It seemed curious at finding two children in the nest.

Hansel's scream hadn't seemed to startle the bird, but what did Gretel know about this peculiar being? Nothing. Maybe it had no fear. Perhaps it thought they were prey.

Gretel felt for her stick, the glass shard, anything she might use for defense.

The odd bird nudged her head gently with its beak. She stilled. "Nice birdy," she sang. "Niiiiice birdy." It picked gently at her scalp, and she cringed, wondering what it was doing. It pushed at her shoulder, then her arm, her torso, her legs. It was examining her, she realized, and picking off ticks, relieving her of the all-over, constant itch she'd had. She heard Hansel inch away, and the bird turned sharply in his direction. "Hold still, Hansel. It's curious. It probably won't hurt you as long as you don't scare it."

"What is it?" he whispered.

It looked like a bird, but with antlers. Kind of like a cross between an eagle and a deer. It had a human-like face, all scrunched and ugly. An eagle, deer, and a goblin? "Ah!" It dawned on Gretel. "An elwedritsch," she said. She'd heard stories about them in school, thought they were mythical.

It opened its great wings, stretched its massive body, exposing breasts she'd seen on stepmother when Gretel walked in on her bathing. Stepmother had been angry and nasty, told Gretel to get away, and screamed foul names at her. The elwedritsch closed its wings over both Gretel and Hansel, like a blanket. It buried its feathered face under its armpit, nuzzled, then began to snore.

Hansel's mouth formed an 'O'.

"Do not scream," Gretel whispered.

"Elwetritschen aren't real," Hansel said, his eyes staring in full terror.

"Tell that to the elwedritsch."

Hansel shivered in fear, and the creature responded. It lowered its body with a comforting weight, bringing Hansel's shiver to a halt. The child sighed, closed his eyes, and to her surprise, he fell asleep. Try as Gretel could to stay alert and awake, she gave in to the security and comfort, and drifted into a deep sleep.

Hansel shook Gretel awake. It was morning. "Did I dream that?" Hansel asked Gretel. The sun shined over the river, and the bird was gone.

"If you did, then I dreamed it too. I don't think that's possible."

"Yeah, well, I didn't think Elwetritschen were possible."

Gretel raised her brow, and sat up. "What is that?" she asked, pointing at two oval, white—

"Eggs!" Hansel replied. "I told you the bird would want its nest back. What if it wants to feed us to the chicks when they hatch?" he asked as he began to crawl his way out of the nest.

Gretel wholeheartedly agreed. They'd been warned many times about bears and their cubs. Elwetritschen were rumored to be harmless beasts, but she didn't want to take the chance. She followed Hansel slowly, carefully.

They trudged away in silence. Gretel was grateful for it; it allowed her to think about their predicament. Lost. Alone. Worse than orphans. They had no home, not anymore, and didn't know where their next meal would come from, or where they might rest their heads if they were even to sleep at all. They'd left everything behind in the nest: bark-bowl, glass shard, the fire, her makeshift spear. But what could they do about it? Not much, other than what they were doing now—surviving.

Days, then weeks went by with monotony. Walk, forage for berries, poop, walk, sleep, forage…

The comforts of home were forgotten. What was left of their clothing had fallen away, along with their shoes.

They could climb trees with ease, and slept in thick branches, huddling together for warmth whenever the space allowed. On colder nights, they dug into the ground with their thickened nails, burying their bodies into the forest bed using leaves and brush as a blanket.

Hansel hardly talked anymore. Instead, he'd grunt, or make clicking noises sounding like the snapping of twigs. He used those noises to communicate with Gretel whenever they stalked rabbits or squirrels. Gretel quit insisting upon washing; there was a benefit to dirt and grime—it thickened the skin and masked the human scent. It had taken time for their stomachs to get used to digesting their food raw, for the vomiting to stop, and the almost constant pooping to subside.

They'd seen nor heard no more from any Elwetritschen.

Until one day, on a walk through the path they'd worn through the forest ground. Hansel suddenly stopped.

Gretel followed his eyes to the ground. There, under an angled rock, lay a black coiled snake. Its diamond-shaped head poked out from the rock, a pink forked tongue darted out, and it began to uncoil.

She went cold. A scream hitched in her throat. The nasty thing slithered towards them.

Hansel backed into Gretel. He tried pushing her backward, but she was rooted to the ground like a stump.

The black snake inched closer, growing in length and threat. Gretel's chin trembled. Her inner thighs felt hot and wet, and a warm puddle of urine steamed underneath her.

Hansel pulled on her hand. But no matter. Gretel was frozen with fear. She wanted to motion for the boy to save himself, to run, but her limbs were filled with cement.

The snake closed in on her toes. Its hard body slithered around her ankles, wrapping itself around her like a rope.

Rustling came from the tree behind, followed by an ear-splitting squawk and a flash of yellow. The snake—it was gone. Gretel looked around, wondering what had happened. Hansel was cowering on his hind legs, whimpering, pointing upward. Gretel's eyes followed where her bother pointed. The Elwedritsch—it hovered in the sky over her, shaking its head back and forth, whipping the black slithery thing—the snake—in its yellow beak. It gave a great slurp, and to Gretel's horrific relief, the Elwedritsch sucked the snake into its mouth, then swallowed it in one enormous gulp.

Gretel sighed, grateful, no longer afraid, reaching up to her rescuer.

With a whoosh, the Elwedritsch gathered both children in its wings, pressing them tightly against its supple breasts. They were flying! Gretel gasped as her breath drained from her. A gentle sensation of weightlessness filled her core, and she worked to regulate her breathing. Hansel whined with terror. Gretel didn't have enough breath to calm the boy down, and besides, by the time she thought of any comfort, they were jolted, and knocked heads. Had they landed?

Indeed. The wings opened slowly, and the children fell into a familiar spot—the nest.

They were not alone. Eggshells littered the nest. With a flurry of fluff, two baby Elwetritschen teetered upon their orange bird-legs and fell against Hansel and Gretel. They were about the same size as Gretel, their round heads level with hers. Bumps protruded on either side of their heads where antlers would eventually form. The chicks were plump and downy. Hansel surprised Gretel when he hugged one of them, his eyes closed, a smile on his face. The chick's beady yellow eyes blinked, and it then responded similarly in an embrace with its puffy wings.

The other baby bird cocked its head, eyeing Gretel curiously.

Their mother had perched on the edge of the nest. She tapped the chick with her wing. It raised its head, opened its mouth, and Mother inserted her beak into the baby's. Her throat undulated, and a thick, chunky substance fell out of Mother's beak into the baby's. She was feeding it the snake. The baby swallowed until gorged, and then mother turned her attention to the baby cuddling with Hansel. After it fed, Mother Bird tapped Hansel. Hansel raised his head, mouth agape. Gretel grimaced. Mother barely flinched. She fed the boy, who gulped greedily.

Gretel continued to watch, now fascinated. Because once she considered it, she realized she had eaten worse things in her lifetime. Who knows how many brambles, poisonous berries, animal feces, fungus, and rot she had ingested over their time in the forest. Gretel eyed her thigh—according to her scarred tallies, it had been over a year.

Gretel felt a soft tap on her head. She looked up to see the yellow beak poised over her. Gretel opened her mouth.

They never had a loving mother, and never knew kindness outside of each other. Sure, their father had done them a service by teaching them what he knew about surviving in the woods. But that wasn't love. That was ego.

The chicks grew quickly; so did Hansel. He and Gretel now clothed themselves in Elwetritschen feathers. And Gretel stopped cutting into her thigh. She no longer cared about how long they'd been lost. In her mind, they'd been found.

Then one morning, while gathering elderberries, they spotted a man in the forest. A raggedly looking woman walked close behind him, heavy shawls blanketing her shoulders, a lantern in her hand. It was a cold, gloomy morning. Winter was on its way.

Hansel and Gretel followed the wayward, elderly couple. Protectively, at first, since they were one of their kind, then suspiciously when the man knelt and aimed up into the tree. He had a gun!

"Go on, shoot!" Gretel still recognized the Germanic tongue. Hansel, however, had forgotten it. He looked to Gretel with question, having no idea what the woman was saying. Did he realize the menace? Gretel clicked and whistled, communicating the potential threat. Gretel, of course, knew the man was hunting for food. Humans had to eat, too. She said as much to Hansel.

It is known that Elwetritschen don't nest in trees. They live mainly underbrush, but respect other birds and their habitats.

And so the man's defiant stance toward the tree was an act of war, as far as Hansel was concerned.

Hansel flared his nostril, his beady eyes narrowing. He released his berries, cupped his hand round his mouth, and cawed. An identical caw answered from a short distance south.

The man fired his gun, blasting an uproar out of the mighty oak. Branches, leaves, and tree-nesting animals exploded in all directions. Torn, bloodied appendages and carcasses flopped to the ground.

Then, a thunderous flapping of wings came from the sky. Hansel's mouth tightened fiercely. His muscular shoulders straightened. He crouched, ready to attack the man with his brethren.

Gretel, however, wished to remind him what it was like to hunt for food, especially with winter coming. Would he remember they had once raised chickens and eaten eggs? That would probably make no difference to him. Circumstances had forever changed Hansel.

Mother Elwedritsch descended from the forest canopy with vengeance in her eyes.

The man and the woman raised their arms in defense. Gretel recalled what it was like seeing the creature for the first time, how she had wobbled on her knees, and wished desperately for the safety of home. Mother Elwedritsch was beastly to behold.

Mother perched on the earthen ground in front of the couple, broad wings spread, sneering like a goblin. The old woman didn't flinch. She leaned into the man's ear. "What ya waiting for, ya fool! Shoot!"

Gretel stepped back. Her heart seemed to stop, and then it pounded. Momentarily forgetting all else, Gretel wondered if it was *her*. Couldn't be, could it, after all this time? Stepmother. Yes, Gretel knew her voice anywhere, anytime.

Filled with hatred, Gretel clenched her jaw, pushed past Hansel, and presented herself to the couple standing under the shadow of Mother Elwedritsch.

Father fell to his haunches, the gun impotent at his side. "Gretel?" he whispered. She took a good, hard look at him as he sat on the ground. She now saw how he had fattened with age, hair gray, skin rubbery.

The woman grunted. She, too, had become corpulent and weathered. "Gretel," said the old crone, looking Gretel up and down with hard, cruel eyes. "What are you wearing, girl? Are those feathers?" She glanced from Gretel to the bird, then back to Gretel. She scowled. "That creature yer pet, eh? Ack, look at yer feet. They're like claws. You've gone feral, haven't ya?" She stretched her wrinkly neck and pointed her gaze toward the woods. "Where's the boy?"

Hansel pounced out of his hiding spot in the woods. He clicked and snitched, summoning Mother Elwedritsch. The bird bent forward.

"Get away!" The old woman swatted at Mother Elwedritsch. Gretel cooed, calming Mother, asking her to wait. Gretel then approached her father, and put a hand on his red, sweating face. He was obviously petrified. His breath came out in gasps, and his pulse raced under her palm.

Stepmother made a move for the gun. And then Gretel saw the shawl around her neck—it was no shawl, but a potato sack. It became clear to Gretel—the fat old couple was not hungry. There were on a snipe hunt for sport. The lantern light was said to be attractive to the

Elwetritschen; they will investigate and then get caught in the potato sack. Elwetritschen were mythical and worth quite a few pieces of gold.

Gretel squawked.

Mother Elwedritsch dove a lethal peck into stepmother's skull, cracking it like an egg. Blood ran down her forehead and into her crossed eyes. She fell like an empty sack.

Mother Elwedritsch whistled, and the brethren descended from the heaven to their Mother's side. They were in fattening-stage for winter, and Stepmother's rotund morsel would add to their weight.

The birds attacked, ripping her apart, gobbling down shriveled, meaty chunks.

Meanwhile, the father had not said a word. He lay dumb with fear. Hansel picked up the gun, then placed it expertly on his muscled shoulder, setting his sight on the father. Ah, the boy had not forgotten everything. The father's chin trembled, and he raised a palm in defense as Hansel fired. "Always aim for center mass," the father once instructed. Gretel heard those words in her mind with the resonating bang. The shot caught him directly in the chest.

Hansel unloaded the rifle, and turned the gun barrel down, using it as a walking stick, like a chieftain. He smirked as their brethren attacked the father, consuming their fill. Mother Elwedritsch nudged her mature chicks aside, then pecked at the body, swallowing down hunks for herself. And then she touched Hansel on the head with her wing. Hansel raised his chin, and Mother Elwedritsch spat her chewed meal into Hansel's open maw. He swallowed satisfactorily.

The familiar tap hit Gretel's head. She looked up into the yellow beak poised over her. Gretel opened her mouth.

***

Catherine Jordan is a horror novelist who edits and writes in different genres. She is the Review Coordinator for horrortree.com, and a contributor to *TheBurg Magazine*—Harrisburg's monthly magazine and news source. Ms. Jordan has been featured in a variety of anthologies and on-line publications. She has also been a judge for the Bram Stoker Award and the ITW Young Adult Award. She facilitates writing courses

and critique groups. Catherine lives in Pennsylvania with her husband
and five children. Her books are available at
    www.sunburypress.com , www.amazon.com and www.barnesan
dnoble.com
and through her website, http://www.catherinejordan.com

Like Catherine on
    http://www.facebook.com/CatherineJordanBooks

    Follow on Twitter @CatherineBooks

HOW THE RABBITS GOT THEIR EARS AND TAILS

BY Robin Lupton

The Messua family were exhausted but happily so, at least for now, but that happiness was stretched. They ran around the campsite all day and hiked through the forest and stomped through streams and it was now past the two children's bedtimes, but they still hadn't eaten. Hunger was about to pounce and Mummy Messua could tell by the set of her toddler, Bhumi's, face that if she didn't feed the girl soon, a tantrum was coming. Hangry toddler tantrums are the worst.

Papa Messua was lighting the campfire, because as the man, he felt it was his job to provide fire for his family. It was taking a long time, and he was getting frustrated and swearing softly under his breath. The little twigs he laid in the fire bowl kept tumbling over and putting out the kindling. The children didn't seem to notice, but Papa could feel Mummy Messua's quietly building frustration.

"You know what my darlings, while daddy gets the fire going, I think because we are out on an adventure, just this once, you all can have a treat before dinner." She reached into a plastic bag and pulled out a chocolate digestive biscuit and handed one to Bhumi and Ravinder.

Ravinder was five and now that they had spent all day in the wilds of nature, he was experiencing the call of technology and whining quietly that he wanted to play *Angry Birds* on Mummy Messua's mobile phone.

"No Ravinder. We didn't pack everything but the kitchen sink to sit in a field so you could ignore everyone and play on my phone. This is a technology free weekend." Mummy said.

"But dad is using his phone right now, look."

Mummy turned to see her husband leaning sneakily over his phone watching a video on how to get a fire started. He had the grace to look embarrassed. She had told him at least four times to pack the fire starters, but he had said that was an affront to his masculinity and he would get the fire going the old fashion way, an idea Ravinder had leapt on with excitement at the time. He imagined them both rubbing sticks until they burst into flame, but in practice he tried for about thirty seconds before announcing it was boring.

Mummy Messua was very close to mentioning the fire starters to him, but then realised Papa Messua was about to throw his own tantrum. Sometimes men are children.

"That's different. He needs his phone to start the fire," she said smiling.

"But that's not fair. Who needs a phone to start a fire? That's dumb. Why didn't the sticks work?"

"Setting a fire is just harder than it looks - okay." That's when she heard a deep whine from Pepper. She turned to see Bhumi sitting on the dog's back pulling as hard as she could on her woolly ears. Pepper was a lovely black and grey labradoodle with a fantastic temperament. For Pepper to whine, Bhumi must have really hurt her.

"Bhumi, what have I told you about pulling on that dog's ears? You're hurting her."

"She likes it mummy" said Bhumi smiling through chocolate smeared lips.

"No she likes you, not having her ears pulled. Do you understand the difference?"

"Wha ha! I got it going now," cheered Papa Messua. The fire crackled behind him casting him in orange and gold, and despite her earlier annoyance, Mummy Messua felt a surge of pride in her husband. He did look good in the fire light. It was almost a shame they only brought one tent.

"Wonderful. Well done, dear. Let's get out the sausages," she said.

In minutes she had the sausages out on long kebab sticks with the ends stuck into carrots to give the kids a bigger handle and more reach, in theory to stop them from burning themselves. She had got the idea from the internet. The family sat around the campfire munching crisps, popcorn, and sliced up cucumber while they watched their sausages cook. After two minutes, Bhumi got bored cooking her sausage and passed her to her mummy to finish up, demanding that it not be burned.

"I don't like it black," she said. She went and sat next to the dog. At first, she snuggled next to him with her little hand dug deeply in the dog's fur, and then for no reason that Mummy Messua could fathom, the girl reached up and yanked the dog's ear as hard as she could.

Pepper whined again, then stood up and licked the girl fully in the face which set Bhumi to laughing.

"Bhumi, I told you not to pull Pepper's ears, you might pull so hard they'll get all stretched out and get stuck like that." Mummy Messua was setting up her story now. She had been planning on telling one of her mother's campfire stories all weekend and as soon as Bhumi had started pulling Pepper's ears she knew which one she would tell. Now was her moment. She would deliver an excellent campfire story, one complete with a moral and she would do so, as well as her mother had. The children would be enraptured and someday they would tell the story to their children.

"No, they won't mummy, that is the dumbest thing I have ever heard," said Ravinder.

"Yeah, mummy that is dumb." parroted Bhumi.

"You think so, do you? Well, let me tell you a story, about a cheeky little girl like you, Bhumi, and you might not think it is so dumb. Cuddle close my darlings." This was the line her mother had always used to start her stories. She watched the line do its work.

Ravinder and Bhumi leaned into the campfire and toward Mummy Messua's voice and she started her tale, just like it had been told by her mother, and mother's mother and countless tellers before, only a little bit differently.

Well my best beloveds, this story starts a long, long time ago when the mountains were living people, the animals could still talk, and the humans like you and me roamed all over the land like nomads, never staying in one place for very long, and always looking for food.

Well in one tribe of humans, there was a man and a woman, their names have long since been forgotten. Well this man and woman, they had 13 children. They had more children than anyone else in the tribe. With so many children the mother and father were always losing track of them, which was a bit dangerous considering they were nomads and always on the move.

One day, one of the little children, we will call her Bhumi, because she was your age, Bhumi, and she looked a lot like you, snuck out of their tent and she wandered deep into the woods.

"Why did no one stop her?" Asked Bhumi.

"Because she was being sneaky, just like you are sometimes sneaky. Besides everyone in camp was busy, because they were packing up and getting ready to move to a new spot. All the food where they were was gone. Anyway, while no one was looking, little Bhumi snuck off into the woods."

While she was there she met a rabbit. Now at this time rabbits looked a lot like guinea pigs. They had little ears and little tails.

The rabbit fell in love with the girl immediately. She and her husband had been trying to have a baby for a long time, but still hadn't been able to have any children, which in rabbit society is frowned upon because typically most rabbits, are very good at making more rabbits.

"How did they make more rabbits, mummy?" ask Ravinder. Poppa Messua, almost snorted his beer out of his nose when he laughed at the boy's question, but Mummy gave him a dirty look over the fire and that shut him up.

"That's another story for another time. What is important to this story is that these two rabbits couldn't have children, so they decided to adopt Bhumi on the spot. They asked her if she would like to come and live with them. Once they told her she wouldn't have any brothers or sisters to fight with, she said, "What a wonderful idea. I'd love to."

At first all the rabbits in the rabbit warren were so happy to meet Bhumi. They welcomed her right away and Bhumi loved it because for the first time she was an only child and didn't have to share her parent's love with anyone. They also got to stay in one place instead of moving around all of the time. Bhumi loved crawling through the tunnels of the warren, looking for berries and edible grasses, and snuggling with the rabbits, but what she loved most of all was tugging on their ears. She loved the feeling of their fur and liked pulling their ears so she could feel the fur slip between her fingers.

As you can imagine the rabbits didn't like having their ears pulled, but they also didn't want to hurt the girl's feelings or offend her adopted rabbit parents, so they tried to ignore it for a while. The problem was Bhumi wouldn't stop pulling their ears and after a few weeks all the rabbits' ears had been stretched extremely out of shape from being pulled repeatedly by the little girl and all the rabbits had ears just like they do today.

Back then, the rabbits also had a tiny seam on their neat short round tails that looked a little bit like a line of stitches. Bhumi liked to pick and pull this seam and watch it unravel and play with the fluff that was stuffed inside. It didn't take long for all the rabbits in the warren to lose their neat little tails and end up with fat fluffy ones. Finally, one day when the girl was about your age, Ravinder, the Rabbit King, said, "This can't go on. We love little Bhumi, but she has destroyed our ears and tails. She will have to go away and live with her own kind."

Well Bhumi and her adopted rabbit parents were obviously very sad about this, but the King's word was warren law and so there was nothing to be done for it and they had to go. The next day the all the rabbits set off on a journey to take the girl home.

Only a quite unexpected thing happened on the way. Whenever a predator came hunting, the rabbits' new long ears were better at picking up the sound and they heard them from far away and the rabbits were able to hide and stay safe.

One of the rabbit's stopped and perked up its ears. "I hear something. Two weasels are hiding in the forest. They're talking. They plan to eat one of us."

All the rabbits sat still and listened with their big ears. The Rabbit King pointed at a berry bush. "The weasels are under that bush. Charge on my command."

Now, Bhumi, rabbits aren't aggressive, but when a hundred rabbits charged, the weasels turned and ran away.

Perhaps these big long ears are not so bad, thought the king of the rabbits.

Then later when they were out in the open, Bhumi's adoptive mother said, "I hear wolves. They're quite close." The rabbits ran into a meadow filled with white flowers and they crouched low behind their fluffy tails and blended in with the little flowers and were unseen by the passing wolves.

Perhaps these big fluffy tails are not so bad, thought the king of the rabbits.

When they finally came close to the humans, who they were able to hear from a long way off with their new long years, the king of the rabbits changed his mind about Bhumi. He no longer saw her ear tugging as an inconvenience, but as a gift.

With the line of tents where the humans live in view, the king of the rabbits, turned to Bhumi and said, "I have changed my mind. Although I didn't like having my ears pulled or my tail picked into a fluffy ball, I can see you have done us a great favour and made our warren safer and stronger. It would be our honor for you to stay and live with us at the warren for as long as you like."

And so she did. Some say she even grew up to be Queen of the rabbits. Anyway, that's why you shouldn't pull Pepper's ears or tail, Bhumi, or you will stretch them out until she looks like a rabbit."

"Yes, but then she will have even better hearing. She will be like the best guard dog in the neighborhood. No one is going to rob us, ever." said Ravinder.

"Oh, that wasn't really the point of the story." Mummy Messua said.

"But it's the lesson the children have learned," said Poppa Messua laughingly. "Any way Mummy, your mother would be proud. She loves those silly origin stories. She is nuts. Always saying you are distantly related to this god or that hero. Now we are going to have a hero dog. Hey. Ravinder, if you pull on his tongue maybe he will learn to talk."

"Shhh! Don't encourage him and don't talk about my mother like that. Besides, how do you know she's wrong? I am undoubtedly a goddess among women for putting up with you lot," Mummy Messua said.

"Yeah! That's brilliant! We can have a dog with super hearing who can also talk. He can be a spy." Ravinder was on his feet now. "Come on Bhumi! You pull Pepper's ears and I'll see if I can grab her tongue. We are going to make a super dog!"

Mummy Messua wasn't really sure where her story had gone so wrong. When her mother told stories it never turned out like this. When her mother told stories about the origins of things, you sat riveted in your seat and when they were over you lived in fear of accidentally upsetting the cosmos for a week. She was tired and disappointed and she really didn't want to fight with the children about the dog anymore. She just wanted to enjoy her drink and watch the flames.

"You know what children." She reached into her pocket. "How about you leave the dog alone and eat your sausages and if you are very good, you can play Angry Birds. Just until bedtime.

In unison, both kids shouted hurray and leapt for her phone.

When she handed them the phone, she felt momentarily beaten. So much for her tech free weekend. Then she looked out over the campsite, at the blazing fires set before the other family's pitches. Camping in England wasn't really wild, but, at least, it was in nature. Beyond more than one campfire she could see the smiling faces of other children illuminated by LED screens, while their parents relished the peace in the firelight. She wondered if they had dreamed of tech free weekends too. At least she wasn't alone.

The kids finished their game, they roasted marshmallows and headed into the tent for bed. The kids were zonked and the entire family was asleep in minutes.

It was pitch black and freezing when Mummy Messua woke to a rustling sound outside her tent. It was probably just the wind.

She needed to pee and she did not want to have to walk to the communal toilet block in the dark. If no one else was up in the campground, she decided she would just pee behind the tent.

She grabbed her flashlight, slipped into her welly boots, and unzipped the tent door as quietly as possible before stepping out into the night.

It was chilly and a light mist had settled on the grass making it slick with dew drops. No one was up that she could see. That was a relief. No trek to the toilet block for her. She slipped behind the tent, and was about to squat before the empty woodland when a dozen pairs of red eyes appeared, reflected in the light of her flashlight. Her breath caught and Mummy Messua made a point of reminding herself there were no wolves in England. Maybe they were foxes or badgers. She had heard stories about badger and fox attacks. She was about to scream for Papa Messua, but the cry wouldn't come. She was as frozen as a hare before a wolf. After a breath, her eyes adjusted to the darkness and she could make out long ears and velvety noses. She was surrounded by rabbits.

One set of eyes was higher than the others. A pretty girl's face peeked through the foliage. The girl looked startlingly like her daughter, Bhumi. Mummy Messua and the girl stared at each other, then the girl smiled, winked, and twitched her nose. Mummy Messua winked and twitched her nose right back.

The girl in the foliage made a small whistle, almost too low to be audible. The eyes all turned away and twelve powder puff tails vanished into the forest.

Mummy Messua, smiled to herself. There was obviously more truth to her mother's stories than anyone including herself had previously believed.

***

Robin Lupton is an expat, currently living, writing, and running in England.

THE WAY OF THE WOLF

By J. F. Terrell Jr.

Introduction

My name is Mary. I am a grey wolf.

How I came to my Hu-mon family is not important. Their story is much more interesting than mine. It is interesting because I love them. Suffice it to say that some four years ago, when My-Boy was about two years of age, I was accepted into the family. I protected them, and they kept me safe. We lived and hunted together.

My Hu-mon family is my pack.

There are three of us in the pack: My-Daniel, My-Boy, and me. My-Daniel is the father and the alpha. Even though I am a wolf, they accepted me, not as a pet, but a family member.

The Grey Wolf is rarer in East Texas than the western side of the state, so I can usually be passed off as "only part wolf." We don't get many visitors, and most folks keep to themselves.

These days most everybody is on edge with World War Two, which started just before last Christmas. For a wolf, I know a lot about Hu-mons, but I've never understood why they seek to destroy everyone and everything around them. Even without war, Hu-mons knock down trees and drill holes for oil that destroys habitats for the wolf. Their road machines kill rabbits, deer, and other animals that could be the wolf's food supply.

It is hard for a Hu-mon to gain the trust of a wolf, but it has been known to happen.

There are a few things Hu-mons do right. The folks here in Tyler, Texas love roses. Hu-mons call Tyler, the Rose Capital of America.

There is an old proverb that I've heard about roses, "A thorn defends the rose, harming only those who would steal the blossom." As a she-wolf who loves her pack, I am the thorn who defends the rose. It is the way of the wolf.

I may be a creature of the wild, but I am happy and comfortable with my Hu-mon family, or in wolf speak my "pack." We were all happy until this story began.

Chapter 1 – Intruders

My family's story began one night in May 1942 when I heard a sound from outside. Through the living room window, I saw a road machine in the driveway. I know that at night when my family is asleep, they don't usually receive visitors.

I watched, through the window, as the car doors opened, permitting four men to approach the house. In the dark, my wolf eyes could see that they carried large sticks. A glint of moonlight in the right spot told me the sticks were boom-sticks. As a wolf, I am well acquainted with guns.

I let loose with a warning howl, and I pawed at the glass. One person banged on the front door. A shadow moved past a side window suggesting the second person was going to the back door. Two more people got out of the back seat and went to the trunk. The racket must have awakened My-Daniel because I saw him run from his room to My-Boy's bedroom, where I could hear he was getting the child dressed.

I continued to paw at the front window and howl until one of the intruders pointed his boom-stick at my window. Instinctively, I ducked below the window just as a shotgun blast shattered the glass where I had pressed my nose just moments before.

My-Daniel yelled for me from My-Boy's room, I made my way to them as fast as I could while taking care to avoid the broken glass. Behind me, I heard the butt of the boom-stick clearing away the remains of the window.

As I entered the room, I saw that My-Daniel had dressed My-Boy, who was then about six years old. I also saw a person at the open window about to fire his boom-stick. I leaped as he discharged the boom-stick just in time to feel the bullet whizz past my ear.

My teeth clenched the intruder's arm, and he fell backed and pulled me through the window. I rode his body to the ground. In the fall, he lost his boom-stick. He tried to push me away with his other hand.

It was not my first taste of Hu-mon blood, but despite my history, it has always tasted bitter to me.

It gave me deep satisfaction to watch he who would attack my pack, squirm in pain. I sank my teeth to the bone and refused to let go. He kicked and shoved at me. He cursed and cried. Oh, what cowards Hu-mons can be when the tables are turned. Take away their weapons, and they are weak nothings. I shook my head as violent as possible and ripped the flesh from his arm. He whimpered and clutching at the useless limb. I pitied him as he tried to regain his feet. I wanted to play with the intruder who would harm my pack, but from inside the house, I heard a coarse voice.

My-Boy needed me.

The Hu-mon house that was their home and my den smelled of death and boom-stick smoke. It stung my nostrils, and with my recent taste of Hu-mon flesh, I found myself reacting to an instinct, nearly forgotten.

My-Daniel lay on the floor covered in blood from a hole in his chest.

Immediately, I went to his side. I nudged him with my nose, but I smelled the advent of death. I put my foot on his chest and I felt only a slight heartbeat. I sensed he had something to say, yet his body was nearly lifeless. I collapsed in a heap at his side and my breath left my lungs. Even a wolf can weep.

The only other thing that could get my attention was a scream from My-Boy. With his outcry, I leaped to my feet and found the first intruder holding My-Boy in his arms His back was to me. The calf of his leg shined like a juicy target beckoning my teeth to sink deep in its flesh.

I caught him in the doorway. He banged his elbow on the door frame as he turned to strike me. He howled better than I could, but he clung to My-Boy while I tried to pull his leg out from under him. I lost my footing on a throw rug and he got away from me. My-Boy cried out for me, and jumped to my feet, and leapt on the intruder's back, and knocked him to the floor.

When I hit the intruder, more than anything, I wanted to sink my teeth into his shoulder. It was within reach of my teeth, but I feared I would bite My-Boy by accident. My teeth only grazed the intruder's back.

He fell and My-Boy was loose upon the floor. I moved quickly while the intruder was still on his knees. This time I went for the shoulder. My fangs sank deep to the bone and I pulled him on his back. He struck at me and cursed, as well. More than anything, I wanted to silence his noise. I released the shoulder, and went for his throat. His hands pushed me away and tore at my fur. I caught his hand in my mouth and snapped two of his fingers. I snapped again and tore a finger from the other hand. Blood squirted everywhere and it sprayed from his leg, his shoulder, and both hands. I reached his throat and his misery ended. The revenge wasn't as satisfying as I hoped. My den, our home, stank with the smell of blood. There was broken glass, one dead body, another wounded intruder outside, two more intruders unaccounted for and what had become of my Hu-mons?

My-Boy stood huddled in a corner where the walls gave him some refuge during the battle. I licked his face and he hugged me. The best that I could tell he had no injuries, but he smelled of fear and sorrow. He climbed on my back as he often had, and then, we went to check on My-Daniel.

I approached the body of My-Daniel cautiously. He wasn't dead, but I could feel him dying. With his last breath he said, "Mary, take him to the cave and stay there." He paused briefly, "The role of the parent is to prepare the child for life…" He stopped in mid-sentence and the icy breath of death fell upon his body.

I knew what he meant by those last words. "It is the way of the wolf," is our mantra. We had shared philosophies and much more, My-Daniel and I.

My howl broke the silence of the night and the night bugs and beasts froze and went quiet. My-Boy tightened his hold on my neck but remained silent. Without a doubt, he was overtaken by shock, but our safety must come first. We had to move – now.

Chapter 2 – Escape

The reality of our situation intensified when I heard sirens in the distance. Even though we lived on the outskirts of town, the police had heard the gunshots. I knew that no matter whatever else had happened, the presence of a wolf would alarm the police.

"Hold tight," I growled in the wolf language that My-Boy understood.

I caught a brief scent of My-Daniel's Studebaker in the driveway. I never understood how Hu-mons could stand the stink of those road machines.

Behind us, I heard the distinct screams of two Hu-mons who sounded like they had encountered wolves, but I couldn't take time to investigate. I didn't voice my victory cry because the victory cry of the wolf is unmistakable as it echoes for miles through the night and over the hills, mountains, and across the rivers and plains.

Quickly, I dove into the woods with My-Boy astride my back. His arms were clenched tighter around my neck than in happier times. I cherished those moments of closeness knowing that one day soon, he would be too big for me to carry, and in a few years, he might be carrying me.

The woods behind our den led into a forested preserve that stretched for miles. The three of us often walked and explored these and other woods. My-Daniel was an avid hunter. The predator that most concerned me was Hu-mons, who often shot wolves on sight. After each outing, I fought the urge to celebrate a successful trip because complacency leads to carelessness.

Moving by stealth, I worked a zig-zag pattern several times, crossing a creek to mask my scent and wash the blood off. What Hu-mons' noses lacked in sniffing was made up for by their tracking dogs. But dogs could be noisy and clumsy and I would have heard them. So far, no such noise was apparent.

When we reached the cave, I noticed an unfamiliar scent, but otherwise, the cave was empty, so we moved in.

I displayed a submissive posture to express my concern for My-Boy. I licked his face, arms, and hands to both show affection and to clean away as much dirt and blood as possible.

I had already taught much of "wolf-speak" to My-Boy and he understood my intentions. I was already familiar with Hu-mon speech.

Wolves communicate with body language, including ear and tail positioning. While showing affection to My-Boy, my ears were laid flat back against my head with my tail tucked between my legs, and I slumped more than I stood erect. After I cleaned My-Boy, I stretched out my front legs and held my rear-end in the air to form a play-bow. Recognizing this pose, My-Boy rubbed me hard and ruffled my fur. I presented an open mouth and made sure not to bite down. This gentle roughhousing brought the laughter I desired. I rolled upon my back for a welcome belly rub.

I didn't know the best time to talk with a Hu-mon boy after he has lost his father and had his home invaded. There were things I needed to know and to say, but after he smiled, I could only mutter, "It will be okay."

He sobbed, and then the outburst of pain I expected and that he needed, burst forth. His cries intensified to wails. I snuggled as close as I could. It was hard to get his attention, but I signaled, "I will take care of you. I will get you to safety."

This six-year-old Hu-mon child whom I dearly loved was dealing with a loss that would impact anyone with shock, fear, and an empty heart. I wondered how a wolf could provide the comfort, reassurance, and guidance he needed.

Through the tears, he spoke, "Mary, I am all alone. What do I do?"

Using wolf-speak I replied, "You have me to take care of you. We will work together. We will be a team." Inwardly, I had no doubt I could mother a wolf cub, but a Hu-mon child was a different matter. I, too, missed My-Daniel. "We must rise to the occasion and learn to adapt."

My-boy rubbed blue eyes that had lost their sparkle. I continued, "It's like playing tag. You must outthink the other guy." I paused to let that soak in. "You will have to be brave and grow up. The business of living is serious." My-boy tightened his hold around my neck. "I will be your guide and teacher. We may both learn some life lessons along the way."

My-Boy cried himself to sleep with his arms wrapped around my neck.

It was a hard night for us both. His father, My-Daniel, was dead, our den was wrecked, and our future uncertain. We had each other and shelter for the moment, but what to do. I couldn't trust a Hu-mon to raise My-Boy. Could I teach a Hu-mon child to live among people? I had a painful choice to make.

I knew I could provide food and nearby stream offered fresh water. Whoever attacked us might still be looking for us. Tomorrow, I would address the issues of basic survival. Tonight, My-Boy needed me next to him for the warmth and comfort I could provide. The internal fires of the mother wolf keep their new-born cubs warm. This was no different. We snuggled for warmth in the cool of the cave.

But the respite was short-lived.

Chapter 3 – Rookie

After an hour or two, in the dead of night, the scent I'd noticed before, grew stronger. I perceived someone in the shadows of the cave entrance. I've heard Hu-mons explain why a wolf's eyes glow in the dark, Tapetum Lucidum, which gives us excellent night vision. I saw young male wolf, smaller than me, but cocky enough to seek dominance, demonstrate with his aggressive stance. Obviously, this young wolf had never read Clarisa Estes' "Run with the Wolves," wherein she teaches "if it is bigger than you, flee."

I emitted a low growl and curled my lips to expose my teeth. I extended my tail straight out and slightly upward to alleviate any doubts he might have that I was standing my ground. I didn't know how high the roof was, but I bent all four legs somewhat, should I need to spring.

We froze in place with our eyes locked and evaluated the other's positioning and preparation. He was physically smaller than me and younger. I was older and wiser. His feet were placed for maximum spring and I expected him to jump. That would be foolish. An air attack is a battle plan typical of the inexperienced.

In wolf-speak I accused him of transgression, "This is my territory, you are trespassing!"

He snarled and spat his response, "This cave is not barren of signs. Have you forgotten the way of the wolf? You seek to take my territory. Only the strong survive."

My eyes did not blink, "You lie. I am not a sloppy pup like you! You failed to properly mark this cave as your territory."

He growled, "All I need are teeth and claw to take back my cave. I'll claim you for a mate."

Had I been a Hu-mon I would have laughed aloud. But this was war between wolves. "Puny balls! I will slap you against the wall, bite your ass, and tear out your fur by the roots."

He began the circle of combat by moving to the right. I responded by moving to the left, claiming no ground, and giving none. His inexperience would betray his attack. The long day had left me with little patience for fun and games. Obviously, his circle was taking him toward My-Boy, who was too frightened to speak and remained wedged in a corner of the cave.

"I will kill your Hu-mon for my dinner and throw it against the wall. I'll leave you to clean up my leftovers." He snarled at My-Boy.

His threat to My-Boy sparked me to strike as quick as a lightning bolt, I caught his tail in my teeth. He immediately whirled about with a leap, just as I had forecast. I dropped to my belly. He sailed overhead and I rose and planted my teeth in his right hind leg. I wanted to bite his ass as I promised, but his hind leg made for a tasty bite. He tore loose from me, then slid against the opposite wall. I signaled My-Boy to stay where he was. I proudly noticed he held a rock in both hands.

My opponent turned and bark at me. "You are slow, old woman." His paced back and forth, visibly favoring the wounded leg.

"I drew first blood. I know where to find more. Your blood has a sweet taste." I bared my teeth in what some Hu-mons would call a nasty smile, and accompanied the smile with the most insane look I could manage. I kept myself between this aggressor and My-Boy.

He was a little smaller than me and probably faster, but our strength was comparable, but my experience should counter his youth.

"I won't kill you, old woman." He spat as he snarled. "But I will take you for my mate. It will be a great honor for you to join my pack." His eyes kept drifting to My-Boy, who was on the opposite side of the room. I stayed between My-Boy and the intruder.

"If your idea of flattery is to call me an 'old woman' you have much to learn." I laughed as wolves do, and then spat in his direction.

He charged straight at me and employed all four legs. Recognizing that I may have overestimated his injury, I stepped to his left side and targeted his left hind-leg. He lacked mobility to counter my move and my teeth sank deep into his thigh. He turned and snapped at me, but my feet were planted, and I jerked him back towards me. His head whipped around and My-Boy met it with a rock to the nose. The interloper yelped in pain. I barked at My-Boy to stay back. My-Boy scampered toward a pile of loose rocks. My opponent shook vigorously and pulled himself free. He attacked at My-Boy. My-Boy was ready and met him with a second rock to the lower jaw. He knocked the young wolf against the opposite wall where he dislodged loose rocks that rained down upon him. A large rock slid from above toward him, but I dragged him out of the way just before the "skull crusher" landed. It hit the cave floor and scattered small stones everywhere.

The young wolf was conscious enough to understand that I had saved him.

My-Boy cried my name and he ran to embrace me about the neck. I licked him in response. I was so happy that we were both okay.

"You were brave!" I exclaimed.

My-Boy smiled as only a Hu-mon child can. "Like my Uncle Bob in the Army."

"Yes, a soldier must have courage." I saw the enlightenment in My-Boy's eyes. "We will need to be brave." He nodded and hugged me tightly. "We must have courage."

"Like a soldier." He echoed with his arms tighter about my neck.

"Yes, a soldier, a hero like Uncle Bob."

He hugged me, and I licked his face to show affection. It is the way of the wolf.

My-Boy pointed to the furry heap on the floor. It began to stir, "Mary, what about him?"

I responded in wolf-speak, "When he awakens, take a rock to your corner and stay out of the way. If he can't beat us, maybe he will join us?"

My-Boy selected his rock and did as I asked.

I placed myself between My-Boy and the young wolf. Gradually he worked his way to his feet. After a few long minutes, my opponent stood upright. I snarled, and he responded with a submissive pose.

I needed to establish the terms of his surrender. "Do you accept me as alpha?"

He maintained the submissive pose. "You saved me from harm, I accept you as my alpha."

"Do you swear loyalty to the Hu-mon? Do you accept him as beta?" The young wolf snarled, but signaled affirmatively.

"You are the omega, submissive to all members of the pack." He was reluctant, but he submitted. As the omega, it would be his task to prove himself worthy of advancement.

In managing a wolf pack, rank and position are essential. It is the way of the wolf to establish the leader, the alpha, who maintains control and will kill to erase all doubts about leadership.

"My name is Mary, but you are not worthy to use my name. You may only call me Alpha. The Hu-mon is called My-Boy, but you are not worthy and may only call him Beta. Whatever past you have is now gone. Your old name is gone. You are now called Rookie."

I signaled for him to speak. He asked, "What is this name, Rookie?"

"It is a Hu-mon name; it is derogatory only if you reject it."

He signaled submission and started to walk away.

I barked for his attention. "One more thing, do you swear to protect and serve My-Boy? If you are a wolf of honor, you will abide by this agreement. It is the way of the wolf."

The young Rookie looked left, then right, and fidgeted until I barked for his answer.

He signaled submission.

"Now let me examine your wounds, and then we'll sleep. In the morning, we travel."

Chapter 4 – Return to the Den

With morning, came the need to feed. Rookie hunted rabbits and My-Boy and I hunted blueberries. My-Daniel used to read out loud and I remembered that Jack London once said, "The aim of life was meat. Life itself was meat. Life lived on life."

My-Boy needed meat to grow, so I regurgitated a few chunks of raw rabbit for him. He already had a few permanent teeth, but I stressed small bites and chewing it well. If he choked, I couldn't help him. He ate without hesitation. I hoped his appendix would reclaim its ancient purpose of processing raw meat.

After finishing with a burp that sounded more like a squeak, My-Boy offered a smile and seemed satisfied, but I needed to know. "How was it?"

"It was good, Mary. You shared your food with me. Why?" My-Boy rubbed his belly as he often did whenever the meal was good.

Without hesitation, I responded, "Because I love you, Benjamin. We take care of people who we love." The Hu-mon name was especially hard for a wolf to utter, but I'd had years of practice.

He hugged my neck, "I love you too, Mary." I responded as all wolves do and gave him a generous lick about the face and rubbed my nose in his belly to spark a giggle.

It was time to be serious. "Last night, our world changed. It's just you and me now."

Rookie interrupted with an "and me too" grunt that sparked a flare of anger from me. Rookie needed to remain silent until he earned his place.

I continued to make my point with My-Boy. "Things have changed, and we have to adapt in many ways, like sleeping in a cave or sharing food. We have a new life ahead of us and a journey worthy of heroes like your Uncle Bob and the soldiers."

My-Boy didn't fidget. His eyes showed that he was fully engaged. "We are a pack, we work together like a Hu-mon family. There are things we must do to meet the challenges. I sacrificed a bite or two of my meal for you because we take care of each other. We are a team, like soldiers on a battlefield." I signaled with my body language to ask if he understood. He responded with a child-like "Un-huh."

I could see this would be a learning experience for us both.

"Besides," I continued. "Rookie is a pretty good hunter. He might catch us a jackalope."

This assertion pulled Rookie into the conversation. "A what?"

My-Boy giggled. "Mary is fooling you. It's a fable."

I explained. "The jackalope is a Hu-mon legend of a jackrabbit with horns. They don't exist."

Rookie gave me that familiar puzzled look. "How do you know so much about Hu-mons?"

I ignored his question. It was nothing I wanted to discuss.

We needed to return to the den for supplies and answers. I wanted to reinforce my memory of the scent of the intruders. I hoped I could find a trace scent of My-Boy's grandparents. I believed I would recognize the smell, but it was not imprinted on me like the scent of My-Daniel or My-Boy.

I set my concerns about Rookie's loyalty aside for the moment. If Rookie rejected my leadership, protocol among wolves called for him to challenge my role as alpha openly or leave without notice. Unfortunately, there is no established protocol for his attitude towards Hu-mon members of the pack. The need for my constant vigilance of Rookie was outweighed by the potential strength that Rookie brought to our ranks. The wolf has a way of looking into the soul. I recognized the potential in Rookie if he stayed loyal to us.

I was more concerned about the effect of recent events on My-Boy.

Rookie brought up the topic after breakfast. "I haven't been around many Hu-mons, but for a Hu-mon child, he seems pretty quiet."

"I know. My-Boy is dealing with a lot. I don't like taking him back to the den, but there are things I need. You will help us, right?" I watched the young wolf closely.

Rookie signaled his agreement.

"Good, I am counting on your loyalty." I punctuated my statement with upright ears and tail. "The strength of the pack is the wolf, and strength of the wolf is the pack."

I began to walk away. Rookie caught up to me. "Wait, what is that from?"

I paused with my tail still erect. "It is from a Hu-mon named Kipling."

Rookie looked perplexed. "Is that the way of the wolf?"

I responded, "It is for us."

I continued to walk away and, Rookie obediently followed, as he should.

"How do you know so much about Hu-mons?"

I didn't respond. I walked in silence.

After breakfast, the three of us set out with My-Boy astride my back and Rookie watching our rear. Traveling in broad daylight across Texas is never a good idea for a wolf, so we did our best to stay out of sight by seeking foliage and avoiding the wide-open spaces that the region is well known for.

About noon, we arrived at the den to find a Hu-mon wandering around the premises. The three of us hid in a secluded spot that offered a good view. Based on prior experience, I thought this Hu-mon might be a Texas Ranger. If I was right, he wasn't one of last nights' intruders. But a Texas Ranger is still a Hu-mon with a boom-stick who will shoot a wolf on sight. I recognized the flash emitted by a camera, so most likely, he was recording the damage. My better judgment told me to wait, but I was anxious to begin the long journey towards the grandparent's home.

Rookie asked what I was doing.

"Can't you see the Hu-mon?" I gestured with my nose.

"So what, we'll come back after he leaves. We are creatures of the night. Hu-mons hide in their den after the sun falls. Moonlight is for howling and prowling in the dark." Rookie's tail wagged with delightful anticipation of howling for fun at the moon.

"We don't have time to wait for a slow Hu-mon. More Hu-mons may arrive. Besides, his cigarette smoke may obliterate traces of the scent that I need." I pawed the dirt to emphasize my point.

Without another word, Rookie left our position. I watch him take a wide swing to the left and approach the Hu-mon from the opposite side. I held my silence. I wished that he had told me his plan. Shortly, he showed himself to the Hu-mon, who took the bait and chased Rookie in pursuit of a clear shot. Proved my point that hunters love to shoot wolves.

My-Boy held on tight and we moved into the den after first taking a quick look for other Hu-mons. We found none. My-Daniel's body and blood were gone and a chalk mark was in its place. The stink of Studebaker hung in the air.

The house was in worse condition than when we left. Fortunately, my shopping list was short and getting shorter by the moment. I fetched a favored blanket for My-Boy that he eagerly took from me. I retrieved a new shirt, a gift from the grandparents that retained their scent. I noticed cigar odor that was new to the house. I stepped around the broken glass and other debris and I picked my way through My-Daniel's bedroom. I snatched up a family photo, passed it to My-Boy for safe storage in his jean's pocket, and then we were off. I told him to retrieve one favorite toy and he returned with his toy shovel. I had no time to question his choice.

Rookie's barked louder to signal the return of the Hu-mon. We met Rookie at our hiding spot in the woods.

"The Hu-mon was a poor shot," The young wolf told us later "And slow of foot, too. I wanted to play the game of hide and find me, but he soon grew tired. I meant to lure him further away."

It was time to exercise my leadership skills. "While you were playing games with the Hu-mon, I found what I needed. Next time let me know what you're going to do before you do it. That is my way."

With that last word, we disappeared into the forest and begin our journey to Nacogdoches.

Chapter 5 – The Watering Hole

We made good time and were near a stream when My-Boy began to fidget. Then came the classic road-trip refrain.

"Mary, can we stop? I have to pee!"

"Why didn't you go before we left?"

"I did, but I have to go now."

I made my way towards a shady spot and then found a suitable rock that offered My-Boy some privacy.

Rookie, who had been in the lead, came back and checked on us.

"Hu-mon children are so needy." Rookie puffed out his chest. "When I was but four months old, I hunted with the adults."

Rookie's attitude towards My-Boy concerned me. Rookie didn't understand Hu-mons as I did. I pondered how to address his lack of compassion.

"Hu-mon children give love," I replied.

"Hu-mon adults shoot you." He responded with a look of first-hand experience.

Our conversation paused when we realized we weren't alone.

A large pack had approached us from downwind, with two males in the lead and more in the distance. One of the pups had already approached My-Boy, who attempted to play with it.

Rookie moved to my side. "I see my old pack has found us."

I twisted my head for eye-to-eye contact. "You could have told me that they were looking for you."

With an almost Hu-mon shrug of his shoulders, Rookie seemed undisturbed. "How was I to know? The two females must have ratted on me."

Before I could respond to my young partner, My-Boy proclaimed, "Mary, look what I found!"

He'd picked up one of the wolf cubs, I bolted over the rock and frightened the cub. I barked at My-Boy to put it down. He did. The pack leaders came within hailing distance. The larger of the two called out, "I see you've found our lost cub. And a lost Hu-mon cub, as well."

I rubbed my side against My-Boy as a sign of affection. "The Hu-mon cub is mine." Rookie moved quietly behind us. I hoped he was watching our rear and not staring at the sky. We were severely outnumbered.

"Why does a mighty she-wolf, a beauty like you, care about a Hu-mon cub?"

The speaker was a majestic specimen. He was easily the largest male and most handsome wolf I had ever encountered. His black coat glistened like the darkest night. His teeth were perfect, and even from a distance, his eyes spoke of a higher intelligence, one comparable to a Hu-mon. He didn't arch his back to appear larger; he was already large. About 175 pounds of pure muscle visibly rolled under his hide. He was probably seven feet long from nose to tail. His canine teeth were more developed than normal. He moved efficiently and with clear purpose.

If I could have I looked up the word "leader" in My-Daniel's dictionary, the wolf's picture would be next to it.

He was magnetic. I was drawn to him. I resisted the idea of a physical attraction, because I didn't have time for distraction. After a moment's pause, I shook off my fascination and answer, "The Hu-mon child lost his family. I'm taking him to a place of safety where I will raise him. He is mine. I claim him. It is the way of the wolf."

The leader sounded doubtful. "It's your right to claim the Hu-mon child if you wish, although I think he is too old." Then a new light appeared in his eyes.

"My name is Apollo. I'm assembling the largest and mightiest wolf pack in all of Texas. Our numbers are declining because Hu-mons kill wolves without provocation. All wolves are welcome to join us. We need the strongest, the smartest, and the bravest to stop the Hu-mon war on wolves. Who are you, my beauty?"

I breathed a Hu-mon curse under my breath. "My name is Mary, and I am not your beauty. My devotion is to the Hu-mon child as its guardian and guide. It is the way of the wolf."

Apollo was visibly disappointed at my rebuff. He growled, "How came you by the Hu-mon child?"

"I don't have to answer your questions," I snarled. "The Hu-mon child's father was killed last night." I heard My-Boy tear up. "He has no one but me. I have studied Hu-mons. It is my right to claim him."

Apollo changed the topic. "Even more intriguing is that you have a Hu-mon name." He paused to scratch the dirt. "Once the Hu-mon cub is no longer your burden, you will be welcome to join our pack. Your beauty and stature would bring the prominence to the pack as well as mighty offspring."

Then Apollo turned towards Rookie. "As to that one, the outcast, he is not to be trusted. I advise you to keep one eye on your Hu-mon and one eye on the outcast. I don't envy your responsibilities, but, it is the way of the wolf."

Rookie started to respond, but I snapped with an intentional miss. Had he been Hu-mon, I would have punched him in the ribs.

Apollo stepped closer and examined My-Boy. I growled lightly and moved closer to signal protection for the child.

Apollo indicated My-Boy, "What is the Hu-mon's name?"

With motherly pride, I responded, "I call him My-Boy."

Apollo growled, "No, his Hu-mon name?"

My-boy held me tightly during this conversation. "It is Benjamin."

Apollo's eyes gleamed, "Ah, that's it, the prophecy from Genesis 49:27. How does it go?" He paused in thought. I could feel him thinking. I've never had that sensation with any other wolf or Hu-mon.

Then he recited the Bible quotation, "Benjamin shall act as a wolf. In the morning he shall devour the prey and at night he shall divide the spoil."

I was surprised to find a wolf who quoted from Hu-mon books the same way I did. "My-Boy is but a child."

Apollo's magnificent tail stood erect to make a point. "Ah, but a Hu-mon child who one day will fulfil his destiny. What will this child become? A healer or a monster, a lion or a lamb. Will he bridge the gap between humanity and wolf, or will he wipe the wolf from the face of the earth?"

I was taken aback. Apollo's comments were much more profound than I expected from another wolf. "How do you know these things? About Genesis and prophecy?"

Then Apollo gave the most Hu-mon of smiles, "Like you, I have studied Hu-mons."

Apollo recalled his pack, who had paused near the watering hole during our exchange. Rookie, My-Boy, and I watched them move off towards the deeper woods. I turned to Rookie. "What do you know about this Apollo? And what did you do to be marked as an outcast?"

Rookie dropped his eyes. "He is serious about assembling an army to fight the Hu-mons, but he doesn't know how to overcome the Hu-mon weapons. Your understanding of Hu-mons could be valuable to him."

I repeated my second question. "What did you do?"

Rookie starred at the sky like a Hu-mon avoiding eye contact. "I tried to get two of his females to leave with me. That was after I challenged him for leadership of the pack."

In response, I growled, "A leadership battle that no doubt you lost?"

He drew a deep breath. "No doubt."

With all this, I had to sit down. "You challenged Apollo? He is one of the most magnificent wolves I have ever seen. What were you thinking?"

Rookie shook his head. "I was young and dumb."

"When did this happen?" I gave him the evil eye.

"Last week, some time," he said and he began to wander away.

I shoved my snout in his face. "I've got news for you, Rookie, if you pull a stunt like that and challenge me for leadership you won't live to tell about it. Don't waste your potential on delusions of grandeur."

Rookie looked positively perplexed. "What does that mean? Look around. You don't have much of a pack."

"It means grow up." I turned my back to him and ran toward My-Boy, who had nearly wondered too far away.

At my approach, My-Boy turned towards me in the tall grass. "Mary, my legs are sore. I'm tired of riding."

"How can you be tired of riding? I'm the one doing the walking and running."

The truth was that we had pushed it hard all day and I could use a break, but I wouldn't admit it.

"Let's try this," I called Rookie to join us. Then I asked him to bend down, so My-Boy could climb aboard. I ensured that My-Boy was firmly astride his back. Rookie objected, but I reminded him who the alpha was. I hoped this would be a bonding experience, but knew I needed to monitor the situation.

I offered encouragement to My-Boy. "Rookie is going to carry you for a while. He is a little smaller than I am so your legs won't hurt." My-Boy dropped his shovel. I retrieved it for him and he stuck it in his belt.

Rookie asked, "Where are we are going?"

"Nacogdoches," I responded. "It's almost due south of here. I'll show you the magnetic wave to follow."

Rookie returned a puzzled look. "I can't read the magnetic waves."

"Yes you can, I'll show you how." Sometimes, I found myself teaching Rookie more than My-Boy.

Chapter 6 - Dreams of a She-Wolf.

One night, during our journey, a recurring dream startled me awake. The dream remained fresh in my mind.

My dream recalled a real memory. My-Daniel, My-Boy, and I were in the pickup truck on a Saturday night in a parking lot. Bob Wills and the Texas Playboys played inside the dance hall. The band it reeled off "Cotton-eyed Joe," "Ida Red," "San Antonio Rose," and other favorites. I always loved the sound of fiddles. I wanted to dance with My-Daniel. I wanted to feel his arms tight around me as we two-stepped with the crowd. The pounding of boots on the barn wood floor provided a rhythmic accompaniment for the music. I was happy snuggling with My-Daniel and My-Boy in the truck as the band played until the early morning hours.

The dream shifted and the three of us were at home with My-Daniel reading to us as he often did. We favored stories by Rudyard Kipling, Jack London, and Edgar Rice Burroughs. I loved the sound of his voice. When he read on of the stories, I could close my eyes to become anyone I wanted to be, including a Hu-mon.

Then another dream took hold, a dream I'd never had before.

I was the she-wolf, Lupa, raising Romulus and Remus. My-Daniel was one of the pups. The other face I didn't recognize, but I believed it was Apollo.

Then I awakened with fright, and I couldn't sleep for the rest of the night.

Chapter 7 - Gunfight at the Old Stone Fort

When we approached Nacogdoches, I confirmed my bearings by finding the replica of the old stone fort on the edge of town. The original building was demolished in 1902, but the replica was only a few years old. It was built during the New Deal, according to My-Daniel. The new building served as a museum and social center.

The magnetic waves that I use to navigate hadn't failed us, but the landmark confirmed where we were. I stopped to get my bearings.

We approached the Old Stone Fort and took care to remain hidden in the woods across the road. Traffic was light that day and I was confident we would go unnoticed.

What I needed to do was get to the building without being seen by any Hu-mons in the area. But when I did so, I recognized the Studebaker parked next to it. I had to know if the intruders were in this area because that would mean they were looking for us.

Before I could speak, Rookie confirmed my thoughts, "I recognize that scent from your den."

I agreed. "That's the same Studebaker and the same person. I smell the cigar from here."

"I caught the scent of the road machine, the Studebaker, when I was playing hide and find me. You know so much about Hu-mons."

Without responding, I ensured My-Boy was hidden quietly nearby.

Then, Rookie called my attention to the activity behind us.

My-Boy pointed and said, "Apollo" loudly enough to get the wolf's attention. I rolled my eyes and kicked myself for not stressing the need to be quiet.

Apollo joined us. Rookie couldn't wait to get a jab in. "So, have you already lost your pack?"

The wolf king gave Rookie a dirty look. "The Hu-mons who attacked you are in that building." He gestured to the Old Stone Fort. Four Hu-mons walked to a nearby feeding place.

I was taken aback by his statement. "What do you know about the attack?"

"I didn't tell you before because I wasn't sure about you. There are some things about you that I am still not sure about." He paused to collect his thoughts. "We have tracked these Hu-mons for some time. They are part of an organized group that we call the Moon-Hunters. They specialize in hunting wolves, but their methods are not always like others. They track and pursue us and sometimes they kill wolves, but sometimes they only trap wolves. We don't know why they trap wolves. They brought equipment to trap you during their attack. They brought a cage for the child, as well. Members of my pack took out two of the intruders and foiled their plans. Their decisive action permitted you to escape that night."

"I heard wolves in the distance as we fled the den." I paused to reflect. "I wondered who the wolves were. I didn't detect their scent."

Rookie chimed in. "Moon-Hunters sounds cool."

I shoved Rookie away. The young wolf never ceased to amaze me.

Apollo continued, "Over time, we have seen many Hu-mon faces. Not all Hu-mons look alike and we have encountered many scents. The Moon-Hunters are part of a large effort to eradicate wolves. I'm confident these Moon-Hunters are looking for you. They begin stirring in late afternoon about this time and when we become active at night, they also become active. Now, maybe you can understand why I'm organizing a resistance."

I bowed and signaled my agreement. "What is your next move?"

"We strike them right now in the daylight when they least expect it."

"Some of your warriors will die," I observed.

"Sacrifice," said My-Boy, who had listened quietly. "Soldiers die so that others may live."

Rookie interrupted us. "Where did he get that from?"

I growled at Rookie to be quiet.

Apollo nodded his head towards the feeding place. "Watch the doorway. It is nearly time."

Four of his wolves appeared at the roof's peak and carefully made their way down the slope where they could peer over the roof's edge.

As we watched, an idea occurred to me. "My-Boy's grandfather Hiram is a veterinarian. He has tended to me in the past. If any of your warriors are injured, he might be able to help. I can take your warriors to him."

"You don't understand." Apollo looked into my soul. "These Moon-Hunters are looking for you. They are better organized than the average farmer protecting his sheep." He paused to let his words sink in. "You should leave before the shooting starts. My wolf-warriors will mask your trail. They are hidden nearby and await my signal."

My-Boy said, "Mary, I want to stay to see the wolves fight."

Apollo smiled, "Someday the child will be a warrior and a leader. He has potential."

My-Boy smiled complete innocence. I said, "In war, soldiers die."

Apollo countered, "Soldiers prepare, train, and work together to fight enemies using weapons and their abilities. They have a plan." His gaze shifted to the feeding place where his wolves lay in wait. "Do you see my wolf warriors on the roof? They were selected for their ability to leap. Other warriors are out of sight on the ground. The Moon-Hunters left their boom-sticks in the road machine. Without their weapons, the Hu-mons will not survive."

"Don't encourage the child." I bristled. "You said you didn't want us pulled into this."

"I don't want either of you pulled in, but destiny is already set and our futures are only a matter of time. I can see it."

His jolting predictions made me wonder. "Who do you think you are, Edgar Cayce?"

Apollo's attention was focused on the feeding place and he pointed at the door.

The four Hu-mons exited the feeding place one at a time. Once all four were outside, the attack began. The first Hu-mon through the door was taken down by a wolf who made a magnificent jump and landed on his head with claws extended. The wolf's teeth snapped at the Hu-mon's face. The Hu-mon dropped to his knees, screamed, and tugged at the wild creature on his head. The three remaining Hu-mons were likewise attacked by wolves, who leaped from the roof. Meanwhile, other wolves emerged from hiding and joined the fray.

Somehow, the last Hu-mon to exit the feeding place, threw his attacker to the ground. He drew a small boom-stick from his belt, fired two shots into his attacker, and a third shot into the wolf attacking him from the ground. The man's friends were overcome and he bolted across the road towards the woods. He ran straight at us, but we hid and let him go past us.

A second Studebaker arrived and more Moon-Hunters piled out of the doors, boom-sticks blazing, and turned the wolf victory into disaster. The men tended to their wounded.

Apollo turned to me. "You must go now. One Hu-mon with a boom-stick is dangerous and they have reinforcements. Leave now. I'll gather my wolf-warriors and counterattack."

I had a decision to make.

I put My-Boy on Rookie's back and I gave them directions. "Follow this road to the railroad tracks, then wait there. At sundown, another magnetic wave will become visible. Follow it until the moon rises. In the twilight, you should see a red water tower. It marks the home of Hiram and Juanita Smith, your grandparent's, farm.

"Wait!" exclaimed Rookie. I can't see colors. I don't know red. I only see shades of grey. What's a water tower? I can't read, and I don't speak Hu-mon."

My-Boy bopped Rookie on the head. "Silly wolf. I know the water tower. It's where Granny and Pappy live. You must learn to adapt." It was heart-warming to hear his confidence.

I licked My-Boy in approval and turned to Rookie. "I will lag behind you and protect your rear. I won't be far behind. Whatever happens, I am counting on you to take care of My-Boy." The young wolf signaled submission. I said, "Keep your ears forward, your tail down, and your nose up." They headed toward the railroad tracks.

I looked for Apollo. He was deep in the woods and positioning his wolf troops in the trees, rocks, and underbrush. If his plan worked, the Hu-mons would walk into an ambush I'd lost track of the one Hu-mon Moon-Hunter who'd escaped the initial attack, but perhaps Apollo knew where he'd gone.

I felt obligated to join Apollo's forces, but my allegiance to My-Boy remained firm. I was taking a chance trusting Rookie. I had confidence in my ability to protect our rear. I denied my urge to watch or participate in the battle, I turned my back to Apollo's forces, and silently wished him success. I chased after Rookie and My-Boy.

I caught up to them and discovered the missing Moon-Hunter with his pistol leveled at Rookie and My-Boy. Fortunately, I had approached stealthily and the Hu-mon wasn't aware of me. I recognized by his cigar scent that he was one of those who attacked us that night at the den. My lips curled back.

I snapped at his gun hand and he fired into the dirt. Rookie and My-Boy took cover. I tussled with his hands for control of the weapon.

We rolled on the ground and I forced him to drop the gun. I released his hand and sank my teeth into his thigh. I regained my feet, but he'd regained the gun and he shot me in my shoulder. I collapsed, but I jumped to my feet and went for his throat. I had only a moment to kill him. We rolled on the ground. He yelled and scratched at my eyes. I'd lost track of the gun, and my shoulder was on fire.

My-Boy and Rookie ran to me. My-Boy rammed the pointy end of his shovel into the Moon-Hunter's side. He dropped the gun and My-Boy kicked it into the bushes. Rookie's teeth found his throat and ripped it open. Blood gushed like a Texas oil well from my dying opponent's throat.

I tried to stand, but I passed out. I was vaguely aware of Rookie and My-Boy hovering over me. They hugged me. I drifted into unconsciousness.

Everything was surreal. I caught a scent that was both strange and yet familiar. I felt lifted up. I was sure I was dying. I sensed my spirit carried down the wolf road to the hereafter.

The last thing I remember was My-Boy calling, "Mommy"!

Chapter 8 – Recovery

I awoke disoriented and confused, but I didn't think I was in Heaven, the other place, or any place where legends said a wolf's spirit could go. There were bright lights, a cold table, and the strong familiar odor of antiseptic. Perhaps the smell kept me from detecting other scents. My shoulder no longer hurt, but I could feel the bandage. I tried to stand, but couldn't. I was still groggy and disoriented. Someone held me down, but I didn't know who they were.

I fought to clear my head. I rubbed my nose and my face. My face felt differently. Nothing was wrong, my face was different. My paws were human hands. After years of living as a wolf, I'd transitioned back into my human form. And I wasn't alone in this room.

I was afraid and I cried, "Where is My-Boy, I mean Benjamin? Is he okay?"

A familiar person opened the door. It was My-Boy's grandfather, Hiram, and Benjamin right behind him. Rookie's claws clicked on the tile floor. He slipped on the slick tile when he tried to go around my bed, and banged into the wall. Benjamin climbed into my bed and hugged me as tightly as ever.

"Mommy, you're back!" I hugged him with my good arm.

"You remember me?" I'd never told him that his mother was masquerading as the family pet.

"Yes, Mommy, I love you." Holding my son with my human hands was the greatest experience of my life. Hearing him say "Mommy," melted my heart as nothing else could. He pulled the family photo from his back pocket. "See, you're right here."

"Take it easy, Mary, you're still groggy." Hiram bent over me and checked my condition. "You've had a rough time, young lady. You held wolf form for too long. John was amazed when I told him."

My daze began to lift and I realized that I was in the treatment room in the veterinarian office at Hiram's farm.

He paused for a response and then realized, "You're still groggy. You need to rest. But someone else wants to see you." I saw him motion for someone to come near. "John, come here."

"Who is John?" I asked. But Hiram didn't answer.

A soft-spoken, but strong, voice responded. "I'm John." I opened my eyes and a giant towered over me. "Mary, we've already met."

"We have?" I didn't know him and I wasn't just confused from my condition.

"Yes, Mary, you know me as Apollo."

I sat up on the table for a better look, Hiram helped me lay back down. "You're Apollo? You're a werewolf, too."

He extended a hand, which was nearly as big as his paw. "Pleased to meet you, Mary. My full name is John Apollo."

We clasped hands for a moment and his grip was firm and strong. My grip was soft as putty.

Hiram cautioned me. "Rest. You're still exhausted. I explained to John that when you were bitten we didn't know anything about werewolves. You were the only werewolf we knew about until I met John yesterday. Take it easy now. You've been through a lot. You lost a lot of blood from the gunshot in addition to the pain you endured in the transition from wolf to human."

That pain revived aching memories. "That's why I held the wolf form for years. The pain of transition to and from human was just too much. I suffered for days every time I shifted."

Hiram smiled. "John here says there is a cure for that ailment in werewolf culture."

Then John chimed in, "Yes, the principle ingredient is a tea made from the Poppy Mallow plant found along the Colorado River. There are other ingredients, but they are easy to obtain."

My memory slowly returned. "What about the Moon-Hunters?"

John breathed a heavy sigh. "All the Moon-Hunters we encountered are dead. My wolf-warriors took heavy losses. I still have to dispose of the Studebakers. I'll need to find a deep lake someplace."

I was relieved, shocked, and a little uncertain about everything. "What do we do next?"

John gently placed his hand on my good shoulder. "What you do is follow the doctor's orders."

He rubbed his forehead and hesitated. "Their attempts to capture us and their war on wolves has forced me to fight back. They wanted to capture you and Benjamin. That means they know about werewolves. We have no choice but to fight them, but I need to develop better tactics and recruit more wolves."

I drew a short breath. "Are we safe here?"

"Yes, take all the time you need to recover. My surviving wolf-warriors are patrolling the property. I've called for reinforcements." He smiled. "As long as I can keep my wolves away from Hiram's chickens, you'll have their protection. I don't know who is behind this, but I'll find out and stop them."

"It is kind of a joke between us." Hiram chuckled. "I keep telling John we don't have any chickens." We laughed. "But I did tell him that you've taught us so much about devotion and compassion and duty and love. You may have been a wolf in appearance, but you were a mother through and through. I grieve for Daniel. His loss is a tragedy, but he loved you as we all do. As Daniel would say, "The role of the parent is to prepare the child for life. Perhaps, you and Apollo will raise Benjamin to lead the pack when he grows up. He might even make peace with mankind."

Together we chorused, "It is the way of the wolf."

***

J. F. Terrell Jr. is best known as one of the administrators in the Facebook discussion group "For the Love of All Things Edgar Rice Burroughs."

Retired from an I.T. career that spanned 42 years, Terrell now devotes his time to the exploration of Edgar Rice Burroughs' legacy.

Terrell regularly contributes essays and short fiction to ERB-APA, the Amateur Press Association chapter dedicated to Edgar Rice Burroughs.

An active member of the Burroughs Bibliophiles, Terrell has also served as a consultant to the Edgar Rice Burroughs collection at the University of Louisville and provided editorial services to Edgar Rice Burroughs, Inc.

Terrell holds an M.B.A. from Sullivan University based in Louisville, Kentucky.

FERAL IS A STATE OF MIND

By DJ Howell

FOREWORD

Fictional or real, feral children are individuals isolated from the culture of their birth and brought up by animals or a culture more primitive than the child's own. Mowgli and Tarzan of the Apes live in fiction, while of reality's many allegedly feral individuals, Itard's Victor, known as The Wild Child, represents the rare case remaining authentic, whatever his origins.

But what if an individual is of a feral state of mind? What if he is an identity in exile? Edgar Rice Burroughs' Tarzan is a case in point. Of British heritage, he was raised by the Mangani, a fictional primate more nearly human than chimpanzees or gorillas. It may be the adult Tarzan's state of mind that fascinates us: he remains always in exile from one heritage or the other: when in civilization he longs for his wilderness, and when there, he longs for civilization. Much of his universal appeal comes from this capacity to reflect our own longings for the extremes of a continuum – civilization at one extreme and wilderness at the other.

What if the individual is of a seventeenth century clan of outlawed Scottish Highlanders who embraces his land's wilderness and its denizens in an enforced isolation from his people and, ultimately, his beloved Highlands? Like his distant literary progenitor, Tarzan, he can speak for all of us as we seek our place on the continuum. Liam Macfarlane can reveal to us our own identity in exile, in our case from the natural world. That is the premise behind the novel *Where You Can Hear the Sea and See the Sound,* from which the following narrative is adapted.

FIRST ENCOUNTER

Foxes and wolves figure prominently throughout Liam's life. His first experience occurs when a toddler.

As late afternoon was yielding to early evening, Liam had rapidly crawled along in the wake of one of Malleta's half-wild cats to the very edge of the forest surrounding her cottage. For once, Malleta herself was nowhere in sight. Flopping down in a patch of sunlight, the wee beastie deigned to accept Liam's gentle stroking and was purring loudly.

Thus, the lad was first astonished, and then deeply insulted when the creature suddenly turned on him.

Ears flat, eyes wild, the cat spat at him and raked his hand with her razor-sharp claws before tearing off in the direction of the cottage. Liam watched her wild escape in astonishment. What had prompted this sudden madness? He never thought to call after her, but he did manage to stand up all too briefly, before crumpling onto his seat. He was working himself into a serious bout of sobbing when a movement to one side caught his eye.

At first, Liam was astonished anew, but then he assured himself this must be a dream, real as it might feel. A wolf pup just about his own size was watching him intently. Suddenly the little creature smiled a smile not unlike Lassie's and gave a tentative wag of his tail. Liam grinned and reached for the creature as he spoke as clearly as he knew how. To the lad's disappointment, his speech was not as clear as it was wont to be in his dream world. Nor did the wild puppy respond in kind. But he was ready to play, and Liam obliged with considerable enthusiasm, hoping this dream would not end so abruptly as too many did, just at the moment of greatest enjoyment.

This time the dream did continue, and Liam found himself in a lively tussle accompanied by his giggles mingling with the pup's growling and high-pitched yips. In the process Liam was becoming quite delightfully dirty – clothes and skin soon covered with grass stains and soil. Here was a dream that could go on forever!

Neither of the two playmates took notice of the pup's mother, who approached the pair with a stealthy silence, uncertainty manifest in her every move. Her other pups watched from where she had left them, hunkered down in the protective shadows of distant trees.

It was not until their frolics precipitated the two into her side with a great thump that the lad and wolfling came up short, both panting. The she-wolf gave her own offspring a lick of welcome, which he accepted as an invitation. Suddenly quite ravenous, the pup settled down to suckle. Liam was at the receiving end of a more tentative lick and was about to join his new companion's repast when he heard Malleta calling out to him. Her voice was unusually soft and carried a hint of urgency unfamiliar to Liam. The lad glanced in the direction of her call. He had not noticed her approach any more than that of the large dog against whose side he was now reclining.

"Come to me, Liam, chiel," Malleta said in a subdued voice. "You need a bath, me lad, and it is time to come to supper and bed."

Indeed, Liam was exhausted from the wild antics of his dream. He wanted to obey, but as so often happens at such times, his limbs declined to cooperate. In fact, he dropped immediately into a slumber hovering about the edges of his dream.

As he slept on, he vaguely heard Malleta cautiously approaching the three of them. Wonder of wonders, the woman spoke to the she-wolf as evenly as she might with any of the human folk of Liam's acquaintance.

"Och, the chiel is mine, friend wolf. And I'll not harm you or your'n. Let him come to me, and we'll all be about our business and none's the wiser nor any come to harm." Liam was unaccountably pleased that Malleta did not share in any insistence upon keeping realms well separated and that the woman shared in his secret conversations with the animals. As to what followed, the lad remained oblivious.

Now the woman held her tongue, bided her time until the she-wolf nudged her own child onto his feet, and moved away from the human one. As the two moved off in innate dignity, Malleta saw regret in the wolf's eyes as the animal glanced back to the sleeping lad before disappearing into the trees.

HIGHLANDS: FROM CHILD TO MAN

As Liam grew into manhood, his teachers were Malleta, a Seer and woman wise in the ways of the natural world; Iain, his loving father, distanced by his outlaw status; and Liam's own intuitive embrace of the wilderness of his Highlands. After a lengthy separation, Iain was taken aback by what he saw in the man who Liam was becoming.

Engrossed in his labor, Iain lost track of time, until he looked up to find the sun high in the cloudless sky. He stopped his work and went to fetch himself a drink from the spring house, first sluicing the icy water over his head and face. As he savored the water, Iain chanced to look toward the opening in the forest. A tall young man was entering the clearing. Iain gulped and nearly choked on the last mouthful of water, as something in the man's figure gave him pause. He had not recognized the lad at first glance.

Until now he had never seen his son as a man grown. Iain returned the ladle to its place and inspected Liam as he strode across the meadow. Family members had assured Iain that the son took after his father. Iain shook his head: One woman's observation had been marked with a mixture of amusement with pride. Too often another's was tart, openly disapproving. Iain studied Liam as he might the stranger for whom he had first taken him. Again he knew the regret of circumstances demanding Liam's rearing by members of Iain's family and that of his late wife, lost in birthing Liam.

The lad was tall with the lean form of one hardened by life in the Highland wilds, and he strode out across the meadow with all the confidence of youth. But Iain was pleased to detect no swagger in Liam's step and knew from Malleta that the lad could be stealthy and downright invisible in the forest, keenly alert to the demands of circumstance, never taken by surprise. For now there was no call for caution, but Liam suspected that the lad was aware that his father was alone at his task and that the stock and help were elsewhere.

Liam's skin was browned from the sun, a marked contrast with the pale rust of his hair, worn loose and almost reaching his broad shoulders. In keeping with the stubborn nature of his clan, Liam wore a kilt of dull green set off by his bronzed skin and the pale saffron of his shirt. As he drew closer, Iain allowed his assessment to continue. Liam halted a few feet away; the two exchanged nods of greeting, but Iain persisted in his scrutiny. The lad revealed neither impatience nor embarrassment but returned his father's frank regard with a faintly quizzical one of his own.

After a moment of reminiscences, some yet to be shared, Iain turned to the business at hand. "Come, me lad, there's much to learn," he warned as he moved out. "No time like the present to begin." With one last lingering glance about the glen, Liam caught up with long strides before adjusting his steps to match Iain's. And so the two walked side by side in a companionable silence. Iain's respect grew as he made the most of his silent observations of his son. It pleased Iain to find Liam so like himself. The lad knew to keep a still tongue in his head and to devote all his senses to taking in his surroundings. It seemed unlikely that anything even slightly out of the ordinary would lie beyond Liam's cognizance.

Uncounted moments into the forest, it was Iain who broke the silence: "I know Malleta has taught ye her healing ways," he began. Liam nodded and waited for Iain to continue. "No doubt ye can locate even the most elusive of the herbs and are skilled in the preparation of her 'magic potions.'"

Iain winked and Liam's frown relaxed into a slight shake of his head. Malleta indulged in no fey magic. Both men knew there was no sorcery in Malleta's powers of healing. She was no witch. The world held a wealth of hidden provisions for any who would seek them out and use them wisely.

"More," Iain continued, his tone now without hint of mirth, "with all your explorations, you know the lands about our Loch and up into the high ground as well as any man, better than most, I'll venture. But what is it that the woman has taught ye of the wee Highland beasties and their ways?"

Though Malleta had sought to prepare Iain for the answer, nothing could prepare a man for the breadth and depth of his own son's empathy with the wild denizens of the Highlands, some inherent wisdom no other could have instilled in him.

As the days of exploration and discovery proceeded, the lad often revealed some element of the teeming life about them, rather than rely on the mere telling. As the men explored their world together, discovering each other in the process, Iain's astonishment grew. How had the lad come upon his awareness? Should the need arise, Iain had every confidence in Liam's innate capacity for instantly assuming the habits of elusive prey although his heart, like that of the auld ones of Highlands history and lore, was more kin to dire wolf and cunning fox.

HIGHLANDS: VIXEN TO THE RESCUE

Given the era as well as Liam's own propensities, capture by the English invaders was inevitable. But, thanks to his knowledge of the Highlands beasties, the outcome was not.

The bound prisoner judged it nigh midnight before he detected the sounds for which he had been hoping. There was a slight skittering in the midden, then the sounds of chewing. Liam suppressed a chuckle. A wayward breeze carried a faint skunky odor mixed with an even fainter milky tinge. Very softly, Liam uttered the mewling cries of hungry kits.

The chewing ceased abruptly. Liam cried again and was rewarded with purposeful skittering. Though he could not detect approaching footfalls, the scents grew stronger. Then he could make out the sleek form of the vixen. She slowed and eyed him with suspicion followed by a disgusted expression so reminiscent of the look his English tormenter had cast at him that Liam felt his face turning very red as he suppressed an entirely inappropriate – and most unwise – guffaw. The vixen regarded him with such uncertainty that Liam feared she would either turn tail and run or simply return to her repast on the fresh scraps of the midden. He remained very still indeed. To his relief, the wee red beastie lifted her sharp nose to scent something even more alluring on the air from behind the man-creature.

With one last suspicious glance at him, the vixen commenced to explore for the source of the promising scent. Inevitably, she was drawn around the tree to which the man was bound with ropes he had slathered with remnants of his meal. Liam held his breath and prayed in silence. He could hear naught, and his nose could no longer judge the proximity of the beastie. He startled when a cold nose and whiskers brushed his hands. Then there was a sharp nip.

"Och, lassie," he barely whispered, "not the hands; the ropes, my wee friend."

To his relief, the vixen complied whether she understood or simply found feeding on the ropes more to her taste. Liam had no expectation of her being able to chew the ropes through. All he needed was enough of a start for him to add his strength to parting them himself. But the fox fooled him. Whatever her own purposes, the little vixen actually worried at the ropes until they fell away from his hands.

Liam did not move. He would not frighten his rescuer. He wished there was some reward he might bestow. But all he could do was to give voice to the soft cries of contented kits sated with milk. The vixen became very still. Then, to Liam's bemusement, she trotted around the tree to face him.

"Aye, lassie, I thank ye," he whispered. But by now the creature had endured enough of these strange proceedings. With one last look at the man, she turned and trotted off to disappear into the darkness. Liam could have sworn he saw her grin, not unlike the smiles of the dogs about the crofts. With a responsive grin of his own, Liam followed the vixen's lead and disappeared into the darkness.

QUONEHATACUT: WOLVES TO THE RESCUE

Upon reaching New-England, the final destination of his exile from the Highlands, Liam, having assumed the identity Kent MacFarland, made his way to along the shoreline of Quonehatacut into the homelands of the Quinnipiacs. Along his way he rescued an injured wolf cub trapped under a boulder. Kent called his new companion Mohegan, the native name for wolves. Some years later, on returning from a diplomatic mission to the Pequots, the People of the Fox, and finding a kindred spirit in their sachem, Sassacus, Kent first encountered the Pequots' sworn enemy, Uncas, sachem of the Mohegans, the People of the Wolf. Uncas was proving to be a staunch ally of the English, known scathingly to the native peoples as Owanux. Thus began Kent's allegiance to the two bitterest opponents, Sassacus of the Pequots and Uncas of the Mohegans, soon to be embroiled in what history would call the Pequot War, setting the stage for battles to come throughout the history of the land the natives called Turtle Island.

The Storm overtook Uncas upon returning home from a diplomatic foray among Narragansets, allied with the tribe he knew as Owanux. He had heeded the harbingers of its coming but had hoped to be warming himself at the fire of his wigwam before it could strike. Instead he was at least one river east of his village and fighting both howling wind and thickening snowfall. If it grew much worse, he would be forced to find what shelter he could and make camp. Otherwise, thoroughly soaked by the heavy snow, even he could find himself hopelessly lost and succumb to exposure.

Not easily swayed from any intent, Uncas persisted. At least he could wrap himself in the blanket gifted him by the Owanux despite their aloof discourtesy. Uncas of the Wolf People would make the staunchest of allies, and he would bring with him all those who would neither be Pequot nor tributary to those People of the Fox. The wolf is mightier than the fox and in numbers at least as cunning. But first Uncas must find a way to forge an alliance. Before that he must survive this storm.

Uncas drew the surprising warmth of the soaked blanket closer and let the notion of alien magic briefly touch his mind before sweeping the unseemly impression away. He wanted at least to cross the river of the Fox People before taking refuge from the storm. He had no desire to encounter any of Sassacus' scouts who might be lurking. But, if he did not make camp soon, no amount of shelter would allow him to ignite a fire with the most protected tinder drenched.

Uncas shrugged the blanket up over his head and continued his miserable slogging through the heavy snow. At the vague scent of a river ahead, Uncas was heartened but resigned. It would be no easy task to paddle across, once he was able to locate a canoe. Yet to be frozen into pathways, the rivers were aroused in fury under the buffeting of the wind sweeping out of the northeast. Upon the successful crossing for which Uncas permitted himself no doubt, he would find shelter within the groves of evergreens beyond. If the spirits remained generous, he would find ample kindling and wood, dry enough for fire. For now, shelter alone was a powerful incentive.

Suddenly, Uncas came to a halt and lifted his head in the manner of the startled forest dweller. All he could hear was the constant hiss of windblown snow, but *something* had penetrated the eerie hush beneath the hiss. He waited. Presently, he dropped the blanket from his head the better to catch any sound.

There! It came again. The cry of a wolf in distress.

The flesh of Uncas' back crawled in reaction. It came again, from the direction of the river. Only one voice, not the cries of a hunting pack. No wolf would be hunting under these conditions. More, Uncas was certain the call was not that of the hunter.

An omen for one who called himself a leader of people associated with wolf-kind? Uncas shuddered, but immediately denied himself the rising fear, however unnatural the calls might prove to be. Uncas had yet to meet a spirit. Whenever such an encounter should come to be, Uncas was quite prepared to hold his own. An unfriendly being of earthly domain or of a realm beyond this one would find a worthy adversary. Uncas might not be the victor, but the being would come away, if at all, with respect for the prowess of Uncas.

Cautiously, the sachem followed the lead of the cries, stopping when he became uncertain of the direction until they came again. As he neared the place of origin, Uncas knew the beast was in or very near the waters of the river. The sachem assumed the very character of wariness itself.

At last, one foot touched the water's edge, and Uncas just saved himself from slipping and tumbling into the wild torrents rushing seaward. The whine of the wind had muffled and distorted the roar of the river. The cry of the wolf came again, very close now and seemingly directed to him.

Uncas was unable to penetrate the wall of snow all but concealing the river itself. Then a momentary change in the direction of the wind and the slightest abatement in the snowfall cleared the way to his vision.

Yes, there was the wolf, stranded atop a small island of tumbled rocks forcing the flow to split into two wildly plunging streams. The creature was coated with snow and suffering the onslaught of river waters whenever they struck the rocks head on to sweep up and over instead of diverging in their mad rush for the sea.

The wolf was steadily regarding Uncas through the snow. Having succeeded in drawing his namesake to him, he ceased the howling. Uncas could feel the eyes upon him even when the driving snow obscured the forms of rock and beast.

How had he come to this plight? As if in answer, the snow cleared again, just enough to reveal a smashed canoe on the half-submerged rocks. Uncas gasped in spite of himself. What magic was this? But then he espied the body of a man sprawled against the rocks. There was plenty of mystery resident here, but it was of this realm, none other.

Uncas wondered at the relationship between man and wolf, but he knew there was one. The man was sprawled as bonelessly as one slain, but to Uncas' thinking, the wolf was not mourning but calling out for deliverance. Alone, the beast would have attempted the swim. Alone, Uncas firmly told himself, the wolf would not have been cast upon the island of stone at all.

Uncas knew he had been called to the succor of these mismatched companions, but he was possessed of no means for effecting a rescue. Nor did he particularly relish any attempt to move the man without taking his protector to safety as well. Uncas was certain only that the wolf would not interfere with a rescue attempt. Beyond that, none could predict.

Uncas scouted the bank. After only a few paces, he literally stumbled upon a canoe hidden under a thin blanket of snow. It proved too small for his purposes, but the shapes of others nearby became apparent, one suggesting a craft larger than the others. Uncas swept the snow away to confirm it would serve to carry all three, assuming Uncas alone could paddle it to the rocks without being swamped or swept downstream, condemning them all to certain death. Should he succeed that far, he must somehow wrestle the man into the canoe, should he still live, and then entice the guardian wolf into the craft without casting them all into the roiling waters to drown together.

Uncas was nothing if not bold to an extreme that Sassacus and most of the Fox People deemed beyond foolhardy. And Uncas was determined to answer the wolf's calls for help. He noted the animal had not resumed his howling and wondered if the beast could have been swept away with rescue so near. But, no, even through the wind and snow, Uncas felt the intensity of that stare. The wolf at least still lived.

Uncas conceived a desperate strategy for reaching the rock island before being swept downstream. He wrenched the canoe from its place across the snow and into the water, judged the crazy currents as best he could, and committed himself to the spirits of river and wolf. He could only hope the one was allied with the other long enough for him to effect his purpose. As the roiling waters swept him along, Uncas fought for enough control to cross onto the path of the rocks. Unlike the two victims, he, at least, was prepared for the collision whenever it came.

Suddenly, without the slightest of warnings, the canoe struck the rocks almost head on. Somehow Uncas was neither thrown into the waters nor crushed on the rocks. Somehow the canoe lifted up onto the rocks to come to rest as if deliberately beached by the skill of his paddling. Both man and canoe had survived the impact unharmed. Stunned, Uncas met the calm eyes of the wolf closer than he had ever experienced the living spirit of this great beast. He saw trust in those eyes and hoped to prove worthy of it.

Uncas assured himself the canoe was securely wedged into the rocks before gingerly swinging himself onto the slippery surfaces to clamber down to the body. A quick examination revealed the man to be thoroughly chilled, but alive. Uncas felt for broken bones but found none. Turning the man face up, he was startled to discover he was of no nation Uncas knew, nor did he look to be English. From the size of him, he might be some kin of the otherworldly ones who sometimes entered this realm, but why would any such being find himself in this dangerous predicament? Not for the first time since initially detecting the faint call of the wolf, Uncas suspected he was somehow being challenged by powers beyond earthly ken. In keeping with his nature, Uncas resolved to rise to the challenge.

Whoever he might be, wherever he might have come from, the man had suffered a terrific blow to his head. That seemed to be his only injury, so Uncas wrestled him into the canoe under the close supervision of the wolf. Then he settled into the craft himself before gesturing for the wolf to do the same. With unceasing calm, the beast obeyed and instinctively settled himself low in the craft.

Having wedged the canoe so thoroughly, Uncas found it no easy task to maneuver it until it was caught by the rough waters, but at length he succeeded. Somehow, he then managed to force his way to the opposite shore. He had no way of judging how far downstream they had been swept, but for now it mattered little. Unless he got the three of them to shelter and a good fire, all three would be dead before the storm relented.

Uncas was a powerful man, but he had no idea how he would get the stranger to the grove of pines ordinarily within sight of the river bank. At length, he determined to let the snow serve his needs. He rigged an awkward harness from the sodden blanket and simply towed canoe and man deep into the trees beyond the reach of the storm. The interlacing branches formed a natural roof neither wind nor snow could penetrate. The trees were so ancient that the lowermost branches were beyond the reach of Uncas and free of snow.

Once within this shelter, Uncas angled the canoe to form a shallow lean-to held in place by a sturdy trunk. After scraping piles of needles underneath for added warmth, he placed the unconscious man in this rude shelter. The wolf watched, shook the worst of the wet snow from his coat, and moved in to press himself against the man. Once he licked the man's face without response and looked back to Uncas.

"Wise, indeed, friend," Uncas approved, "but I will see what more I can do to give us warmth. And we must eat for strength to survive in this cold." Once again he was startled by the intelligence in the wolf's calm eyes.

"Who *are* you?" he muttered under his breath, but the animal merely dropped his head to his paws in apparent exhaustion.

"Ho-o-o," Uncas drew a long breath, "I agree, but what must be done only I can do." And he left the immediate shelter in search of enough wood to see them through the night and to melt snow for a healing tea and a thick gruel suitable for providing sustenance for the wolf and himself.

His foraging at last complete, Uncas uttered a brief prayer of thanksgiving as he returned to gather pine needles and cones and ignited them to start the fire. To his vast relief, his firestone threw a spark upon only a few strikes, and the tinder burst into life. With shaking hands, he forced himself to add heavier pieces of wood slowly to avoid snuffing out the first tentative flames. The smoke found a sinuous pathway up through the branches overhead.

From the pouch at his waist, Uncas withdrew a small tightly woven basket in which he melted snow first to offer water to the grateful wolf and then to brew healing tea. Some of this potion he managed to dribble between the injured man's teeth. The remainder Uncas drank himself before starting to warm the gruel. While it simmered, he ventured out one last time for additional wood. After sharing the simple meal with the wolf, he added the warmth of his body to the two and arranged his blanket around them. Gratefully, Uncas felt the combined warmth of their bodies and the fire suffuse his body. Certain they would survive the night, he allowed himself much needed sleep.

While the companions were sleeping, the wind died away and the blizzard faded until it was no more than an occasional drifting flake of snow. With the perversity of the season, the new day proved to be sunny with a warmth more in keeping with mid-summer than late fall. Uncas awoke to find himself comfortably warm despite the fact that the fire had burned itself out. From his position under the pines he was unable to judge where the sun was in the sky. He suspected it was midday or later.

At the man's first stirrings, the wolf rose to push through the blanket and lifted his nose to test the air. His coat, like the blanket, had dried during the night. Uncas discovered his own clothing to be mostly dry. Judging them all to be better off in the sun, he turned to the stranger, who seemed to be sleeping rather than unconscious. Again accepting the watchful eye of the wolf, Uncas rolled the man out of the sheltering canoe and then lifted him to one shoulder and carried him out from under the trees. The man murmured under his breath but did not awaken. The wolf looked from one to the other in what Uncas interpreted as relief.

The welcome heat of the bright sun filled Uncas as pleasantly as a belly replete with roasted venison. He found a smooth expanse of rock where he stooped to place the sleeping man. Although there was no sign of fire starting in the blood, Uncas left his charge in the keeping of the wolf to go in search of a grove of willows. A tea of the bark might prevent the coughing and internal fires which so often trail such an ordeal as the man had suffered.

When Uncas returned with the bark, the man was sitting up, the wolf settled between his knees with his head supported in the embrace of the man's hands. At the same time, the two of them sensed Uncas' approach and turned to face him. The wolf lifted his head to whine a low greeting.

"Aye, Mohegan, ye know him, then?" The words sounded like English, but then the man surprised Uncas by speaking in his own tongue, "I thank you for the rescue. I am Kent MacFarland." He stopped there, expecting Uncas to reveal his identity and go on to reveal how he and his unlikely companion were brought to this place.

"I am Uncas of the Wolf People; some call us Mohegans. *Your* Mohegan called me to you."

JOURNEY'S END

And then it was that events proceeded into war without regard to personal relationships. Kent MacFarland was forced to make choices among combatants he deemed friends as the Pequot War and its repercussions ravaged the land he had come to love. As Sassacus had once warned him, "The Fox and the Wolf are two different beasts. Each goes its own way. They do not range the lands or hunt as one kind. Can the Fox and the Wolf live together in a man's heart?"

Shortly after the Treaty of Hartford determined the fates of the People of the Fox and all who dwelled in New-England, English planters were arriving too close to Kent's holdings for comfort. Kent knew he and his family would be forced into yet another exile for him. At the insistence of his Quinnipiac wife, he embarked upon what she knew as a belated journey-quest to resolve the matter of his true identity. And disappeared from the ken of all somewhere in the wilds of what would become the states of Vermont and New Hampshire. Had the land finally claimed his person for its own as it had claimed his heart and soul?

***

Inspired by childhood on the Connecticut shoreline combined with fascination for Native Americans and Tarzan of the Apes, Howell proceeded from ecology to environmental law to engaging hearts and minds in addressing environment matters. She focuses on how formative places help make each of us who we are and what happens when we are separated, often involuntarily, from such places, in short: self, place, and identity – and identity in exile. Tarzan is compelling as the ultimate identity in exile, at home in the extremes of wilderness and civilization. In both he moves with intelligence, grace, and dignity while most of us are caught closer to the civilized extreme.

Her publications include *Intellectual Properties and the Protection of Fictional Characters* and the environmental trilogy: *Scientific Literacy and Environmental Policy, Ecology for Environmental Professionals, Environmental Stewardship: Images from Popular Culture.* Her self-published *Where You Can Hear the Sea and See the Sound* is the culmination of her "mission."

ELISE'S WARD

By: Stuart Conover

"The child cannot be trusted."

Elise could not believe the words that the Mother Superior was uttering. They peered down at the child in question from a darkened window high above the keep's holding area. He hadn't spoken a word since being taken captive and once they had let him loose, he slithered along the ground like the giant lizards which their order was sworn to fend off.

"Not be trusted?" Elise couldn't keep the astonishment out of her voice, "He is but a boy. A boy who has likely never known his own kind."

The Mother Superior looked at her coldly.

"When the great Dragons forsook our lands, taking magic with them, they left these drakes and some of their lesser breather behind to inflict as much damage on the enlightened races as they could. You know we have defeated almost all of them aside from these pests. If the drakes raised this boy as one of their own, there is no way he can find his way back to his humanity."

Elise wasn't about to take no for an answer. It wasn't her place to speak out, but how could she not?

"If we can restore the light to his eyes, he could lead us to their dens. We could possibly end these abominations for good."

"Mmm." The Mother Superior replied.

Once a great warrior priest, her body had long ago failed her. The Mother Superior was beyond old. It was whispered that her rage against the drakes, who bred like rabbits, was all that kept her going. Though, lately, it was rumored that her ties to the great general Zenlan was responsible for her continued existence.

The idea of finally wiping out the drakes wasn't just her reason to live, it was a legacy that she believed would be honored for thousands of years. A cruel grin slowly fractured her usual stoic face.

"Very well. Let us see what this boy, whom you so ill-advisedly wish to save, can tell us. He shall be your ward. You have a month to provide progress or he'll be judged by the city's council. In the meantime, you will be held responsible for his actions."

"As the Mother Superior commands."

Elise turned and strode away from her master. She knew that a slow and agonizing death was the only verdict the boy would see. She couldn't let that happen. He was not responsible for how he was raised. More importantly, if he could be brought back to his humanity, she would have helped the leader of her order make progress toward their greater purpose. She would secure a higher position within the order.

The Draconic Order had been the power behind the throne - all the thrones in all of the kingdoms for years until the great rebellions. The Order had lost so much, but thanks to their ties with Zenlan they were regaining their lost prestige.

Elise needed this win to position herself for a place of power for when their influence was rebuilt. She didn't want much, all she wanted was to be the next Mother Superior and the power which came with the crown.

Nothing would stop her from this.

A week went by without much progress.

Now, Elise was worried that she might have bitten off more than she could chew. Standing outside of the boy's cell all she could hear was his snarls from the other side of the locked door. Two guards leaned against another and limped away from the prison.

There was no progress with the boy. None. He would not listen. He attacked anyone who came near. He resisted all forms of civilization from clothes to proper eating.

Elise wanted to scream. Her fists tightened. She forced her anger from surface as quickly as it had risen.

She couldn't let anyone else see her so emotional. More importantly, she couldn't admit that the Mother Superior was right. There was no room for weakness in their order.

Forcing a saccharine smile onto her face, Elise slowly walked into the room.

Instantly, the boy looked at her. His eyes were still enraged at whatever the guards had just done to him. She pictured the guards limping away from the prison. He must have made them pay for it.

"Boy," she stated in a soothing tone, "This simply will not do. You need a name, boy. Even objects have names and you aren't an object."

He hissed at her.

She spoke more. Of her life. Her dreams. The words didn't matter. The inflection did. She spoke slowly, rhythmically, quietly.

He still hissed, but the rage was draining from his response. That was part of her order's training. Control from seduction to persuasion to negotiation. They were all abilities in which they were trained, in addition to their warrior skills.

At the very least, her abilities were once again keeping the boy from attacking her. A small success at best, but one none of the others had been able to accomplish.

She slowly moved toward the child. Her voice flowed in rhythm, the cadence and inflection calmed and relaxed the child. His eyes sagged and the tension started to ease from his shoulders.

Until Elise put her hands in the pouch at her side. Anger flashed in his eyes and he hissed in warning.

She smiled again and slowly withdrew her hand. In it was the largest mutton leg she had been able to find in the pantry. She had forced the cooks to prepare it while she stood outside the kitchen to avoid the room as it filled with smoke.

Knowing it would take some time, she had slipped into the cellar for a quick glass of wine to sooth her nerves.

The boy never took his eyes off the meat, but he quieted down. He watched it in her hand.

Elise finished approaching the child. It was time to do the same thing she had done every day for the last week.

Pointing to herself, she said her name out loud. Pointing to the child she said "slither" for the first time, instead of boy. Finally, pointing to the meat, which was new today, she said "mutton." She paused and repeated the process two more times before pointing to the meat.

The boy looked at it.

He looked at her.

He looked at it.

"Mmmustenss" the boy hissed out and looked at her.

Once again, Elise let her emotions get the best of her. Her laughter filled the room as she handed the meat over to the child.

"Yes!" she cried, "mutton!"

"Mmustens!" the boy said with a smile that would terrify anyone else. He grabbed it and devoured the meal until there was nothing left but bone.

He sat down with that same sadistic smile plastered over his face and his hands on his full belly.

"Elise" she continued pointing to herself. "Slither" she said pointing to the child.

He jumped to his feet and came dangerously close, raising a hand that could easily have struck her, but he stopped short. Pointing, he said "Eleesss." She smiled again, pointing to herself she repeated her name, pointed to him she said "Slither."

Hand covering his face, the boy responded "Sslithher."

Another week passed.

Slither hadn't attacked a guard in three days, not that he was any less intimidating around them. He was able to say a few more words now as well. He could call multiple things by name, mainly food. However, anything beyond that was still out of reach. He used simple nouns only, and was unable to express actions, tenses, and concepts. Elise wondered how she had ever thought teaching this creature ten years of communication skills in the span of a month had ever seemed feasible.

With only two weeks left she wanted to throw in the towel.

But she couldn't. She wouldn't. There had to be another tact she could use on Slither. Something to jumpstart his language. Or, at least, get him to lead them to where the drakes nested so they could finish this war once and for all.

Entering the room, Slither jumped up and shouted her name. For the first time, it was clear without any signs of the hiss that usually accompanied it. Perhaps, the boy was learning faster than she's thought.

She spent the next two hours going over items in the room, food, and a list of things she had brought with her. Progress was being made but only on items, not actions. He couldn't seem to grasp even simple ones and had spent most of the previously day calling the chair "sit."

He seemed happier. It wasn't clear if it was from the solitude or the rewards of new food, but Slither seemed to enjoy the time he was spending with her.

The third week had kicked off on a high note. Pride blooming in her chest, Elise was thrilled. The child had learned what sit meant. Not only that, but walk, stand, eat, and more had become common place. It wasn't what she needed to help the Mother Superior, but it was a start.

She also had begun using pictures to teach items and locations which couldn't be brought into the room such as trees and ponds, but Slither seemed unresponsive to this way of learning.

She thought it unlikely that the child would be ready in another week. However, Elise had a plan. If she could show the progress which she had made and make it clear that this would be continue, even if it took a few more months before it was useful, it should still secure her future in the order.

Also, she was ashamed of having developed a soft spot for Slither. Her progress would likely spare his life. Not that it was clear what kind of a future the boy could possibly have once he gave them the location of the drakes. The child's life was probably forfeit, but maybe she could have him spared if he were to join their ranks.

After the training was finished for the day, Elise put her plan in motion. She retired to her quarters and penned a lengthy letter to the Mother Superior.

At the start of the fourth week, a response was received. The Mother Superior was eager to see the results which Elise had written about. They should expect her to arrival the following day.

A week before her deadline.

Elsie was shocked. She wasn't ready, and more importantly, Slither wasn't ready.

Elise patiently waited outside of Slither's room. With news of her progress, the Mother Superior, herself, had come to view the results. Communication with the boy was still rough, but she believed that she had formed enough of a bond with the boy to stay his execution.

At least, that's what Elise hoped.

The Mother Superior rarely was known for granting extensions on one of her decrees, but with the chance of potentially wiping out the remainder of the drakes at their source, it was a real possibility. It seemed like the best motivation Elise could ask for.

Elsie was impatient, but nearly an hour passed before the leader of The Draconic Order made her way down the hallway. Even dressed casually, her clothing and jewels were worth more than what most of the guards would earn in a lifetime of service.

Elise feigned stoicism while the Order's elder made her way down the hall and finally stopped before her.

You have news?" she uttered, clearly not impressed with what she saw.

"Yes, Mother Superior, we've made great strides with communicating with the boy and…"

She was cut off.

"Has he told you where they breed? Where we can eliminate them all at once?"

"No."

The Mother Superior sneered. "Fine, let us see this progress you claim to have made before I decide what to do with the cur."

The two walked into the room. She could tell the Mother Superior was surprised. Before them, Slither sat quietly at a desk. The boy was no longer naked, covered in hair, and snarling. He sat before them fully clothed, and appeared to be studying a children's puzzle.

He was so lost in working on solving it that he hadn't heard them come in until Elise cleared her throat.

Slither jumped up, startled, a look of his old self briefly flashed across his face before he broke into a smile at seeing her.

"Elise!" he laughed.

It was clear from the Mother Superior's face that the last thing she had expected was for the savage boy to look normal. Not only that, but he had spoken.

Maybe, just maybe, this wasn't a lost cause after all.

Elsie spoke calmly. "Now Slither, today we're going to have a talk with the Mother Superior here."

He looked between the two and seemed to understand.

"She has a few questions for you. I don't know if you'll be able to answer them, but I'd like you to try."

The three sat down.

"Slither." The Mother Superior began, "I'd like you to tell me about the drakes."

"Drakes?" he said questioningly.

'We haven't gone over that word yet. I told you we weren't ready for that."

The Mother Superior took a pile of scrolls from within her velvet robes.

She looked at the writing on the sides and slowly lined them up in them in order and looked at Elise.

"How do you teach this cur something new?"

"Well, usually I bring in food, and after a meal, I show him a new object and say *this is called* and say the new word."

"Have you tried pictures?"

"Yes, but he hasn't learned to respond to pictures. We're still on names, mostly. Sentences and abstract ideas are out of his reach at this point."

The Mother Superior unrolled the first scroll and showed it to her. It was an intricately drawn image of a drake. The small dragon in the drawing stood on its hind legs with its claws extended and its mouth filled with teeth.

"Teach him."

Elise looked at the image and up at Slither. She took the scroll and moved around the table. She placed it before the boy and his entire face lit up at the image. That same unnerving caricature of a smile was once more plastered across his face. He laughed.

This wasn't the type of reaction that would go over well.

"Slither," she pointed at the image, "This is called drake."

He was so lost in the picture that Elise had to repeat herself and finally waved her hand in front of his eyes to get him to focus.

Once more she pointed at the picture, "drake."

"Drake!" he said with enthusiasm. He snarled in a tone she had never heard him use before, "Drake!" he said again, followed by the same tone and snarl.

She couldn't tell if the young boy was excited, or, if he was trying to teach her in the same way she had been teaching him the last month.

Her order's leader quickly unrolled another scroll and Elsie had no time to consider what that could mean. She need more time to think, this was important.

The scroll was another image of a drake. Only, this one was a female and she was surrounded by eggs.

Elise's mouth tightened in a straight line. She knew that even if the boy could learn these words, he wouldn't be able to understand that Mother Superior wanted to know the location of them. Even he did understand, could he explain it to them with his limited vocabulary?

"Drake egg." She pointed to the new picture. Slither still had problems combining words, but she wanted to be clear exactly what they were looking for.

He looked at the picture, back at her, and back at the picture. Elise couldn't tell what he was thinking.

Slowly, he pointed to the eggs in the image and quite perfectly repeated, "Drake egg."

The Mother Superior jumped up with a look of triumph on her face quickly unrolled another one of the scrolls.

This one was larger than the rest, and instantly it was clear that it was an intricate map of the area. Elsie could identify most of the area from the local landmarks on the map. Anyone who had travelled in the area at all should recognize many of them. For someone who had lived their entire existence here...

Slither studied the map. His eyes shone in a way that Elise had never seen before. Slowly, he moved his finger over the castle they were in. From there, he pointed to the woods where he had been taken prisoner. A look of anger flashed across his face.

"The drake eggs." The Mother Superior shouted. She pointed first at the image and then waved her hand over the map, "Where are the drake eggs?"

He raised his eyes and stared into the face of the woman he hadn't met before today.

"Drake eggs" he repeated and moved his hand over the original picture. He smiled again.

"Yes. Yes, you cur, where are the drake eggs? Tell me." Mother Superior again moved her hands over the map. Elise could tell this was going to go nowhere fast.

Only, this time when Slither responded, the voice he used was not his own.

Slither's fingers traced over the map and a strange deep voice that spoke in complete sentences came from the child's mouth. "You wish to know where the drake eggs are."

"Yes!" The Mother Superior shouted. She hadn't noticed the change in his demeanor, or that he had asked a question in a complete sentence, but Elise had noticed and she slowly backed away from the table.

Something was wrong.

"You've spent a lifetime in hate. You pretend to worship the dragons, but all the while you use the powers at your disposal to hunt down the last descendant they left upon this world. And all because one of them hurt you when you were a child."

The color drained for the Mother Superior's face. For the first time that Elise could remember, her face showed emotion. The fear flared in her eyes and was etched in the wrinkles around her tightly clenched mouth.

"No. I..." her voice trailed off.

"You would trade the one belief you claim to have for revenge on an entire species. And all to punish one who you provoked in the first place. He may have scarred your body, but you are the one who took it as an insult, you are the one who scarred your mind."

Slither threw his head back and Mother Superior backed away.

His entire body arced and he screamed in pain and rage. The smell of sulphur filled the room. He held onto the desk before him with both hands and flames erupted from his mouth. Tears streamed down his face as his fiery breath turned the parchment scrolls to ash and scarred the table before his fire reached its intended target.

The Mother Superior screamed, but the sound only lasted a moment as the flames engulfed her.

Elise hugged the far wall of the room and huddled in terror while the leader of her order burned before her eyes. Leathery skin and muscle peeled away and her bones blackened within the inferno.

Then. As quickly as it had happened, Slither closed his mouth and the fire went out. Smoke and the reek of burning flesh filled the air, but the flames were gone.

Slither, slumped backward into his seat.

He sobbed.

Elise quietly slipped along the wall toward the door.

The metallic voice spoke once more from the child's mouth.

"The Draconic Order once worshipped the dragons and all their brethren. The order was betrayed by this woman. She has led you astray for her own purposes. You have been betrayed by her alliances."

Slither turned to look at her and old eyes, not a child's eyes, shone in anger in his face.

"When you lead them, and from this day forth you will lead them. Seek not revenge, but understanding. Seek not to conquer, but rather seek peace. Spare this child and seek the old ways. Or one day, maybe hundreds of years from now, you'll know her pain. I can come back. You won't like it if I come back."

Suddenly, Slither's head jerked up and his hands reached for his throat. Pain flashed across his face. He looked at the smoldering remains across from him, and he tried to scream, but yet was unable to utter a sound.

Elsie crossed the room and took the silent boy in her arms. She wiped away his tears. She used her perfectly modulated calming voice. "It's alright. You and I will stay together. We have much to teach each other. It's alright."

***

Stuart Conover is a father, husband, rescue dog owner, horror author, blogger, journalist, horror enthusiast, comic book geek, science fiction junkie, and IT professional. With all of that to cram in on a daily basis, it is highly debatable that he ever is able to sleep and rumors have him attached to an IV drip of caffeine to get through most days.

A resident in the suburbs of Chicago, most of Stuart's fiction takes place in the Midwest if not the Windy City itself. From downtown to the suburbs to the cornfields - the area is ripe for urban horror.

'Oceans' was released on April 14th, 2020, and contains five of his drabbles: "His Last Days at Sea", "Lost Beneath the Waves", "The Last Resort," "The Lost Isles," and "The Self-Sustaining Outpost."

'Solitude' was released on January 14th, 2020, and reprints his story "We Lost Charlie Today" which was originally released in 'Soul Survivors Volume II.'

'Horror USA: California' was released on December 13th, 2019, and reprints his story "Fry Machete's Monsters, Munchies, and Mayhem" which was originally released in 'Dead of Winter.'

'Trembling With Fear: Year 2' was released on July 5th, 2019 which he co-edited with Stephanie Ellis and contains a number of his drabbles.

GOING NATIVE

By Rie Sheridan Rose

Grimspiltzafit was lost. Tired. Where were the Olders? Had they left him behind? The ship was not due to depart for several time-units. Surely, they wouldn't have gone without him. The Olders would have noticed him missing...wouldn't they?

They *had* been arguing over soil samples, and he hadn't been able to get their attention despite his best efforts. He'd gotten bored with the bickering. So, he decided to go exploring on his own...but now, he could no longer hear their voices, and he hadn't paid attention to the path as he daydreamed his way down it. He had no idea which way would lead him back to the Olders.

What should he do?

His lower appendages ached. The ground was full of stones, and they bit into his unshod phalanges. It was hard to breathe in this heavy air. He was miserable.

Slumping down on the cold hard ground, he shuddered himself to sleep. A piercing cry started Grimspiltzafit awake. He bolted upright then cringed against the wavy vegetation around him. There was a strange creature about a meter high pointing a thin tentacle at him. He didn't understand the language the creature was speaking, but the excited tone came through clearly. Grimspiltzafit couldn't understand what the squeaking creature was trying to communicate, but he did understand the tentacled appendages reaching toward him.

He bit down hard on his back teeth twice, and the translator device built into his molars clicked in. Now the shrill noises resolved into words he could understand.

"Mama! Mama, look! What is it, Mama? Can I keep it?"

His internal defenses kicked in, and he played dead.

As he lay there, he felt the creature's pointy tentacles prodding him, and then the sensation of being lifted from the ground. There was a feeling of being crushed that brought a squeak of surprise from him.

He opened his eyes a crack to see the squeaking creature now clutched him to its chest, rocking back and forth crooning a little song. The creature's warmth was actually quite pleasant. This close to the creature, he got an impression of youth. The being seemed much the same age as he, if skin texture and limb length were any indication— perhaps even slightly younger. Long strings of a muddy brown color grew from its head, and, when it opened its mouth, he could see a hole where its two front teeth were missing. That must make eating difficult...

It saw that Grimspiltzafit was awake and bent even lower, exhaling a warm, sweet breath into his face. His nose wrinkled as he attempted to unravel the complex components of that breath. He recognized none of the notes involved. This world was so different from his own. How would he survive without the Olders? He didn't know what was safe to eat or drink; where he could safely sleep; how he could get away from the ugly creature now clutching him in a death-grip.

***

It turned out the creature's name was Elsa, and it was a she—much to Grimspiltzafit's surprise. He would never have expected someone so tiny to be female. In his experience females were huge, and the males the small ones. It was just one of many assumptions he had to learn to reject.

Elsa proved a good teacher. Well, aside from the doll clothes thing. At least that didn't last too long.

Once she had taught him the rudiments of her language, he spoke to her Olders. They were surprised by his plight, but listened and reacted well. The female Older—much more what he expected of a female—even took him "shopping" to buy clothing of his own. They fit much better than the doll clothes.

As the days began to shorten, it came time for Elsa to enter the education center for daily instruction. Curious, Grimspiltzafit—who now went by the name of George—decided to go with her. The "Mom" Older had written a note to the officials of the education center to insure that the two of them would not be separated...though he wasn't sure what "interpersonal dependencies" meant.

Still, it was comforting to be together. He held Elsa's hand as tightly as he could, afraid he might lose her in the crowd chattering in the hallway. Though he had been with Elsa's pod for several weeks now, he had never seen so many "humans" in one place—and these were mostly small like they were.

He tugged on his cap anxiously. No one else was wearing a hat in the education center. He followed Elsa into a room where a tall, slender female stood greeting the "children" as they walked into the chamber.

The female stuck out an arm to block his entrance.

"Hold on there, mister. No hats allowed in the classroom."

George—he had to get used to thinking of himself as that—froze. "I—"

Elsa thrust out another of Mom's notes. "My brother has a condition," she said confidently. "He has a note from the doctor."

They had decided the cap was easier to explain than the fact that he had no hair and two small breathing horns on his head. The horns were only used in cases of emergency, but he couldn't hide them if he had to remove the hat.

The "teacher"—that was the word for the human education dispensers—frowned slightly as she skimmed the note.

"Well, if the doctor says it's necessary, I suppose we have to deal with it. I'll explain to the class so that we don't have a dozen caps in the room tomorrow. Come stand by me at the head of the class. Elsa, you can save him a seat, but go sit down now."

Elsa squeezed George's hand, and moved to the back of the room where she set her backpack on the desk next to the window and sat down in the next desk over. George mouthed a "thank you." The window would help him feel stabilized in this tiny room.

"Class, my I have your attention please."

The whispers stopped as the children assumed a face forward position of expectant interest.

"My name is Mrs. Wright, and I will be your teacher this year. There won't be too many rules, as long as you listen and behave. Now, this is George. He has a medical condition that makes it very bad for his head to be in the sunlight. That is why he gets to wear his cap in the classroom. As none of the rest of you seem to be exhibiting the same condition, don't expect to get the same treatment. No one else gets to wear a hat in school."

George felt his interior heating rise. They would think him a sissy...but it couldn't be helped. The horns were worse.

"Go and sit down now, George, so we can begin class."

He nodded, practically running to the saved seat.

There were a few more whispers, but generally his "classmates" seemed more interested in the teacher's instruction than his anomalies. He opened the book that Elsa indicated, and found the place.

Mrs. Wright had an engaging style of teaching, and he was soon quite engrossed in the studies. Though rudimentary compared to his studies on the home-world, he felt that this "education" of theirs had potential. The studies she was providing would definitely aid his understanding of this world and its language.

***

"C'mon, Georgie...it's prom! I don't have anyone else to take me..."

George yawned, running a hand through the wig he'd taken to wearing instead of a hat when they hit middle school. He rocked back on the rear legs of his chair. "What about Freddie?"

"He's going with Anna...c'mon!"

"Maybe I already have a date. It's possible."

"Grimspiltzafit, you cut that out!"

He let the chair crash to the floor. "Damn, Elsa! You haven't called me that in a long time."

"Well...you are acting like an alien at the moment. So superior and smug and...and..." She burst into tears. "I just want to go to prom. It's my last chance before we graduate."

George rose to his feet and threw an arm around her shoulder. They were almost of a height—short for a man, tall for a woman. "Of course, I'll take you, Elsie. I was just teasing. You're my best friend *and* my sister—and if I didn't, Mom would kill me."

She swiped at the tears, favoring him with a watery grin. "Darn right, mister! And don't you forget it."

George pulled her into a hug. Getting found by the Flynns was the best thing that ever happened to him. Without them, he probably would have died out there in the woods, but they had accepted him, given him food and shelter, and helped him feel like part of a family again. He wouldn't let Elsa down for the world.

Memories flowed through his mind. The time they built a lemonade stand and forgot the sugar—but still sold out because people felt sorry for "the cancer kid" as he was perceived. The tree-house in the woods where he told her all about his world—the purple trees swaying like palm fronds, the glitter of the crystal buildings in the sunlight, the ships zipping about like fireflies in the night. The time they snuck out with a pack of cigarettes and a beer to see what they were like—they both took one puff and immediately felt sick...and the beer was left untouched.

Elsa was the truest friend, the closest family he had ever had. If she wanted to go to prom, he'd make it the best experience of her life.

***

The night of the prom was spangled with stars twinkling in a midnight sky. George looked up at them with none of the yearning that had wracked his heart in the early days on Earth. He smiled. His heart was here now.

He looked over at Elsa, her eyes shining almost as brightly as the stars.

"You ready?"

Biting her lip, she nodded.

"Let's do this then." He took her hand, and they stepped into the gym.

The hanger-like building had been transformed into an underwater paradise. Blue gels softened the lighting, and large cardboard sea animals had been taped to the walls. The refreshments were set up on tables made to look like large rocks.

He leaned over and whispered, "They went a little overboard, don't you think?"

"I think it is beautiful," she breathed, squeezing his hand. "I feel like a mermaid princess."

"You look like one, too," he answered with a grin. "Just don't trip on that train."

He led her over to the punch-bowl and got them a couple of drinks. "Shall we find a table?"

They dropped their things onto an empty table out of the main flow of traffic and sat sipping the punch. It had an odd aftertaste, but he put that down to nerves. He'd been practicing in secret for weeks…

"Would you like to dance?" he asked Elsa, as the music changed from pounding rhythm to something slow and sensual.

She blinked. "Really?"

"Well, it isn't much of a prom if you just sit here in the dark and watch, now is it?"

The radiance of her smile took his breath away.

"Sure." She placed her hand in his, and he took her onto the dance floor.

He twirled her into his arms, and she lay her head on his shoulder with a sigh. "This is perfect, Georgie."

"Don't say that until you're safely back at the table. I'm not quite sure I've got it right."

She laughed softly, and his heart swelled. Yeah, this was perfect…

A sense of euphoria began to bubble up inside him as they glided across the floor. The night was the best thing ever. She was the most beautiful girl he'd ever met. Things were absolutely per—

"Watch where you're going, numb-nuts!" growled a masculine voice behind him. The words were followed by a sharp shove that almost pitched him to the floor.

Elsa cried out.

George let go of her hand and turned…into a punch to the jaw. This time he did crash to the floor.

"What the—?" He tried to focus his eyes on the youth leaning over him, but something was wrong.

"You've been asking for that for twelve years, Georgie-boy," said his attacker. "Thinking you are too good to follow the rules. Don't need no cap now. Why is that? What makes you so special?"

George's heart sank. Billy Sullivan. He'd had it in for George ever since Mrs. Wright sent him to the principal's office in the first grade. He'd made George's life a living hell every chance he got.

"S-sorry, Billy. Did I bump into you? I'm not that great a dancer."

"You and me have a score to settle, son. Outside. Ten minutes."

George worked his jaw as Billy stalked off. "What the hell did I do to him?"

Elsa offered him a hand up. "You were different. You did too well in class. He's been a bully all his life. He wanted to be better than everyone, and he's not better than you."

George got to his feet. "Let's finish our drinks. I need a minute to think."

"Yeah. I don't feel like dancing anymore."

They wove their way back to their table, only to find their drinks a purple stain in the center of the white tablecloth. Elsa's purse had been dumped atop it.

She began stuffing things back into her bag, obviously blinking back tears.

George struggled to control his own temper. "C'mon. We'll grab another drink on the way out."

"You aren't going to fight him, are you, Grimspiltzafit?" she whispered urgently. "You'll kill him!"

"No. I'll try not to hurt him. But if I don't show up, he'd ruin the rest of our night—and maybe our lives."

"I guess you have a point." She accepted a new drink and took a sip. "Why are some boys just stupid like that?"

"A universal question, sis." He chugged his own drink, the odd aftertaste spiking a rush of restless energy through his nervous system. He felt like he could lift a car in one hand. "Let's go take care of this once and for all."

Elsa looked up at him with a frown. "Do you have to, Georgie? Can't we just pretend he's gone home and enjoy the prom?" Her tone was wistful.

"I wish we could, Elsie, but you know we can't. It would just make him suspicious. We can't have that, can we?"

He slipped a finger under her chin. "Don't worry, sister mine—I promise not to hurt him...too bad." He felt every nerve in his body vibrating like a tuning wire. He'd never felt this way before.

Striding back into the star-filled night, he took a deep breath. His night-vision was better than human, and he could see Billy lounging against his car on the other side of the lot. "You wait here, Elsa," he called over his shoulder as he started for the car.

She opened her mouth to protest, but he shook his head. "I mean it, Elsa. You don't want to see this up close."

Her hand flew to her mouth. "What are you going to do?"

His brow lowered. "Be myself," he replied grimly.

He squared his shoulders and stalked across the dark parking lot. Billy Sullivan had six inches and at least fifty pounds on him, but he was tired of pretending to be a weak little nobody. Especially with the energy running through him. Tonight, he would show the bully his *true* self.

As he reached Billy, his hands automatically formed fists. His chest filled with air, and he willed the muscles to tense. It had been a long time since he let himself *be* himself. He was almost looking forward to this.

He raised his fist, ready to smash it into Billy's face. Before he could follow through, a beam of light pierced the darkness from over their heads.

Grimspiltzafit raised a hand to shade his eyes. The beam shimmered with refractions of light that he hadn't seen since he was a mere podling. He could make out the shape of the ship now.

They had come back for him! After all this time…

Billy was on his knees on the tarmac of the parking lot, rocking back and forth as he stared at the descending ship.

It was just a shuttle. Not that much larger than one of the school buses. Down it came, to rest on three supports. A hatch opened in the side of the shuttle, and a ramp extended.

Grimspiltzafit came to attention automatically, his early training clicking into gear. He heard running footsteps coming their way. Damn...Elsa.

She skidded to a stop beside him, her mouth dropping open as she saw the being coming down the ramp. "Is that...?" she whispered, clutching at Grimspiltzafit's arm.

"An Older," he said out of the side of his mouth.

The being coming down the ramp wasn't one of his pod. He'd never even seen it before. Its size argued it was a female, and the breathing horns curling above its head said it was of high rank. Why was it here? And why after all this time?

The being surveyed the three of them, eyes sweeping them coldly. Then its eyes locked on Grimspiltzafit. "You are the podling who was left behind?" it said in the language of his people.

George stepped in front of Elsa. "Yeah. What of it?" He spoke the old language, but in the idiom of his upbringing.

The alien recoiled as if slapped. "How dare you speak so familiarly to a member of the Nine!"

"Why would a member of the Nine come to find me after all these years?"

"It should be enough for you that I *have* come to retrieve you and take you back to the home world."

"It's been a dozen years. Why would you bother?"

"Since when would a podling from a third-class pod question its betters? Your Olders were concerned. They felt unease when you did not return to their ship. It was not their place to remain on this world and search. They had duties to fulfill. They reported to home world as was proper. They petitioned the Nine for intervention as was protocol."

"I wasn't far away from the ship. Why didn't they take a few minutes to look? It wasn't against protocol to spend an hour looking!" Grimspiltzafit felt his chest heaving with anger. Why hadn't they looked for him? Mom and Dad would have looked for Elsa until they found her. Any human parent would have.

The alien looked down her nose at the three youngsters, then focused once more on Grimspiltzafit. "You may have been born to a pod on Celene Selta, but you are no longer Celena. To speak so to a member of the Nine; to raise your hand to another; to fraternize with an…" It shuddered. "…inferior creature like this one." It gestured toward Elsa. "You have been raised…*human*. There is no place for you on Celene Selta."

It turned and ascended the ramp, which withdrew behind it. The ship rose into the night, banked, and disappeared into the stars.

"W-what the hell was that?" Billy shrieked.

"Apparently, I am too human to go home," George sighed, shaking his head. "And to think I've spent half my life trying to be *more* human."

Elsa threw her arms around him. "I guess you are stuck here, Grimspiltzafit."

George hugged her back. "There's no place I'd rather be stuck, Elsie."

"Uh…sorry about earlier, Geo—Grimspil…whatever. I promise I'll leave you alone from now on."

George reached up and pulled off his wig. His breathing horns uncoiled in the night air. "From now on, I'm not pretending to be what I'm not anymore." He tossed the wig to the ground and reached a hand to Billy. "But if I am going to reveal myself to the world, I could use a friend who knows the truth."

Billy looked at the outstretched hand, and then reached out and took it. "Proud to help."

George hauled the other boy to his feet. "Let's get back inside. I promised Elsa we'd dance."

***

Rie Sheridan Rose multitasks. Her short stories appear in numerous anthologies, including On Fire, Hides the Dark Tower, and Killing It Softly Vol. 1 and 2. She has authored twelve novels, six poetry chapbooks, and lyrics for dozens of songs.

SWIM WITH THE BEAVERS

By Robert Allen Lupton

My first view of Castor National Wildlife Refuge was from the air. The helicopter circled the ranger's cabin in the wilderness and made its approach to land. The refuge consisted of a large pond created by a beaver dam on a large creek. There were several hundred acres of virgin forest surrounding the pond in every direction. I could see the tops of aspen, alder, and cottonwood trees among the pines and firs that dominated the forest. Willow trees drooped over the edge of the pond.

The pilot continued his approach by skimming over the pond. Cattails, lilies, and other water flora speckled the glistening surface. The ducks and geese squawked to protest our passage and scrambled madly into the air.

A ranger standing in front of the cabin shielded his eyes from the sun as he watched our approach. The pilot put us gently on the ground, killed the engine, and removed his headset.

"Let's hurry, Don, I've only got about thirty minutes' turnaround time. We need to get your supplies unloaded and I need to get back in the air."

We climbed down from the aircraft, automatically keeping our heads lower than we needed to in order to avoid the slowing helicopter rotors. The ranger approached, and I stepped forward to meet him.

"Hi, I'm Donald Blaine. Call me, Don."

"Gary Davis," he said. "Glad to have you here. Let's get the plane unloaded. Jim is a great pilot, but he's a real crybaby when you mess with his schedule."

Jim made a rude gesture to Don and helped unload the supplies and my duffel bags from the plane. He made a quick run to the bushes and washed his hands at the pump outside the cabin. He shivered and said, "Damn, I always forget how cold this water is. So, Gary, I'll be back in a month with the next supply run. I guess this is your last month here. Don, if there is anything you want me to bring next month, use the satellite phone to let me know."

After the helicopter left, Gary said, "We need to get the supplies inside and secured. The raccoons will be in the food if we don't. What the raccoons don't eat, the bears will. I'll show you where the storage lockers are."

It took about an hour to get everything put away.

There were three benches on the front porch. I took the glass of sun tea he offered and we sat in the shade of the cabin. "How long have you been here, Gary?"

"Ten years. When my wife died, I needed to be by myself. You know, the Forest Service has a couple dozens of these small refuges in inaccessible locations around the country. This one is not even on any list. It's a secret, but you know that."

"Yeah, they made me sign a non-disclosure agreement when I took this assignment. I only signed up for a year. You've been here for ten years?"

"I've always felt like this is where I belong. The only people I see are the supply pilots. My bosses came with him three times. I expect they wanted to be sure that I hadn't gone completely native. Every time I got a new boss, I got a visit. Our last boss, Mrs. Wilkins, seemed happy that I wasn't running around barefoot in a loincloth. You have to keep up the rituals of daily life or you will go crazy. Shave, wash your clothes, wash yourself, and wear your uniform."

"Shave and take showers?"

"You bet. The Forest Service put in a solar system right before I took this assignment. You don't get television, but you can get television and movie recordings delivered with the supplies. You don't have internet, but if you'd wanted internet, you wouldn't have taken this job. The solar electric system will give you lights at night, make sure you have hot water, and power the electric appliances. There's no air conditioning, you don't need it this far north. There's no heat, either. I have enough wood chopped and cured to get you through the first winter. I always told myself, if you want to be warm every day, you have to chop some wood every day."

We stayed quiet for a moment and watched the birds returning to the pond. The ducks fly the last few seconds parallel to the water and take some ragged steps as they walk on top of the water until they finally settle on the surface. Geese, swans, and cranes land the same way on water. "I've never seen this many waterfowl on one pond."

"This is a large, active beaver pond. It's been here a long time. A healthy beaver pond is attractive to migratory waterfowl. You will have birds all year, but they'll change with the seasons. The beaver families keep up the dam and the pond. The birds enjoy the benefits without doing any of the work. I have minks and otters living here, too. They typically live upstream this time of year. The otters like to play and hunt in the running water above the dam. The mink tend to hunt on shore most of the time. During season, they'll spend hours catching crawfish in the shallows and eating them."

I finished my tea and he refilled my glass. "I didn't know there were any secret refuges when I went to work for the Forest Service. Do you know why this is a secret refuge?

"You bet. There's a ranger's log inside the cabin. The first entry is in 1905. It's by the first ranger assigned here. He started building what became this cabin. The first log entries are about how and why this refuge came to be. He tells it better than I ever could. I've been by myself too long to talk much. Let's take a walk and I'll show you around the refuge. You can read the log tonight and we'll talk about it in the morning."

The beaver dam was over a hundred feet long. That was big, but not the biggest. There's a dam in Canada over a half mile wide. That's wider than Hoover Dam. Several beavers were doing maintenance on the dam or gathering food. A large part of the forest was covered with new growth timber. When beavers harvest the older trees, new shoots come up in the area newly open to sunlight. The new tender aspen and other trees are some of the beavers' favorite foods.

The beavers I could see were all a pale brown, almost tan or beige in color. When the sunlight glinted off their wet fur just right, they appeared to have golden fur. The California Beaver was sometimes called the California Golden Beaver, but these weren't California beavers. The American Beaver normally comes in colors from a black brown to a very light brown. These beavers had fur much paler than light brown. It had a distinctive yellow hue. I mentioned it to Gary.

"Yes, these are the most golden colored beavers that I have ever seen. They're larger than normal, too. The adult males weigh over one hundred pounds and can stand over three feet tall. The females are nearly that big. At least two hundred beavers live in this colony. The large size and light coloration gets reinforced with every generation. Like all beavers, this group is aggressively territorial. Interlopers are violently encouraged to leave."

"Doesn't the golden color make them easier for predators to see?"

"Probably, but a hundred-pound beaver is not easy prey. These guys outweigh everything in the area, except bears. They're bigger than a bobcat or a lynx. The owl or eagle that can carry off a beaver this size hasn't been hatched. Beavers are great parents and protect their offspring very well. The young are guarded until they reach breeding age, two or three years old. This colony takes protection to a new level. See the sentries posted around the pond and the beaver lodge? One tail slap on the water and every beaver will be under water in seconds. These boys even fight as a team. You know how big their teeth are? One of the big males could break your leg with one swipe of its tail. They won't bother you if you don't threaten their kits. I've watched them lure a mountain lion into the water. They climbed on top the lion's head and held it under so that it drowned in a matter of seconds."

"Sounds like you really like these beavers."

"I named a bunch of them, but I'll let you come up with your own names for them. The first ranger used to make up sayings 'bout the golden beavers. I've amused myself over the years by continuing that tradition. The golden beaver waddles, but it does not run. The golden beaver watches, but he does not intervene. The golden beaver bites, but he does not chew. I know my sayings sound silly, but I like them. One you will want to remember is, 'when the golden beaver sounds the alarm, look to your own safety.' You don't want to fight off a bear, a lion, or even a pissed off bobcat."

We laughed and hiked back to the cabin. After dinner, he gave me the logbook. I settled into the rustic chair, poured myself a scotch, and opened the book. The brittle pages were yellowed and the edges had crumbled. Someone had placed clear tape on the edges to keep them from crumbling any more. The ink had faded to a deep brown. The hand was quite legible. That night, I read the entry written by the first ranger. Gary and I talked about it the next day.

We talked about it every day until Gary left me alone at the refuge. During my years at the refuge, I copied every word in the first ranger's log. What follows is what he wrote. I haven't edited it or commented on it. You can read it exactly as I did that night in the cabin.

Get something to drink and make yourself comfortable. Once you start reading the ranger's story, you'll want to finish it. I think it helps to be sitting in an overstuffed chair in front of a softly burning fireplace, but that's up to you. Just make sure your phone is turned off and you have the time to read without interruption. When you're ready, start at the beginning.

My name is Benjamin Castor. It is March 3, 1905. It is only fitting that I am the first Forest Ranger here in this national refuge created by Teddy Roosevelt and named after my family. Actually, it is named after my great grandfather, Nathan Castor. This is the way my father told his grandfathers' story to me.

You learned about Paul Bunyan, Pecos Bill and Johnny Appleseed in school. You know their legends and their stories, but you don't know the story of my grandfather, Nathan. Nathan and his parents had started west in a Conestoga wagon just before the War. Nathan was a blond-haired, blue-eyed three-year-old. His father, like all his family, was a loner. The family was headed west alone in their wagon. "I don't need to pay no trail guide," Nathan's father said, "We just need to go west until we find the mountains."

Unfortunately, along the way were rivers and streams to cross. The family had no experience in finding or making safe crossings. This shortcoming made fording every swollen creek an exercise in terror. During an attempted crossing of a stream that was just below flood stage, Nathan was washed out of the wagon and swept downstream. The family searched for a couple of days and then headed west toward the next dangerous river crossing.

Nathan struggled to keep his head above the rushing waters. He was able to grab a branch that he instinctively used as a flotation device. Unable to swim and too young to understand how to work toward either bank, Nathan just held the branch and rode the current until it deposited him, cold and exhausted, against the side of a pile of mud and sticks blocking one side of the stream. He lay there shivering until he cried himself to sleep.

While Nathan was riding the current, Chee, a female beaver, returned after a full day working with the rest of the colony to repair the damages that the rushing water was doing to their dam. She had fed well and her teats were heavy with milk. She needed to feed her kits. She swam down and entered the underwater passage to her living chamber. When she climbed onto the first level, the drying off level, she knew something was wrong. She didn't hear the kits, who should be whining for food. There was light in the chamber, there shouldn't be light. She hurried onto the higher nesting level. The top had been torn away and her kits were gone. She could smell bear. A bear had done this.

Chee climbed out of her chamber through the hole the bear had torn open. She looked and sniffed for the bear. It was gone. She could smell the bear and she could smell something else. It was a new animal, one she had never smelled before. She followed the scent along the top of the dam. She found Nathan plastered with mud and debris laying halfway in the water.

She cautiously approached the creature. It woke up while she sniffed and it hugged her with both arms. Chee knew this was a child by its smell. She needed a child and she could tell that this child needed a mother. She rolled gently onto her back and offered the food that only a mother can provide. After the man-child finished nursing, Chee eventually taught him by trial and error to hold firmly to her fur. She pulled Nathan along the edge of the dam. She didn't hesitate to dive when she came to the section outside of her chamber. Nathan automatically held his breath for the few seconds they were underwater.

She deposited him on the drying floor and climbed to join her mate, Snik, who was already repairing the damage caused by the bear. Snik knew the kits were gone. The mated pair acknowledged each other's sense of loss and then got on with the business of repairing the chamber roof. The golden beaver is sad, but it does not grieve.

Snik and Chee used their noses to encourage Nathan to climb from the drying floor to the sleeping floor. Snik followed Chee's lead and they accepted the young human into their lives.

Snik took charge of Nathan's training. Nathan accompanied Snik on his daily rounds. There were trees to cut, lilies to be eaten and repairs to be made. They don't say busy as a beaver for no reason. Nathan would hold on to Snik's fur and Snik would carry him through the water.

Snik and Chee were excellent parents. Three-year-old Nathan weighed about thirty-five pounds. All of the adult beavers were over twice his size. The other beavers came to accept Nathan. They called him Tis-Chik, which means 'no-tail' if you speak beaver. My grandfather called himself Tis-Chik most of the time. At first, Tis-Chik traveled around the pond carried on the back of Snik. Little by little, he learned to swim for himself. He couldn't swim like a beaver because he didn't have a tail. He developed his own method of swimming. He kept his feet together and undulated them up and down. He used his arms in a three-quarters sideways motion. By the time he was five, he had beaver-like speed in the water. Tis-Chik could hold his breath for ten minutes or more. This wasn't as long as a beaver could stay underwater, but it was amazing for a human of any age. His body strength was more than any civilized twelve-year-old. He was faster on land than on water and could outrun the fastest member of the colony.

He learned that he could eat lilies and cattails. Unlike the beavers, he needed meat. He taught himself to catch crawfish and minnows, which he devoured whole. He learned to catch fish by building small dams and waiting until the fish swam into the areas he had dammed up. He would quickly break the dam and then pick up the fish when the water drained out.

He never hunted waterfowls or the birds that lived in the trees around the pond. However, he would raid their nests for eggs on a regular basis. Waving a large stick overhead, he was a match for the most protective duck or goose. He discovered that he could climb trees. He could serve as guard for the colony or he could steal eggs from a bird's nest. Frequently he climbed the trees just for fun. Like children everywhere, the young beavers played games like tag, king of the colony, and keep away. Tis-Chik would snatch a choice aspen branch from an unsuspecting beaver and dash for the nearest tree. He would climb up just far enough to be out of reach and then torment his pursuer with a barrage of insults and small branches.

Whenever Chee saw him in a tree, she would scold him for his behavior. His mock apologies, accompanied by some tender choice bark stripped from the upper branches, were always accepted.

The language of the beavers is a collection of clicks, whistles, squeaks, barks and grunts. Inflections inaudible to the human ear give the same word many different meanings. Tis can mean no, nothing, never, or leave now, depending on how it is used. This was easy for Tis-Chik. However, beavers also communicate by slapping their tails on the water. Tis-Chik used cupped hands to mimic a tail slap. Two hard, fast slaps are the beaver danger warning. Three slow slaps call for help to dismantle a fallen tree or to share a new found crop of water lilies. Grandfather thought three slow slaps meant, 'good food', come and join me.

The young beavers teased Barton about his small teeth and lack of tail. He tried making a tail from birch bark. He shaped it carefully and tied it around his waist with vines he selected for that purpose. The birch bark tail looked good enough on land, but it was a problem in the water. The bark interfered with swimming. Once, it had even caught on a branch underneath the water. Tis-Chik almost drowned before he could free himself.

Beavers store food for the winter, they call winter the cold time. Like ants, squirrels, and even some mice, beavers harvest during the warm time and hide the food away for the winter. Beavers take young branches with new bark and embed them in the underwater mud. Perhaps this is the origin of the phrase "food bank." During the winter, a hungry beaver swims from his chamber, bites off a branch, and carries it home to eat at its leisure.

The first cold time was the hardest for Tis-Chik. He couldn't live on bark. He was able to catch fish occasionally. He would dig freshwater mussels out of the mud and break them open between two rocks that he kept on the drying floor. Chee would whistle her displeasure until he had cleaned every piece of broken shell from the chamber. She kept a neat house. Lord knows how she would have been if he had tracked a single broken shell into the sleeping room.

He became inured to the cold. Chee, Snik and their new twins spent most of their time sleeping during the cold time. Except when hunting food, Tis-Chik snuggled with them for warmth.

That first winter, he mastered the beaver language. He also learned of the dangers that faced beavers. He learned about bears, mountain lions, bobcats, and lynx. Snik explained that even a badger, a mink, or a weasel would take a kit left unprotected. Eagles, hawks, and owls were always looking for young beavers. The colony had to guard against these beaver killers.

When spring came, Tis-Chik joined the other beavers inspecting and repairing the dam from the ravages of winter. Food was plentiful. The lilies and cattails were spreading, new shoots and branches were everywhere. The cries of the newborn filled the air. But this spring brought more than new life and good food. This spring brought the bobcat.

After the bobcat took the first kit, the beavers held a council to discuss the problem. The beaver colony's approach to defense against predators was to post sentries, sound the alarm, and hide. Everyone would hide and hope the bobcat took someone else.

Tis-Chik was only four, but he understood that waiting your turn to be sacrificed was a bad idea. He tried to explain that to the colony, but they were not receptive to new ideas from a no-tailed child. The traditional method of dealing with predators was to keep the kits inside the dam. The adults would watch carefully and not stray too far from the water. Eventually, the bobcat would move on.

Tis-Chik argued that many beavers were stronger than one beaver or one bobcat. The council did not agree. The kits would be sequestered and the adults would be vigilant. Three days later, the bobcat took a young female.

A group of young adults that Tis-Chik had played with the previous fall approached him. Chib was a female and the largest in the group. The males would soon outgrow her, but for now, she was the largest. "I lost my friend to the bobcat today. You think we can kill it. Tell us how."

Tis-Chik devised a simple plan. He was the fastest on the ground, not as fast as the bobcat, but faster than any beaver. Tis-Chik would pretend to be hurt and would make loud noises of pain to attract the bobcat. He would pretend to limp as he tried to return to the pond. He would roll around on the ground. The other beavers would lie in wait to attack the bobcat in mass. Tis-Chik did not know the term, but he was creating a gauntlet for the bobcat to run.

They group set up the trap for bobcat the next day. They cleared a narrow trail through a blackberry thicket. They dug out small depressions where they could hide at almost ground level on the side of the trail. Tis-Chik scooped mud over their backs, leaving only their heads above the ground, which were screened by the blackberry foliage.

Tis-Chik positioned himself at the start of the newly cleared trail just outside the thicket. He sat on the ground and cried and moaned as loud as he could. He stood and limped around in a small circle. He fell down and rolled in the dirt.

The bobcat soon came and watched his performance. It watched for a while and began to slink into the opening where Tis-Chik continued his performance. With the confidence of a top predator, the bobcat slowly left cover and stood facing Tis-Chik. The cat pulled his ears flat back and snarled. This display usually froze his prey.

When the bobcat's ears went back, Tis-Chik broke through the blackberry patch toward the pond. The bobcat leaped after him.

A male beaver butted the bobcat hard in the side and rolled it over. As it tumbled, it raked Tis-Chik's haunch with one paw, leaving three deep cuts in his left buttock. Tis-Chik fell to the ground under the blow.

The bobcat hissed, regained its feet, and whirled to face the beaver who had head-butted it. Before the cat finished turning, Chib hit him with her tail. The blow broke both of the cat's hind legs. The other beavers, whistling and chirping in fear and mutual encouragement, surrounded the cat and clubbed it to death with their tails.

The beavers covered the dead bobcat with mud and sticks. They marked the burial site with their scent glands to warn the rest of the colony to stay away.

Chib and Chee took Tis-Chik upstream to where the clear water flowed. They helped him wash his cuts and prepared a poultice of willow bark, chewing the bark to a pulp.

The wound festered and a fever set in. The beavers cleaned the claw marks and changed the willow dressing daily. Tis-Chik chewed the fresh willow bark that the females brought for him and the cuts healed and the fever passed.

The rest of the warm time went without incident. Tis-Chik stored food for the cold time. He laid in a supply of nuts, seeds, and cattails. He also collected mussels from around the pond and from upstream and downstream and placed them near his living chamber. During the cold time, insects and rodents occasionally invaded his food source. Tis-Chik didn't mind, a little protein is always welcome.

Over the next few years, the occasional predator would range into the colony's territory. The beavers had learned to fight together. Occasionally, a beaver was injured or lost, but the Golden Beaver Colony was not easy prey for any animal. The carnivores learned to stay away.

Occasionally, a rogue beaver would wander in from upstream or downstream and try to move into the pond. Beavers are fiercely territorial, and the colony was no exception. Interlopers were met by a squad of angry beavers. The colony thrived. Births were up and the death rate was down. Food was plentiful.

Tis-Chik helped build lodges and dams nearby when young beavers left to start new colonies. He excelled in selecting sites that required the least labor and least material. Soon, he was making all the decisions about repairing and extending the massive dam that housed the colony's many family lodges. When Chib and her mate decided to relocate with their extended family, Chib asked Tis-Chik to help them pick a site.

The beaver pioneers travelled overland for over a week. They passed three streams where other beavers from the main colony had already located. Once the location for Chib's dam was selected, Tis-Chick stayed long enough to help get construction well underway.

Tis-Chik was larger and stronger than any beaver by his fourteenth year. His kept his golden hair chopped to shoulder length using broken mussel shells as clumsy knives. He had learned to throw rocks when he hunted for food. He could stun a rabbit or mouse with almost every throw. Hunger improves your aim.

He became aware that the male and female beavers paired off for their lifetimes and produced one or two young just before spring. He wondered why there was no one for him to pair off with. The female beavers had no interest in him and he felt the same way about them.

That spring, while he pretended to stand watch to help guard the colony, he was actually resting in a walnut tree. He watched two robins build a nest, thinking about how all the animals paired up with another of their kind. He had never seen another of his kind. Chee had tried to explain how the creek had delivered Tis-Chik to her, but he didn't understand. He watched the robins as they worked and hoped there was another beaver like himself somewhere.

A new sound caught his attention. He heard clumsy footsteps tramping toward him. He laid as flat as he could on his tree branch. His dark tanned skin and mud splattered body made him virtually invisible from below.

The thing making the noises walked upright like Tis-Chik. It was covered from head to toe in the skins of dead beavers and deer. It had dead deer skin strapped on its feet. It was dragging a bunch of tree branches tied together, which had a large pile of dead skins and other things tied on top.

Tis-Chik watched while the man made camp near the pond. The man constructed an enclosure from fallen branches, which he covered with beaver skins. He packed his food supplies into another skin and hung his food in the air from a tree branch. He unpacked several shiny things from the pack. He carefully buried these things, one at a time, along the trails where the beaver left the ponds. The man attached each of the things to a tree or to a sharpened branch that he hammered deep into the ground.

Shortly, a beaver waddled from the pond and stepped onto one of the shiny things. There was a loud snap and the beaver was caught by its front paw. He rolled and struggled but could not escape the shiny thing. The man made the rounds of his traps later in the day and found the beaver trapped. From his belt, he took a stick with a sharp rock on one end. He killed and skinned the beaver. He hung the skin to dry on a frame made of branches.

After the man went to sleep, Tis-Chik retrieved the drying skin and put it on the bottom of the lake. He used large rocks to hold it down. He spent the rest of the night moving or destroying the traps. He didn't know the word "trap," but he would learn it later. He threw most of the traps into the water, but he moved two of them into the path the man took when he checked his traps. He attached them to trees, just like the man had done.

The next morning, the man was angry when he saw the hide was gone. He believed some predator, a bear or a cat, had carried it off. He stomped out to check his trap line and immediately stepped on one of his own traps. The sound of his leg breaking was louder than the sound of the trap snapping.

The man sat up and tried to open the trap and remove his foot. Tis-Chik immediately began throwing rocks at him. Hunting birds and rabbits had sharpened his aim. The man screamed and yelled, to no avail. A well-thrown rock knocked him unconscious.

Tis-Chik killed the man with his own skinning knife. He kept the knife, axe, and deer skins. The beaver skins were weighted down on the bottom of the lake. The rest of the man's supplies were scattered. The traps were hidden inside Tis-Chik's sleeping chamber. Such was his first experience with his own kind.

Tis-Chick practiced diligently with the knife and axe. He wore the deer skin pants that he had taken from the trapper. They gave him a way to carry the weapons while leaving his hands free to swim or climb.

This first man was only the beginning. Mankind's demand for beaver coats and hats sent trapper after trapper into the American wilderness. Tis-Chik and his colony met them with the same violent territorial protection that kept mountain lions, bears, and rival beavers away from their home. Men learned to hunt somewhere else.

By the time Tis-Chik was fifteen, the tales of the tall golden beaver and his haunted beaver pond had spread across the society of trappers. They whispered it in taverns. They told it like a ghost story as the firelight faded in camps across the country. The warned each other about the beaver that walked like a man. Many a trapper claimed to have seen the man-like beaver and his pond. "A man can pass through his territory safely. A man can even camp for a night. But, if a man unpacks his traps, he has signed his death warrant."

After the trappers came pioneers. Tis-Chik followed the small bands of families as they moved past his area. He would hide in the forest and watch to learn their ways and their words. The wagons and horses seemed vaguely familiar and he was sure that he knew many of the words that they spoke to each other. Mama and papa seemed familiar.

In his sixteenth summer, he found a large group of pioneers making a permanent settlement three creeks to the west of his pond. They were building their village where two creeks joined to become a river. He watched as they built houses out of logs. He thought this was very intelligent, but didn't understand why the people didn't use mud to hold the logs together. They built their houses too far from the water. He noticed that there were more than one kind of person. There were big people and little people. There were men and women. When he watched the women cleaning themselves in the creek, he got strange feelings inside. He didn't understand, but it made him feel anxious and unsettled. He moved downwind and sniffed. There was no scent of the mating smells the female beavers produced when in season.

He watched through the summer. He watched through the fall. He watched as the men built a dam upstream from the camp. They used their tools and carved large rocks and carefully shaped them. They were making millstones. By winter, they had a functioning mill installed on the creek. They ground acorns and other found nuts that year. The women had cleared an area to plant grains in the coming spring.

Tis-Chick would not have placed the dam where the people built it. It was not a good place. The land was too steep behind the dam. The water backed high up the creek bed instead of spreading out into a placid pond. This narrow, but steep, dammed watercourse provided steady and strong water flow to keep the mill turning, but Tis-Chik knew that, come the spring thaw, this dam could wash away.

There was one of the people that the others called Ruth. Tis-Chik spent much of his time watching her. His colony was doing fine without him. He checked regularly and the lessons that he and Chib had learned were being taught to the new kits. No trapper or predator would dare approach the pond.

Tis-Chik learned some of the people's words. Actually, he was remembering the words, but he didn't know that. He took to leaving small gifts for Ruth. A shiny rock, a pile of mussels or even a beautiful collection of feathers would turn up in her path. She suspected one of the boys in the community was an admirer, but wondered at the bare footprints that she found left in the mud when an offering appeared.

Tis-Chik marked the area around each gift, but the Ruth never acknowledged his markings. She never so much as sniffed a single tree. Perhaps her nose didn't work. He decided to show himself to her when the warm time came.

The cold time came and went. Trees were budding and grasses were sending up new shoots. The colony was filled with the cries of the newly born kits. The waters were flowing fast, fresh and clean beneath the not yet thawed ice coverings over most of the creeks and ponds. The thaw was just beginning.

The people in the village watched the creeks with concern. The creek without the mill rose steadily. It was now impassable and getting higher every day. The mill dam was still holding the other creek back, but the water level in the pond behind it was getting higher and higher. The men worked like beavers, cutting more trees and raising the height of the dam.

Tis-Chik watched their frenzied efforts. This was foolishness. The higher they raised the dam, the more water that would be trapped. The longer it took for the dam to fail, and it would fail, the worse the flood would be. Tis-Chik would have told them if he knew how to tell them, that the right thing to do was to lower the dam and let the water flow evenly, not raise the dam and increase the weight of water pushing against it.

His experience told him that this dam would not hold for another day. Whenever it broke, the rushing water would wash away the houses and people in the village. It would wash away Ruth. What was to be done? Tis-Chik would ask Chib. He would ask the beaver council.

He hurried back to his colony and barked for a council. The beaver gathered at his request and listened as he explained. At first, the beavers had no interest in helping the people. They saw people as just another predator. Chib took his side and insisted that the colony owed Tis-Chik help. "I think these are his creatures," she said. "They smell like him. If we can help, we must. I don't see how we can help, but we must do what we can."

Chee, who was now almost a white beaver, said. "Remember how Tis-Chik would hold onto our fur and we would carry him around the pond? We can go to the people place and Tis-Chik will show them how to hold on to us and we can carry them across the fast waters."

A beaver asked, "What if they won't let us carry them to safety? They could be afraid of us."

Tis-Chik said, "If they won't let us help them, then they die. I have watched them in the water. Some of them can swim, but not many. Even those who can swim, swim badly. Please, let us try. There is no time to lose. The ill-placed dam they built will break today."

The beavers agreed to try and over a hundred beavers set off toward the village. Beavers don't move fast on land and the journey that took Tis-Chik less than an hour was a four-hour hike for the beavers. They arrived on the opposite shore of the creek from the village. The beavers lined up on the edge of the water and stood on their hind legs.

When the people noticed the beavers, they were afraid. The people knew they were trapped by the waters. They thought the beavers had come to watch them drown. They gathered on their side of the ever-widening water and pointed at the beavers and shouted at each other. They waved their arms and ran around in circles. They stopped when Tis-Chik stepped into view. The villagers watched while he and one beaver entered the water. The beaver towed Tis-Chik into the middle of the stream and back to the edge. The maneuver was repeated with a different beaver and then repeated for a third time.

Before Tis-Chik could make a fourth repetition, the first of the men who had been working on the dam ran into the village. "The dam is going, the dam is going," he shouted. "We have to get out."

The people knew that the waters were already too high for them to cross. While the dam had not yet broken, it was failing and the water was flowing faster every minute. The rest of the men staggered into the village. The rising steam was carrying logs torn from the dam past them every second. The streams were too swift for anyone to swim across.

Chib pulled Tis-Chik through the fast waters. The people backed away when they came ashore. Tis-Chik said, "Mama, papa, damn fool, amen." The people stared at him. He unwrapped a small bundle that he had kept dry, pointed to Ruth, and placed a collection of feathers, mussel shells, and shiny rocks on the ground.

She said, "Oh my! This must be the person who been leaving things like this for me all year. I do believe they are here to help us."

"Help, help," said Tis-Chik. He pantomimed holding the beaver's fur one more time and then turned and motioned to the assembled beavers to cross the water. They did so.

Ruth set the example and went first. She approached Chee. Chee moved to the edge of the water and waited while Ruth took her fur in both hands. Chee quickly pulled Ruth to safety on the other side of the raging torrent. The other people, singly and in family groups, came forward to find a beaver waiting to carry them across. Tis-Chik guided several hands to proper placement on a beaver's back. The beavers pulled every person to safety.

The dam broke and the village was washed away. No one was ever foolish enough to try and build in that location again.

Their task finished, the beavers melted into the forest and returned to their colony. Tis-Chik stayed with the people while they built shelters. Their supplies were gone, but he showed them how to find food. He learned to speak their language. The people followed the river downstream until they found the large permanent settlement that eventually became the capitol of this state.

The villagers dispersed and spread throughout the community. Tis-Chik stayed with Ruth and her family. They told everyone that his name was Tristan Castor. Castor is part of the formal name for beavers. He eventually went to school and became an engineer. His understanding of dams, bridges and hydraulics was unsurpassed. Many a bridge that you have crossed during your lifetime was constructed based on the principals he designed. The Massachusetts Institute of Technology still uses a beaver as its symbol.

Tristan and Ruth eventually married. Their oldest son became the first United States Senator from this State. Their youngest son was the Secretary of the Interior Department under Theodore Roosevelt. He and his family accumulated several thousand acres of land surrounding the pond where the golden beavers raised Tis-Chik. The people in the state never forgot how the beavers had saved the settlers. The story grew with the telling. The flood waters became faster, deeper and colder through the years. The number of people saved by the beavers became larger and larger with the telling and retelling of the story. It was said that Tis-Chik could bite through an axe handle. The legends claimed that the man raised by the beavers could swim faster than the fastest racing boat could travel. He could hold his breath for hours on end. Some even claimed that he was a mystic spirit of the forest and would protect good people, but would punish evildoers who would despoil the land or the wildlife.

No matter how much the story became exaggerated, the settlers and their descendants never forgot the debts that they owed Tis-Chik and the beaver colony. Tis-Chik, now Tristan, used his power as a senator to establish perpetual protection for the land of the golden beavers. The land he carefully assembled was donated to the federal government and designated a wildlife refuge. I was pleased to be the first ranger assigned to the refuge. I have written this so that you understand why this place is secret and why it must be protected. The beavers saved my family, it is my job to save them. If you read my grandfather's story in this logbook, it is your job, too.

The log entry ended there. I put the ranger's log away and went to bed. I spent a sleepless night because I had so many questions. I must have finally fallen asleep because I woke to the smell of bacon and coffee, got dressed, and staggered into the kitchen.

Gary said, "Good morning. Coffee's ready. How do you like your eggs?" He poured a cup of coffee, slid it toward me and pointed to the sugar bowl. "Scrambled? Fine. You drink some coffee while I finish this bacon and cook the eggs. I know you have questions, just hold them until I have breakfast ready."

The coffee was good and so were the eggs. I ate everything, washed the dishes and poured us both another cup of coffee.

I looked at Gary and said, "I know about Senator Castor and his son, the Secretary. If I believe the log, his father was a feral child raised by beavers. Romulus, Remus, and Bucky, oh my! Do you believe it?"

"It is absolutely true, that's why the story has been suppressed. The truth is the reason this refuge is hidden. The press would never leave this beaver colony alone. They saved a small village that included some very important people. They deserve better than that. It's my family's obligation to see that they get that protection."

"Your family?"

"Yes, my family. I am a direct descendant of Tis-Chik and Ruth. Every ranger has been a member of our family. We work and live an outside life and then, when we reach what most would consider retirement age, we take our turn guarding the beaver colony. My father crossed Europe with General Patton. He supervised the construction or repair of numerous bridges during the allied advance. He could tell the places where the tanks could cross without building a bridge. He knew whether to dam a creek or river or to build a bridge. He helped make the advance go quickly. He stayed on after the war for a while. He helped repair dozens of dams. He even spent a year with the Dutch repairing dikes. I never fought, but I designed and built hydroelectric dams across the world."

"I'm pretty sure I'm not a Castor. I've never built anything in my life. So why am I here?"

"I'm old and I'm sick," said Gary. "I don't have any relatives that are the right age to take my place. The oldest is only in his early fifties. We need someone to be the ranger for the next ten years or so. We've watched you for years. You have no family and you truly believe in protecting the animals in our national parks and refuges. I'm to spend this month with you, making sure that you are the person we can count on until my nephew can take over."

"What if I'm not?"

"If you're not, then I'll send you back and spend time with the next person on our list. The cancer won't get me tomorrow, so I have time to check out the next two or three candidates, if necessary. In the meantime, the refuge perimeter fence won't check itself. We can talk while we walk."

We dressed, packed lunch and then spent the day walking the perimeter. We ended up by the beaver pond before sunset. Gary said, "Let me show you some things."

He pointed to a blackberry thicket, "This is where Chee, Tis-Chik, and the young beavers killed the bobcat. Right up this trail is the tree where he watched the trapper. Look closely, you can still see scars on the trunk from where the trapper tried to pull the chain loose while he was being stoned. We can find evidence of where other trappers were waylaid and either killed or frightened off if we keep looking around."

I noticed the beavers who were positioned as guards around the pond, and they took notice of us but did not sound an alarm. The beavers continued working with no concern about our presence.

"The beavers know me. Within the month, they will know you, too. It's like in the Sherlock Holmes story, a dog doesn't bark at its own people."

After I had been with Gary for a little over a week, he brought out an old suitcase after dinner one evening and placed it on the table. "You are going to work out just fine. I can tell. These are the last things I need to show you."

Inside the suitcase was a bundle wrapped in oilcloth. He carefully unwrapped it and picked up the first item. "This is the axe that Tis-Chik took from the first trapper."

He handed me the axe and reached down and held up a bone handled knife. "This knife was taken from the first trapper or perhaps a later one, no one is quite sure. It is quite old, isn't it?"

I stood and looked at the remaining items on the oilcloth. There were more knives and a dozen or so animal traps of various sizes. I looked questioningly at Gary and he said, "Tis-Chik destroyed most of the traps, but he always kept enough of them around to use against any human intruders."

"Why are you showing me this?"

"I told you how we descendants of Tis-Chik have watched over the lodge and pond all this time. I haven't told you the rest of what the family does."

He rolled the antiques back in the oilcloth, returned it the suitcase and stored the bundle in the closet. "When every man child is three years old, he is brought to the lodge. Each young man, myself included, spends three years with the beaver colony. This tradition has continued since the senator, Tristan and Ruth's first son, was brought here years ago. One of my nieces gave birth to a baby boy last month. In three years, he will be brought here to live with the beavers. You must not interfere. The only thing you are to do is to leave the oilcloth-wrapped axe, knifes, and traps under the scarred tree. The beavers will handle everything else."

"You expect me to watch your family abandon a three-year-old?"

"The child is not being abandoned. He is being fostered to the beavers for three years. The beavers will be the better for it and so will the boy. I know. Remember, I lived three years with the beavers. I need your word that you will do as I ask. It is possible that you may be the ranger during the fostering of more than one child. Whenever a child completes his time with the beavers, either he, his parents, or the beavers will return the knives, axe and traps to the scarred tree. You must keep them safe until the next child arrives. You will be the first ranger here that doesn't speak beaver, so the colony can't talk to you. The children may be able to communicate with you if necessary, but you can't count on that. My family and the beavers have been doing this for years, so just trust the beavers. They know how to do this."

I had already made up my mind to do as Gary asked. Nevertheless, I asked the same questions over and over again until Gary left. His answers never changed. It was really simple. Keep the perimeter fencing intact, deal with any human intruders, and don't bother the beavers.

I woke up one morning about two weeks later. The cabin was quiet and empty. There was no evidence that Gary had prepared breakfast for himself. His bed was neatly made and all his belongings were in place. I went onto the porch and called for him, but I got no response. I continued to call his name as I followed the well-worn trail to the beaver pond.

I stopped calling for him when I got to the edge of the pond and saw his clothes. His shirt and trousers were neatly folded and his Smokey Bear ranger hat was sitting on top of them. His boots were sitting to one side of the clothing. Socks were stuffed inside them. There were bare footprints leading into the water.

For a moment, I considered the possibility that Gary had drowned himself in the pond. I shielded my eyes and scanned the placid water. The beavers were working like only beavers can do. I didn't see Gary anywhere. Perhaps the worry showed on my face, I don't know. I turned to go and before I could take a single step I heard a clear whistle echo across the pond. 'Shave and a haircut, two bits.'

I knew Gary was fine, he was where he wanted to be. The oldest golden beaver had come home.

***

Robert Allen Lupton is retired and lives in New Mexico where he is a commercial hot air balloon pilot. Robert runs and writes every day, but not necessarily in that order. More than a hundred and fifty of his short stories have been published in several anthologies including the New York Times best seller, "Chicken Soup For the Soul – Running For Good". His novel, "Foxborn," was published in April 2017 and the sequel, "Dragonborn," in June 2018. His first collection, "Running Into Trouble," was published in October 2017. His collection, "Through a Wine Glass Darkly," was released in June 2019. His newest collection, "Strong Spirits," was released on June 1, 2020.

His third novel, "Dejanna of the Double Star," is scheduled for publication in October 2020.

"Swim with the Beavers" was first published in "Uncommon Origins," by Fighting Monkey Press in 2016. It was selected for the anthology, "Best Indie Speculative Fiction" by Bards and Sages Publishing.

FERAL CHILDREN IN FACT AND FICTION

By Serena DuBois

Author's Note: The article below was written in 2006 for the Leanta Press edition of "Tarzan of the Apes." *Due to its length, only the first half of the article was printed at that time. This is the first time that it has been available to the general public in a print version.*

We all know the tale of *Tarzan of the Apes*. His birth parents dead on an African shore, animals raised Burroughs' titular hero. Burroughs calls these animals "great apes" or *Mangani*. Philip José Farmer in his "definitive biography of Lord Greystoke" *Tarzan Alive,* suggests that the creatures that adopted Tarzan were not animals at all but rather an almost extinct precursor of *Homo sapiens,* "a giant variety of *Australopithecus robustus* ... a hominid supposed to be extinct, but possibly surviving in the remote jungles even to this day." He states that they had speech, which made them human no matter what they looked like.[1]

If Burroughs had known or read the stories of real feral children available at the time he wrote *Tarzan of the Apes* in 1912, he would have suggested something very like this. Almost all of factual literature regarding feral children indicates that if children do not learn human speech at an early age, and if they are not living in the vicinity of human beings that have speech and talk to them, they never learn to talk. As we shall see, the ability to speak is critical to a feral child's living as a functioning adult member of a human community—the usual definition of "human".

This lack of speech in most feral children appears to have nothing to do with lack of intelligence, autism or neurological impairment. Rather, speech is learned, and learned at a certain time in a child's life, with repetition being a good part of the learning process.[2, 3]

Tarzan picks up languages easily. He speaks over nine to a greater or lesser extent, and more than twenty dialects as well. To the contrary, most feral children chronicled in the last several hundred years cannot even speak their native tongue. They know only the language of the animals that raised them: barking, growling, wolf howls. The meaning of this language is for the most part incomprehensible to humans.

Cases of actual feral children are comparatively few and hard to come by. Researchers have discovered around 120 examples of children confined, isolated or found living with or around animals. After sorting through these stories, we find that several were hoaxes, and many are sad tales of children confined in small cages or isolated from humanity in other ways. A small percentage of the children were in the wild on a temporary basis, lasting only a few days or weeks at most.[4]

Less than half of the children listed were actually living with, or appear to have been kept alive by, animals. These reports and anecdotes range in time from our own era back through the Middle Ages, with one lone story from Roman times of a child discovered with goats. A few tell of feral children in modern times, who have also been found with herbivores such as gazelles, cows, sheep and again goats.

More often the animals the children are taken from are carnivores of one kind or another or primates such as chimps or monkeys. There are around thirty stories where wolves, dogs or jackals are the parental figures, eight with apes or monkeys (all of them in the 20th century), seven with bears and one each for leopards and panthers, both of which came from India. One wonders if Kipling heard of these before he wrote *The Jungle Book*.

Most of these stories are not backed up with any proof that could even begin to be called scientific, and in modern times newspaper articles about these children are "rescued" are usually without any follow-up since the writers move on to newer stories. When these reports appear in more than one paper, the chances are that they all go back to a single source.

As we dig back into the early legends of feral children, we enter the realm of mythology or perhaps mythologized history. The best-known ancient story of feral children is that of Romulus and Remus, the founders of Rome, twin sons of Mars via the rape of the Vestal Virgin Rhea Silvia. They escaped death through a series of happy circumstances, including being fed by woodpeckers and suckled by a mother wolf. This last well-known part of the Romulan legend brings their story firmly into this article.[5]

While their story has many mythological elements, modern Italian anthropologist Andrea Carandini, among other modern scholars, believes in the historicity behind the Romulus legend. He bases this on the discovery of the *Murus Romuli,* or Romulan fortifications, found in 1988 on the north slope of the Palatine hill in Rome.[6] We have the same problem here that we will have with many of these accounts. We have no way to verify the anecdotes, and even archeological discoveries are open to interpretation. Most historians would not agree with Carandini, and one suspects that even the Romans of the time of Augustus, 750 years after the founding of the city on the Tiber, may have had doubts about the more fanciful aspects of the story.

More than a thousand years after the founding of Rome, we come on a tale of "…a baby boy, abandoned by his mother during the chaos of the Gothic wars in about AD 250, was found and suckled by a she-goat." When the survivors of the war returned to their homes, he was living with the goats. The returning survivors named him Aegisthus.[7]

This story is told by Procopius of Caesarea, a prominent Byzantine scholar, who lived during the time of Justinian in the 6th century AD, in his *History of the Wars; Books VI-VII, Gothic War (De Bello Gothico*, published originally around 551 AD). He states that he saw the child himself.[7] However, the Fortean Times web page, source of the above quote, gives the date of the boy's abandonment at around AD 250.[8]

So the question arises: Which date is correct? Is Procopius passing on a story he heard as something he actually saw? Did the web source get the date wrong? Or do we have here something as simple as someone's typographical error making the date 250 AD when it should have been 520 AD? The several web sites that quote this story, all cite the Fortean Times web site. None of them noted the discrepancy between the 250 AD date given and the dates of Procopius' life.

The 6th Century Gothic Wars, at the beginning of the period modern historians call the Dark Ages, certainly were dark on the subject of feral children. The only extant story prior to the 14th Century is the "Green Children of Woolpit", in Suffolk, chronicled by Ralph of Coggeshall and William of Newburgh in the late 12th century. This tale of temporary isolation mentions no animals, so falls outside the scope of this article.[9]

The next three examples appeared in Germany in the 14th century. All three children were described as being raised by wolves, and all were found between 1304 and 1344. The information, however, is incomplete and written centuries after the children lived. Two of the wolf boys were found in Hesse. Alexander Ross in his *Arcana Microcosmi,* published around 350 years later, in 1652, has this to say about the first wolf boy who was discovered in 1304:

> In the Lantgrave of Hesse … was found a boy who had been lost by his parents when he was a childe, who was bred among Wolves, and ran up and down with them upon all four for his prey. This boy was at last in Hunting taken and brought to the Landgrave, who much wondring at the sight, caused him to be bred among his servants, who in time left his

Wolvish conditions, learned to walk upright like a man, and to speak, who confessed, that the wolves bred him and taught him to hunt for prey with them. This story is rehearsed by Dresserus in his *Book of new and ancient Discipline, Hist. Med.* part. 1. c. [10]

His source is Matthaues Dresserus (Matthieu Drescher) writing in 1577. The Feral Children web site also mentions an undated Benedictine chronicle, which may have been Dresserus' source. This certainly pushes this information into the area of hearsay.[11]

The second wolf boy of Hesse had a much shorter and probably sadder existence than the first. He was located in 1341 at the age of seven. He fought his captors, running around on all fours and hiding from them, refusing to eat the food they gave him and died soon after. His story is told in the *Hessian Chronicles* by Wilhelm Dilich in 1608, so again there is a large time gap between the happening and the written record that has come down to us.[12]

The third medieval German wolf boy was found in Wetterau in the winter of 1344 and captured by nobles out deer hunting in a dense wood. The story goes that he had lived with the wolves for twelve years, and after his capture lived to about 80 years. No other information is given, so we don't know if he learned to speak, or to live as a human does.[13]

The records of medieval feral children remain scanty. One other wolf boy mentioned by Ross was discovered in the forests of Ardenne, France around 1500 after having been carried away by wolves and nourished by them. He writes that the wolf boy "could neither speak nor walk upright, nor eat anything except raw flesh, till by a new education among other children, his bestial nature was quite abolished." No further information was given.[14]

We jump another century and discover that in the 17th century the reports are of children found with bears—one from Denmark, two from Lithuania, and from Ireland a tale of a boy living with wild sheep, eating grass and hay, and a second briefly told story of a boy living in late 16th century Bamberg, Germany, with cows. This last story is an anomaly in many ways. While he grew up with cattle in the mountains, running on all fours and fighting with dogs, he was eventually civilized and even married. It appears that he could not have been totally denied human companionship in his early youth.[15]

The bear boys follow the pattern of the wolf boys and other feral children we have seen. They run on all fours, eat what bears eat, and don't easily learn human languages. For example, Joseph Connor says the following about Joseph the Bear Boy of Lithuania found in the 1660s:

> ...his manners were altogether bestial; for he not only fed upon raw flesh, wild honey, crab-apples and such like dainties which bears are used to feat [*sic*] with, but also went ... upon all-four. ... he was not taught to go upright without a great deal of difficult [*sic*], and there was less hope of ever making him learn the Polish language, for he ... continued to express his mind in a ... bear-like tone.[16]

We have scant information available regarding the other two incidents of feral children found with bears, the Danish bear boy of around 1600 and the second Lithuanian bear boy discovered in 1694; however, accounts of the second Lithuanian boy report that he did learn some speech and to walk upright.

The 18th century saw a number of cases of isolated children, which are outside the scope of this article as well as that of a bear girl in Fraumark, Slovakia in 1767 and a wolf boy of Kronstadt found in Brasov, Romania around 1780. In both cases they were practically dragged from their wild homes and taken to nearby towns to be civilized, but without success. The bear girl was locked in an asylum where she would eat only raw meat. *Wolf Children and Feral Man,* by Singh and Zingg contains a long discussion of the wolf boy of Kronstadt, who like others never learned to speak, would howl pitifully when he saw trees or mountains, and preferred raw meat, although he learned to eat human food including legumes after a time.[17]

As we come into the 19th century, we find that most of the stories available come from India and are about children raised by wolves or found with them. The feral children web site lists 11 cases in 19th century India of children found with or raised with wolves and one case in Texas of a girl raised with lobo wolves. Three other 19th century children were reported raised by or with animals: one each by bears in India, gazelles in Mauritania, North Africa and sheep in Greece. All of the Central and Western European cases are sad stories of children confined or isolated by humans. These stories include one of Clemens, a boy in the Netherlands as told in an 1863 article in *Anthropological Review* who was

> ...set to keep swine, and shut up with them at night. The peasant, his master, gave him scarcely enough food to sustain life, and he used to suck the milch sow and eat herbage with the pigs. ... he would go on all fours in the garden, and seize and eat the vegetables ... He never lost his affection for pigs; and ... they would let him ride about on their backs. His

pleasantest recollections and his favorite stories were about his life with them in his childhood.[18]

The article dates the account in the early 19th century, some forty or more years prior to the publication date. It is interesting to us because of the animal aspects of the story and the fact that it indicates that due to his being near humans as well as with the pigs he was able to speak as an adult and become a part of the human world, though it appears that given a choice he would have preferred to stay with the pigs.

The next half dozen examples of feral children are all from the 1840s in India. Major-General Sir W. H. Sleeman tells their stories in *A Journey Through the Kingdom of Oude, in 1849-50.* [19] These stories collected by General Sleeman all come from the same part of India and have a number of elements in common. The children, all boys, were taken from their parents at about three years of age (when age could be confirmed) and were between nine and twelve when found and removed from the wolves. None of them learned to speak more than a word or two of the local tongue though most of them could eventually respond to signs. They all preferred raw meat to other food although some learned to eat cooked or vegetarian food. Sleeman commented on their lack of cleanliness and their smell in almost all cases.

All of these wolf boys wished to return to their lupine parents in the jungle and tried very hard to do so. Although the "Second Sultanpur Wolf Boy" [20] died three years after he was "rescued", the others survived, albeit one can't really say that they thrived. Like Burroughs' hero, they wanted very desperately to go back to the jungle and were apparently no longer suited to living with humans.

This quote from Sleeman's book is of interest:

> In all parts of India, the Hindoos [*sic*] have a notion that the family of a man who kills a wolf, or even wounds it, goes to utter ruin; and so also the village within the boundaries of which a wolf has been killed or wounded... Some Rajpoot families in Oude, where so many children are devoured by wolves, are getting over this prejudice. [21]

This attitude is demonstrated throughout the extracts from Sleeman's book where children are taken from their wild homes, but the wolves with them are often not killed or otherwise hurt; apparently they have not completely gotten "over their prejudice." When you consider the important role that both reincarnation and transmigration play in Hindu belief, it is no wonder that East Indians balked at killing wolves, particularly a local one who might have been someone's grandfather.

They might have even assumed that a person previously related to the child, now in the form of a wolf, "adopted" him.

There are common elements in all of these stories. Troopers find a boy running with a mother wolf and her "whelps". With the best of intentions, the troopers take the child forcibly from the she-wolf. They either dig him out of her den or grab him up and carry him back to live with humans, who usually only keep him for a short while before finding that this wolf child is too hard to raise and to deal with.

As with most of the feral children seen previously in this article, all of these children that Sleeman discusses learn little or no spoken language, but often can be directed by signs much as a dog can be taught to respond to hand signals. They almost always prefer raw meat to other food, and human captors find their smell repulsive. The boys pine for their lupine families and continually attempt to return to them.

We see a particularly interesting example of wolf/human interaction in the case of the child known as the First Lucknow Wolf Boy. The story of this boy followed the pattern above. After being taken from his wolf family by troopers and brought back to Bondee, he had several different caretakers, all of whom tried to civilize him without succeeding. After a time he was put in the care of a cashmere merchant's servant, Janoo, who taught him to eat human food and to walk on two legs. When directed by signs, he could prepare a hookah, light it and bring it to Janoo. Then…

> One night while the boy was lying under the tree, near Janoo, Janoo saw two wolves come up stealthily, and smell at the boy. They then touched him, and he got up; and instead of being frightened, the boy put his hands upon their heads, and they began to play with him. They capered around him, and he threw straw and leaves at them. Janoo tried to drive them off … but, after going a little distance, they returned, and began to play again with the boy. … They came four or five times, and Janoo had no longer any fear of them; and he thinks that the first two that came must have been the two cubs with which the boy was first found, and they were prevented from seizing him by recognizing the smell. They licked his face with their tongues as he put his hands on their heads. [22]

Janoo's master wanted him to get rid of the boy, but Janoo insisted on keeping him. However, whenever they passed a jungle area, the boy tried to escape. Janoo had to leave the boy behind for a few days while he went on business for his master, and when he returned, discovered that the boy had run off and was not found again.[22]

Furthermore, in those cases in which parents found their missing child, the boy had little or no feeling for the parent and in several cases the parent rejected the child for this reason. The boys had all bonded so completely with the wolves who raised them, that they apparently had no memory of or caring for their birth parents.

We can see the spiritual sister of the First Lucknow Wolf Boy in another similar case half a world away in the wilds of Texas. The tale of the Lobo Girl of Devil's River has many points in common with the Lucknow Wolf Boy's story, the main one being the unwillingness of both to be bound by human customs.

The Lobo Girl was born to Mollie and John Dent, trappers at Beaver Lake in Texas in 1835. Lightning killed her father, and her mother apparently died in childbirth. When the people whose help the father had sought arrived at the Dents' cabin, they found the child gone and the tracks of lobo wolves in the vicinity. They assumed she had been killed and eaten.

But ten years later there were several sightings of a girl hunting with a pack of lobo wolves. The feral children web site states that the

> ... hunt was mounted, and after three days the Lobo Girl of Devil's River was caught after fighting wildly to keep her freedom. She was taken to a ranch ... and locked in. Her howling attracted answering cries from wolves far and wide, and a large pack of wolves rushed the corrals, attacking the goats, cows and horses. Shooting started, and in the confusion the girl managed to remove the board nailed over the window and make her escape.[23]

Seven years later in 1852 frontiersmen surveying for a new route to El Paso saw the Lobo Girl "suckling two wolf cubs on a sand bar in the river." She ran off carrying them and was never seen again. At that time she was around seventeen years old.[24]

One has to wonder what happened to the Lobo Girl in the years after this last sighting. We can only hope that she lived out her days with the wolf family who raised her, just as we would want to see the Wolf Boy of Lucknow who escaped back to his jungles find his own true lupine family again.

Our next sightings appear in the late 1850s in the aftermath of the East Indian Sepoy Rebellion of 1857 to 1858.[25] Between 1858 and 1900 there are five more cases of wolf boys in India, as well as a girl found with bears. While far away from India, a boy living with sheep in Greece in 1891 and a second boy with gazelles in Mauritania in Western Africa in 1900 are also discovered.

The five stories of boys found with wolves follow the same pattern as before. The story of the Third Sultanpur Wolf Boy found in 1860 is discussed in a letter to *The Field* in 1895 about 35 years after; it follows the usual pattern of these stories with one major difference. The child, discovered with the wolf cubs, is taken from the den and adapted successfully to human society. H. Ross, the writer of the letter admits he is told this and did not see it happen, but it was verified so he had no reason to disbelieve it. He goes on to say that

> As regards the child, I saw him when he was just brought in, …and until I left …. He seemed to be about four years old, and sat up like a dog, both arms straight down in front of him, with his hands flattened out on the ground, and his legs drawn up under him like a dog; he moved by hops something like a monkey, but never stood up on his legs, and always kept his hands on the ground. He gave vent to snarls and sounds, not actual barks like a dog, but something between a bark and a grunt. He would not touch cooked food, but ate raw meat ravenously. The police officer took charge of him, and gradually broke him in to taking milk, then milk and bread, and so on. He certainly was not an idiot, for, **after being tamed, he was sent to school, and eventually taken into the police force** [emphasis added]. Everyone at the time considered it a clear case of a wolf-child.[26]

This boy stands out because he crossed the barrier between the lupine world and the human. Mr. Ross doesn't mention that he learned to speak, but one assumes that it is a given in this case. We are left to wonder if the boy had language before he lived with the wolves. Since he later joined the police force, it seems evident that the force became his pack, his replacement for his lupine brothers and sisters.

The other four late 19th century feral children did not fare so well. None of them learned speech or were assimilated into human society, and all had the characteristics of wolves that we have seen previously. The Shajehanpur wolf boy,[27] found in 1858 in the aftermath of the Sepoy Rebellion, lived for years in a hut without human speech or integration into human society.

Dina Sanichar,[28] having been removed from the wolves' cave when he was about six years old, was taken in by the Sekandra orphanage, lived till 1895 and never learned to speak. During his time at the orphanage, he befriended the Second Sekandra Wolf Boy,[29] who arrived in 1872, age 10, and lived only four months after his arrival. The last 19th century wolf boy, the Batispur Wolf Boy[30] was found in 1893 at the age of 14. The *Calcutta Times* report at the time of his discovery is the only one we have, and we cannot know what happened to him later.

The last 19th century reports move away from wolves. There is the brief story of Skiron from Greece mentioned by Singh and Zingg in *Wolf Children and Feral Man.*[31] Around 1891 Skiron's father died. His mother left him with someone and returned to her homeland; he lived with the sheep for four years on "milk from the sheep in the summer and acorns and roots in the winter." [32] He later found a home with a shepherd, and nothing else is known about him.

Our last Indian feral child in the 19th century is different in many respects from those discussed previously. This child, the Jalpalguri Bear-Girl, was according to a newspaper article published five years later, found "… by some coolies … in the den of a bear. It is presumed that she was brought there … and when very young was nursed by her bear-mother." [33] This article goes on to detail the girl's ursine behavior:

> …she was a strange combination of a bear and a man, she was ferocious like a bear, and attempted to bite and scratch men when she saw them. In her locomotion she used her legs as well as her hands and moved like a bear. She growled at intervals like a bear and ate and drank as a bear; in short, all her habits were like those of a bear, while by her features no one could fail to recognize her as a human being.[34]

The people that discovered her took her to a hospital in Jalpalguri where she stayed three years and "learnt to walk, eat, and drink like a human being, and showed certain emotions which were peculiar to man. The hospital authorities retained her about three years, and afterwards thinking her an incurable discharged her." [35] She apparently roamed the streets for about two years getting her food where she could and sleeping outdoors at night. Five years after she was removed from the bears, the missionary who took her off the streets, with the help of the *Unity and the Minister* newspaper (organ of the New Dispensation Church of the late Babu Chunder Sen) eventually found her a home at the

> …Das Asram, a philanthropic institution of Calcutta … where she is now taken care of. … By contact with society she is now generally acquiring human habits. It has been pronounced by medical men that she will gradually regain her humanity.[36]

Since this article was written at the time the events happened and once again there is no follow-up, we can only hope that she did "regain her humanity".

The last 19th century feral child is even more of an anomaly in many ways than the ones previously discussed. His home was Mauritania in Western Africa, and he survived by living with gazelles. The Feral Children web site does not give a source for this story, but says that around 1900 a boy, whose mother put him out to wet-nurse with her tame gazelles because she was unable to feed him, went with the gazelle he was tethered to when it wandered off "to follow a herd of wild gazelles. Eventually the herd became accustomed to the gazelle and her strange companion, and the Mauritanian Gazelle Boy lived with the herd for some years before he was eventually captured." [37] After a long time the boy learned to speak and became a hunter. The story ends with the boy dying of grief because he realizes he has killed his gazelle wet nurse. Needless to say we have no way of knowing the truth of any part of this tale which the Feral Children website calls "a likely story."

As we move forward into the 20th century, we find that until the 30s all of the stories of feral children found with animals are still from India. From this time and place we also find our only stories of feral children and big cats, The Leopard Boy of Dihungi found in 1915 and the briefly mentioned Indian panther child from 1920. All we know of the latter is that he was a Hindu boy returned to his parents after being nurtured by a panther.[38]

There is more information about the Leopard Boy of Dihungi. He was stolen, while his mother worked in the fields, by a leopardess that had two of her cubs killed by local villagers. A sportsman killed the mother leopard three years later. Subsequently the villagers found the boy and two living cubs in her den and returned the boy to his parents. The report does not say how old the Leopard Boy was when he was stolen or if he ever learned to speak. When first rescued, the boy could run very quickly on all fours, had an acute sense of smell and ripped apart and devoured any fowl he could find. Stuart Baker, who visited the Leopard Boy and wrote the story for the *Journal of the Bombay Natural History Society,* said that the boy had learned to walk like a human when he saw him five years after he was taken from his leopard mother.[39]

Our next feral child is Goongi, a girl who was found in the Indian state of Uttar Pradesh. Researchers believe her to be non-speaking because her name meant "dumb" in the local tongue. The Feral Children web site says: "She exhibited characteristics common to feral children: she was supposedly covered with hair, and ran on all fours." [40] They take their information from *Jim Corbett's India.* It is that author's suggestion that she was brought up by bears because she ate what bears ate, had great climbing ability and also had deep scratches on her body that could have been made by bears.[41]

Except for one "Jackal Girl"[42], the feral children of the first part of the 20th century were found with wolves. Little is known about three of these, all boys, who follow the usual pattern of lack of speech and animal habits. Two of them were found in wolves' dens but in both cases preferred to eat roots and plants and not raw meat, which suggests that they might have been isolated children who found unused dens to live in.[43] The history of the third, the Satna Wolf Boy, indicates that he was carried off by wolves as a baby and rescued years afterward as told by a Mr. C.H. Burnett who stated that "he couldn't speak and 'had very peculiar habits'." [44]

Now we come to two of the most famous Wolf Children: Amala and Kamala, who are the primary reason for Singh and Zingg's book, *Wolf Children and Feral Man,* which is based on diaries Singh kept when they were in his care. There is far too much material to go into detail here, but the interested reader will find complete excerpts from this book on the Feral Children web site.[45] Amala lived only a short time after they were taken from the wolves' den and the mother wolf killed, while Kamala lived for nine years more in Singh's care before succumbing to typhoid.

In these nine years he had far more success in socializing Kamala than is found in any previous case that we have on record. The work was hard and slow. After perhaps a half-dozen years with Singh, Kamala had a vocabulary of about 40 Hindi words, not always completely pronounced and could make short sentences. Singh was able to get Kamala to walk, eat and sleep as the other children in his orphanage did, but at the time of her death he was still far from seeing her become socialized. As with almost all the other feral children, she could be neither fully wolf or fully human. [46]

In the middle part of the 20th century we find a potpourri of parental animals for feral children. Several children lived with monkeys and apes[47] (the first recorded instances of these); a bear mothered a girl in Turkey[48]; two more boys were discovered with gazelles, and several more wolf boys[49, 50] turned up. From 1945 we have our only instance of a boy who lived for ten years with ostriches in North Africa before hunters found him and brought him home. It is said that he lived on grass while he was with them.[51]

In all these cases there is little or no mention of the children learning to speak. While some of them learned to walk on two feet, they tended to drop back to four to run. As with all the stories we have heard previously, they behaved like their parental animals and ate what these animals preferred. This 1930s report of one of the "monkey children" illustrates the pattern. In the 1930s, "Assicia ... moved around on all fours, on knees and fingertips, with ankles bent, scratched herself in the manner of a monkey, and uttered quivering cries... her favourite food was bananas." [52]

The boys that ran with gazelles, one in Syria (1946) and one in of the Sahara Desert Mauritania were both as fleet as the animals they were found with. Both were reported racing beside jeeps at speeds up to 50 kilometers per hour. One report said that the Syrian gazelle boy could run at 50 **miles** per hour.[53] The Feral Children web site says "at first the Syrian Authorities wanted to study him and refused to let American doctors or French doctors take him for study. When the funds weren't forthcoming, the young man was left to live in the streets." There are a number of stories of gazelle boys from Syria, and while the Foretean Times and Feral Children web site suggest that some are fabrications (referencing *Pursuit* [54]*)*, some prove to be real.

According to the Fortean Times, Jean-Claude Auger, a Basque anthropologist saw the Saharan Gazelle Boy while traveling in the Spanish Sahara in 1960. He patiently waited for the herd and won the animals' and the boy's confidence. Auger stayed with the herd for some time and wrote:

> The boy walked on all fours, but occasionally assumed an upright gait, suggesting to Auger that he was abandoned or lost at about seven or eight months, having already learnt to stand. He habitually twitched his muscles, scalp, nose and ears, much like the rest of the herd, in response to the slightest noise. Even in deepest sleep he seemed constantly alert, raising his head at unusual noises, however faint, and sniffing around him like the gazelles.[55]

Auger came back two years later with companions who "chased the boy in a jeep to see how fast he could run. This frightened him off altogether, though he reached a speed of 32-34mph (52-54km/h), with continuous leaps of about 13ft (4m). Olympic sprinters can reach only 25mph (40km/h) in short bursts." [56] While several attempts were later made to capture him, none were successful. There are no photographs, so once again we are left to wonder if the story is true or a fabrication.

The Turkish Bear Girl and the two wolf boys, Djuma from Turkmenistan and Ramu, the Second Lucknow Wolf Boy from India, all follow the pattern we have observed throughout this article. They fight their captors, don't learn civilized ways, and all three of these hapless children ended up in mental hospitals. Ramu spent fourteen years in the Lucknow hospital, dying there in 1968. The others were still in the hospitals they had been place in when last heard from. Ramu lapped milk from a glass, chewed bones, and "when taken on an outing to the zoo became very excited by the wolves." [57] Djuma had learned a few disjointed words. Nothing was said about the others learning to speak.

In the last third of the 20th century, two-thirds of the thirty feral children on listed were confined, isolated or hoaxes. As we examine the documents concerning the remaining children that were said to have lived with animals we see that this is a time of change. Wild animals are disappearing from the picture, and more domesticated ones are taking their place. We have our last record of a wolf child, Shamdeo in India, in 1972, and in 1984 and 1998 our first and second cases of children living with dogs. Seven children were found with monkeys, and one with goats, Daniel from the Andes, who lived with them for eight years, drinking their milk and eating roots and berries. [58]

Shamdeo, whom we could call the Last Sultanpur Wolf Boy, followed the pattern of the other East Indian wolf children. He was found with five wolf cubs, fought his human captors, preferred wolf food and never learned human speech. When last seen he was living in Mother Teresa's Mission of Charity orphanage.[59]

Four of the five children found with monkeys exhibited all of the usual feral child traits as well. None of these learned to talk, and they appear in many cases to have ended up with the monkeys because of unrest in their countries, which is also part of the feral child pattern as we have seen throughout this article.[60][61]

The fifth monkey child, John Ssebunya, is one of the anomalies we find occasionally while sifting through these stories. He left his home at the age of four, escaping his father who had just killed his mother, and was accepted by a troop of monkeys living in his part of Uganda. James Butler, producer/director of a BBC documentary about John, goes into great detail about John and his life with the monkeys. In a letter to Feral Children he relates that John *told him* that he

> ...came across a group of monkeys. He says he was able to eat crops that the monkeys raided from the fields and that he went into the fields and stole food as well. There is no proof that the monkeys fed him — primatologists would regard this as very unlikely but are quite happy to accept that the monkeys stole more food than they needed and dropped some on the ground and John picked it up from the ground and ate it.

>John identified the monkeys as *Cercopithicus Aethiops* (the common African Grey or Green Vervet Monkey). This is very significant as this is one of the very few species of mammal that lives in social groups *and will accept and tolerate a lone individual of another species of monkey living alongside their group* [emphasis Mr. Butler's]. Other monkeys and apes will not do this…

What stands out in this quote, of course, is that John was able to give such detail to James Butler. Unlike most, he was old enough when he left his family to still be reacclimatized into human society when he was found. According to the Feral Children web not only did John learn to talk but to sing as well, and tours with the Pearl of Africa Children's Choir.[63] Further on in the letter, Mr. Butler states that "… these findings are **not** evidence that the Tarzan myth is true (although they may show how the myth could arise apocryphally from a basis in fact)." [62]

Ivan Mishukov from Russia is the last feral child from the 20th century. The boy had lost his family in the chaos surrounding the collapse of the Russian economy in 1998 and "earned the trust of a pack of wild dogs by offering them scraps from the food he managed to beg, and in return for the food, they provided him with protection from the winter temperatures on the streets of Reutova, west of Moscow, which can reach 30 below zero (Celsius)." Ivan was quickly reintegrated into society after he was taken from the dog pack because he could speak before he was with them. [64]

We come finally to the three remaining feral children found with animals, those in the 21st century. These three were all were found with dogs, one each in Russia, Romania and Chile.

According to the feral children site, Axel Rivas, the Chilean dog boy, was "…thrown out of his home by abusive parents when he was five years old, and was then placed in a children's home. He … escaped in 1998, at the age of eight," and lived with dogs in a cave suckling on a bitch for part of his food. He was captured again and escaped again after begging to be allowed to go back to the dogs that he said were his family.[65] No further reports are given, so we do not know if he stayed with the dogs or was rescued again.

The second 21st century dog boy is Traian Caldarar, a Romanian and also a victim of family brutality who left home at the age of four to escape his violent father. He was found three years later and eventually returned to his mother and her family. He was in poor health when located, with rickets and other signs of malnutrition. The doctors who cared for him thought he had been with dogs because of his animalistic behavior patterns. His caretakers nicknamed him Mowgli, and for that reason he was called "the Wolf Boy." He was written up in a number of news stories that appeared from February 14 through 22, 2002 after he was found and in a lengthy follow up article in the April 14th *Daily Telegraph,* when his mother took him home. We have nothing after that. Considering that he must have had speech when he left home at four, there is a very good chance that he is integrating into human society at the current time.[66]

The last feral child raised by animals is Andrei Tolstyk found in Russia in 2004 at age seven. He was first abandoned at three months when his mother left home; his alcoholic father then left him as well, and he somehow survived in the care of the family's guard dog reverting to a totally feral state. After examination by doctors, he was moved to a local orphan's shelter where he struck up a friendship with an orphan girl with whom he communicated with signs. The doctors were hopeful that he could be integrated into society, but if everything we have seen so far is correct, this will probably not happen since it is unlikely that he will learn to speak.[67]

We only had twenty cases of feral children of all kinds prior to the 19th century. Of those, eight were isolated and the other twelve, or 60%, were with animals. The Feral Children website found twenty-three cases in the 19th century, fifteen of which lived with animals, or a little over 65%. In the 20th century there were 58 reported cases of feral children, only twenty-eight of which were connected to animals, a drop to a little over 48%, and as we noted earlier, by the time we got to the last third of the 20th century, only one-third of the feral children cases were connected to animals. In the first six years of the 21st century there have been eighteen cases of feral children reported, only three of which were connected to animals—all dogs, that the children went to when their parents were not there for them. This is a drop to fewer than 17%.

We no doubt saw more total cases in recent centuries just because of better newsgathering. The decreasing numbers of children raised by animals is not remarkable either considering the drop in wild areas and animals available to children. We would continue to hope that one day we will see a similar drop in children confined or isolated by the people who are supposed to love and care for them.

John McCrone, in his book *The Myth of Irrationality: the Science of the Mind from Plato to Star Trek,* [68] discusses feral children including Kamala and others from this article. This book goes to the heart of the question, "What makes a feral child different from a 'civilized' one?" and is worth reading by anyone pursuing this interest. To quote the web page devoted to this book, it "…presents a compelling case for a new psychological model of the human mind, one based on the division and interaction between a hard-wired evolved half and a language-oriented learned half." [69] His suggestion is that without language and the continual monologue going on within our minds we cannot form societies, bind time with written history, or develop civilizations at all. We are what we think, and thought is based in that internal monologue.[70]

If a child is brought up with wolves, monkeys or other animals, and is taken in by them before it learns human language, the internal monologue (if such exists in animals) will probably consist of barks, growls, yips or other noises that are the language of the animals. Those few children we have found throughout history who are anomalies either spent part of their time when very young with humans, as did Clemens, the boy living with his family's pigs in the early 19th century, or were taken in by animals after they were three or four years old and had learned language as with John Ssebunya of Uganda and two of the 21st century dog boys. The rest were caught in a halfway world, not allowed to be animal and unable to be human. Tarzan was indeed lucky that Kala, a member of that obscure band of *Australopithecus robustus* that Burroughs called Mangani, rescued him.

****

End Notes

[1] Phillip Jose Farmer. *Tarzan Alive: A Definitive Biography of Lord Greystoke*, Popular Library, NY, NY, 1972, page 25

[2] Peter Hobson. *The Cradle of Thought: Exploring the Origins of Thinking*, Oxford University Press, USA, 2004.

[3] Jonah Weston. *Wild Child: The Story of Feral Children*, Optomen TV, 2002, an interesting documentary on isolated children and also how all children learn language. This film is often shown on the Learning Channel [TLC], and deals with several modern feral children, including Genie, a 20th century child tied down and isolated by her parents for 13 years. It is not available in VHS or DVD at the present time but can be found on IMDB TV per a 2020 search.

[4] See http://www.feralchildren.com/en/children.php for this complete list or http://www.feralchildren.com/en/children.php?tp=0 for their page with just those feral children raised by animals and information about this process.

[5] For more information on Romulus see Plutarch's *Life of Romulus* and online in Wikipedia http://en.wikipedia.org/wiki/Romulus_and_Remus

[6] See http://www.cbsnews.com/stories/2005/02/14/world/printable674077.shtml for more about Andreas Carandini's discoveries of the early Roman palace dating back to Romulus' era.

[7] For the story of Aegistus and much more about feral children see the Fortean Times web site and their article at http://www.forteantimes.com/articles/.161_feralkids.shtml.

[8] For more on Procopius (late 5th Century CE, — c. 565 CE) see http://en.wikipedia.org/ wiki/Procopius and http://www.vortigernstudies.org.uk/artsou/procop.htm.

[9] Glyn Maxwell. *Wolfpit: The Tale of the Green Children of Suffolk*, ARC Publications, 1997-09-1, http://www.feralchildren.com/en/pager.php?df=keightley for Ralph of Coggeshall's version of the story.

[10] Alexander Ross. *Arcana Microcosmi,* London, 1652, Tho. Newcomb, printer, Book 2, chapter 4, pages 112 to 116, http://www.feralchildren.com/en/pager.php?df=ross1652.

[11] Matthaeus Dresserus (Matthieu Drescher). *De Disciplina Nova Et Veteri, Tam Domestica, quam scholastica : ad consolandum erudiendumq[ue] parentes, praeceptores, ac liberos,* Basel, 1577.

[12] Wilhelm Dilich and Johan Carl Unckel. *Hessische Chronica [Hessian Chronicles],* Frankfurt, 1608, II, page 187 quoted on http://www.feralchildren.com/en/listbooks.php?bk= dilich1608

[13] Ross.

[14] Ross.

[15] Philipus (Philip) Camerarius. *Operae Horarum Subcisivarum Sive Meditationes Historicae,* Frankfurt, 1609, P. Kopffij (printer) pt 1 page 343ff as recapped in English on http://www.feralchildren.com/en/showchild.php?ch=bamberg

[16] For detailed information about Joseph the Bear Boy of Lithuania see *The History of Poland in Several Letters to persons of Quality, giving an account of the antient and present state of that kingdom, historical, geographical, physical, political and ecclesiastical ... : with sculptures, and a new map after the best geographers : with several letters relating to physick*, Bernard Connor (O'Connor), London, 1698, Dan. Brown & A. Roper page 342ff to be found at http://www.feralchildren.com/en/pager.php?df=connor1698

[17] Rev. J. A. L. Singh, and Professor Robert M. Zingg *Wolf-Children and Feral Man,* Harper, 1942. Out of print, excerpted on the Feral Children website at http://www.feralchildren.com/en/showchild.php?ch=kronstadt.

[18] E. Burnet Tylor. "Wild Men and Beast Children", *Anthropological Review*, Vol. 1, No. 1 (May, 1863), pp. 21-32, http://www.feralchildren.com/en/showchild.php? ch=clemens.

[19] W. H. Sleeman. *A Journey Through The Kingdom of Oude, in 1849-50,* Richard Bentley, London, 1858 and New Delhi, 1995. Extracts at http://www.feralchildren.com/en/ pager.php?df=sleeman1858 and other URLs cited. Sleeman tells the stories of the following children: The Hasunpur wolf boy (1841), Bankipur wolf boy and First Sultanpur wolf boy (both 1843), the First Lucknow wolf boy (1844), the Second Sultanpur wolf boy (1848) and the Chupra wolf boy (1849). Because they bear so many similarities, this article is dealing in detail with only the First Lucknow Wolf Boy.

[20] Sleeman as extracted at http://www.feralchildren.com/en/showchild.php?ch=sultanpur2 for the story of the second wolf boy of Sultanpur.

[21] Sleeman again via http://www.feralchildren.com/en/showchild.php?ch=sultanpur2.

[22] Sleeman. For the complete story of the First Lucknow Wolf Boy see http://www.feralchildren.com/ en/showchild.php?ch=lucknow

[23] Barry Lopez. *Of Wolves and Men,* Scribner 1979-09-01, and J. Frank Dobie. *Straight Texas (Publications of the Texas Folklore Society #13),* University of Texas Press, 2000-04, pages 79-86. http://www.feralchildren.com/en/showchild.php?ch=felipe.

24 http://www.feralchildren.com/en/showchild.php?ch=felipe.

25 Also called The Indian Rebellion of 1857, the First War of Indian Independence, and the Indian Mutiny. For a lengthy discussion of this war and the reasons for it see http://en.wikipedia.org/wiki/Indian_rebellion_of_1857. Germane to our discussion is the fact that in India the officers were British and the troopers were natives, which helps to explain why many feral children were taken from their lupine packs and the wolves allowed to live.

26 H. Ross. Letter, *The Field,* London, no 9, 1895, no 2237 p 786, http://www.feralchildren.com/en/showchild.php?ch=sultanpur3

27 *Lippincott's Magazine,* LXI, 1898, pg. 121, and H.D. Willock. Letter, *The Field,* Jan. 11, 1896, no 2246 pp 36-7, http://www.feralchildren.com/en/showchild.php?ch=shahjehanpur

28 Singh and Zingg. See also Valentine Ball. *Jungle Life in India, or the Journeys and Journals of an Indian Geologist,* London,1880; republished as *Tribal and Peasant Life in Nineteenth Century India,* and also George Chauncey Ferris. *Sanichar, the Wolf-Boy of India,* New York, 1902.

29 Singh and Zingg, Ball, Ferris, and http://www.feralchildren.com/en/showchild.php?ch= sekandra

30 *Indian Mirror* (of Calcutta), Sunday, February 19, 1893 as quoted in detail at http://www.feralchildren.com/en/showchild.php?ch=batsipur

31 Singh and Zingg.

32 http://www.feralchildren.com/en/showchild.php?ch=trikkala

33 *Amrita Bazar Patrika [Daily English News].* December 14, 1892, as quoted in detail in http://www.feralchildren.com/en/showchild.php?ch=jalpaiguri.

34 *Amrita Bazar Patrika [Daily English News].*

35 *Amrita Bazar Patrika [Daily English News].*

[36] *Amrita Bazar Patrika [Daily English News].*

[37] http://www.feralchildren.com/en/showchild.php?ch=mauritania

[38] André Demaison. *Le Livre des Enfants Sauvages,* André Bonne, Paris 1953 http://www.feralchildren.com/en/showchild.php?ch=panther.

[3] E.C. Stuart Baker. "The Power of Scent in Wild Animals" *The Journal of the Bombay Natural History Society,* Vol. 27, July 1920, pgs. 112-118, also reproduced in Singh and Zingg's *Wolf Children and Feral Man,* and discussed at http://www.feralchildren.com/en/showchild.php?ch=dihungi.

[40] http://www.feralchildren.com/en/showchild.php?ch=goongi

[41] Jim Corbett and R.E. Hawkins. *Jim Corbett's India,* Oxford University Press, USA, 1987-03-01.

[42] At http://www.feralchildren.com/en/showchild.php?ch=jackal there is a brief mention of a European girl rescued from jackals in Cooch Bahar, India in 1923. No reference is cited and the web site states that she "longed to return to the jungle, and died within a few months."

[43] See http://www.feralchildren.com/en/showchild.php?ch=maiwana for more about the Maiwana Wolf Boy and http://www.feralchildren.com/en/showchild.php?ch=jhansi for the Feral Children web site's discussion of the Jhansi Wolf Boy. Information for both of these children was taken from Singh and Zingg's book cited in Endnote 28 above.

[44] J.H. Hutton address to the Folk Lore Society later published as "Wolf-Children", by J. H. Hutton and J. P. van den Brand de Cleverskerk, in *Folklore,* Vol. 51, No. 1 (Mar., 1940), pp. 9-31. Also http://www.feralchildren.com/en/showchild.php?ch=satna.

[45] At http://www.feralchildren.com/en/pager.php?df=singh the reader will find 41 web pages of extracts from Singh's diaries having specifically to do with Kamala and Amala.

[46] John McCrone. *The Myth of Irrationality: The Science of the Mind from Plato to Star Trek,* (Carroll & Graf Pub., 1994-08) See http://www.feralchildren.com

/en/listbooks.php?bk=irrationality for Amazon customer reviews of this book and more information about it.

[47] André Demaison [endnote 38] discusses both Assicia, the Liberian Monkey Girl [http://www.feralchildren.com/en/showchild.php? ch=assicia] and The Monkey Boy from Casamance in Guinea-Bissau [http://www.feralchildren.com/en/showchild.php? ch=casamance].

[48] *American Weekly,* September 5, 1937 and *Sunday Despatch* [*sic*], July 31, 1938 for http://www.feralchildren.com/en/showchild.php?ch=turkey.

[49] *Agence France Presse,* February 8, 1954, originally wrote the story of Ramu, the second Lucknow wolf boy, next seen in India's national newspaper, *The Hindu,* of February 10, 1954 (reprinted on February 10, 2004, and at http://www.hindu.com/2004/02/10/ stories/2004021001470902.htm) and then in the *Illustrated London News,* "Ramu: the Wolf Boy of Lucknow", February 27, 1954, and finally in the *Sunday Express* of April 21, 1968. See http://www.feralchildren.com/en/showchild.php?ch=ramu.

[50] *Daily Mirror,* April 17, 1962 as quoted in http://www.forteantimes.com/articles/ 161_feralkids.shtml; also http://www.feralchildren.com/en/showchild.php?ch=djuma.

[51] Several web sites tell this story including http://www.forteantimes.com/articles/ 161_feralkids.shtml and http://www.feralchildren.com/en/showchild.php?ch=sidi. No articles dated at the time this event took place could be found, but see Mitch Case, "No more babies for Mkombozi", *The Decatur Daily,* May 17, 2005, Decatur, AL, which article recaps the ostrich boy story and a number of others discussed in this article: http://www.decaturdaily.com/decaturdaily/columnists/mitchchase/050517.shtml

[52] André Demaison. [http://www.feralchildren.com/en/showchild.php? ch=assicia]

[53] http://www.feralchildren.com/en/showchild.php?ch=gazelle which uses *Pursuit,* #3, April 1970. Stories of Gazelle boys in Syria were written up by a number of newspapers, pooh-poohed by *Time Magazine,* in "Triumph of Civilization", September 9, 1946, [http://www.time.com/time/ magazine/ article/0,9171,855406,00.html] and "Gazelle Talk", October 7, 1946

[http://www.time.com/time/magazine/article/ 0,9171,778833,00.html] and have been checked out by the Fortean Times [Endnote 7) as well.

54 *Pursuit, #3*, April 1970, Pg. 31

55 Fortean Times [see Endnote 7] web site whose source is Jean-Claude Auger (writing under the pseudonym Jean-Claude Armen). 'Un Enfant-Gazelle au Sahara Occidental' in *Notes Africaines* No.98 (April 1963, pp.58-61) and in *L'Enfant Sauvage du Grand Désert* (1971), which appeared in English as *Gazelle Boy* (Universe Books, NY, and Bodley Head, 1974).

56 Fortean Times.

57 http://www.feralchildren.com/en/showchild.php?ch=ramu

58 *The Sun,* London, March 5, 1990, and *The Fortean Times,* 59:20

59 Bruce Chatwin, article in the *Sunday Times Magazine*, 1978-7-30, compiled in his book *What Am I Doing Here?,* Penguin (Non-Classics), 1990-08-01. See also C.Y. Gopinath, *Sunday Magazin* (Calcutta), March 4, 1979.

60 Fortean Times [Endnote 7, "161 Wild Things"] quoting Sunday Mirror, June 26, 1973; *INFO Journal*, No.11, Summer 1973 [Tissa of Sri Lanka]; Harlan Lane & Richard Pillard: *The Wild Boy of Burundi* (New York 1978);.*Fortean Times, 25:9.* [The Burundi Monkey Boy]; and *FT,* 49:12 [Robert of Uganda].

61 http://www.feralchildren.com/en/showchild.php?ch=bello [Bello, the Nigerian Chimp Boy].

62 See http://www.feralchildren.com/en/showchild.php?ch=ssebunya for a letter from James Butler, the producer/director of *The Boy Who Lived with Monkeys,* a video presentation for BBC, written by PJ Blumenthal; see also Chris *Brooke,* "The Boy Who Was Raised by Monkeys", *Daily Mail,* September 23, 1999; Sally Magnusson, "Taming the Monkey Boy", *The Scotsman,* October 17, 1999; Daniel Thomas Cook, *Symbolic Childhood (Popular Culture & Everyday Life,* Peter Lang Publishing, 2002-06, page 65-85; and Michael Newton, *Savage Girls and Wild Boys: A History of Feral Children,* Picador, 2004-03-01.

63 Feral Children, …?cg=ssebunya.

64 http://www.feralchildren.com/en/showchild.php?ch=ivan; see also Newton's book from Endnote 62, and Richard Tyler, "Homeless Russian Boy Raised by Stray Dogs", World Socialist News, July 23, 1998, [http://www.wsws.org/news/1998/july1998/ivan-j23.shtml] quoting *The Guardian,* July 16, 1998.

65 *Taipei Times,* June 20, 2001, "Dog Boy Found Living in Cave", Reuters, June 19, 2001, Santiago, Chile [http://www.taipeitimes.com/News/archives/2001/06/20/0000090750] with follow up "Chile's 'Dog Boy' Flees Care Center", Reuters, November 14, 2001, [http://www.rense.com/general16/chiliDogBoy.htm]

66 *The Scotsman,* February 14, 21, and 22, 2002, retold in *Far Shore News,* February 22, 2002, "Romania's Wild Boy Reclaimed by His Mother" [http://www.100megsfree4.com/farshores/nwild.htm], with follow-up in *Daily Telegraph,* April 14, 2002, "Wolf Boy is Welcomed Home by Mother After Years in the Wild" [http://www.telegraph.co.uk/news/main.jhtml?xml=/news/2002/04/14/wmog14.xml].

67 Andrew Osborn, "Abandoned Boy Said to Have Been Raised by a Dog", *New Zealand*, April 8, 2004 [http://www.nzherald.co.nz/section/2/story.cfm?c_id=2&objectid=3582191].

68 McCrone.

69 http://www.feralchildren.com/en/listbooks.php?tp=3. This reference also includes information regarding most of the other books listed in my endnotes.

70 McCrone.

***

Serena DuBois has been writing for both pleasure and publication for most of her adult life. She has had poetry published in the University of California at Davis literary magazine Parados and From Anugraha to Amanecer: The SWI 10th Anniversary Anthology and in other two anthologies. She wrote a regular column for the Rainbow Magazine, and has written articles for

Explore for the Professional. Her short story "The Visitor" can be found on ERBList's Pulp Fiction page, http://erblist.com/fanfiction/index.html#shortstories. She is currently working on a series of futuristic novels laid in 2060, well after "the Year of Shaking and Burning" and preparing her cross-genre novel A Thousand Ancestors for publication.